THE SEVEN

D1608114

Sean Patrick Little

First published by Dog Ear Publishing
4010 W. 86th Street, Ste H
Indianapolis, IN 46268
www.dogearpublishing.net

ISBN: 978-160844-066-5

Printed in the United States of America

Acknowledgements

Many thanks to those who purchased my first book and liked it enough to encourage me to write more. Without the occasional badgering, I don't know if I would have ever gotten around to actually publishing another book.

I would like to extend sincere gratitude to the initial readers of this book whose criticism and keen eyes helped to make it better: Brandon Schmidt provided a keen eye for detail and helped with the science parts. (*Gimpus, if you ever decide to give up the scientific pursuits, you are a natural literary editor.*) Nancy Malecha provided moral support as well as caustic insults that ate away at my soul little by little, but I usually need that. Jessi Ehlenfeldt, Holly Lauth, Ann Sarazin, Tina Blondell, and Vicki Spindler all read through early versions and were extremely supportive. That support is very much appreciated. Jason Ehlenfeldt, whose taste in books mirrors my own, contributed some ideas. And Helen Lauth was one of the pickiest typo-spotters this side of the Pecos.

Many thanks go out to my art guru, James McGee, for once again taking time out of his workaholism to put together a cover design.

I want to thank my long-time friends Steve Kittleson and Rachel Nacion for being comic book nerds with me. I also have to thank my sister, Erin. For what, I have no idea, but she complained when she wasn't in the acknowledgements of my first book...which she still hasn't bothered to read.

I would like to thank Rush, Marillion, Cheap Trick, Colin Hay, House of Large Sizes, Fish, and Type O Negative, the bands whose music provided background noise much of the time I was writing.

I need to mention the comic writers I have long admired for weaving their words and worlds: Neil Gaiman, Warren Ellis, Garth Ennis, Frank Miller, Mike Baron, Chris Claremont, Bill Willingham, Brian Michael Bendis, Alan Moore, Terry Moore, and Mike Mignola.

I would also like to thank the other independent writers and authors I met at conferences and book festivals who exchanged books with me, spent the long (often disappointing) days talking and commiserating with me, and gave me advice, jokes, and bits of wisdom: John Harrigan, Jennifer L. Miller, Sue Christenson, Michael Allan Mallory, Marilyn Victor, Lois Greiman, C. Hyytinen, Marston Moore, and Arvid Lloyd Williams.

Finally, I would like to thank Craig and Judy Johnson for breakfast.

For Annika

THE SEVEN

Sean Patrick Little

Book One
Origins

Sarah knew where to find him. She always knew where to find him as if they had a psychic bond. When they were kids, he was always the first one she found when they played hide-and-seek; Andy could never hide from her for long. Sarah could always make a beeline for Andy's hiding spot.

She walked deep into the woods behind the Home, meandering along the old logging road with a flashlight in her hand. It was still daylight, and would be for a while, but where Andy was hiding, a flashlight would come in handy. After a time, she came to an old game trail and veered off the dusty tire rut into the heart of the forest. Tall, overhanging oaks laid down a thick blanket of shade and kept the late August sun from being unbearable. Locusts droned constantly in the trees and birds twittered mindlessly, cheerful despite the heat. A steep embankment along the path angled into a low, narrow valley. At the bottom of the valley was a dry creek bed that led deeper into the woods and to a small cave that Sarah and Andy had discovered years ago, not long after they first came to the Home.

The cave was carved into a hillside, a vein chiseled through limestone. The opening was small, barely big enough to squeeze though. When they were kids, it was huge. Now, Sarah eased her narrow frame through the opening feeling a hint of claustrophobia. Once through the opening, there was a gently sloped descent that opened into a small, round room. That's where she knew he would be.

Andy was in the middle of the cave, flat on his back, his bulky frame taking up a good portion of the space. Andy wasn't tall, but he was wide and thick, powerfully built, the true definition of "fireplug." He had thick, beefy arms and legs like tree trunks. His broad stomach, slightly paunchy, rose and fell slowly with his breath; his arms and legs were spread-eagle. Sarah trained her beam on him. His eyes were closed, but the light made him squeeze his eyes shut a little more.

"Andy, are you okay?"

For a long time, Andy didn't move. He didn't acknowledge Sarah in any way. Then, he inhaled sharply and blew out a long slow breath. "I'm tired, Sarah."

"I know." Sarah sat down cross-legged in the dust and dried leaves next to him. She caught the thin outline of a cave spider in the flashlight and quickly turned off the beam, shuddering.

"They ask so much of us, you know?" Andy's voice cracked a little. It wasn't like him to get upset. He was usually a rock, the one everyone else went to for a shoulder to lean against when they felt low. Sarah felt a tinge of worry creep into her belly.

"I know."

"I can't keep it up."

"Yes, you can. You're strong," said Sarah. "Stronger than the rest of us."

"Whatever," said Andy. He rolled to his side and pushed up to one elbow. "They keep saying that we're all going important to some stupid research thing and that we'll all understand one day...but, you know what I think? I think they're full of crap."

"You just have to keep working, Andy."

"No! No, I don't! I've been doing everything they asked of us. I haven't complained once, have I? I just keep on going through the tests, the surgeries, and the pain and therapy afterward, and I keep putting up with Cormair's crap and for what? For nothing. Nothing has happened to us in all this time! We're seventeen now! That means we've been under Cormair's control for ten years, can you believe it?"

Sarah shook her head. "It doesn't feel like ten years."

"To you, maybe. To me, it feels like twenty." Andy flopped back down into the leaves and closed his eyes. "Remember what it was like when we first came to the Home?"

Sarah remembered it clearly. It wasn't one of those things a person could forget. She remembered the long, dark bus ride with six other children. She remembered the crisply uniformed soldiers on the bus, large, muscular men in dark gray fatigues who gave them candy and soda. She vaguely remembered her parents' faces, filtered through a smudged, grimy bus window as they waved good-bye, before the soldiers put up the metal window covers blocking out her final view of her family.

The Home. It was a strange, run-down, oddly-angled Victorian-style house in the middle of a forest, a relic straight out of a Grimm Brothers' fairy tale. As the bus approached, Sarah thought it looked like the haunted mansion from Disneyworld. Dr. Cormair, the man who would rule their lives for the next decade, had been waiting at the door to greet them when the bus pulled up to the entrance. He was a thin, almost frail-looking man with dull, graying hair and severe, gray eyes behind wire-rimmed glasses. His face was a permanent mask of impassiveness. He wore a starched, brilliantly white lab coat. Through the next ten years of their lives at the Home, none of the seven would ever see him without the coat, no matter the time of day.

Sarah was ushered to the porch with the other kids and they were photographed, once as a group, and then individually, front and side. They were shown to their rooms, each one sparse and devoid of character. Over the years, they would each collect a few mementos, some posters, and colored blankets or pillows with lace edges, but the walls remained the dull, light gray color they were when they moved into the Home. The rest of the rooms were just as dull. The couches in the TV room, the chairs in the kitchen, even the shower curtains, were all dull and colorless. The entire place felt barren and muted.

"I remember," said Sarah. "I was scared. I think we all were."

"Not me," said Andy. "My dad was a drunk. He hit me a lot. My mom never even bothered to stop him, because then he'd smack her around, too. When my dad was at work, my mom's depression was overwhelming. She just sat in front of the TV and stared blankly. She never played with me or my brother, or interacted with me except to tell me not to do something. The Home seemed like Heaven to me, at first. Kids to play with, I had a purpose, and best of all no one hit me. That's why I believed in the research more than everyone else at first, I think. I wanted to be special. I wanted to be important. I wanted to help people and to be able to be strong for kids like me, kids whose parents hit them and treated them badly."

"And you will be, Andy."

"When, though? Ten years of this crap. Ten years of electrodes and scans and tests and surgeries and training and…and…all that other crap. When does it pay off? When do we get to see results?"

"Maybe it doesn't," said Sarah. "Maybe this will all be found out to be a colossal waste of time and money and none of us will ever do whatever it is we're supposed to do. Then Cormair will have to abandon the project and we'll all get to leave here, go back to our families, and live normal lives."

Andy sat up. "I'll believe that when I see it."

"We're almost eighteen, anyhow; I can't see that they can hold legal adults against their will for long without breaking some sort of international law or something."

"You've been reading the news online, right?"

"Of course," said Sarah.

"Two words: Guantanamo Bay."

Sarah's face fell. "But we're American, right? They can't hold Americans, right? We're not terrorists."

Andy shrugged. "As far as I know, we're government property. We have been for ten years. I don't know if we can even be called 'citizens' anymore. With all the money and research they put into us, I don't think they're just going to let us go trotting free any time soon."

Sarah reclined back in the leaves and dust and touched her head to Andy's. Neither spoke for some time, both listening to each other's shallow, measured breathing. "Maybe I should stay here with you for a while?" Sarah whispered.

"I was going to go back eventually, you know."

"I know."

"So why did you come after me?"

"Maybe because I wanted to be away from the Home for a while, too."

Indigo was always a bit different from the other six. She was the first one to discover punk music and hair dye. She was the only member of the seven to ever sneak away from the Home and go to the little town down the road. Though she was never busted by Dr. Cormair, this was still a major offense the other six would never have dreamed of committing. She was a wild spirit and often butted heads with Cormair or the cadre of teachers brought in to educate them over the past decade. She was artistic and liked to read books the other six wouldn't even touch—Camus and Kafka, Ayn Rand and Dostoyevsky. She was arrogant, blithe, and sometimes cruel, often picking fights with the others for no reason. She was the only member of the seven who was Asian, Japanese to be specific, and she was the smallest and thinnest. She was also the one who endured the most testing.

Dr. Cormair began a trial of rigorous, near-daily testing from the first day she was in the Home. Indigo wasn't entirely sure what they were testing her for, but she knew it was something about her brain because every time they strapped her to a chair, they slapped electrodes all over her head and made her do mental exercises. She'd had to have a shaved head for a while two years ago because the researchers put electrodes onto the skin of her skull and a metal neuro-net on her brain. The doctors at the Home even implanted a device into her brain that could be plugged into a jack at the base of her neck, at skin level, that connected to electrode plots in her brain to run tests, among other fiddling they had done in her head. It had all been extremely painful. In ten years, Indigo had her head opened up a dozen times.

She stood in the middle of the Home's main laboratory, an impressive room tiled on all four sides with dark gray metal sheeting and filled with all manner of instruments, scanners, electrographs, and monitoring devices. Indigo was wearing a blue plastic skull cap that was wired heavily with electrodes. On a table ten feet in front of her sat a fist-sized, bright red plastic block. She was being tested…again.

"Indigo, I want you close your eyes and try to reach out to the block on the table with your mind, okay? Pretend that you control an invisible hand that juts out from your forehead, okay?" said Doctor Sebbins. She was a pretty, young doctor who had only been at the Home for two years. She had been brought in to teach Chemistry and Biology, but her personable manner made her one of the few teachers that the kids had actually liked. At the urging of the kids, Cormair hired her on a full-time basis. She moved into the Home and became Cormair's chief assistant.

"You got it, Doc," said Indigo. She scrunched up her face and gave the big red block on the table an evil-eye stare. She even reached out one of her own hands and made dramatic sweeping gestures with it, imitating the old wizard she'd seen a few nights before in the late movie on television. "Rise! Rise, I command thee! Rise!"

Nothing happened.

From the bank of computers in the corner, Sebbins said, "Okay, that's good, Indigo. Now I want you to *actually* try. This time without the theatrics, please."

"How do you know I wasn't *actually* trying then?"

"I'm reading your brainwave patterns over here," said Sebbins. She tapped the computer monitor in front of her with the end of her pen. "When you *actually* try, other parts of your brain light up. When you pretend, it looks different."

Indigo sighed. "Fine. I'll *actually* try."

"That's all I ask."

"What are you testing me for, anyhow?"

"I'm measuring activity levels in your hypothalamus. Now stop talking and concentrate."

Indigo sighed and flopped into the comfy wing chair in the testing room. She looked at the table where the red block lay on a plain, single-mold, white plastic card table. Indigo had been used to this sort of test. She'd figured out years ago they were training her to be some sort of psychic or clairvoyant or telekinetic or something. That's why they kept testing her brain. Ten years of pointless tests and still she hadn't been able to move so much as a mote of dust in a sunbeam or see two seconds into the future. She was beginning to think the doctors were wasting their time.

Indigo bit her lip, concentrated, and stared at the red block until it felt like it was burned into her brain. She closed her eyes and concentrated, forming the red block on the table in her mind. She concentrated on the block, fixing it in her mind's eye. She imagined an invisible arm extending from her head; she could feel the fingers closing around the block. She could feel the block's resistance. It was solid in her mind. Indigo paused. It had never been like this before. She could feel something! She began to feel elated; her heart began to race.

Using the invisible arm, she willed the fingers to grip the block and she pulled back. In her mind, she could feel the actual weight of the block as it lifted off the table. There was a tug, a pulling sensation as the weight of the block actually registered with her imaginary arm. Butterflies jumped in her stomach. She was doing it! It had never felt more real. Indigo opened her eyes, nervously, excited, fully expecting to see the block hovering before her, gripped in the invisible, telekinetic hand.

It hadn't moved an inch. It hadn't shifted. It was still on the table, stubborn and defiant.

"Damn it!" Indigo swung out with her heavy-soled Doc Martens' and kicked the leg of the table. The leg bent inward and the table collapsed, the block bounced away into a corner.

"It's okay, Indigo," said Sebbins. "Come here and look at your brain activity. This is a huge step forward. Honest. Your hypothalamus lit up like a Christmas tree just then. That's exactly the type of activity we've been waiting to see!"

"No. No, it's not. It's the same junk that has happened since I was brought here. I'm so tired of this, Seb! I thought something was supposed to be happening by now!" She ripped the cap off her head and flung it into a large, glass tank in the corner.

"Frustration is a natural reaction, Indigo. Don't let it get to you. Take a moment and then come try again."

"No! Maybe you don't let it get to you, but I let it get to me! This is useless and you know it! What are we doing? Most people stop beating their head against the wall the first time it hurts. I've been slamming my head into spikes for years and there hasn't been one iota of progress!"

"Indigo—come look!" Sebbins turned a computer monitor toward Indigo. A pattern of red spikes jutted wildly across the screen. "Look at the activity!"

"No! Screw this. I'm going to go take a nap." Indigo spun on her heel and made a perfect, huffy drama-queen power-stride out the door, as any good teenager throwing a tantrum should.

Indigo raced out of the lab, down a corridor, and into the elevator. The elevator let her out in the kitchen. She walked through the kitchen and into the entryway of the Home. She turned left at the large, spiral staircase that lead upstairs to the residence hall. At the top of the stairs, she turned right and walked down the hall to her room. She kicked the door open leaving a dent in the wood. She slammed the door behind her and threw herself onto her bed, fuming. Tears pricked at corners of her eyes. She had *felt* it this time. It had been real! For ten years, she had jumped through the hoops and been a good little trained puppy. She had done all the tests, no matter how ridiculous she felt they were. She had dealt with the pain of the poking, prodding, and needles and scans. Beneath her hair, her scalp was a weave of scars. She had put up with the constant invasion of privacy. She had buried the pain of being sent away by her parents.

But why?

What hurt the most was that deep down Indigo really wanted these alleged abilities to work. She wanted to have the abilities that Cormair hinted she might have. She wanted to be psychic, or telekinetic, or clairvoyant, or whatever the hell it was she could do with her supposedly "special" brain. To be truly unique—not just in the way she dressed or the books she read or the music she listened to—to be unique among the unique was what kept her in the Home. It kept her from running away. It kept her submitting willingly to the tests. And now she felt it was all for nothing, a pointless exercise in futility.

A fire of rage burned in her gut. Indigo didn't want to give into the tears. She swallowed the lump in her throat and tried to push away the years of failure. A scream welled up in her chest and she let it pour forth, pushing her face into the pillows on her bed so that she could scream as loudly as she wanted without alerting Nurse Hathcock or the housekeeper, Ms. Miller. She wanted to feel aggression. She wanted some sort of emotion to counteract the failure and sadness.

Her stereo suddenly blared. The Ramones CD she had been listening to the night before blasted out of the speakers at maximum volume. Indigo jerked her head up, ready to punch a new hole through whoever dared invade her sanctuary, but the room was empty. Joey Ramone wanted to be sedated, and Dee Dee supplied raucous riffs, but no one had been in her room to turn on the stereo. The stereo remote was across the room on top of a stack of books on her desk. She hadn't nudged it by accident in the midst of her tantrum.

Indigo slowly stood up and turned the volume down on her stereo. She sat back on the bed and looked at the stereo receiver.

Had she done that?

Indigo walked back across the room and closed her eyes. She visualized every inch of her room, mapping it in her head. She focused on the stereo on the wire shelf across the room. Concentrating, she imagined the invisible arm again; she extended a finger from the hand at the end of the arm and pressed the power button on the stereo. The music didn't stop, but she began to get a headache, a dull throb in her temples.

Indigo slouched back against the wall and slid to the floor, dejected. Maybe one of the others had turned on their stereo and the signal from their remote turned on her stereo. Maybe she hadn't depressed the power button all the way and vibrations of her heavy boots on the old, wooden floor made it slip back to the on position.

Indigo put her fingers on her temples and rubbed in slow circles until the headache receded. She stared at her stereo. Why hadn't it ever powered on by itself before?

"Do you remember your last name, Holly?" Posey asked.

Holly's freckled nose wrinkled in thought. She picked a daisy from the flower garden and absently plucked petals, letting them flutter from her fingers. Her mousy brown hair blew into her eyes and made her scratch her forehead. "I think it was Braun. Holly Marie Braun. I haven't thought about that in years, though."

"Posey White. That was my last name." Posey stretched, arching her back. She was Holly's physical opposite: tall and slender, with sharp, dark features and an aquiline nose.

"So?"

"Don't you think it's weird that none of us even use our last names anymore?"

"Not really. I mean, our families pretty much gave us up. Who would want to retain the name of someone who didn't want to fight for you? I think Sarah's parents kept up correspondence the longest and even that dwindled out after our third year here. I haven't heard from my parents in eight years. So what? I don't even like my name. Holly Marie. It's so plain."

Posey nodded. "Do you remember the last names of the others?"

"No."

"I do."

"Why?"

"Because it struck me as funny when I first came here."

"Why?"

"Didn't you notice we were all named after colors?"

"No. I didn't pay attention, though."

"Posey White, Holly Braun, Andy Greenberg, Indigo Maru, Kenny Schwartz, Sarah Blusendorf, and John Redmond. White, brown, green, indigo, black, blue, and red. Like a rainbow. You never noticed that?"

"Never saw a rainbow with black and brown stripes. Are you sure Schwartz means 'black?'"

"Yeah. The actor Michael Ian Black's real name was Michael Schwartz. He changed it when he started acting. It means black in Yiddish. I looked it up a while back."

Holly threw the daisy stem over her shoulder and looked at Posey. "Are you thinking there's some big coincidence in the fact that we all have a color in our name?"

"Maybe. I don't know. I was just saying. How many of the others do you think remember their last names?"

"None, if they're lucky," said Holly

They walked in silence for another fifty yards. They crested the small rise of the hill in front of the Home. John was coming toward them in a slow, graceful lope. He was holding his shirt in one hand and every well-defined muscle on his bare torso shone with sweat.

"Oh. My. God. Catch me. I think I'm going to faint," said Posey.

"Grow up," said Holly. "He's like our brother."

"Our brother from another mother," said Posey. "Doesn't change the fact that he's gorgeous and we never get to leave this place to go find real guys to date."

"Are you really that boy-crazy?" Holly sighed. "I swear you want life to be like those stupid romance novels you read all the time."

"A little romance never hurt anyone," said Posey. "To be swept away by love, to be loved like that, it's the greatest thing in the world, Holly."

"Maybe to you," said Holly.

John jogged up to their side and stretched his arms above his head to help him catch his breath. He got control over his breathing almost immediately. His short dreadlocks hung down into his face. "I feel good," he said. "I just ran almost twenty miles on the track out back. I think those treatments they did to increase our stamina are finally kicking in."

"Or, maybe it's the fact that you've run almost twenty miles a day for the last five years," said Holly, ever the pragmatist.

"Spoil-sport," said John. He playfully tugged the ponytail that hung down the middle of Holly's back. "You guys seen Kenny?"

Posey sighed. "He's probably locked in his room, pouring over some dumb novel about orcs and trolls or something. Either that or he's chatting online again. If they catch him doing that one more time, he's going to get solitary for a month."

"The only way they'll catch him is if they walk in on him. Kenny's practically reprogrammed the whole computer system of the Home," said John.

A long, low horn sounded from the front porch of the Home.

"Supper time," said Posey. "We have to head back."

"I wonder if Sarah found Andy yet."

John shook his head. "I have a feeling they're still on the property or else Cormair would go mental and call in a S.W.A.T. team or something."

"Well, we have about two thousand acres of land to hide on. That's a long way to roam while still being 'on the property,'" said Holly. "Andy doesn't miss meals, though. They'll be back."

"You guys have any testing tonight?" asked John. Posey cringed a bit. Every time he said 'guys' was a reminder that he didn't see her as a woman.

"I don't," said Holly. "You figure out what they're testing you for yet?"

"I think I'm supposed to be some sort of soldier," said John.

"Soldier? Like G.I. Joe or something?"

"No—a real soldier…with guns and tanks and stuff. Lately, that's been what all my testing has been about. Shooting and throwing knives and running and such. They've been making me run the obstacle course out back every night."

"Well, you have the running down," said Posey.

"You ever figure out what you're supposed to be?" asked John.

Posey shrugged. "I don't know. My tests are all bizarre. They keep showing me pictures of birds and skyscrapers and asking if I feel anything. They made me climb the old silo out back one day. They look at my brain patterns and stuff. They put me in the virtual reality goggles the other night and it showed aerial pictures of the Home from really high up. I think that maybe I'm supposed to fly."

"That would be so cool," said Holly. "I'd love to fly."

"Me too," said John. "First thing I would do: Get out of this place. I'd go fly to some city where I could get lost and they'd never find me again."

The trio walked up the front steps of the Home. The wooden boards of the stairs creaked under their feet. Sarah and Andy came out of the woods at the far edge of the yard of the Home and jogged down the hill to join the trio on the steps. "Did we miss dinner?" said Andy.

"No. Just in time."

"Good," said Andy. "I don't need the demerits."

"And you have never missed a meal since you got here," said John patting Andy's stomach.

"Got to keep my girlish figure, don't I?" said Andy.

Kenny was in the dining hall when the group walked into the Home. Indigo was missing from dinner, but that wasn't unusual. She only ate with everyone else once or twice a week.

Kenny was a shy boy, always had been. He also was very serious. He had short hair, dark, sullen eyes, fair skin, and he wore thin, circular wire-rimmed glasses that gave him an almost sinister look. John often compared his look to Arnold Toht, the sadistic Nazi from *Raiders of the Lost Ark*. Kenny was sitting at a table with a plate of grayish gruel in front of him. His nose was buried in a thick book about physics.

"Aw, man. Mushroom gravy over noodles again!" sighed Andy. "Isn't this like the fourth time in the last ten days we've had to eat this slop? What happened to decent food? Remember when they used to give us steak? Or remember the filet mignon at Christmas?"

"It's not so bad," said Holly. "We've had worse."

"I think maybe the grant money is running thin this month," said Posey. "We had good food at the beginning of the month. Towards the end of the month they always try to stretch the budget a little to cover the tests and whatnot."

Vera Miller came out of the kitchen with a pitcher of milk in one hand and a tray of Rice Krispie treats in the other. Vera was the cook and the housekeeper of the Home. She'd been there the whole time that the Seven had been there. She was matronly and polite, but never really much of a mother-figure. She wore her silver hair in a tight chignon and her countenance was stern and severe. She glared, never looked.

"I 'eard you complainin' Andy! You'll eat what you're given and you'll like it or there won't be anything!" she said with her thick British accent. "I don't cook to get insulted by the likes of you. If you want to eat better, then you join me in the kitchen and you give me a bit of 'elp, you ingrate!"

"Sorry, Vera," said Andy, blushing. He sat down next to Kenny and ladled a heap of noodles onto his plate.

"Where's the skinny girl?" barked Vera. Even after ten years, Vera still pretended she only had a passing, casual knowledge of them. "She'll not be raidin' me kitchen after I'm done wit' the evening meal. She'll eat wit' the rest of us."

"I only want coffee," Indigo announced from the top of the stairs.

"There'll be no coffee, either," Vera said. "You know the doctors don't want you all screwing up your systems wit' caffeine and sugar."

"Too late for that," said Indigo. "Hell, look at Andy. He wolfs down the gross national product worth of chocolate each week."

"Oh, shut up," said Andy.

"And don't you be cursing in front o' me," growled Vera, smacking her wooden spoon against the side of the pot on the table. "I can't keep you from sayin' it, but I can keep you from sayin' it in front of me. I hear language like that, you'll be tastin' the business end of me bottle of dish soap!"

"No coffee or sugar, but the heap of chemicals in detergent is okay? This place is stupid," said Indigo. She flopped into a chair next to Posey and idly played with her napkin.

"Posey, darling, spoon some noodles onto Indigo's plate," said Vera. "And Indigo—you will eat. You're getting far too thin. I've 'alf a mind to have the doctors strap you down while I shove a few platefuls of fish and chips down your gullet."

"I'll volunteer for that," smiled John. "I can never seem to eat enough."

"That's because you're a growing boy," said Vera.

"It is because your body consumes fuel at three times the rate of a normal boy your age." The kids turned their heads and saw the thin form of Doctor Cormair entering the hall. His measured steps were deliberate and slow and his shoulders were slightly hunched from years of pouring over data sheets and computer keyboards. His hair, now a silvery-gray, was slicked back without a strand out of place. His eyes surveyed the table through thick, round glasses. "It is perfectly normal. You need the food to be better to compensate

for your advanced energy consumption rates. I apologize for no
resources to properly feed you every night. I hope to atone for that so...
Cormair's voice was thin and wheezy, as if he was constantly struggling for
breath.

"No worries, Doc," said John with a good-natured smile. John, more so
than any of the others, had always tried to be friendly with the doctors.

"Indigo," said Cormair, "you will eat what you are given. And you must
eat. Not having the proper resources in your body can corrupt test results."

Scowling, Indigo picked up a fork and took a small bite of pasta. "Can't
have your precious tests corrupted now, can we?"

Cormair tactfully ignored Indigo's jab. "I trust the rest of you are well.
Andrew, I am glad to see you back. I assume you got your tantrum out of your
system?"

"Yes, Doctor," said Andy. He blushed brightly, his face filling with a
fiery red that almost matched his hair.

"Sarah, I thank you for going to find young Andrew," said Cormair. He
sat at the far end of the table, opposite of Vera Miller, and accepted the bowls
of pasta and gravy as Holly brought them to him.

Dr. Sebbins walked into the dining hall and sat next to Cormair, as was
her custom. "Any plans for tonight?" she asked brightly. "I was thinking
maybe of watching a movie in the TV lounge. Say, nine o'clock?"

"I could be up for a movie," said Posey, smiling, "as long as the boys
don't choose it. I don't think I could handle another violent bloodbath
movie."

"Hey, *Full Metal Jacket* is not a violent bloodbath," said Andy, heaping
his plate with noodles for the second time.

"That means you'll want to watch some sort of girly flick," said John.

"Romances aren't just for girls," said Posey, sticking out her tongue at him.

"Sure. They're for girls…and guys who want to be girls."

"Enough, you two," said Sebbins. "Kenny? What about you? You up
for a movie tonight?"

Kenny raised his head from his book and blinked twice. He swiveled his
head slowly, looked at Sebbins, gave a brief shake of his head, and returned to
his physics book.

Sebbins stared hard at Kenny with concern for a long moment before
giving her plate her attentions.

"Has anyone experienced anything out-of-the-ordinary today?" Cormair
asked. He asked the same question at every evening meal. He had been asking it every night since they arrived.

Indigo bit her lip. The stereo was definitely out-of-the-ordinary, but it
wasn't something she felt like she wanted to bring up. She knew that men-

tioning it would bring an all-night battery of tests and experiments. It had happened to John once. He had let it slip that his eyes had felt like they were bulging out of his skull for a while and that bright lights were hurting his head. Sebbins and Cormair had exchanged strange looks and had scuttled John from the table. They had him sequestered in the labs for most of a day and a half while subjecting him to an inhuman amount of testing. When he came back to the other six, he swore he wouldn't mention anything ever again, even if he was shooting fire through the top of his skull at the dinner table.

"Anyone?" asked Cormair again. Indigo felt like his eyes were staring a hole through her. She forced her gaze to remain down on her plate while she shook her head a few times. Cormair didn't ask again, but Indigo didn't look up from her plate again.

"I have finished," Kenny said. "Thank you, Ms. Miller." He nodded at Vera and stood. Before the doctors could ask any question, he turned and left, headed up the spiral stairs to his room. He was always the first to leave the table. He also was the only one who remembered to thank Vera each night, no matter how weak the meal.

"I'm going to go, too," said Andy. He'd wolfed four times as much as anyone else. He dropped his fork on the empty plate and was gone before Cormair could say anything.

"Me too," said Holly. She gave Cormair a withering smile and left the table, her plate still half-full. The other four quickly found reasons to excuse themselves and disappeared, leaving the three adults alone at the table. None of them wanted to be around Cormair when they didn't have to be.

The atmosphere in the dining room became heavy and sullen. Cormair was silent, but his face showed frustration and hidden rage. He drummed his long, thin fingers against the table top. "They are lying."

Sebbins frowned. "Is that hypothesis, Doctor?"

"That is fact, Doctor Sebbins. Look at the scans, the blood work, the X-rays! Those children have changed dramatically in the last few years according to their internal workings, and I refuse to believe that none of them have experienced manifestations of their abilities. According to my data, they should be going through dramatic shifts of power by now."

"Perhaps they are, and they are unaware of it. It is happening at a genetic level, correct? If you take a child who was meant to be brunette and alter their DNA so they are blonde, will that child even know unless she looks in a mirror? These kids don't have a mirror to look into for what they're becoming."

"But I haven't altered a hair color. I've altered brain chemistry, physical structure, musculature—"

"Look at Posey though, Doctor Cormair," interjected Sebbins. "She has nearly unbreakable bones and those bones have less than a tenth of what a normal bone mass should be in a girl her age. Ten years' of change in those bones and all she's complained about is acne and her height. Those bone structure changes aren't changes that she's aware of, Doctor. She's oblivious to her physical alteration because her DNA has been altered and spliced so that she's growing without knowing that she's different. That's a success, Doctor."

"Doctor Sebbins, I am not one who celebrates the completion of the first mile of a marathon. If I do not finish it, it is not worth celebrating. My research, this program, was meant to create the next evolution of man. I am doing nothing short of playing God and if I am not successful, it is not worth celebrating because I will have committed far too many sins to repent."

"Then give them some more time. You know as well as I do that the teenage brain is not fully developed. Their higher thought processes are still arranging themselves, their frontal lobes are still adjusting to the treatments. I've been seeing a lot of positive steps lately. Indigo's hypothalamic activity is increasing every day, Kenny's brain patterns are unlike anything we've ever seen before. I'll bet we'll begin to see change any day now."

"Doctor Sebbins, you are young. You are in that rare age where you are too old to remember teenagers, but too young to be a true adult," Cormair's voice wasn't condescending, only cold and rational. "Teenagers have made a living throughout the centuries by knowing more than they let on and effectively evading the prying of adults. It's a contest to them. They are constantly hiding information from us. It's how they survive. They are lying. They have begun to notice the changes. They may not have fully completed their genetic shifts, but at the very least some of them have noticed. Mark my words, Doctor. Some of them already know."

Kenny's room was more spartan than those of the other six. His bed was plain, without extra pillows or thick comforters. He kept it adorned with the same simple, gray, military-issue blanket that was on the bed the day he arrived at the Home. His desk was bare except for the computer Dr. Cormair gave him to use for his studies. He had bookcases along one wall of his room and each bookcase was absurdly organized, each book rigid and in its place, alphabetized and organized according to a system of Kenny's own design. Each bookcase was full, but not crammed full. Kenny read everything he could get his hands on, but kept only books of information—computers, electronics, astronomy, physics, complex mathematics. Kenny's education far surpassed the education of the other six thanks to his reading and private study, but he never showed it in class or in Cormair's tests. He guarded his intelligence carefully. He had plans. They could only keep him at the Home until he was eighteen. The law books he read told him this. At eighteen, he would leave and never look back. It was almost time. He endured the arduous saga of testing and surgeries. He had survived ten years of torture and isolation. He was going to leave.

Kenny logged an entry sequence on his computer. Immediately it presented him a series of passwords. Everything he did on the computer was meticulously encrypted. He didn't want Cormair taking advantage of his intellect or discovering what he was doing online. It might compromise his plans.

Computers had always been Kenny's refuge from the Home. He was a self-taught hacker, utilizing the Home's computer systems to figure out how to effectively "leave" the Home via the cyber-realm in chat rooms, bulletin board systems, and instant messengers. He had conversations with men and women all over the world, even though it technically was outlawed because Cormair didn't want them or searching for their families or being directly influenced by individuals in the outside world. Kenny never bothered relocating his family. They'd never written to him, nor had he written to them. When he stepped onto the bus ten years ago, he had considered himself an orphan. The computers did allow him to discover things about himself, though. He found his actual date of birth. The first thing they did in the Home was told all seven of the kids that their birthdays were to be celebrated on December 31 each year. Kenny knew it was done to keep them at the Home as long as legally possible. He'd discovered his birthday, though: September 29. Only a few more weeks and he would leave the home under the cover of night, a legal adult, to find a new life, a real life.

The computer flashed an error message. Kenny frowned. He retyped his access code.

INVALID.

Kenny squinted and retyped his access code slowly, making certain the keystrokes were clean.

INVALID.

Kenny frowned. Cormair had blocked his encryptions. It happened occasionally. Cormair brought in top hackers every so often and attempted to get them to break through Kenny's defenses and restore Cormair's authoritarian control. It never worked. At the most, it only served to inconvenience Kenny for a while.

Kenny pushed back his chair and knelt on the floor next to his computer's hardware tower. He popped the side panel off, exposing the computer's assorted chip board-and-wire guts. Kenny took a deep breath and held it. He slowly stretched out his finger and touched it to the motherboard. Instantly, his body went rigid as he felt the hyper-flow of information. Data streams from the motherboard flowed directly into Kenny's mind and were instantly processed, a broken levee of information. In his mind, the data streams became three-dimensional building blocks and lengths of yarn, waiting to be strung like a game of Cat's Cradle. As easy as thinking, Kenny reset the passwords. He looped the security firewalls. He restructured the programming into a complex fortress of data for which only he had the key. Kenny then reversed the flow of information in his mind and channeled the data back into the motherboard and across the network. His hand fell from the motherboard and Kenny wiped away the sweat from his forehead. His breath was shallow and his chest hurt. He closed his eyes and waited for the stabbing pain in his head to subside.

PASSWORD ACCEPTED. GOOD EVENING, KENNETH.

The monitor displayed his desktop icons and awaited his command.

Kenny coughed and the chest tightness began to evanesce. He popped the panel back onto the tower case and pulled himself off the floor. He had been communicating with computers for three years now. As far as he knew, he was the first of the seven to gain his or her powers.

Kenny's body was heavily scarred from surgeries that Cormair had put him through when he was first brought to the home. Cormair had implanted computer hardware in Kenny's brain. He had installed pieces and parts—Kenny himself didn't know how many or what they were, but hacking into the Cormair's private files shortly after his powers manifested, he learned that Cormair was trying to create a cyborg. Part human, part machine. That was Kenny. The cyborgs in the movies were always super-strong war machines, more robot than human. Kenny was still the weak-looking, wire-rimmed glasses wearing über-nerd he had always been, but the only difference was that Kenny could speak to computers—to the entire Internet if he had to—and bend them to his will.

As far as he was concerned, that was more powerful than being a super-strong war machine.

Holly was resting her arms on her windowsill and she stared out into the night. Years ago, she had kicked out the metal screens so that she could have an unencumbered view of the gardens and the forest behind the Home. She loved to watch the wind blow the leaves, especially in the spring when the flower petals would stream down from the cherry trees like snow. She loved to take deep, cleansing breaths of the pine-scented night air. She loved to see her breath in the air in the fall. Most of all, she loved the animals she could see in the trees and the gardens.

Holly's birth family had been farmers. She could still remember the red barn with its chipped and peeling paint and the old, square farmhouse she lived in until she left for the Home. She remembered the baby animals: lambs and kids, calves and kittens. She loved animals. Perhaps that was why she developed the ability to talk to them.

A crow, elegant and dark, landed in the apple tree at the edge of the garden. Holly locked her eyes on it and the crow froze. *Bring me a flower. A white flower.* She sent the animal mental images of what she wanted it to do. The crow bobbed its head as if it was acknowledging her command and leapt down from the tree, spreading its wings to glide to the cobbled garden path. The crow cocked its head, found the flower, and with surgical precision, it used its beak to sever the stem and flew the flower up to Holly. It landed on the windowsill and dropped the flower into her open palm. Holly produced a small square of bread she'd sneaked from dinner and gave it to the crow, which quickly ate it and flew back to the apple tree.

Holly held the petals and inhaled deeply. The fragrance was almost overwhelming to her, a colossal medley of powerful scents. Two years ago, Holly had noticed that her sense of smell had become much, much stronger than it had been. She had noticed because a mouse had died in the garden and the stench of its rotting flesh had woken her from a sound sleep. It had been foul. Since then, she had realized that she could smell everything better. Smells weren't just smells anymore. When she walked through the fields with Posey and Indigo, she noticed the urine spray of territorial animals. Posey and Indigo couldn't smell the ammonia residue, the marks were so old and faded, but to Holly they had texture and meaning as easy to read as a billboard sign. Stay Away. My Field. They were so plain and direct that Holly had felt uncomfortable walking near them.

Shortly thereafter, Holly learned her hearing was enhanced as well. Her room was next to Kenny's room and the first thing she noticed was the constant, rhythmic pattern of his fingers on a keyboard at all hours of the night. Even a pillow over her head couldn't block the sounds. She began to realize that she could hear a grasshopper's mandibles severing through a stalk of grass at twenty paces. It took some time, but when she concentrated, she could force herself to not hear as well. It protected her from some of Cormair's tests, like the ones where he would jam tubes in her ears and pump white sound through them until her teeth shook.

"Holly?" Posey's voice was outside her door.

"What?"

"Can I come in?"

Holly reluctantly left the window and opened the door for Posey. The lanky girl had her hair back in a ponytail and was in a short-sleeved nightshirt. She held up an uncooked bag of microwave popcorn.

"Movie night, remember?"

"What movie?"

"Doctor Sebbins got *Notting Hill* and *The Rundown*. I think she wanted everyone to be happy. C'mon! Hugh Grant—British cutie!"

"You are desperate for action, aren't you?"

"We're not all asexual like you," said Posey, poking Holly playfully in the shoulder. Holly shut her door and followed Posey down the hallway.

"Pose?"

"What?"

"You feeling okay?"

"Fine. Why?"

"The back of your neck is all rashy."

Posey sighed. "These stupid zits. I swear: Billions of dollars of research and they can't do a thing about acne."

Holly reached a finger up and touched Posey's neck. Posey yelped.

"What was that for?"

"Sorry…it just looks…odd."

"Odd?"

"Yeah, like it's not acne."

"Great, now I've got some sort of cyst or something. Just what I wanted."

Holly frowned. "It's on your arms, too."

"What?" Posey stopped and craned her neck back to look at her arm. She swiveled it back and forth. "Gross." Small, white dots were outlined down the back of both her arms to her elbows. Posey touched one and jerked her finger away. "They're sharp!"

Holly put her hand on Posey's shoulders, tracing between her shoulders along the line of spines. "They're across your back, too, Pose."

"What?" Posey shot an awkward arm over her head and felt them with her fingers. "Oh my god. What is this? Why me?" She turned and looked at Holly, her face was gaunt. "What am I going to do, Holly? This is what they're looking for isn't it? This is what they've been waiting to see from us all these years."

Holly couldn't say anything. She'd been hiding her abilities for everyone for some time, even from Posey, who was like her sister.

Posey turned back to Holly, her eyes were wide. "You cannot tell anyone. Okay, Hol? You can't tell. I don't even want to know what they'll do to me if they find out."

"But Posey, if these get worse, you might need help."

"Don't tell them! I'm serious, Holly! Do not tell them!"

"I won't," said Holly. Worry began to gnaw at her.

Fat, wet tears began to pool in the corners of Posey's eyes. "Why does bad stuff always happen to me? I'm tall. I'm ugly. I have this stupid zit face and big beaky nose. And now I'm becoming the freak-of-nature science project that Cormair wanted."

"Don't cry, Posey. Sebbins will know something is up."

"Don't tell me what to do, Holly. Look at me! I was never pretty, and ever since I got here, I've just been getting uglier and uglier…and now I'm some sort of mutant."

"You're not."

"I am!" Posey shrieked. Her voice cracked into a painfully high octave that seemed to scrape against Holly's eardrums like razors.

"Pose!" Holly reached out and grabbed Posey's arm.

"Stop it! Just, leave me alone, Holly. I need to be alone!" Posey yanked her arm away and threw the bag of microwave popcorn at Holly. "Leave me alone!" Posey stormed down the hall.

Andy's door opened and he stuck his head into the hall. "What's going on?"

"Nothing!" yelled Holly. "Leave it alone, Andy!"

"I didn't do anything!" Andy protested. "Is it illegal to ask a simple question?"

Posey suddenly arched backward in pain and crumpled to the ground screaming.

Holly raced to her side, sliding to a stop. "What? What's wrong? What hurts?"

"My back! My shoulders! It feels like my skin is tearing apart!"

Doctor Sebbins suddenly appeared at the top of the stairs. "Posey? Posey, I'm here!"

Posey was sobbing and twisting in agony. "Oh god! Please help me, Doctor!" Blood stains began to show on the back shoulder area of Posey's nightshirt, red and wet through the cotton.

"Hold her still for me, Holly. Andy, I can use you, too." Doctor Sebbins produced a latex glove from her pocket, ripped it on, and began to palpate Posey's back while Andy fell to his knees next to Posey and held her by the shoulders.

Posey shrieked in pain again. "Please help me! It's burning!"

Dr. Sebbins grabbed at the back of Posey's nightshirt. She used a pair of scissors from the pocket of her lab coat and made a cut through the ribbed neckband. Then, she jerked the nightshirt open to reveal Posey's back. "What are those?"

Two bloody lumps had appeared on Posey's back, jutting out from her shoulder blades. Each of the lumps had a gnarled, bony-looking knob in the center.

Holly pointed and stifled a yelp. "What is happening to her? What are those things?"

"What? What's wrong with me?" Posey shrieked. "What's happening?"

"We've got to get you to the labs, Posey," said Dr. Sebbins. "Andy, I need you to carry her down there for me. Gently, now. Holly, I need you to call Doctor Cormair and tell him to come to the lab right away. Also, I want you to page Nurse Hathcock and ask her to come on the double." Holly ran to one of the intercoms on the wall and pressed the numbers that summoned Cormair and Nurse Hathcock to the lab.

"What is wrong with my back?" cried Posey.

Andy lifted her gently. "I don't know, Posey," he said. Andy smiled at her reassuringly and headed down to the labs with Doctor Sebbins on his heels.

Holly watched them go. The other doors in the residence hall opened and John, Indigo, and Sarah joined Holly in the hallway, wrapping her in a sidelong hug.

"I guess this is it," said John. "I guess it begins. This is what Cormair has been working toward."

Sarah looked down at Holly. "Was this her power?"

Holly was in a daze. Her mind was spinning. Was this sort of thing going to happen to her, too? Would it happen to all of them?

"Cormair's going to keep her away from us, isn't he?" said Holly.

"He's finally got his lab rat," said Indigo. "Posey's going to be examined, worked over, and tested to death."

"Don't say that, Indigo," said Sarah.

"At least he won't be coming for any of the rest of us for a while," said Indigo. "We pretty much get a 'Get-Out-of-Being-Tested-Free Card' here."

"That's a heartless bitch kind of thing to say," said Sarah. "Posey is our sister."

"Maybe your sister, round-eye, but she ain't my sister."

"Indigo, stifle it. We don't need attitude right now. This is a time when we need to stick together more than ever," said John. "If Posey has begun to show the changes from all our years of testing, you know that the rest of us probably will, too."

"I already have," said Holly quietly.

"What?" said John.

Holly swallowed hard and tried to get some confidence in her voice. "I said I've already changed. I have powers."

"What?"

"I can talk to animals. I can speak to them. I understand their languages." Holly was so scared she was shaking. She had come to terms with her abilities some time ago, but to actually speak about them out loud—it sounded like the rant of a crazy woman. "I can make animals do things for me. I can hear and smell really well, too."

"That's insane," said John.

"You had a Swiss Cake Roll this morning for breakfast," said Holly.

"You saw me have it," said John.

"I slept in this morning. I didn't have breakfast. I can still smell it on your breath."

John slumped back against the wall. "That's messed up."

"And Indigo—I know you smoked a cigarette this weekend when you snuck out. I can still smell it in your hair and on your skin."

Indigo blushed. "I did. But I showered like five times since then."

"Doesn't matter to me," said Holly. "I can still smell it."

"That's impressive," said John.

"And Sarah—you were in a cave today, a cave that's usually inhabited by pine martens in the winter."

"What?" yelped Sarah. "Gross! What's a pine marten?"

Andy came back up the stairs. He looked worried. "Sebbins took Posey away from me as soon as we got to the labs. Cormair was already there. They slammed the doors shut and locked them. I don't even know what they're going to do. What are we talking about?"

"Powers," said Sarah. "Holly's got 'em."

"I talk to animals," Holly whispered.

Indigo sighed. "I turned on my stereo today."

"So?" Holly said. "Big deal. So did I."

"With my mind. From across the room."

"Oh," said Holly.

"I'm pretty sure I'm telekinetic. That stereo thing was the first time anything like that ever happened, but that's what I think they've been training me for. Every time I go into the labs lately, Seb's been all like 'Pretend you have an invisible arm.' They want me to move blocks and stuff. It's got to be telekinesis."

"Aw, man," sighed Andy. "Nothing has happened to me, yet. This sucks." He and Sarah exchanged a look.

"Me neither," said John. "Telekinetic! That would be so cool."

"Are you sure that nothing has happened to you?" asked Indigo. She was eyeing John suspiciously.

"I am," said Andy.

"I wasn't asking you, big dummy. John—look at yourself. You have muscles like a weightlifter. How many weights do you lift each day?"

John shrugged. "I don't. I wish I did, though. This place doesn't have a weight room. I just do a lot of sit-ups and pull-ups and run that obstacle course."

Indigo suddenly lunged forward throwing a punch at John. He fluidly swiveled to the side and blocked her arm with one arm, shooting out his other arm in an elegant counter-punch. His extended fingers stopped millimeters from Indigo's throat. It had only taken fractions of a second. He moved so fast that even he didn't know what had happened. John and Indigo stood frozen for a moment. John's eyes were wide and he jerked his hand back, staring at it incredulously. "I didn't mean to do that. I just sort of *did* it. It was involuntary, I swear, Indigo! You know I wouldn't hurt you!"

Indigo swallowed hard and touched her throat with her fingers. "I shouldn't have done that. It's my fault, but I had to test a theory I've been working on. I think you're a weapon, John. I've been watching you. You never, ever get tired when you run, even when you sprint. You never trip. You're never clumsy. Everything you do is graceful. What other purpose would you have than to be a living weapon?"

John opened his mouth, and then closed it. He looked at her stupidly. "Maybe I'm just an athlete."

"Yeah," said Andy, "because all athletes are trained to shoot guns and throw daggers while running an insanely difficult obstacle course. I remember that event from the Olympics."

"Or remember why we stopped playing darts?" said Sarah. "You *always* won. It wasn't fun anymore. You hit any spot you aim for. You never miss."

"So what? That doesn't mean I'm a weapon."

"Look at the facts," said Indigo. "Holly can control animals. I have telekinesis. John's a super athlete who is also a deadly marksman. What's the purpose of that?"

"Cormair says he's advancing human evolution. Maybe that's the future of mankind," said Sarah. "We develop abilities that help mankind."

"How is being a marksman *helping* mankind," said Indigo. "Unless your version of 'helping' means killing them with a single shot."

"That's not what I meant," said Sarah. "There might be other purposes for John's ability."

"Are you that dense, blondie?" said Indigo. "John is a trained killer. He never gets tired, he can hit anything he aims at, he moves faster than he thinks.

Those are tools of an assassin if I've ever heard it. He's a killer. Unless you think that sort of thing is helpful as an attendant in a nursing home."

"Well, what about you?" said Sarah. "Telekinesis would be a helpful ability. So is talking to animals. Think about what we could accomplish if we could openly communicate with animals."

"Telekinesis as helpful? Maybe. If I was a quadriplegic, I could see it. But as someone who can get things for herself? I don't see much use to it."

"I do," said John. "There's a lot of uses for it."

"Like what?"

"Like, what if a telekinetic could pull the pins on the grenades attached to a soldier before he has a chance to use them? How about turning off a security system from across a room? Maybe a telekinetic could drop a mountain on a platoon in the field? I think there are probably a lot of uses for a telekinetic, but I'm only coming up with military aspects."

Indigo's lips were moving, as if she were talking to herself, going over facts in her head. She suddenly stopped and looked up, her face was ashen. "Think about it: John's a killer, I can kill, Holly can communicate with animals that could kill. We're all killers."

"Don't be stupid," said John. "I don't kill. Neither do you or Holly."

Andy was squinting at Indigo. "Hold it. I think she's on to something. What else could it be?"

"We're all weapons," said Indigo. "If your powers show up, there's going to be something weapon-like about them; I'm sure of that. I'll bet Posey's changes will give her some sort of weapon ability. Andy, Sarah, Kenny—if their abilities show up, I'll bet there's some weapon aspect there, too. That's the point, right? They want to make us some kind of superhero soldiers...genetically 'fix' us so we're beyond human...then, send us overseas to kill their enemies. There's no 'next step of human evolution' like Cormair keeps harping about, we're turning into weapons. We're humans with superhuman weapon abilities."

"I'm not a weapon," said Holly.

Indigo slumped against the wall and slid to a squatting position. "Right, Holly...because there's nothing at all useful about someone being able to tell every bird, bug, and beast in the area to attack and maul a person...Or how about being able to tell a swarm of yellow jackets to maliciously sting a man to death? Yeah, sure, there's no weapon potential there."

"I wouldn't do that."

"Would you have a choice?" Andy said.

"What do you mean?"

"If you were a weapon, you could be detained under some stupid Homeland Security policy or something. You could be *forced* to use your powers."

"I wouldn't," said Holly. "I'm never going to tell Cormair about my powers." She shuddered. The idea of commanding animals was appealing until Indigo put those thoughts into her head. Holly wasn't a killer; they couldn't make her kill. She had never thought of herself as powerful, but perhaps Indigo was correct: Maybe she could be a weapon. Holly quickly forced the idea out of her mind. It was frightening. She couldn't let herself be manipulated like that.

"I think keeping our powers secret is the best idea for everyone," said Indigo. "Unless something happens like it did to Posey—but we have to keep anything physical like that hidden as best we can." Indigo paused and her eyes flicked down the hallway. But, we've got to be together on this one."

"We need to get Kenny in this, too," said Sarah, following Indigo's eyes. The group shuffled to Kenny's door—the only door on the second floor that wasn't adorned with comic strips, pictures of bands, or even a name plate and a "Do Not Enter" sign. Sarah knocked and the door opened. Kenny's stoic face peered out. He didn't speak.

"Kenny, do you have any powers yet?" blurted Indigo. "Posey had a massive breakdown tonight. Something happened to her and Sebbins took her to the lab."

Kenny blinked twice. He peered around at the faces of the others. He shook his head briefly.

"No powers?" said Indigo. "None at all?" Kenny started to shut the door but Andy jammed his foot into the base.

"Hold up, Kenny. We're coming in," said Andy. Kenny backed up, startled. He quickly turned off the monitor on his computer. As the five of them entered his room, Kenny slowly backed into the far corner like a trapped rat.

Holly shut the door and looked around at all of their faces. "We need to keep our powers secret, agreed?"

There was a chorus of nodding heads. Kenny stood staring as if they were going to gang up and beat him down. His arms were up in a semi-defensive posture.

Holly sighed. "Oh for the love of macaroni, Ken. What is wrong with you? We've known each other for ten years and you still act like we're strangers. Just answer like a human being for once: Will you keep your powers secret if they manifest themselves?"

Kenny nodded. He cleared his throat. "Yes, I will." His voice sounded hollow and strange. Holly watched a red flush creep up the back of his neck.

"Good. I shudder to think about what is happening to Posey right now," said Holly.

"Maybe we should go help her?" suggested John.

"What?" Sarah yelped. Holly knew what she was thinking. Going into the labs without one of the doctors meant big-time trouble, and going in with the idea of getting one of them out of testing! Holly could not even begin conceive of the punishments. Once, when she was eleven, Holly and Posey had wandered into one of the classrooms without permission and rifled through the papers in the cabinets. When they were caught, they had been sentenced to a month of solitary confinement in their respective bedrooms. No music, no movies, no communicating with any of the others. That had been harsh enough. An unaccompanied foray into the labs was insanity. Who knew what Cormair would do to them?

"Seriously! Indigo says I'm a weapon, right?" said John. "Well, maybe it's time I figure out exactly what kind of a weapon I can be. I'll just sneak down there and bust her out. Bring her back to her room."

"What if she's really sick?" asked Sarah. "What if this…reaction…she had tonight was because the testing and stuff is going wrong?"

"Maybe it is," said Indigo. "I don't have any side effects. Neither does Holly or John."

"So what if breaking Posey out of the labs might kill her?" said Holly. "We can't let that happen, either."

"What should we do then?" asked Andy.

"We go down as a group and offer moral support. We be there for her and let her know we don't think she's a freak," said Holly. "Posey would be there for us. She's like that. You all know it. She's the only one of us who makes out birthday cards for everyone. She likes being in this place, I think. She still remembers all of our last names."

"Our last names?" John said. "I don't even remember my own last name."

"Redmond," said Holly. "Posey knew it. We talked about it today. She remembers all that stuff."

"Jeez," said John.

"Holly's right. We have to go to her," said Sarah. "Remember when John was down there getting those horrible tests? Remember how helpless we felt up here? I'm not going to leave Posey alone down there. I think we need to break her out."

"What will we do if we do that?" Andy asked. "That's a major violation. We'll all be punished severely."

"Screw that," hissed Indigo. "I am sick to death of them treating me like an object."

A slow smile crawled over John's face. "I've got an idea. You know how we all said we were going to leave here some day?"

Sarah looked horrified. "We said some day! Not…today!"

"Why not today?" said John. "Good a day as any. What makes today different from next week or next month?"

"What about our…abilities?" Sarah's voice wavered. "Andy and Kenny and I haven't changed yet. What if things happen to us like they happened to Posey? What if we need help? I thought that Doctor Cormair was going to help us learn to use our powers and such."

"I didn't need any help," said Holly. "I just kind of did it."

"Look at me! That punch!" said John. "I don't know that we'll need a lot of training. I think it'll just come naturally."

"What if it doesn't?"

"Sarah, c'mon!" Indigo sighed, throwing up her hands. "This is a chance! We've been going through the wringer here for a decade, just counting days and clock-watching until we got old enough to leave! Maybe we've all just been waiting for a spark to help us get up the courage to leave? This is a spark! We pack our bags, meet in the lobby before dawn, bust Posey out of the lab, and get out of Dodge before Cormair can force us all into brain scans and muscle stimulation tests."

Sarah bit her lip. She looked over at Holly.

"Let's do it," said Holly.

"Andy?" Sarah looked at him.

He nodded. "It's time."

Indigo frowned. "They're not going to just let us go down there and stroll into the lab. It's not a walk in the park. We can't even get past those security doors."

"I…" Kenny suddenly spoke. He stopped, cleared his through and started again. "I…can."

Doctor Cormair placed the girl into a tank of a special solution of his own creation. He didn't have an official name for it; for lack of a better term, he called it the hyper-womb. It was a cylindrical glass tank filled with an oxygenated syrup of steroids, antibiotics, and stimulus agents that was meant to provide accelerated rehabilitation to his charges. When their bodies began to change, the hyper-womb would heal them, and get them through the transformation process with minimal stress and at a greatly accelerated rate. The girl was suspended in the tank now, completely submerged. Her lungs had filled with the syrup, as had her stomach. By now, her blood stream was pumping medicine and steroids through her system to help her cope with the changes.

Cormair sat and watched with self-satisfaction. He knew the children had been lying to him and now here was his proof. Doctor Sebbins monitored the girl's vitals on a machine next to him. She hadn't spoken since the girl had been brought down.

Posey's hair hung in damp tendrils around her face and shoulders. From her back, the appendages were growing at a visible rate. The bones had at first looked like simple finger bones, but now they had elongated and thickened. A pair of gangling, slender bones jutted out from her shoulders and muscle tissue was ebbing from her body in long, corded strips to surround the bones, slowly crawling around them like caterpillars. The bony spines from the back of her arms had lengthened and thickened as well, curving in thin arcs toward her latissimus muscles. The spines pierced into her flesh, connecting with the muscle, but becoming wrapped thickly with muscles of their own. At the point where the bones originally broke through her back, her own skin was growing to cover the bones and the muscle without so much as a scar.

"Brilliant, is it not?" said Cormair. He felt a need to break the tension in the room. He had respect for Dr. Sebbins as a scientist, but felt that her emotional attachment to the experiments had been too strong. Dr. Sebbins saw them more as people and not as projects and that was her biggest weakness.

Sebbins looked up from her machine's monitor. "I'm sorry, Doctor. I wasn't listening. What did you say?"

"I said it is brilliant. We scanned through hundreds of thousands of individual DNA profiles to find this girl who had the proper body mechanics for the experiment and was at the proper pre-pubescent age to begin implanting secondary DNA splices. This particular girl's DNA was complementary to bird DNA, thus she became an experiment to create something avian. Those appendages will develop into actual wings if my research was correct. Feathers and all!"

"I know, Doctor. I've read the files."

"But, are you not amazed? We are on the cutting edge of the future here, Dr. Sebbins. We are creating a new type of human being, an entirely new species."

"People have been destroyed for playing God, Doctor."

"Dr. Sebbins, you will not scare me with your fairy tales."

"I'm just saying, Doctor: Look at literature, history. People have been punished for reaching above themselves. Does the name 'Icarus' mean anything to you?"

"I am not worried. I have too much to lose to be worried."

"I'm worried about the wing structure," said Sebbins. "It doesn't look as if she will be able to utilize those wings for propulsion. The muscle structure looks too weak."

"She will be able to propel with the wings," Cormair's voice was firm and sure. "She is not going to take off like a game bird or a finch, but she will fly.

I imagine she will be much more like a condor or an albatross. Perhaps her human legs will give her an advantage for lift-off that condors do not possess. The wings will allow her to utilize thermals to glide for hours, maybe days if she can stay awake. They will also allow her to glide from high places, escape routes and the like. Surveillance. That will be her forte. Her eyes were genetically enhanced to be as powerful as a falcon's eyes, you know."

"I know," said Sebbins, rolling her eyes. "I said I read her file."

"The only thing I'm worried about is her vocal chords. I wonder if they will be able to stand up to the enhancements I tried to implant. That was my idea, you know—turning her voice box into a weapon."

"'Shrike Scream' it's called in your files."

"A voice box that's been mechanically enhanced and amplified to the point of being able to cause physical damage with a scream. Wonderful!" Cormair never smiled. His face only gave hints to his emotions, but he was happy. Ecstatic, even.

A pneumatic door slid open at the back of the lab. Cormair and Sebbins both stood up. A slightly overweight man in a dress military uniform walked through the door. He was bald with a thick mustache. A dark gray service cap was tucked under his arm and he walked with a brisk, smart step.

Cormair swallowed hard. He rubbed his palms on his lab coat and nervously straightened the lapels. He extended one hand genially. "General Tucker! I was not expecting you for some time, yet."

"I received a message that you finally had a major development," Tucker said. He ignored Cormair's outstretched hand and kept his eyes on the tank. "What has happened? That looks like Subject Six in that tank."

"Posey," said Sebbins. Cormair hushed her with a stern look.

"Yes, General. That is Subject Six. We have had an extremely exciting development. The project has finally borne fruit. It has begun to sprout its wings."

"*Its* wings?" Sebbins hissed.

"Why is it in that tank?"

"Why is *she* in that tank," said Sebbins. This time, General Tucker turned and looked at her. He narrowed his eyes.

"Why is *it* in that tank?" he reiterated.

Cormair felt his chest tightening. "The subject is undergoing an accelerated mass transformation process. In the past few months, we have been administering a cocktail of gene development serums and pituitary stimulants to Subject Six. The subject has also been given bone growth enhancers in order to stimulate the scapulae growth that we hoped to achieve. Combined with the avian DNA splices and injections administered over the past ten years, it appears that Subject Six is precisely on schedule. The subject remains in the tank in order to facilitate fast, pain-free bone-and-muscle growth as well as to allow us constant monitoring to all chemical changes in the body. I expect the subject to be operational within fifty hours."

"Excellent," said General Tucker. He approached the glass of the tank and examined the wing stubs on Posey's back. "Excellent," he said again. "And it will be able to fly?"

"She—" Sebbins began, but Cormair cut her off quickly.

"If everything works as I have planned it: Yes, the subject will fly. At the very least, the subject will be able to glide for extensive amounts of time."

"And the eyes?"

"I believe the eyes may already work. I have not confirmed this, but I have my suspicions."

"Such as?"

Cormair cleared his throat. "This subject used to wear glasses, General. However, the subject has not worn glasses or contacts in almost a year, except when she knew she was going to be brought to the lab. I believe the subject's vision to be quite incredible."

General Tucker nodded. "Excellent," he said again. "Doctor Cormair, I believe this development may save you from...unpleasantness. I don't have to tell you that the investors in this project have become extremely...impatient...waiting for you to finally produce some results."

"Thank you, General."

"However," the general continued, "once I bring them this result, they are going to be extremely *hungry* for more. Do we have an understanding between us?"

"Of course, General," said Cormair.

"If this bath is going to speed up their...changes...why aren't they all in the baths?"

"It's not like that, General," said Sebbins. "If they are subjected to the serum without confirmed change to their structures, the steroids and enzymes in the serum will tear the flesh from their bones and destroy their muscles. They have to go into their changes on their own, and I don't believe any of them will be undergoing as dramatic a physical shift as Posey. Perhaps Andy, but none of the others will require the serum to survive their shifts. At the most, they will experience some discomfort, some soreness."

"Why haven't you figured out something different then? Why haven't you been figuring out some way to speed the rest of them through it, then?"

"Are you some sort of sadist who—" Sebbins began. Cormair grabbed her by her shoulders and spun her away from the general.

"General," said Cormair, "you have children, don't you?"

Tucker's eyes darted from Cormair to Sebbins and back. "Why?"

"If you have children you understand how difficult they can be to deal with, am I correct?"

Tucker hesitated. "Affirmative."

"That is because their brains are basically like a chilling pudding. There are some bits that are solid and some bits that are still trying to become solid. Their brains are trying to determine who they are, what they are, and what they can do and cannot do. I have made this whole proposition even more difficult for these seven subjects because I transplanted DNA, tampered with their muscles and skeletons, spliced their genes, stripped out their immune systems and implanted systems that I customized to each of them, and I added bits and pieces to their brains! If I tried to expedite that before I knew where their heads were going to be, I would essentially be sentencing them to death. Their brains would attempt to solidify at such a rate that the necessary components that control their new skills and their bodies would be forced into places that they don't belong. They would become brain-damaged. They would lock down into a vegetative state and all the billions of dollars that has been invested in this project would be wasted. That is also why I have tried to make them live as normal a teenage life as I could in these surroundings. I encouraged them to find hobbies, watch movies, watch TV, and think for themselves, despite your desires. I was attempting not to ruin this entire project by having the research subjects become unresponsive, dead tissue." Cormair finished his speech with a dominance posture, crossing his arms and staring hard at the general. He hoped the general would blink first.

General Tucker's mustache twitched. "Very well. I will give you an extension. However, I want to have facts on Subject Six's abilities—documented with digital video as soon as it is removed from this tank. Your investors will be expecting it as well."

He nodded at Cormair and Sebbins and turned on his heel, military fashion, and strode to the door. He turned back. "Now that this project of yours is bearing fruit, Dr. Cormair, I will be increasing security on this base. We do have…enemies…that might wish to intervene on this project. They may know of its location. You can expect to see an increase immediately. I would prepare the experiments for this, of course. A swift-attack vehicle parked on the lawn may disturb them." He nodded again and walked out of the room. The pneumatic door hissed shut behind him.

Cormair blew out a long, slow breath. His knees felt weak and shaky. His heart was beating rapidly, painfully. He collapsed feebly into his chair, hands falling limply to the sides. Tucker was the sort of bully that Cormair feared since he was a boy. Science was his work, his life. It was his only desire. Putting up with people like Tucker was the price he had to pay in order to indulge his desires.

"Water, please," he said. Sebbins reached into a small cube refrigerator under the desk and handed him a bottle.

"You kowtowed to him," she said. "All this time, I've only see the legendary ice-cold Doctor Cormair, the fabled emotionless stone gargoyle—heartless, soulless, relentless in his work, driven and single-minded. But, I see you have a weak spot."

"I will thank you not to mention it again, please," said Cormair. He drained the bottle of water in a single breath. "General Tucker is the liaison of the group that has funded this project for the past decade. He pays your checks, my checks, and enables us to be able to do this great work of ours. He has been the only person to check on our work here. He has had the only say on whether or not this project continues since its inception."

Cormair stood up and walked to the tank, staring at the young woman suspended in the brilliant orange serum. "This project…is the culmination of my life's work, Doctor. I have been doing recombinant gene therapies and working on creating the next order of life since I was an undergraduate student! This is all I have ever done. It's all I ever wanted to do. If I must kowtow to General Tucker to do it, I will. I am nearly seventy now. That is five decades of work. It is a lifetime of labor in which I have advanced the collective knowledge of humanity more than any scientist before me. I realize, of course, that I will die before the true value of what I have done is know, but the important thing is that I have done it. My name will be legend amongst the learned the world over. The work I'm doing here will eventually lead to cures for cancer, AIDS, Alzheimer's, and who knows how many other diseases and syndromes. I have created something great. I cannot have it taken away from me now; you must understand me!"

Cormair turned and grabbed Dr. Sebbins by the shoulders. "Do you understand? This project is my entire life! It *must* succeed. I will not allow it to fail." His heart pounded and a vein throbbed in his head. He could feel himself sweating. Now that he was so close, he needed to finish this project. He was on to something on a fundamental level that could change the future of humanity. His whole life as a research scientist—his whole life in general—was wrapped in this project. Without the research, without seeing the success of the research, his whole existence was for naught. It could not happen that way!

"This project will go through no matter what!" Cormair stormed to the door of the laboratory. "Keep an eye on her. Alert me the second anything changes!"

"What about the rest of the kids? The military protection? They're bright kids, Doctor. They're going to figure things out."

"I will tell them tomorrow morning, first thing."

Cormair walked to his room. He kept a basic living quarters in the laboratory level. It was decorated in a modern, sparse style. The furniture was black, white, or gray. The walls were white and decorated only with a few famous pieces of art works, mostly old masters. They were prints, of course. Posters, really. Cormair would never waste resources on real art.

There was a small, utilitarian kitchen in his living quarters. Cormair only used it to heat water to brew tea. He set the kettle on a burner and prepared a tea infuser ball of a leafy, strong peppermint tea. It would calm his stomach. It would calm his beating heart.

Sebbins was a good assistant. No. Sebbins was a great assistant. But, if she tried to get his project stopped, he would have to fire her. She was too close to the subjects. That was jeopardizing the project.

If she tried to stop the project…

If she tried to stop his research…

If *anyone* tried to stop his research…

Cormair knew that he would have to stop her if she tried anything to jeopardize the project. He would kill if he must.

Kenny's palms were sweating. He knew he could do it, of course. He could open the doors. He could rewire the passkeys. He could make it so no door to this lab ever opened again. He *knew* he could do it…but he had never tried it with someone else watching. Now, as he stood in front of the door to the labs, it was all he could do not to feel their eyes boring into his back as he flexed his fingers in preparation to make contact with the security system.

"C'mon, Kenny!" Indigo hissed. "It's almost dawn. Cormair and Sebbins have to sleep some time. This is the best chance we've got to rescue her."

Kenny wasn't a hero. He was a computer nerd and he accepted that long ago. He was going to leave the Home and blend into the ether, using his computer skills to make a great living and have a real, human existence for the first time in his life. He'd even met a friend online, a girl, and they were going to get an apartment together in Seattle. Kenny didn't love her or anything; that would be stupid to fall in love with someone you'd never seen or spoken to, but she was a kindred spirit, someone who wanted to hang out with Kenny because she liked talking to him, not because they were forced into some horrible, B-movie science experiment together.

He touched the keypad of the door and the data flow hit his brain like a tornado. Rewiring a basic firewall security program through a computer wasn't overly difficult, slightly taxing at best. However, getting into an actual security protocol, a door on a vault or a computerized gate, was a different matter. The data streams weren't like they were in a computer, like wooden building blocks to be pried apart and restacked. The stream in a heavy-duty electronic lock was more like an old brick-and-mortar wall. Kenny had to break through the security streams and hack away the individual locks with his mind. He had to force, not finesse. It was physically draining. He wasn't actually moving, but the toll on his body was immense. He knew he was sweating. He could feel sweat trails sliding down his back, soaking his shirt, and making it cling to his skin. He could feel the tickle of sweat beads crawling down his forehead and clinging to his eyelashes. His chest began to hurt as his heartbeat increased. The wall was falling, but it was taking too much time. Kenny didn't know if he would be able to stand at the lock long enough to do it. His face flared red with the stress and his eyes rolled back into his head. It was all he could do to cling to consciousness…and suddenly the wall fell. Kenny collapsed in a heap, weak as a newborn, sweating, straining for breath, dizzy and sick.

Holly knelt down and felt his forehead. "He's burning up!"

"I'll be…okay," Kenny whispered. His throat was dry; his tongue felt swollen.

"Did you get through the door?" asked Indigo.

"Indigo! Be sensitive! Kenny's hurt," Sarah hissed. Indigo glared at Sarah.

"Be…okay," Kenny reiterated. His head felt as if it was being crushed by waves of pain. He had to grit his teeth and seethe in order to keep from passing out. His stomach churned and he became sick.

"Gross!" Sarah's face screwed up as if she were going to throw up, too.

"Does that always happen, Kenny?" asked John.

Kenny nodded. "It's the trade-off." The pain began to lessen. "I've never had it that bad, before. But, I've never tried anything that difficult before. I usually just stick to the computer…it's less—" he wretched again, "—physical. Leave me here for a while. I need to rest. I'm not…strong enough…to walk."

"We're not leaving you behind," said Holly. "I'll stay."

"Andy, can you carry him?" asked Sarah.

"Sure. No problem." His thick arms lifted Kenny off the ground as if the lanky hacker was an infant.

Kenny felt like a rag doll. He lay limply in Andy's arms. It made him feel even weaker.

"What's the new passkey, Kenny?" asked Indigo.

"One…one…one…one."

"Eleven eleven? That's it?"

"Didn't want it to be too difficult."

"Why not just one number then?" said Andy. "Seems to me that'd be even less difficult than four numbers. How about no numbers? That'd be easier, yet!"

Indigo punched the numbers and the pneumatic door hissed and slid open. The six made their way down a dimly lit corridor and opened a second door—same pass code. Kenny had recoded the entire security system.

The main lab was at the end of a system of corridors and down several stories. It was buried deeply beneath the Home. The elevator at the end of the hall was rigged with a security camera and another security code separate from the pneumatic doors.

"Security might see us in the camera," said Sarah.

"Anybody got a power to disrupt a camera?" asked Andy.

"I might...but, I don't know if I have the strength," said Kenny.

"Anybody got a better idea, then?" said Andy.

"Let me do it," said Kenny.

"We need you to get through the elevator code," said Indigo.

"Why don't you just telekinesis it off the wall or something?" said Holly.

Indigo stuck out her tongue at Holly. "If the camera just stops transmitting, they'll know."

John shrugged. "We've all been in the elevator before. We could just go down as a group, no big deal."

"You don't think they'll get suspicious—six potentially powerful teenagers just out for a morning elevator ride before dawn?"

John gave Indigo a shove, sending the small girl stumbling.

"Jerk!"

"Wait!" Holly hissed. "Do you hear that?"

They all froze. Holly walked over to a door along the corridor; one of the adjacent labs where secondary experiments were examined. Holly opened the door and froze.

Andy peered into the room over her shoulder. "Bugs!"

"They want to help," said Holly.

"You can hear them?" said Andy. "Creepy."

"I can," said Holly. "They want to help." Holly walked over to a floor-to-ceiling cage where dozens of bright green swallow-tailed moths were fluttering in desultory patterns.

"How?" asked Sarah.

"Watch," said Holly. Her eyes began to mist and haze to a foggy white. She opened the cage and the swarm of moths began to flit out of the cage, looping and crossing, bumping into lights and objects, but heading out of the room as a green-and-red cloud, nearly silent, with fuzzy red antennae guiding them as they flew. They landed on everything, tasting, sensing, and moving on once again.

"This is so gross," said Sarah.

"It is not," hissed Holly. "And watch your tongue. They're sensitive. They think they're pretty."

"Oh, they are," said Sarah. "Very pretty. But, they're still *bugs*!"

The moths meandered toward the elevator. The door was standing open. The moths entered and began to gather over the light in the ceiling and the lens of the camera. In moments, the entire elevator light was covered and the camera was blanked.

"If I hadn't seen it, I wouldn't have believed it," said John. "Holly, you have one truly wicked power."

Holly didn't say anything, but the look on her face was not pride.

"Let's do this, then," said Indigo. "Kenny? You ready to break into this elevator?"

Kenny swallowed again. His throat was parched. "Yeah. I think I got one more in me. Andy can you…move me over there?"

Without a word, Andy moved him into the elevator and held him in front of the keypad by the door. Kenny reached out his hand and placed his palm onto the buttons. Instantly, the electrical tingle and the data streams began to wheel through his mind. This combination wasn't nearly as difficult to reroute as the pneumatic blast doors, but given how drained he was, it was still a Herculean task. The cement blocks did fall, though, and Kenny reclined in Andy's arms, too weak to speak or keep his eyes open. The elevator doors closed, plunging the six teens into blackness. Kenny inhaled deeply and fell into unconsciousness as well.

Andy was always strong, even when he was a kid. He could remember wrestling with his older brother before being taken to the Home. He easily manhandled his brother, throwing him about the room with a strength that seemed unnatural for a six-year-old. When he really stopped to dwell on it, the fact that he couldn't remember his brother's name bothered him.

He held Kenny in his arms and barely noticed the boy's weight. Kenny would never be considered a big guy, but Andy wasn't even fatiguing. Could this be his supposed "power" finally manifesting? Sebbins once told him that he was meant to be the strongest of the seven. He didn't know whether she meant emotionally or mentally or physically, but he guessed it had something to do with physical strength since he was easily the worst student of the seven.

The group rode down in darkness and the elevator stopped at the bottom of the lift. The level the lab was on was home to Cormair's private living quarters, Sebbins' private office, and the massive structure of the lab itself, the size of half a basketball court, but cluttered with machines and scanners and implements and devices. It was dimly lit and full of fear and shadows. None of the seven liked it down there. That room only brought memories of pain.

Indigo lead the group from the elevator. "What are the moths going to do?"

"They're going to stay in the elevator until someone collects them. If we're fast, we'll be able to use them to get back upstairs."

"Let's remember what we're going to do here, okay?" said John. "Kenny's already got us the passkey to get into the lab. Cormair and Sebbins should be asleep. If anyone's awake, it'll be Nurse Hathcock. She won't be too tough to handle. She's small and fat. All we need to do is keep her from pressing the alarm button. Sarah, that's your job. You're the fastest of us all. You sprint in and block her from hitting the wall alarm. Then, we get one of the sedative hypos from the wall cabinet and put her under. She's a nice lady, but she can't follow us."

"Got it," said Sarah.

"Then, we locate Posey and get her out of the lab. We beat feet back up to the lobby of the Home and run like we're on fire. We make tracks for the nearest road, get away from here and regroup, then we take our next steps, whatever those might be. If there's trouble, we split up, try to stay alive and just get out of here; we'll meet up at that old abandoned barn down the road."

"What if she's sick or something?" said Indigo. "What if we can't move her?"

"Then, we deal with it when it happens. I think we should stay with her, a show of unity and all that."

Holly whistled lowly. "Cormair will be mad."

"Unity wouldn't work," said Andy. "Think about it: Kenny hacked through the system and Holly commanded a horde of moths. Cormair will review the tapes and know that their powers have started, too. They'll end up in here doing whatever it is they're doing to Posey. The rest of us will never see daylight again."

Indigo and Sarah exchanged looks. "What's our alternative?"

Andy bit his lip. "There is no alternative. We either break her out of there or we don't. If we go in, we go all the way. There's no backing out. If we can't break her out, we're going to be pinned to the wall by Cormair—loss of privileges, no movies, no books, no talking to each other. We will become lab rats, pure and simple. This is it: Gut-check time. We either back out like cowards or we get Posey and blow this place."

Indigo didn't hesitate. "Let's do it."

Andy looked at Sarah. "There's a bigger world with plenty of better caves."

Sarah gave him a half-smile. "If you go, I'll go."

"I'm in," said Holly. "I've been meaning to leave for years."

John scratched his head. His mop of dreadlocks bounced. "I'll go if you all go; no point in me staying here all alone."

"What about Kenny?" said Holly. "He's unconscious."

"Kenny would be the first one out the door," said Andy. "In ten years, he's never, ever even been *here*."

"Then we do this," said Indigo. She reached out her finger and keyed in the four digit passkey. Andy held his breath.

"Holly…wow."

John felt like someone punched him in the gut. There before him, in some sort of glass tank filled with an orange-amber fluid bubbling like a champagne glass, was Posey…only, she wasn't Posey anymore.

"What happened to her?" Indigo could hardly spit out the words.

Andy knelt down and laid Kenny's unconscious body on the floor. "I don't know, but it can't be good."

Holly looked even smaller than normal. She moved behind John and put a hand on his arm. "Is…is she alive?"

His tongue felt thick and he felt a little dizzy, but John whispered, "I…I don't know." The testing had never been this rigid. They had never submerged them in some sort of tank. What was worse was what had happened to Posey's body. She was grotesque, but strangely beautiful. There were large, fleshy mounds on her back, long and pointed; a framework of bone and skin jutted from them in lengthy arcs. A thin membrane of skin hung between the bones like mesh webbing.

"Wings," said Holly, barely above a whisper. "She's growing wings. Like an angel."

"They gave her wings," said Andy. "What were they trying to prove? She looks like she's dead." He punched the wall next to the doorway in the hall and cracked the plaster. John saw a vein standing out in Andy's face that he had never seen before, a thick, obtuse blue vein that ran into his neck.

John put a hand on Andy's shoulder and stepped into the lab. Nurse Hathcock was asleep on a cot in the corner. "Sarah?"

Sarah's face turned to John, her blue eyes were wide and confused.

"Get Hathcock."

"Oh, yeah," Sarah mumbled. She started to walk toward the nurse, but her eyes never left Posey's limp form.

Indigo strode forward boldly and pressed her hands to the glass on the tank. "Let's get her out of there."

John shook his head. "What are you thinking?"

"She doesn't belong in there. It's like she's a specimen in a jar of formaldehyde. Get her out."

"She's in there for a reason, Indigo," said John. He grabbed her wrist and pulled her back from the tank. "Look at her! She's hurt! She's changing! How do you know that taking her out of that fluid won't kill her?"

"How do you know it isn't killing her right now?"

"Stop it, both of you!" said Holly. Fat tears were crawling out of the corners of her eyes.

Nurse Hathcock chose that moment to wake up. The portly, fifty-something woman sat up suddenly and looked over at Posey, seeing the teens in the lab. She scrabbled to her feet, struggling to get her girth out of the cot, her chunky fingers grasping at the eyeglasses that hung from her neck on a chain. "What are you all doing here? You should be in your rooms! Leave now!"

"We came to get Posey," said Holly. "What are you doing to her?"

"Posey's sick, Holly. Indigio! John! Get away from that tank!"

"Get her out, first!" said Indigo. "She doesn't deserve this!"

"This is ridiculous." The nurse made a move toward the wall alarm. "I'm getting Dr. Cormair in here." Hathcock moved unimpeded by Sarah, whose eyes were so focused on Posey in the tank that she completely forgot about her duties to the plan.

"Sarah!" John shouted. She didn't snap out of her trance. Hathcock hit the alarm and a hollow, metallic klaxon began sounding.

"This is not good." John ran over to the series of keyboards and control panels that Dr. Cormair usually sat behind while he was being tested. "One of these has to get her out of there!"

"We could really use Kenny right now," Holly said. She rushed over and began to push buttons and flip switches.

John swatted her hands away. "What are you doing? You don't know what those things do! One of them might electrocute Posey or something." Holly yanked her hands away.

The door to the lab suddenly slid open. Dr. Cormair walked in and looked about with unflappable calm. "What is Kenneth doing in the hallway and why are the rest of you in this room?" His voice was low and measured.

"Get Posey out of the tank!" shouted Holly.

Dr. Cormair walked over to the control panels and adjusted a few of the controls that Holly had messed with. "I am afraid that it will not be possible to release Posey right now, Holly."

"Why not?" Indigo said, drawing herself up to her full height, which wasn't imposing.

"As you can plainly see, Posey is undergoing massive physical change. Releasing her from the hyper-womb would be extremely detrimental to her development, and not to mention fatal at this stage."

"Why? What are you doing? Tell us what's going on, Doc." It was time for them to stop being jerked around. John had enough of the secrets and the half-truths and the tests and the condescension. He was tired of being a team player.

"When you need to know, you will be told," said Cormair. "Please understand."

"I don't think this is your call, Doc," said Andy. "How many years have you been keeping us in the dark and treating us like trained monkeys?"

"Yeah!" Indigo chimed in, "Ten years of being your pets is enough, Doctor! We want to know what all this is about right now."

"No," Dr. Cormair replied coldly. "It is not the time."

"No!" shouted Holly. It was the loudest she had ever yelled. "You don't think we've figured out what you're doing to us? You think we're so stupid that we can't figure out that you're trying to make us into some sort of government weapons project?"

"What?" Cormair's eyes narrowed. "Holly, I am attempting to achieve the next elevation of human development, not weapons."

Holly mirrored Cormair's cold look. "I know there is a hive of wasps in the other room. How about I bring them in here and you can tell me how controlling animals isn't a weapon."

Cormair's face registered slight surprise. "I knew you were lying to me. You have had control for some time, haven't you?"

"Long enough to know how to use this so-called 'ability' I have!"

"What about the rest of you? Have you all manifested your abilities, yet?"

Doctor Sebbins' voice crackled over the intercom. "Dr. Cormair? The passkeys have been changed. I can't get into the lab areas."

The barest hint of a smile tickled at the corner of Cormair's mouth. "Kenneth. I knew his powers were in full use. That is why I kept bringing in specialists to challenge him. I did not know he would be able to reroute physical security systems, though. This is a lovely development."

"Stop changing the subject, Doc! We want to know," Indigo said. "If you know what I can do then I think you'd best cooperate."

"Prove it," said Cormair. "If you truly have telekinesis, Indigo, then please demonstrate it for me."

"What?"

"You heard me," Cormair sat down at his desk. "Make something fly across the room. Here—" he flipped a pen to Indigo's feet, "—use your powers to imbed this pen into my skull like a dart. If you have control, this should not be a challenge."

Indigo glanced at John, her mouth hanging open like a guppy. John shrugged and nodded at her.

"You wouldn't really do it, would you Indigo?" said Sarah. Her voice was wavering.

Indigo looked at the pen, then at Cormair. Her shoulders slumped a little and her head tipped forward, her bangs hiding her eyes. She was defeated.

"Indigo, your power is controlled by your brain. That is, perhaps, the easiest thing for us to monitor. You were hooked to a scanning machine yesterday. I know that your power hasn't manifested itself. Your power was the most implausible. If it manifested at all, I would be surprised. Telekinesis might just be beyond our capabilities. I was actually going to write you off as a failure."

The klaxon continued to go off in the background. Cormair motioned to the speaker where the sound was emanating. "That is bringing the military down here as we speak. I would recommend that you all return to your rooms and we will pretend that this…incident was a mistake."

"Military?" John's mind was racing. The plan had fallen apart. Cormair still controlled them. "What is the military doing here?"

"Protecting you," said Cormair. "They are here to protect the interests of the investors who have financed your education."

"Our education? More like your research," spat Andy. The veins in his arms seemed to be bulging. "We've been your pets, not students. We're tired of it, Doc. We're leaving tonight. And Posey is coming with us."

"Again, that will be bad, Andrew. If you remove her from the hyperwomb, the sensation of the unpurified air on her flesh will cause her levels of pain that she has never experienced before. She will be in intense agony. The shock of it will most likely kill her."

Holly stepped backward. "It's over, then. We're screwed."

"He's bluffing," Andy puffed out his chest. He seemed to get bigger, thicker.

"What if he's not?" shouted Holly. "What if Posey is in pain? What if that tank is helping her?"

"Look at her, Holly! She's barely alive!"

"That medicated coma is for her best interests," said Cormair. "Being submerged in the serum without a breathing apparatus is not something most people adjust to well."

"How do we know you're telling the truth?" Andy said. "You've lied and told us half-truths all our lives! If you're lying, you know we're leaving tonight and your money dries up."

"That wouldn't be a problem," said Cormair. "This research was never about the money."

"It was about being God, wasn't it?" John's voice was low. "The next evolution in mankind…the powers, the abilities…you were playing God."

"This research is bigger than God!" shouted Cormair. He was suddenly angry. He had never raised his voice in ten years. He had never looked angry or frustrated. His face had been an unreadable mask for a decade—and suddenly he was screaming. "This research was about the next step of human life! It was *my life*!"

"Well, now it's about *our lives*, Doctor," John's said calmly. "We deserve to live our own lives now. A decade is more than enough time to make us your lab rats. It's time to let us go."

"The work is not over yet," said Cormair. "I will not permit it to end!"

"It's not your choice anymore."

"John…" Kenny's voice was low and crackling with wheezes. "I have control of the tank. I can get Posey out." No one had noticed him crawling to the banks of hard-drives and servers along the wall. He was slumped back against the rack, his hand on one of the processors; a thin line of blood trickled from his left nostril from the stress and strain.

"Get her out, then," said John. He backed away from Cormair and headed toward the tank.

"No!" Cormair shouted. He reached into a drawer and produced a small handgun. "John! Back away from the tanks. Kenny, relinquish control of the computers. You are jeopardizing Posey's life!" He leveled the handgun at Kenny. "Now, Kenneth. I will wound you if I must."

"You'd shoot your precious research?" Holly looked incredulous. "You're insane. You'd shoot one of us? How many billions of dollars would you waste?"

"It doesn't matter," said Cormair. "Only the end results matter. My life's work matters! You are just a part of that! I must see this project through to completion. Shooting Kenneth in the leg or the arm—that won't kill him. It will stop him, though. Kenneth, you must not empty the tank."

"Too late, Doc," Kenny smiled.

Doctor Cormair whirled around and saw the level of fluid in the tank rapidly decreasing. As the fluids drained, Posey's body sunk to the floor of the tank. "No! You fool! You utter fool!" Cormair raised the gun at Kenny.

The pen at Indigo's feet suddenly lifted up from the ground and flew through the air, piercing the doctor's forearm between the radius and the ulna causing him to drop the gun. It clattered to the ground loudly. Indigo smiled triumphantly. "Telekinesis, Doctor. I'm no failure."

Cormair clutched at his forearm, his hand was curled into a ball, the Bic pen sticking out of both sides of his wrist, the end covered in blood. "Very good, Indigo," the doctor's voice was low and precise again. "I will very much enjoy studying your brain now. This is a delightful development."

Indigo suddenly twisted and extended her fist. A brief flash of silvery-white light generated from the end of her fist and blasted forward, smashing hard into Cormair's chest. The thin, elderly man flew backwards as if he had been hit by a truck.

"Holy cow!" Andy breathed. "Indigo, that was amazing!"

"Let's get out of here," said Indigo. She winced and closed her eyes, bringing her hands up to rub her temples. John could see her gritting her teeth. "He's done. Andy, please get Kenny."

The fluid had drained completely out of the tank. Posey was motionless, slumped against the glass, a dead seabird washed on the shore.

"Posey?" Holly said. She was crying. "Posey, please wake up."

"She can't hear you," said Indigo. "We need to get the lid off of the tank."

"Leave it to me," said Andy. He crawled up the ladder on the side and put his hands on the sides of the metal lid. There were tubes and mechanisms all over the top. Andy slipped his fingers under the metal and began to pull. He braced his legs on the ladder and began curling his arms up. The lid trembled. The veins in Andy's arms jumped out and his neck muscles bulged and seemed to double in size. A low, guttural scream drew out from Andy's stomach, and broke into voice in his throat. Glass began to crack and splinter down the sides of the tank. Suddenly, the entire tank shattered and rained down in razor shards of glass. Andy fell backwards off the ladder, landing on the ground with a brutal thump that made the floor shake.

"Andy! What's going on?" John fell to his friend's side and put a hand on his arm. It felt like a bag of snakes was twisting beneath the skin. "Look at him!"

Andy's arms seemed to be heaving, doubling in size and mass. His chest was bubbling with muscles. He seemed to be becoming something twice his already impressive size. He wasn't getting taller, only increasing in muscle and girth. His chest expanded, his stomach became broader, his neck thicker.

"Something finally happened," said Sarah. "He's changing, too."

Andy's eyes blinked open and he began to scream. His eyes were wide and scared and his scream sent chills through John's bones. It was a scream of absolute agony.

"Nurse Hathcock! Do something!" Holly shouted.

The nurse bustled over and tried to hold Andy's head. He reached over his head and grabbed her by the shoulder. With the flick of his wrist, Nurse Hathcock was sent flying across the room and smashed into the rack of servers. She fell to the floor motionless. Sarah was at her side in an instant. "She's still breathing!"

Inside the tank, Posey stirred for a moment.

"She's alive!" Holly pointed.

Posey's eyes snapped open wide. Her dark brown eyes were gone, replaced with brilliant, reflective, golden eyes—the sclera and iris had turned a dark, molten gold color, with only the tiniest pinpoint of black where the pupil should be. Even from across the room, John knew she was in pain. And then Posey opened her mouth and screamed.

All the glass in the room exploded. John collapsed in agony; his eardrums felt punctured. Holly crumpled to the floor, clutching at her ears. Indigo and Sarah both grabbed their heads and fell to the ground. The scream clawed and punched their brains. John could only writhe in pain and pray for the pain to end.

Posey felt like she was on fire. Every nerve in her body crackled with a thousand sensations and the only thing registering in her brain was pain. Pain at the end of her limbs, pain in her chest, pain in her back, pain in her head— it wouldn't stop. It couldn't stop. The only thing she was able to do was scream, and that caused more pain. Her throat felt like a thousand pins were being dragged down the back of her esophagus, and when the noise blasted from her throat, all hell broke loose.

She couldn't stop screaming, though. She knew she was hurting people. She could see Holly, doubled over in pain. Every detail in Holly's face was crystal-clear and sharp. Every minute dollop of agony that was heaped on Holly registered in Posey's eyes. She knew she was hurting her, maybe killing her, and she couldn't stop. The scream seemed to have a life of its own, turning over and over in her throat and her chest, and destroying everyone she loved.

The pain kept intensifying and burning in her. She struggled to raise her arms, causing more pain; malicious waves of flames seemed to be licking at every inch of her flesh. She clapped her hands over her mouth and tried to muffle the sound. She could feel the pressure of the noise against her hands. Her scream had physical presence, it had body and weight. It was a beam of destruction.

In the muffled din, John somehow got to his feet. He was hurt, she knew, but John was tough. He never got tired, he never gave up. He staggered toward the med-kit on the wall by the hyper-womb tank. Posey watched him, wide-eyed with fear, the scream still blasting from her throat. She didn't know what had happened to her. She didn't even remember being brought to the lab. She remembered the spines, and the bones jutting out of her back. She kept one hand over her mouth and reached back with the other hand, feeling a large appendage. It hurt to touch, like prodding an open wound. She flinched when her fingers contacted the flesh, and the appendage moved. Posey discovered a new sensation in her brain—she could *move* that appendage. It was like suddenly discovering you had an arm you never bothered to use. Posey mentally checked her other shoulder and found another appendage that she could move independently.

John grabbed a jet-hypo of sedatives from the med-kit. When they had first begun testing, the doctor told all of them that he placed just such a sedative in there for just such a reason. When John had asked why, the doctor had only replied, "You'll know when it happens." John took two running strides and propelled himself to Posey's side. He slid to her on his knees, jabbing the hypodermic into her neck, and released the spray.

Posey felt the delicious burn of the sedatives traveling through her bloodstream. She started to get sleepy. The scream dwindled in her throat as the pain decreased. She began to drift into that terrible blackness beyond sleep. It was better than being awake.

Holly scrambled to her feet. Her sensitive ears were still throbbing, a loud, squelching, ringing noise echoed in her head; the sound had actually made her physically sick. She clutched her stomach and fought the urge to vomit. Kenny tossing his guts had been enough for her to witness for one night. Holly stumbled to Posey's side and cradled her friend's head in her lap.

"What did they do to her?"

"I don't know," said John. Andy had stopped screaming, toning his discomfort down to pained grunts. "Let's help Andy." He stumbled away from Posey and dropped to his knees next to Andy. "You okay?"

Sarah was at Andy's side in an instant. She grabbed his wrist and slipped her hand into his. "Andy, I'm here. You're not alone."

Andy's head turned to look at Sarah and John. Blood vessels had burst in his eyes and they were now a vibrant crimson, giving him a demonic appearance. His skin was still rippling and surging as his muscles roiled in intense transformation. His arms were bulking up ridiculously. He looked cartoonish, an exaggerated caricature of his former self.

In the distance, somewhere down the tunnel, a loud, low "boom" reverberated down the corridors, down the elevator shaft, and into the lab. Everyone froze. Holly looked over at John and Sarah. "They're coming."

"They blew the first door," said Indigo. "We need to get out of here."

"What about Posey and Andy?" said Holly. She had never known fear on this level before. She hadn't felt terribly sad about leaving her family. There was a sadness there, yes, but it hadn't been tragically sad. It was almost as if they had been kind strangers raising her while she waited for her real parents to return from a trip. Posey was her *sister*; Andy was her big brother. She cared for them on a deeper spiritual level.

"We'll carry them," said John. He grabbed Andy's hands and tried to lift him into a sitting position. A strange look crossed his face. He braced his feet and tugged again. Andy's torso didn't move. John sank low and grabbed Andy under his arms and pulled. Andy remained on the floor. "Oh geez," John breathed. "His weight increased."

"I can see that," said Sarah. "How much?"

"Ten times? Maybe twenty? It took everything I had to just lift his arms." John shot a furtive glance around at the others. Holly could see that he was scared, too.

"Indigo? Can you lift him?" asked Sarah. "Please?"

Indigo shook her head. "It was all I could do to pick up that pen and fling it. I don't know if I could manage anything better."

Holly felt frustration welling up in her. She felt like crying and screaming and hitting something all at once.

Another low "boom," louder than the last, sounded down the corridors.

"That's door two," said Indigo. "They'll be at the elevator shaft in a bit. Then, they'll be in here."

A back door. That was their only hope. Dr. Cormair was so fastidious that he had back-up plans for everything. He had always been one-step ahead of them when they were kids, figuring out plans for mischief before they could even think of it themselves. There had to be an escape hatch.

Holly gently set Posey's head down and crawled over to Cormair's body. "Doctor?" She eased him off the floor gently and cradled him. He coughed slightly and looked up at her. "Doctor, we need to get out the back door. The military is coming."

Cormair coughed again. Red flecks of blood colored his lips. He looked up at Holly with a confused look on his face.

"Doctor," Holly said again. "We need to leave this lab. We need to get out the back door so the military can't take us and make us into weapons."

Cormair's face lost the confused look, and for a second, the cold, hard face Holly knew so well returned. For a long, terrifying instant, Holly was scared that he might not help them. He reached a hand up, grimacing in pain, and pointed at a dusty, unused monitor in the back corner. It stood on a simple wheeled cart and appeared to be attached to an antique bank of black servers. A new wave of coughs overtook him and he curled into a ball.

"The back corner somewhere! There's a back door! There's something we can use!"

Kenny staggered to his feet; blood from his nose had run down his neck and stained a wide spot on the front of his shirt. "I'll get it." He staggered forward clutching his chest. He put his hands on the monitor and his body went rigid. He took his hands off. "There's a security protocol here. We can get out of here."

"So do it!" should Sarah. A third low explosion rattled the lab.

"They're coming down the elevator shaft," said Indigo. The pneumatic door to the lab was still open from when Cormair had entered. Indigo closed her eyes and concentrated.

Holly watched as nothing happened. "Indigo! Close it manually!"

Indigo's eyes popped open and she flushed red. "Oh yeah!" She jogged across the room and entered the passkey. The door slid shut. She glanced about the room. "That won't hold them for long!"

Kenny had already returned to his rigid state. His body trembled as he cracked the security protocols. A door, dusty with disuse and poor housekeeping, suddenly popped open with a loud metallic creak. Kenny collapsed.

Holly looked around the room. Andy was immovable. Posey was light enough for Sarah to carry, or Holly could handle it if she must. John could get Kenny.

"We have to leave Andy," said John. Holly had been thinking it, too, but she didn't want to be the one to bring it up.

"No!" Sarah was horrified. "I'm not going to leave him!"

"We don't have a choice, Sarah!" John shouted. "The military is going to be in here in an instant. We can't move Andy! He'll be okay. We need to get Posey and Kenny out of here!"

"No!"

Andy's mouth opened. His breath was coming in short, seething gasps. "Go! Get out...of here!"

"You have to come with us, Andy!" Sarah shouted. "All for one, one for all and crap like that. Please!"

Andy grabbed her with one oversized hand. "Don't...make me...throw...you!"

Indigo stepped in and yanked Sarah from Andy's grip. "Come on!"

Holly delicately lifted Posey into a fireman's carry. The difference in their sizes was painfully evident as Posey's dangling arms and legs almost touched the floor when Holly stood up. John ran over and grabbed Kenny. Indigo pushed Sarah through the door first, and the others, without Andy, followed. John kicked the door shut behind them and the newly re-programmed security protocol locked the door shut.

They were in a long, dark tunnel. Holly's sensitive ears could hear drips of water in the distance. She also heard…the soft shuffle of leathery wings. A bat!

"I can't see anything," said Indigo.

"Hush!" Holly said. "There's a bat in this tunnel! He can get us out." Holly reached out mentally, implanting images of friendship and assistance into the bat's mind. The bat replied in kind rather quickly. Holly caught images of what the bat was experiencing, walls and shapes being lit up by echolocation. In seconds, she began to receive images of the tunnel's surroundings. There were some boxes near the door, but the rest of the tunnel was vacant. It had a damp floor from being subterranean, but it wasn't muddy or flooded. The tunnel went straight for about two hundred and fifty yards, and then began to lead upward in a long, low, shallow incline. "This way," said Holly. She began to walk forward, Posey's feet bouncing off the ground occasionally as she walked. The others followed closely behind her, silent, listening to her footsteps.

As the tunnel began to incline, Holly could see a pinpoint of light in the distance. The bat projected images of freedom into her head: Cave mouths, open sky, a forest. It was a long way, but it was freedom.

"We're almost there," she said. "The bat says we're almost there."

"Thank him for me," said John. "And ask him not to fly into my hair."

Holly could feel the fresh air on her face. The air was becoming cleaner and pine-scented. The entrance of the tunnel was blocked off with tree boughs and leaves. To anyone walking through the woods, it looked like a lump of branches. Holly set Posey down and pushed through the tree branches. She popped up in the thick, pine forest, not far from where Andy and Sarah had emerged the previous day. From her vantage point she could see the yard of the Home lit-up like a Friday night football field from portable halogen lights and vehicle headlights.

"This isn't good," she said. Indigo, John, and Sarah quickly scrambled up to see what Holly was seeing.

The yard of the Home was full of soldiers. Military vehicles had set up a perimeter around the Home. A helicopter was in flight to the west with a searchlight swinging from its belly.

John cursed under his breath. "Get back into the tunnel!"

"What?"

"Get back in!" John shoved Holly and she nearly lost her balance. "This is bad! They've got a copter!"

"So? A helicopter can't see us in the dark!"

"Didn't you ever watch an episode of *COPS*? Those helicopters are probably equipped with those high-tech infrared cameras. Our body heat stands out in the forest like blips on a radar screen. If that helicopter passes us, they'll locate us for sure!"

They ducked back under the relative security of the tunnel. John pulled the tree boughs back over the entrance. He slumped against the wall next to Holly. "We screwed the pooch on this one."

"Don't say that," said Indigo. "We got Posey. We escaped the Home."

"We haven't escaped anything yet," said John. "In fact, we're going to be in trouble soon."

"How?" said Indigo.

"Food," said John. "I know you don't eat much, Indigo, and maybe that's a side-effect of your power or something, but the rest of us need to consume a lot of protein and carbs to be able to fuel up. No food means we're going to be weak as kittens in this tunnel."

"I can get us food," said Holly. "But it won't be pretty unless we can cook it."

"Trapped like rats," said Indigo. She flopped backward against the wall and slid to a sitting position. John followed suite, and Holly knelt beside Posey and held her head. Posey was still slick and slimy with the serum from the tank. Holly could feel goosebumps on her arms.

"We should have brought a blanket for Posey," said Holly. "She's still naked and I think she's cold." John tugged his sweatshirt off and handed it over.

"This is the warmest thing I packed," he said. "I don't really get cold. I think it's part of my gene programming."

Indigo rooted in her backpack and came up with an oversized hooded sweatshirt of her own. "I got this."

Sarah took off her plain denim jacket. "She can have this. It's not much. I might have a pair of trackpants, too." She rooted in her duffel until she came up with a pair of insulated black vinyl pants.

Holly took all of the proffered items and began to dress Posey. She tugged the pants on, and then draped her naked torso with the sweatshirts and jacket. She didn't pull them over her head for fear of causing so much pain that Posey would awaken again. After dressing Posey, Holly laid her down on her side and spooned up behind her, draping an arm over Posey and trying to hold her close enough to share heat.

"So now we wait?" asked Sarah.

"Until we figure out something else to do," said Indigo.

The tunnel became quiet and Holly began to feel sleepy. She yawned. John was looking at her.

"Go to sleep," he whispered. His whisper was as loud as a shout in Holly's ears. "I'll stay up. I want to watch the yard, anyway. Maybe I can figure out a way to get us out of here."

"Yeah, like sleep is even possible right now with a battalion of soldiers looking for us."

"You exaggerate," said John. "It's not a battalion. It's maybe a fifth of a battalion, maybe less."

"It's enough," said Holly. "It's probably more than enough."

Andy couldn't believe what he was feeling. If he was undergoing even a fraction of the pain that Posey was undergoing, he could understand why she screamed. Under his skin, his muscles were expanding, rolling, churning like wild animals. His biceps rippled and the skin of his arms stretched like the bicep was going to rip through it. He was sweating and the sweat was oily and gave off a thick, foul odor that made him gag when he accidentally breathed in through his nose.

His jeans tore open at the calf and the thigh. His shirt bulged and stretched until it ripped along the seams. The copper button that fastened his jeans at the waist popped off and ricocheted off one of the walls. The neckband of his shirt became so tight that it threatened to strangle him. He reached up and tried to slip a finger beneath it, but his fingers had swelled so much that they were almost useless. He tensed his neck; rolling waves of pain shot through his body and the neckband tore open. Andy could feel tears rolling down the corners of his eyes and he shook with sobs that he stubbornly refused to vocalize.

Dr. Cormair crawled over to Andy's side. He reached into his pocket and produced a jet-spray hypo. "This is a sedative. It will not put you to sleep. You have too much mass and muscle for this to affect you like it once did. It should ease your pain, though. It might also make it difficult for you to move." Andy felt the cold metal of the hypo touch his neck and a slight pulse as the fluids were released into his system. In moments, the pain in his body lessened to a bearable level, but Cormair had been correct. He was unable to move. His arms and legs became dead weight.

A gruff male voice shouted through the pneumatic door. "Attention! We are about to blow the door to the laboratory! Stand away from the door!"

A second later, the door buckled from the force of a contained explosion and fell into the lab with a horrendous crash. In the span of a heartbeat, a dozen soldiers with machine guns and shotguns burst into the lab. They were screaming orders and commands and checking behind cabinets and under desks. They moved with an amazing proficiency. In seconds, the screaming stopped and another solider walked into the room, followed by Dr. Sebbins.

Dr. Sebbins rushed to Dr. Cormair's side and checked his vitals. "I am afraid I will require an ambulance, Doctor," Cormair coughed. "I believe I have some internal injuries. Indigo has manifested some striking abilities."

The soldier who walked into the room with Sebbins flipped open a two-way radio and called for a gurney and medics. In moments, several military corpsmen sprinted into the room and placed Cormair and Hathcock on gurneys.

"Andy, where are the others?" asked Dr. Sebbins. Andy could detect an edge to her voice. She was nearly pleading with him. "These men need to find them before anything happens to them. It's for their own safety; please understand."

Andy gave her a half-smile, but didn't say anything. He turned his head to face up to the ceiling and stared. The medicine that Dr. Cormair had shot into his neck was already fading. The pain was returning slowly.

The soldier who seemed to be in charge strode over and pulled Dr. Sebbins away from Andy's side. He consulted a chart. "You are Subject One. Codename: Brawn. You are under our employ. You will do as you are told. This is non-negotiable. Where are the other subjects?"

Andy smiled at the soldier. He could see captain's bars on the man's shoulders. A cloth nameplate on the man's shirt read "Krantz." Captain Krantz. His face was heavily scarred on the left side. He had an eye-patch. Captain Krantz the pirate. Andy pictured him with a tri-cornered hat and a parrot. The image made Andy smile more.

The captain turned to Sebbins. "Is this subject retarded?"

"No. He's fine...I hope," said Sebbins. "He's undergoing a physical change, though. His pain level must be through the roof. It's probably all he can do to keep from screaming."

"How do we deal with this?"

"We need to get him to a hyper-womb. There used to be one in this room, but it was apparently destroyed. There are more on this floor."

"You put me in one, and I'm going to destroy it," grunted Andy. His voice seemed foreign to him. His voice seemed to have dropped an octave and it was thick and gravelly.

"I do not know if you will be able to get him off the floor," said Cormair. "His mass has increased exponentially."

"We'll get a forklift down here if we need to," said Krantz. "Can you walk?"

Andy shook his head. His thigh muscles were still rippling like water, swelling and getting thicker. His legs weren't his own currently. Any mental signals he could send to make them move seemed to be ending at his trunk. He could only lie on the ground like a twisted lump of flesh.

"You four," Krantz pointed at a cadre of soldiers. "See if you can get this subject off the floor."

The soldiers quickly surrounded Andy and slipped their hands around his shoulders and legs. On a three count, they all lifted as a group. Andy quivered for a moment, but remained on the ground. In a moment, the soldiers gave up. "Captain, this subject must weigh more than ton, currently."

"Then let's get the forklift." Krantz flipped open the radio again and barked out orders. In moments, the sound of a small engine could be heard in the tunnels. A forklift, painted in sand camouflage, came into the labs. The tines of the lift scraped the floor as they moved toward Andy.

"You're going to hurt him!" Sebbins cried. "He's strong, not invulnerable!"

"Do you have a better idea, Doctor?"

Sebbins bit her lip. "No."

"Then we proceed," Krantz gave the forklift driver a signal and the forklift moved forward. Several soldiers had to slide thick, corded ropes under Andy's neck and arms, and then a dozen of them pulled on the ropes to roll Andy to his side. The forklift crept forward slowly until the tines touched Andy's back. The soldiers let go of the ropes and Andy crashed down on the forklift tines. The driver started to lift Andy and the hydraulics groaned and protested. A few soldiers leapt onto the back of the forklift to keep it from tipping forward. The tines were able to lift Andy a few inches off the floor, but the balance point of the forklift was close to being compromised.

"Get him down the hall; get the doctor to the infirmary," shouted Krantz. "Doctor? Will you be accompanying the subject?"

"I will accompany *Andrew*, yes," Sebbins spat. "He's a human being! Treat him like one!"

Krantz ignored her completely. He turned to two of the corpsmen standing by. "McCloskey, DeWitt—get the subject into a hyper-womb immediately. Get the tank filled and start monitoring his vitals. According to the doctor's records, this one may be capable of extreme strength. Use extra sedation in the tank. I don't need him punching his way out."

Andy gave Sebbins as much of a smile as he could muster. "They better knock me the hell out, because if I can swing my arm in that tank, I'm going to blast out of it."

"I know you will," Sebbins said. She patted his arm and the forklift started crawling out of the lab, straining and slipping with Andy's weight.

Dr. Sebbins bit her lip. She felt like the whole experience was too surreal, too chaotic to be actually happening. Combined with smoky haze from the explosions that took out the doors, the lab felt more dream-like than real, as if she could pinch herself and wake up safe in her own bed. The acrid smoke in her nose and the noise and the diesel smell of the forklift told her that it was all too valid.

The corpsmen were preparing to move Dr. Cormair out of the lab. "Give me a minute with him, please!" Sebbins said. She knelt down next to the gurney. "In private, please, Doctor-Patient confidentiality. I am his personal physician, I have to ask him some relevant medical questions. A patient is entitled to a private conference in this matter."

Cormair arched an eyebrow at Sebbins and Sebbins winked back. The corpsmen exchanged confused glances and shrugs and reluctantly moved back several paces. Sebbins lowered her lips to Cormair's ears. "Where did they go?"

Cormair wheezed and coughed. He whispered as quietly as he could. "The...hidden entrance. The tunnel."

"Do you know where they're heading?"

Cormair shook his head. He tried to speak, but a cough stopped him short.

"Will they leave without Andy?" asked Sebbins.

Cormair coughed and shook his head. "I don't...think so."

"So they'll be on the property."

Cormair nodded.

"How do I stabilize Andy so he can get out of here? I want to find them and take them to the Safe House."

The Safe House was a hidden lab just over a hundred miles away. Cormair had set it up in case of an emergency. He had quietly funneled money to the creation of the Safe House from the incoming grants. The investors didn't know it even existed. Cormair had the foresight to hire several independent contractors to build the lab in sections. It was completely off the grid, supplied with energy by a hydroelectric generator and a geothermal steam vent.

Cormair nodded. Sebbins hoped he knew it was for the best. "The serum," Cormair croaked. "It's the only thing that can help him...but,

Andy…he might be able to take the pain. Posey cannot; her transformation is the most extreme. She must be placed back in a hyper-womb. You might…be able to get Andy out—" Cormair was wracked by a cough that made him wince in pain and brought a trickle of blood to the corner of his mouth. "Inject him with a massive dose of serum straight into his blood-stream, preferably in his carotid artery. He may be able to get enough use of his body. He will need the serum consistently until he…finishes his change." Cormair gasped for air, and then his head lolled to one side.

"Corpsmen!" Sebbins called out. The soldiers rushed to the gurney and began administering oxygen. "Is he going to be all right? I think he might be bleeding internally."

"He just passed out," said one of the men feeling for a pulse. "We need to get him into surgery fast, though. We have a surgeon on the way. He should be at the base in twenty minutes."

Sebbins bit her lip. She walked over to a refrigerator in the corner of the lab where Cormair kept his supply of medicines. There were several IV bottles of serum and a few hypos of sedatives and steroids. She pocketed them all, whispering a prayer of thanks for the oversized pockets of her lab coat.

The soldiers had unceremoniously dumped Andy's body onto the base plate of one of the hyper-wombs. Sebbins could see him struggling to deal with pain. The soldiers were lowering the glass encasement over Andy's body.

"Wait!" Sebbins walked in and injected Andy with two hypos of serum. She lowered her voice and whispered in his ear, "When this takes hold, you should be able to move. Whatever happens happens, okay?"

Andy smiled at her with gritted teeth. "If I start, find a place to hide, Doc. I'm going to trash this place like a Led Zeppelin hotel room."

Sebbins walked over to the life support monitor for the tank and instructed the soldiers to continue lowering the tank. Andy's bulk took up nearly the entire base plate, but tank locked securely into place. The vacuum seal on the base engaged and the tank became water-tight. The serum began to pour down into the tank around Andy, splashing him and covering him with viscous orange syrup. The serum filled the tank quickly.

Sebbins could see the look of peace on his face; she could tell the serum had removed his pain. She leaned over the microphone on the control board. "Andy? Can you hear me in there?" Andy nodded.

"We didn't have time to wholly sedate you. In a few moments, the serum will be up to the top of the tank. You will not be able to breathe air anymore." Andy's face jerked out of its passive look. His eyes focused hard on Sebbins.

"Don't worry," she said. "You will not die. You will panic, however. The serum is oxygenated. It will keep you alive. You need to trust me on this.

Swallow as much as you can so your stomach gets full. Then, when the serum is over your head, you have to breathe it in. You have to suck it into your lungs. Big, deep breaths. You will panic. Your body is going to try to fight it. It's a natural instinct. It's your body wanting to keep you alive."

The soldiers came over behind Sebbins to watch the monitors with her. She slipped a hand into her lab pocket and lightly fingered a sedative hypo.

Andy began to suck down big mouthfuls of the serum, grimacing as he swallowed it. He gagged slightly and coughed. The last foot of room in the tank filled quickly and Andy was submerged.

He was holding his breath; Sebbins could see it. "Andy, if you don't try to breathe normally, you're going to have a tougher time adapting to this tank!"

Andy closed his eyes and his mouth opened. His eyes popped open and his body went into spasm as the survival instinct took over. He began to seize.

"Blow the air out of your lungs, Andy. The inhalation will feel more natural. Don't worry! This will only last a few seconds!"

Andy shook and twitched. His arms began to tremble.

"Andy! This is normal! Listen to my voice: You will be okay, Andy! You *will* be okay."

Andy suddenly uncurled, flinging out his arms and legs. His fists and feet slammed into the glass of the tank and shattered the thick glass. The serum poured out of the tank in a glossy orange wave.

Sebbins pulled the hypo from her pocket and jabbed the nearest security guard in the neck. His eyes closed and he fell over almost immediately. Andy stepped out of the tank and took two steps that shook the room. He reached out and grabbed the two-way radio that the other soldier was fumbling. Andy squeezed his oversized hand around it and crushed it. He extended a finger and poked the soldier in the head. The man's eyes rolled up into his head and he fell to the ground in a heap.

"How do you feel?" Sebbins asked. She started pulling dull blue surgical gowns out of a drawer and tying them together to make some makeshift clothes for someone Andy's size.

Andy was sputtering and coughing up serum. "I feel okay," he grunted. His voice was thick and hoarse. It was a stark contrast to the mellifluous tenor voice he had before the change. "Let's get out of here."

Dr. Sebbins started draping him with the gowns. "I don't know that we're going to be able to hide you. I think we have to make a break for the hidden corridor in the lab."

"Soldiers won't be there?"

Sebbins frowned. "I don't know. Stay behind me and I'll go check." She opened the door to the auxiliary lab and glanced down the hall. A guard in gray camouflage holding a Kalashnikov rifle was pacing the intersection of the main corridor and the hall to Cormair's living quarters just outside the door to the lab.

"Everything all right, Doctor?" he called.

"Everything is fine. I could use a hand, though." The soldier slung his rifle over his shoulder and walked down the hall, moving quickly. Before he could turn the corner into the lab, Sebbins had injected him with a sedative in the upper shoulder. He had just enough time to see Andy, comprehend what was happened, and start to draw his weapon before he passed out. Andy took the end of the rifle in his hands and bent the end like it was rubber.

"I'm strong," said Andy.

"Very much so," said Dr. Sebbins. "You were engineered to be a human tank."

"Are we going to escape?"

"We're going to try."

"How strong am I?"

"I don't know. I couldn't tell you. You might be able to bench-press a Greyhound bus. Follow me."

Sebbins moved quickly and quietly down the hall, each step with the light touch and grace of a trained dancer. In contrast, Andy took earth-shaking, thundering steps behind her. Each time his foot fell, she could feel the vibration through the floor. Sebbins knew that Cormair had compensated for his mass by giving him a squat, powerful, unbreakable skeleton, but Sebbins worried about the boy's joints. How could his knees continue to hold up?

"Doc?"

"What, Andy?"

"I think we're going to have a problem."

"What's that?"

"I saw the escape door when they opened it earlier."

"And?"

"I'm not going to fit."

The door had been made to fit a normal human being. The tunnel behind it was not much larger than the door. Andy's body, wider and thicker than any human, would never make it to the end of the tunnel. Sebbins began cursing silently and searching her mind for an alternative escape route.

"The only other way is the front door, isn't it?" said Andy. "This lab is below ground. There are no fire escapes. We can't jump out any windows."

"Andy, how fast do you think you can run?"

"Doc, have you looked at me? 'Run' just ain't in my vocabulary anymore. 'Stagger' maybe. How about 'Galumph?' 'Trudge?' 'Lumber?'"

"Will you be able to lumber, then?"

"Not very fast. I was never very fast. I'm probably ridiculously slow now."

"Did I ever tell you I ran track in high school?"

"Nope."

"State Champ in the four hundred meters. Let's go through the front door."

"It's probably going to be difficult. If there are soldiers here, they will probably want to stop us. I don't think I can hide behind a tree."

"Walk while we talk. I'll tell you what I know about your abilities. You are exceptionally powerful. Your musculature has been artificially enhanced making you incredibly strong. Your muscles are so tightly corded that they can stop bullets Your bones are unbreakable. Your skin will still bleed, you will still feel every bit of pain that comes from skin damage, but you will heal at a slightly higher rate than anyone else."

"I like this so far."

"I have no idea how strong or powerful you will be. Dr. Cormair was anticipating you would be able to exert maybe twenty thousand PSI in a punch, maybe more. We won't know until we test you. To put it in perspective, a heavyweight prize fighter only punches in the high three thousand range."

"Whoa."

"Of course, Cormair was being conservative in his estimates. You may be able to produce much more than that. One thing you have to know, Andy: If you hit a person full-force, you will kill them. The human skeleton will not be able to take it. You will shatter their bones into rubble and rupture all of their internal organs. They will be dead before they hit the ground." Sebbins glanced over her shoulder to make sure Andy knew she was serious.

"Sounds like I'm a beast, then."

"You were built to be a tank, Andy. They are vehicles of destruction, and so are you now. You are no longer going to be capable of being lax in your actions. Everything you do is going to have consequence because of your strength. You can't even flip a pencil at someone without making sure you check yourself because if you don't, you could turn that pencil into a dart."

"I'll be careful," said Andy. His face was somber. He was looking at his cartoon fists, each inflated and unreal. One of his fists was almost the size of Sebbins' torso. His forearms were as big as her waist.

The elevator was unoccupied and a few Luna moths were still clinging to surfaces. "Holly's work?" Sebbins asked brushing a moth away from her lapel.

"Of course."

Getting into the elevator was a tight squeeze. Andy had to go in sideways and Sebbins squeezed into the corner by the buttons. The doors closed and the elevator began the upward journey.

"Is this going to hold me?"

"It's a freight elevator. Dr. Cormair requested that it be able to move ten tons."

"Will it hold me?"

"If it doesn't, we'll know how much you weigh."

The cables strained, but the elevator moved normally. "I'm less than ten tons, I guess." His breath began to get labored. "The pain is coming back, Doc."

"You need more serum. Cormair said it's the only thing that will help you get through the change. I have to keep you injected with massive quantities of serum."

"So do it," Andy's fists suddenly tightened into boulders. "I'm starting to not feel my arms or legs."

The door opened and they were suddenly face-to-face with several soldiers. Andy shoved Sebbins behind him and blocked her body with his own. No one moved. Sebbins reached into her pocket and slowly withdrew another heroic dose of serum. She reached up and pressed the end into Andy's neck and injected it. "Don't punch them, but you can still throw them, as long as you're careful."

A slow smile spread across Andy's broad chin. "Done."

The soldiers reached for their guns, but the one nearest to the door was lifted off the ground like a child's toy and thrown into the rest sidelong toppling them like bowling pins. Andy thundered out of the elevator. He grabbed a handgun from the soldier on top, ripping it away from him and dwarfing the pistol in his massive hand. He squeezed and opened his hand, dropping a lump of useless metal onto the ground.

Dr. Sebbins rushed for the front door. "Andy! Let's go!" She flung open the front door and froze in her tracks.

An armored personnel carrier and a large, off-road truck with a mounted machine gun in the back were parked on the lawn. A few dozen soldiers, holding various rifles and assault guns were milling around the vehicles. A helicopter buzzed overhead, sweeping a painfully bright searchlight across the ground. Two soldiers, each leading a barking and excited Belgian Malinois at the end of a leash, were making a sweep down the road leading to the front door of the Home. From the sounds in the distance, there were more vehicles and soldiers surrounding the Home.

Andy looked at the fiasco over Dr. Sebbins' shoulder. "I guess this wasn't supposed to be that easy."

"Let's go back."

"No," said Andy, his blue surgical gown kilt flapping in the wind. "Let's test out these bulletproof muscles of mine. Just get behind me, Doc. Hit me with another spray of serum and keep low. I have a feeling this will be ugly."

John snuck out of the tunnel when he was sure the helicopter wasn't overhead. He hunched in the darkness by the trunk of a rotting oak, staring down at the Home. From his vantage point he could count at least fifty soldiers and four vehicles; there were probably more that he couldn't see, more crawling through the darkness, looking for them. Every soldier was armed of course, and three of the vehicles had visible guns.

It was a deathtrap. They would not be able to rescue Andy. John couldn't see how it would even be possible, yet something in his brain was thinking independently of his common sense. Something in his mind was putting angles together, highlighting points of weakness and places where he could get through them undetected. His mind was calculating probabilities and looking for things that could be used as weapons. He noticed a good, sharp stick, straight and thick, with a nice heft. The programming in his brain told him that stick would make a weapon if he had no other choices. He could calculate in his head exactly how long he would have to make a break for the Home from the relative safety of the forest tree line. He could look at the soldiers posted around the perimeter and knew how fast they would react, what angle they would have to shoot from, and he could mentally project the telemetry of the bullets, so he would know how to jump, turn his body, and avoid them all together. These were calculations that no human should be able to make, yet his mind was putting it together as fast as his eyes could take it in. Was he always able to do this? It didn't feel like it was a new experience. His mind wasn't rebelling against the information. He wasn't shrieking in pain. Instead, it felt like he was actually *living* for the first time in his life, tingling threads of excitement crackled along his brainstem as this information brimmed in his skull.

A cracking stick behind him brought him out of his trance. In the dim light of the forest, John could see Sarah's golden hair poking out of the tunnel.

"I just gave Posey another sedative. She was starting to moan in her sleep."

"How many more do we have left?"

"Only two."

"Well, let's hope it holds out long enough."

"I think we've maybe got enough for four hours."

"It's going to be light by then," John said. The eastern sky was beginning to become lighter, but it was still a dark gray without a hint of rosy hues. "We're not going to be able to escape in broad daylight and if we stay in this tunnel too long, we're going to get caught, too. I can hear dogs. You think they're going to find us?"

"Maybe," said Sarah. She hunched down next to John and peered into the yard. "Is it hopeless?"

"I don't know." He was surveying the soldiers with a grim look.

A niggling thought twitched in Sarah's mind, a warning alert that what she was witnessing had some sort of issue about it. She was drawing a blank as to what, however. "Something isn't right down there," said Sarah. "I can't put a finger on it, but something about that scene bugs me."

"I know," said John. "I spotted it first thing. I think Indigo was right: I'm hard-wired to be a perfect soldier. I instantly sum up a situation with a militaristic intelligence. I didn't even know I knew how to do that."

"Well, what isn't right?"

"Look at the vehicles and the soldiers."

"Yeah?"

"No flags. No insignias. No emblems of any sort."

"What?"

"There are no American flags anywhere. Not on sleeves, not on the vehicles, not anywhere. There are no markings to identify any country anywhere down there."

"So?"

"You've seen the same movies as I have. I don't think the U.S. Military goes anywhere without designations or flags flying. I'm too far away to tell if the writing on the vehicles is English or not. I don't think it is, though."

"You think we're in some foreign country?"

"Maybe," said John. "That might make sense. We were only allowed to watch television brought in from a satellite dish. We were never shown where we were on a map, not even when our tutors were teaching us geography. We were never allowed to see a newspaper. Indigo never saw a newspaper or a town name sign when she would go to the town down the road."

"So?"

"It doesn't make sense," John's mind was wheeling, trying to put pieces of a puzzle together. The picture he was getting was fuzzy, but it was the base idea of a theory. Non-American military, strange vehicles, a remote location...What for? Something clicked in John's head.

"This is going to sound stupid, but I think that maybe town was a set-up. I think it might be a military outpost made up to look like a town."

Sarah shook her head. "You sound like some crazy conspiracy theorist. We rode here from our *American* homes on a bus. We have four seasons with wicked cold winters, so if we're in another country, we're in Canada. Big whoop."

"We might be," John agreed. "But, I still don't think this is any sort of *American* government military. Look at the weapons."

Sarah glanced at the soldiers she could see. She could make out the black steel rifles with the wooden stocks and the graceful, curved clip sticking out of them. She shrugged and looked at John quizzically.

"Kalashnikov's. AK-47's. They're not American weapons. Russian, originally. They're favored by paramilitary groups because they're cheap, light, and accurate. They're also easy to pick up at gun shows or on the black market. This has to be a militia outfit. It's not the official army of any country."

Sarah's brain was trying to follow John's train of thought. "We're not American?"

"I don't think we are anymore. I think America doesn't know what's been going on here. We might be in America, but if that's the case, then these guys are underground. The government probably doesn't know they exist. A military group like this, with massive funding, a full arsenal of weapons, and fleet of vehicles that's still hidden from the government has to be paramilitary, and what do paramilitary groups try to do in third world countries? We read about it online every so often, usually in smaller African nations."

"Military coups?"

"Exactly. They try to take over."

Sarah's eyes were dinner plates. John could see in her eyes that she was putting the pieces together. She gasped. "You're saying that you think we are some sort of project that is an attempt to overthrow America!"

"What else would it be? America has the biggest guns in the world, one of the largest armies, the most resources, and the means to keep up supply and communications for a long war. I could see how that could make some people upset."

"But why?"

John had it figured out. John loved his history textbook, he loved seeing how the past had a direct influence on the present and the future. Maybe it was part of his new genetic hardwiring. "The Second Amendment."

Sarah's mouth gaped. "Say what?"

"The Second Amendment, the Right to Bear Arms, was put in place by a government who realized that if it hadn't been for the personal munitions of the militias and minutemen, they would not have had the ability to combat England's armies. Therefore, they instituted the Second Amendment to allow citizens to have a means of protecting themselves against intruders—even armies of the government itself. It was supposed to be a check-and-balance against the military power of America becoming too cocky and becoming like the British soldiers."

"That was well over two hundred years ago! Times have changed!"

"Of course they have, but don't you see it? America has nuclear weapons, bunker-buster bombs, laser-guided missiles that can hit a target the size of a teacup from five hundred miles away. A homeowner with a deer rifle can't stand a chance against that."

There was a long silence between them. "So they build super weapons. Something the government doesn't know about and can't know about," said Sarah.

"The government keeps tabs on dangerous chemicals like plutonium and uranium. If there are weapons-grade mass-destruction components out there, the government can probably track them. But people…"

"People are harder to track."

John didn't feel a need to elaborate any further. It had been scratching at his brain since he first saw the soldier with the Kalashnikov. He felt in his gut that they were still on American soil, but probably hidden someplace that the government would never look. Keep your friends close, but your enemies closer. He remembered reading that the terrorists who had orchestrated the World Trade Center attacks had been living in America for some time prior to that fateful morning. He also knew that there were functioning anti-government militias in America, but usually they were run by anarchist country nut-balls who had read one too many Ayn Rand novels. What if someone with a militia mindset, but real military brains got together with some rich people who were a little perturbed at the government's rampant spending and didn't agree with their foreign policies? Was it too far-fetched to think that they might get together, pool their monies, and invest billions in a project to help create a new breed of soldier that could combat a heavily armed army? Regular weapons weren't enough and even if they got a nuclear weapon, they couldn't nuke a country if they still intended to live there afterward. An army that could take down the government had to be fast, light, lethal, and efficient. It had to be able to hide or blend in to the populace, strike without warning and make precision attacks on single targets with a minimum of disturbance. Most of all, they had to be able to adapt and accomplish things without the military hardware that the government possessed. The hardware needed to arm a regular human army big enough to take out the US Military could never get into the United States without the FBI, the CIA, or the NSA knowing. However, if the army didn't need hardware—if it could use anything…

John looked at the sharp stick and he could feel the exact throwing motion he would need to hurl it into a man's neck from a distance of twenty steps. His brain ran him through the motion. It would be too easy. Sick realization dawned on him like a ray of light.

"We were meant to stop the government."

"What government?"

"The government of the United States of America. We're thinking, capable soldiers, right?"

"Right."

"So, we were taught all about America's injustices in the last thirty years. Remember that one tutor they brought in to teach us about the invasion of Iraq? And remember how he showed us the fourteen things fascist nations have in common?"

The light seemed to dawn on Sarah. John saw her eyes light up. "And we had to find examples of a country that it worked for outside of 1940's Germany!"

"I think we all chose Italy, right?" said John. "But, those rules would have worked for America, too. Think about it. The flags, the patriotism, the finding a scapegoat to blame troubles on, the Patriot Act—They were trying to teach us that America had supposedly turned fascist on its base and were duping the people."

"So, they want to go to war against the government."

"They make *us* go to war to prove that the government is vulnerable and that small groups of people can take out major targets, the president perhaps. Once that happens…"

"It's open season on America."

"Terrorists will come out of the woodwork, won't they?"

"And they'll be controlled by whomever started this army down there."

"Chaos."

"Anarchy."

"And once that ends, once the government is replaced by the group that funded us, they are free to begin to take over other countries because America, the World's Policeman, is no longer functioning."

"Without the world's army, there'd be no one to stop them."

"If you watch a guy knock out a five-hundred pound weightlifter, you don't step up to that guy. This would be the same thing: We take out America—who would dare to stop us?"

Sarah slumped back against a tree. "This sounds like five pounds of crazy in a four pound sack, John."

"It is," he agreed. "But it fits! You see that it fits, right?"

"It does, but it's also crazy. You sound like a rambling, paranoid conspiracy theorist. It doesn't prove anything, John."

"It might someday. I just need to find proof."

"What if it is the U.S. government doing this to us? They wouldn't want insignias and flags all over stuff if they were doing some sort of illegal operation inside American soil."

"The AK's, though. U.S. troops don't use AK's!"

Sarah fell silent for a long while. She watched the troop movement and watched the helicopter spin lazy circles in the north, just over the tops of the trees. "Do you think Cormair knew?"

"He had to have known."

Sarah's lips tightened into a line. "He knew and he was willing to turn us over to a terrorist cell operating inside this country with aspirations to take America down."

"If I ever see him again," John seethed, "he's going to answer some questions."

The noise in front of the Home suddenly doubled. Soldiers began shouting and a few blasts of machine-gun fire rang out.

"Something's happening," said John. "You don't think that they found us, do you?"

"No look!"

A grotesque blob of something that once looked human bolted from the doorway of the Home and ran to the side of an all-terrain truck. He hunched down, gripped it, and suddenly stood up. The truck was picked cleanly into the air and hurled into the side of another truck, flattening it.

A few bullets struck the beast in the arms and he yelled out in pain.

Sarah recognized the cry instantly. She blanched. "John, that's Andy!"

Sarah watched in absolute shock as she watched Andy toss the truck. She didn't see the fun-loving guy she had known for ten years, the guy she split popcorn with on movie night, the guy who used to make stupid hats out of cardboard to make her laugh after she endured surgeries; instead, she saw a massive bulk of a human, a living comic book beast of ridiculous, over-pumped muscles. She saw several of the soldiers draw their weapons, but Andy charged forward, scattering the soldiers like bowling pins and smashing through the wreckage of the trucks.

"We have to help him." Sarah felt suddenly sick.

"How?"

"I don't know!"

John frowned. "Rushing in like idiots could get us killed. Right now, it seems like Andy knows what he's doing. Hang back for a second and see if he needs us."

The dog handlers released the two Malinois and they took off like bullets, baying and snarling in anticipation of the attack.

"I'm going to help!" Sarah hissed. She began darting through the trees, ducking low branches and leaping over shrubs. The first Malinois hit Andy's forearm, sinking its teeth into his wrist. Instinctively, Andy flung his arm and the dog was forcibly thrown thirty feet across the lawn. It landed hard and tried to get up, but its hind legs wouldn't work.

From inside the tunnel behind her, Sarah heard Holly scream. Her animal senses: She probably "heard" the dog's pain when it landed, Sarah thought. John would have to deal with Holly's trauma. Sarah was only concerned with Andy at the moment.

The second dog, witnessing the first dog's punishment, fell back to barking at Andy in an intimidating manner. Soldiers were beginning to swarm toward the front lawn. The helicopter rushed to the scene, bright, white illumination flooding the lawn from the massive halogen spotlight.

Sarah could see the tree line and she knew she was going to have to do something when she got there. She started glancing left and right, scanning for weapons. She wondered if she could sneak up behind a guard and steal his gun. They had been taught hand-to-hand combat. At one point, a former Israeli Mossad agent came in for several months to teach them all Krav Maga. She knew how to disarm a man with a gun, even a soldier.

She leapt over a bush and landed hard on her left heel. A shockwave of pain shot up her left leg, all the way through her pelvis and stomach. When her right leg landed another shockwave of pain blasted through her, this one more intense. Her knees buckled and she fell forward, crashing through the scrub at the tree line and sliding into the clearing. Sarah rolled with the fall, trying to find footing again, but when she tried to stand, ripples of electric anguish rolled through her legs making her lower body feel like it was being dipped into flames. A terrifying thought flashed through her brain: It was a transformation. She was changing, just like Posey, just like Andy.

Her ankles felt tight, like the skin around them was going to explode; her feet were jerked into rigid angles. She couldn't even flex her toes. Her leg muscles felt like they were twitching, a thousand muscle spasms a minute. Pain bit into her with sharp teeth. Her Achilles tendons tightened and her feet pointed involuntarily. A split-second later, muscles around her shins inflated and jerked her feet back to a ninety-degree angle. Her hips were alternately burning and going numb. Her groin muscles were in spasm and her lower abdominal muscles were contracting violently.

Down at the yard, several soldiers drew tasers and fired on Andy. He fell to his knees, screaming. Someone ran out of the Home to help him. Sarah saw a long ponytail and white coat. She saw Dr. Sebbins try to run through the soldiers, but one grabbed her and threw her to the ground.

Sarah pushed herself up with her arms and willed her legs underneath her. They hurt; she had never known pain like this, but it wasn't a time when she could sit and complain about it. Andy was being attacked. Dr. Sebbins was being attacked. They needed her help. Sarah started to stumble, her legs on autopilot, lurching awkwardly like a tin man. Her arms flailed wildly, trying to gain balance. Her left leg thrust forward, followed by her right leg. Suddenly, she felt a distinctive hard click in her hips and the rest of the world slowed to a crawl. She was in the yard in a heartbeat, and past it in another. She shot straight through the action and all the way into the forest on the opposite side of the yard. Everything was a blur, flying past in the blink of an eye. She was moving so fast that she couldn't even take in a breath. Tears streamed from the corners of her eyes. Her eyes felt dry and she wanted to squeeze her eyelids shut. She could barely think. When she finally was able to gain conscious control of her legs and forced herself to stop, she was several hundred yards away from the Home. Her face stung from where bugs had hit her. The skin on her upper arms was scratched and bloody from the tree branches. A stick had gashed her forehead and a line of blood ran down the right side of her nose and to her lip where the salty, metallic taste surprised her. Her legs hurt less, but they still ached like she had just finished a marathon.

She turned around and focused on the men with the guns. At least seven rifles were being trained on Andy and Dr. Sebbins from what she could see. Sarah started to run again and the click in her hips happened. She went from a stumbling jog to blinding speed in an instant. She angled her body slightly and ran between Andy and the soldiers, slashing a hand out at the barrels of the guns. It felt like she punched flaming spears, but the guns flew out of the hands of the soldiers, many of them broken from the impact of Sarah's speed.

The soldiers recoiled, falling backwards with expressions of shock and fear. The only glimpse of Sarah they saw was a blur of color.

Sarah stopped herself at the tree line again. She looked down at her hand. The palm of her left hand was swollen and red. Her middle finger looked strange. She touched it and it hurt a lot. It was definitely dislocated, probably broken. Speed had its disadvantages.

John and Holly broke through the tree line next to Sarah. "What's happened so far?" said John. He had a thick, pointed stick in his hand.

"They've surrounded Andy. I broke their guns, though."

"How'd you do that?" Holly asked.

"I ran really fast," Sarah said. "And I mean *really* fast." She curled her left hand into a fist, manually bending down her middle finger and gritting her teeth through the pain. "My abilities finally manifested. My legs are killing me."

"How do we get Andy out of there?" Holly asked. She squinted down at the yard. "It looks impossible."

"Let me see if I can help," Indigo's voice broke through from the trees behind them.

John glanced over his shoulder at her. "Can you move any of those soldiers or lift Andy?"

"No. But, I think I can move some of the lighter stuff. Maybe I can throw dirt in their eyes or something."

"That might help," said John. "Here's the plan: Sarah, I want you to sprint down and get Dr. Sebbins to safety. Bring her back here, but take a roundabout way. Go around the Home. Hide in shadows as you run. Don't give them an open look. I don't want soldiers running directly to us. Holly, do you think you might be able to bring some animals?"

"I don't know. I can hear them in the trees around us. There's birds and some smaller mammals. I can hear ants and flies, too. But, they're all scared. They know something bad is going on. Sometimes, if they're scared, they won't come. Heavy fear can override my abilities."

"Well, see what you can come up with."

Holly nodded and took a couple steps backward, her eyes becoming milky as she concentrated.

"I'm going to sneak down to the Home. You see over there on the dark side? There's an unmanned vehicle. It's an APC. It'll be big enough to carry all of us. I'm going to steal it. Once I start it up, Sarah, I'll need you back to help me get Andy into the back. Once that happens, we'll need to get Posey and Kenny into the back as fast as possible and we'll need to get out of here fast." John was oozing an aura of command. Sarah didn't know why, but she was willing to do whatever he asked of her.

"The squirrels. The squirrels can help, said Holly, her eyes were completely white. "They're scared, but they also like the adrenaline rush."

"Perfect! How can I use squirrels?" John chewed his lower lip for a moment. Then, he smiled. "Can you get them to chew through the fuel lines of those other vehicles down there?"

"I can try."

"What about me?" Indigo asked. "Let me help."

John glanced into the sky. The helicopter was still hovering overhead, flashing its spotlight and cutting the air with loud rotors. "Can you bring that thing down? I need to kill that spotlight."

Indigo bit her lip. "I don't think so. It's huge."

"Remember David and Goliath," said John. "It's not the size of the rock—it's where you hit the giant."

Indigo smiled. John's stick suddenly ripped out of his hand, and glided easily to Indigo's open palm. Her fingers curled around it. "Got it."

"Once that helicopter is down," said John, "go and get Posey and Kenny. Bring them out of the forest the best you can. Holly, you help her once you can, too."

"Okay," Holly said. She crouched down and held her hands on the side of her head. Her face was wrinkled up in concentration.

"Sarah, go!" John said. He, in turn, spun on his heel and hauled down the hill toward the APC in the shadows of the dark side of the Home.

Sarah locked her eyes on Dr. Sebbins and angled her body to the most direct route. This time, she concentrated and was able to make her hips pop before she started to move. When she took her first step, she was flying. In an instant, she was at Dr. Sebbins' side. Before the doctor could question her, Sarah grabbed her and slung her into a fireman's carry. The doctor was fit and didn't weigh much, but the additional weight seemed to make Sarah's knees compress and her legs felt shorter. "Hang on, Seb!" Sarah grunted. *Click!* And Sarah was a blur. She was still moving at an intense speed, but the additional weight made it hard to compensate. It made her knees hurt and her ankles felt like they were going to explode with each step. Sarah still couldn't take in a breath while she was running. She looped around to the back of the Home before she had to stop to breathe. When she tried to stop, she had to take several extra steps to keep from sending Dr. Sebbins flying.

She set Dr. Sebbins down and bent over, gasping for breath and trying to rub the soreness out of her knees.

"Sarah! Your powers!"

"Just came," gasped Sarah. "Just happened a few minutes ago."

"How are your ankles and knees?"

"Sore and stiff."

"Your tendons are becoming thicker. Speed like yours will require a lot of ligament changes. Your tendons are going to become like high tensile-strength steel. They need to be strong to keep from blowing out at speed. Your bones are going to change too. Imagine them like the shocks on a car."

"Doc! Science lesson later! If you haven't noticed, there are guys with guns."

"Oh, right! I'm just so proud of you!"

"I need to take you to the rendezvous point."

"The what?"

"John has a plan to get us out of here. We're making our break tonight. He figured out the project. He figured out what those goons were going to do with us. We're leaving, Seb."

"I'll come with you."

"No," said Sarah. "We have to do this on our own."

"Sarah, I know where there's a safe house! I know where we can find the things you're going to need to get you through the changes without excess pain. There's a hyper-womb there. If Posey doesn't get into it, she will die."

Sarah felt cornered. "It'll be John's call," she said. "Now, get back on my shoulder. I think I can make it to the meeting place in one more jaunt."

"You couldn't just run there outright?"

"I can't breathe when I run, Doc."

"That wasn't in the files."

Sarah grabbed Sebbins and ran again. She was able to make it to the spot at the tree line just as her body was screaming for air. She came out of speed and collapsed. Dr. Sebbins flew off her shoulder and bounced on the ground once before sliding to a stop. "Sorry, Doc."

Before Sebbins could reply, Sarah was up again and sprinting back to Andy's side. Her knees and ankles hurt less. She could tell that her speed was much, much greater when she didn't have to carry weight. She made it to Andy's side and was able to stop quickly, coasting out of the burst and coming to a stop in front of Andy. "We're getting you out of here!"

"Good. The ground is cold," said Andy.

Sarah looked around and saw more soldiers coming. She clicked into her powers again and shoulder-charged the nearest soldier.

An old physics adage was running through Sarah's head. It was the one about objects in motion, and how they tended to stay in motion. When Sarah made contact, physics took over. The impact sent her spinning off at speed, tearing through the soil like a plow as her feet tried to regain footing. The solider blasted off his feet through the air, a human projectile fired from a very angry cannon. He careened into several other soldiers, toppling them violently, sending them rolling, a mound of flailing arms and legs.

When Sarah finally found her balance again, she was able to turn a hard, sharp corner and blast back down the line of soldiers, slapping weapon barrels with her left fist, trying not to make bone-on-metal contact or hit her broken finger. The wooden stocks and grips shattered like kindling as the metal was smacked out of place. Her left hand was becoming a mound of black-and-blue flesh.

The APC fired up and rumbled from around the side of the house, black diesel smoke pouring from its pipes. John leapt out and grabbed one of Andy's arms. "Sarah! I need you! Now!"

Andy was already struggling to his feet. "Out of my way, Spaghetti-head." He stepped on the bumper of the APC, and it tore off under his weight and was mashed into the ground beneath his feet. "My bad. Bill my insurance company for that, will you?" Andy jumped up, landing heavily in the back of the APC. It creaked and the flyleaf springs groaned as they struggled to compensate his weight. "That does it. After we get out of here, I'm calling Jenny Craig."

"Sarah! Let's go!" said John. He ran back to the front of the APC and threw it into gear without bothering to close the door. Soldiers were rushing the vehicle as he peeled across the lawn sending chunks of sod and mud flying.

Sarah heard gun shots. A few bullets bounced off the metal sides of the APC.

Bounced?

Sarah realized the soldiers weren't firing live metal rounds; they were shooting immobilizers—rubber bullets meant to injure, but not kill. They were riot control devices, non-lethal ammo. She leapt into speed and realized that the bullets were visible to her as she ran. She could see brilliant black spheres seemingly crawling through the air. She was actually moving faster than they were! She could catch them, slap them with her fist, and knock them off trajectory! She connected with the first bullet, slapping it hard with her palm. A jolt of pain shot through her arm; it felt like a large, nasty insect had sunk two fangs' worth of venom into her hand. The old physics teacher's voice came back to her: For every action there is an equal and opposite reaction. The jolt wasn't horrible, though, and Sarah knew that she wasn't really being bitten; she had to suck it up and deal with the pain.

In the distance, Sarah heard the sound of engines coughing and growling into action. She could see headlights through the trees near the end of the long driveway. More vehicles were coming, mobilized from the town down the road. Sarah cursed under her breath. John was right; the town down the road was a secret paramilitary installation. It had to be.

The APC slid to a stop at the tree line. Holly had Posey on her shoulder and Indigo had dragged Kenny through the scrub by his wrists like she was dragging a corpse. Dr. Sebbins was tending to Posey as best she could in the dim light. John bailed out of the cab and rushed everyone into the back of the carrier.

"Stay down! Stay low! I think they're going to be shooting."

"I can help," said Sarah. "Give me a chance."

"Do your thing," John said. "And make it fast. Follow when you can!"

"I will!" Sarah turned and sprinted to the oncoming soldiers. Her speed was so great that the soldiers were like frozen statues. She plowed into them sending them flying. Soldiers farther back from the initial line began firing the riot bullets, full auto. The air became vibrant and buzzing with gun fire. The bullets were all around her; Sarah had to angle her body oddly, spinning like a dervish through the hail of bullets. She could see them approaching, ten bullets in a close line, burped from a single barrel. They were coming faster and faster. More and more soldiers fired. An APC was unloading at the top of the circlet drive by the front of the Home. Soldiers were taking defensive positions around the vehicles, falling to the ground and remaining flat and low, taking aim at the blur that was Sarah, and firing short bursts of ammo in flat pattern, aiming in front of where they thought she would be running, trying to slow her down.

The bullets were coming in too fast for Sarah to dodge now. There were bullets high and bullets low. A soldier in the back of the APC was setting up a strange, silvery apparatus that resembled a cannon straight out of a sci-fi movie, a large silver tuning-fork with wires and pipes all over its sides and a generator at its base. Sarah turned away from the bullets and ran down the driveway. She moved faster than she had when she was trying to control her run in the relatively confined space. It felt more like she was flying than running, each toe barely grazing the ground. She blasted down the road and into the empty field. Her lungs were screaming for oxygen. Thigh-high weeds scratched at her jeans and, at her speed, began to strip the material. Suddenly, Sarah felt a burning sensation from her thighs. She stopped, several hundred yards from the Home. The burning increased. Sarah smelled smoke. Her pants were on fire!

Sarah fell to the ground and quickly stripped off her jeans. The inner thighs and crotch had rubbed together so fast that the friction had caused them to burn. She breathed a silent thanks for choosing underwear that day that made her look semi-sexy, but still offered significant butt coverage.

Her leg muscles had changed. She had always had lean, lithe thighs, but now they rippled with hard strands of muscle. Her knees were more pronounced and her calves were tight and powerful, remarkably chiseled. Even her ankles, especially her Achilles tendons, seemed to be more pronounced, more sculpted.

Sarah stood up and stamped out the remaining embers so the field wouldn't catch fire. In the distance, she could see the APC wheeling away from the gunfire, attempting to roll down the tree line toward the road. Its headlights bounced wildly as it banged its way over the rough terrain. Sarah turned and launched herself toward the APC. As soon as she jumped into speed, she could see the thick wall of bullets heading toward the tires of the truck, attempting to take it down. The bullets glistened silver in the halogen spotlight's glow. The soldiers had switched to live, lead ammo in order to take down the truck.

It felt like it took forever, when it really took only fractions of a second, but Sarah flew toward the line of gunmen. She slapped away the bullets with her other hand and felt the skin on her palm burning. She turned back at the end of the line to take down the guns, slapping them with her right hand, feeling the soft tissues swell and bruise from the impact. She slowed down to turn around for a third pass. The soldier manning the futuristic cannon engaged his weapon. The air suddenly became filled with white noise, a wall of pure sound that hit Sarah like fiery talons. She arched backward in pain, losing her footing, and spinning to the ground, landing hard and sending a roostertail of dirt and debris flying as her body paid the price for stopping while inertia still carried it at insane speed.

Sarah lay still, gasping for breath, feeling like every bone in her body was broken, her eardrums exploded, and her brain was jelly. She could see the searchlight of the helicopter overhead illuminating the yard. She could hear the shouts and commands of soldiers. She could hear the engine of the APC in the distance. John was still going. He was getting the others out of there. She had been successful.

There were several metallic clicks as a half-dozen rifles were suddenly locked, loaded, and pointed at her. She craned her head and saw a cadre of soldiers with guns leveled at her. The sonic cannon on the back of the APC targeted her again. A tall, powerfully built man in gray camouflage and a red beret was sneering at her, his hands behind his back. Half of his face was horribly scarred with burns and he wore an eye patch.

"What...what happened?" Sarah gasped. She tried to sit up, but the soldier in the beret put a foot to her shoulder and smashed her back to the ground. He stepped down hard with his toe, pressing into her collarbone painfully. He drew his sidearm, a particularly lethal looking semi-automatic handgun, and pointed it at her forehead.

"Subject Two. Codename: Blink. Do not attempt to get up. I will be forced to blow out your kneecaps. You were just hit with a prototype Sonic Cannon. If you attempt to flee, I will not hesitate to shoot you with it again. You are under arrest." The soldier nodded at one of the men with a rifle. "Cuff her. Hobble her ankles with the polywire, too."

"What? What are you doing?" Sarah tried to sit up again, but the toe of a combat boot dug hard into her clavicle and she could only choke out grunts of pain. "You're going to break...me."

"You'll heal," the soldier growled. Sarah felt thick cord wind around her ankles. Handcuffs were snapped on her wrists. "Throw her in the truck. One of you keep a hand on her at all times."

One of the soldiers, semi-toothless and sneering, gave Sarah a smile that made her skin crawl. He spoke with an accent that hinted toward Eastern Europe. "With pleasure."

"They got Sarah! They got Sarah!" Indigo watched out the back of the truck with horror as she saw Sarah's body hit the ground and spiral out of control. She shoved her head through the small window into the cab of the truck. "John! Sarah's down! What do we do?"

John didn't take his eyes from the road. "Now we need that distraction, Indigo. Take down the helicopter. Take out the lights. Darkness can help us."

Indigo went to the back of the truck and looked out. She could see the white bricks that surrounded the garden of the Home. One of those would work if she could get it airborne. The pen was a small, light object. The rocks would be a much greater challenge. Indigo could feel the ability within her now, a small spark in the center of her brain, but it was still difficult to control. The past two times, when she had been able to use it, she had been upset. When Cormair had called her a failure, she felt the tears crawling into her eyes, she felt the frustration of not being able to utilize her power and the frustration of feeling trapped and confined. Was her power was tied to emotion?

Gunfire burst around the metal sides of the APC, clanking against the thick body armor of the truck and sending up sparks where they connected. Indigo ducked back inside the truck, and covered her head with her arms. If there was ever a time to be under emotional stress, it was now.

She stuck her face back around the edge of the truck and focused on a single brick. She concentrated and struggled to grasp the brick. She could feel its heft, its solidity. Gritting her teeth, Indigo pulled back and saw the brick give way. She broke out in a cold sweat. The brick was heavier than it looked. She could feel the mental stress tearing through her brain; lightning strikes of pain exploded in her head. The pen had been so light, merely a tickle in her head. This was more like cat's claws digging into flesh, razor-sharp slashes of agony. Indigo swung the invisible arm and the brick flew into the air. Indigo took aim at the searchlight on the helicopter and flung the brick at it with her mental fist. The cement missile flew fast and true and smashed into the Plexiglas over the big, concave mirror shattering the searchlight. The yard was plunged into a dim light from the halogen lamps by the Home and the driveway. Two more bricks took those out quickly and efficiently and the yard was lit only by the headlights of trucks.

"Yes! Outstanding work, Indigo! Outstanding!" John called from the front of the truck. "Holly! I need you and a bat to guide us up here! I'm going to kill the lights! Indigo, I need you to take out the helicopter!"

Indigo slumped down. Her head was killing her. Waves of pain, the worst headache she had ever experienced, seethed from the center of her brain outward. She put her hands to her head and squeezed, trying to lessen the sensation of her skull splitting in half. "I don't know if I can!"

"Remember!" John cried. "Placement, not size!"

Dr. Sebbins crawled over to Indigo. "Indigo, I know it hurts. Your brain is doing something no one in the history of the world has ever done before. You are an advanced human, the next step in evolution. Your brain is still primitive compared to the power it now controls. You're going to experience pain! But, think small. Small items are easier for you to lift."

Indigo still had John's sharpened stick. She threw it into the air behind the truck and caught it with her mind. It was light, much lighter than the bricks. The cat scratches in her brain receded slightly. "John! Where's the gas tank on a helicopter?"

"Low! In the back!"

Indigo focused on the stick and aimed it at the swirling body of the helicopter. The lights on the copter's belly made it easy to spot. She waited until she had a clear shot and used every last ounce of energy in her body to hurl the stick. She could feel the stick snap from her telekinetic fist. The helicopter continued to churn the air overhead, its rotors cutting the night sky.

"I missed!" Indigo couldn't believe it. "What now?"

"I smell gas!" Holly shouted.

"What?"

"Gas! Do you smell it?"

"No," said Indigo, but after a second the chemically sweet smell of high octane fuel hit her nose. "Yes!"

"You hit the tank! It's got a leak!" Holly shouted.

"Well, a leak hasn't brought the helicopter down! Will it?"

As if it was answering her question, the helicopter's engines gave a wheeze and the helicopter moved away from the yard, lowering in altitude as it went.

"Now what?"

"A spark!" cried John from the cab of the APC. "Spark the grass! Get it to ignite! Fire is good for confusion and fear!"

"I can do that!" Indigo cried. She quickly picked up two small rocks, flat, black rocks from the garden, and sped them at the cast-off barrel of a rifle that Sarah had broken. The two stones hit the barrel with incredible force and two sparks leapt from the metal. The vapor of the gas ignited and there was an immediate cloudburst of flame throughout the yard. Soldiers were screaming and beating out small fires that seemed to cling to them in places where the helicopter fuel had doused them.

"Did I do that? Was that me?" Indigo felt weak. There was more fuel on the ground than she had thought. A wave of pain suddenly wheeled through the center of her head and stole her breath away. Indigo clapped her hands to her ears to steady herself. Overhead, the helicopter, losing fuel rapidly, began to move away to a safe spot to set down.

"Let's get Sarah," Andy said, his voice a low, rumbling avalanche.

"No time," John shouted back. "The fire's too thick and we've got to roll. The road is just ahead of us. We have to get Posey into a hyper-womb and we've only got a limited window to do it. Sarah will have to hold her own until we can come back. We will get her, though."

"Screw that, you go. I'm not leaving Sarah!" Andy cried.

"She would tell us to go," Dr. Sebbins said. "She wouldn't want us throwing effort after foolishness."

"No!" Andy yelled back. He started to get up from the ground, but Sebbins was quick. She pulled a hyper-needle loaded with sedative from her pocket and hit Andy in the neck. His eyes rolled back in his head and he flopped back onto the deck of the APC.

"That'll only last for a little while. His body is going to metabolize it very, very quickly."

"A little time is all we need, Doc," John called back. He wheeled the APC on the road and punched the gas to the floor. Indigo lost her balance and had to grab the canvas drape on the back of the truck to keep from falling out.

Indigo looked out the back of the truck at the yard of the Home. The yard was in flames, bathing the Victorian façade of the Home with eerie, dancing orange lights. There was something hellish about it, like a scene out of Dante's imagination. Soldiers were screaming, an ambulance was rolling down the road from the town to the east, and short, angry bursts of gunfire were still being blasted in the direction of the APC. Somewhere in the midst of all that, Sarah was being held by soldiers. Sarah, who had so valiantly defended them and helped them to escape. It didn't seem fair.

"How will she find us?" Indigo asked.

Dr. Sebbins looked up from Andy's side. "We'll find her after we've escaped. We can't help her if we all get captured."

"Am I supposed to believe you?"

"What do you mean by that, Indigo?" Dr. Sebbins pushed her hair out of her face, tucking it behind an ear. There was an edge to her voice. Indigo had never heard her speak like that.

"I mean, you're a doctor, Doctor. You're one of *them*, one of the people who have been putting us through experiments for the last ten years. How do I know you're leading us to safety? I have half a mind to just chuck you out the back of the truck right now. You might be bringing the soldiers to us."

"You do realize that I was being shot at just as much as you were."

"You realize that none of us were hit? How do I know the soldiers weren't aiming low?"

"Indigo, I had no idea that they were moving in on the Home."

"If my power was lie detecting instead of telekinesis, I bet you'd be in trouble right now."

"Indigo!" Sebbins' voice was tinged with anger and she was pursing her lips.

"Seriously, Doc! How am I supposed to believe you? Just last week you pushed a needle into my brain and told me it wasn't going to hurt. It was excruciating! And now you expect me to think you're trying to save us? You're just as bad as the soldiers."

Dr. Sebbins' face flared red. For a moment, Indigo thought she was going to stand up and punch her. But, Sebbins did the opposite. She sat back against the far wall of the APC and looked down at her own feet, utterly dejected. "That's fair."

"Fair?"

"You're right. You have no reason to trust me. For two years now, I've been breaking my Hippocratic Oath in the name of science. I justified it by thinking that I was a balance to Dr. Cormair. I thought I was there to protect you from him, but in reality, I was every bit as bad as he was, wasn't I? No, I was worse. I was worse because I thought I was treating you well. You have no reason to trust me, Indigo. You're right. However, I have to ask you trust me. I know where there's a safe house. That safe house has a hyper-womb. That tank is Posey's only chance to get through her transformation alive. Her body will not be able to handle the physical stress of the change. So, I have to ask you trust me."

Indigo glared at her. "Will you answer questions when we get there? Will you come straight?"

"Come straight?"

"I don't want to hear more lies, Doc. We've been lied to all our lives. I want to know about what you did to all of us and what our purpose was supposed to be. I want it straight and factual. I don't want half-truths and vague answers. We're all going to be legal adults soon. Some of us probably are already, but we had our birthdays taken away from us. We deserve to know the truth.

Dr. Sebbins rubbed her face with her hands. She looked ten years older. "Fair enough. I'll tell you everything I know, but you have to believe me when I tell you that what I know isn't much. I've read the dossiers on your powers. I know what you're supposed to be capable of doing. I know precious little else, though. Dr. Cormair kept me on a need-to-know basis."

Indigo sat down across from Dr. Sebbins and pulled her knees to her chin. "And you're going to help us, right?"

"You've got to trust me."

Indigo inhaled slowly. "All right. But, if I think you're screwing us over for a second, I'm going to use my telekinesis to push a Q-tip through your heart."

Dr. Sebbins nodded. "If that's how you feel."

"It is," Indigo said. And what scared her was that it was precisely how she felt.

Holly sat in nervous silence next to John. She gripped the handle on the door tightly to keep from bouncing around. Military vehicles are not known for their comfort. The bat that lead them through the tunnel, a plain little brown bat, had been mentally conscripted into service to lead them away from the Home. Holly gave directions to John as the bat flew rapid circles high above the truck and projected images and information into Holly's mind. At the same time, Holly had discovered a barn owl in the trees near the Home; most of the other animals had fled when the shooting began, but the barn owl was curious and watched the flames with great interest. Holly slipped into its brain, she could "feel" the heat radiating to the woods, collecting in its facial feathers. Holly gave the barn owl a little nudge and got it to fly above the Home, perching on one of the gables. Its eyesight was fantastic. It was able to give Holly mental pictures of Sarah. Holly could see Sarah seated in the back of a truck with a thick, green cable around her ankles, and her hands were bound behind her back with handcuffs. Sarah's face was contorted, not in pain, but for another reason. Holly used the eyes of the owl to zoom in on the scene. A soldier was seated in the back of the truck with Sarah. He was turned toward her, his hand roughly groping her breasts. In his other hand, he held a gun. Holly's stomach pitched. "John, we've got to go back!"

"We can't, Holly," said John. "Sometimes, in battle, no matter how much it hurts, you have to leave your soldiers. The unit is more important than the individual."

"She's being assaulted!"

"Sarah's tough. She can handle it. I'm sure she's just waiting for the right moment to break free."

"Sexually assaulted! Some perv is touching her!"

John's face changed. His cheeks became hollows as he clenched his teeth. "Rape?"

"No, but she's not happy. We've got to go back."

John checked the side mirror and saw the headlights bouncing behind the truck. Holly watched his eyes dart to the roadsides. She could see him thinking, debating. She could see him putting ideas together. It was a good thing he was trained to be a super soldier, because the only thoughts in Holly's mind was getting the barn owl to swoop into the back of the truck, talons bared, and claw the pig's eyes out of his skull.

John called into the back of the truck. "Doc? How soon until Andy's on his feet?"

"He's starting to come around now. I can give him enough serum to get him mobile," Sebbins called back.

"Do it!" John said. "How close are our pursuers? Can your bat see if they've got weapons?"

Holly quickly tapped into the bat's psyche and it sent her mental pictures of a pair of Humvees, on fast assault. Twin, turret-mounted fifty-caliber machine guns were on the back, a soldier manning each one. The bat's eyesight was very good. "Step on the gas, they're almost on us. If we stop, they'll catch up fast. There are only two trucks, though. I think the squirrels incapacitated the rest of the vehicles."

"Gotta love those squirrels. Doc! We need Andy up on his overly-large feet!"

"I'm almost there, Spaghetti-head," Andy thundered.

"Andy, there's trees alongside the road. Think you can you pull one of them down?"

"I think so. We'll find out pretty quick, eh?"

"If you can't, we're going to be screwed."

"Then I guess I better not mess up."

"Batter up, big boy. Swing for the fences." John stepped heavy on the brake and the truck slid sideways in the road.

Andy rolled out of the back of the truck and landed on his feet. Holly watched as he wrapped his bulky arms around the trunk of a medium-sized Maple and began to strain. The tree began to waiver. Andy braced his legs and strained again. There was a violent ripping sound and the tree was suddenly out of the ground. Andy let it fall and it crashed into the ground along the side of the road. He wiped his forehead. His shoulders sagged. "No sweat. John! Drive away. I'm going to need the room."

"I'll help him!" Holly threw open her door and jumped to the ground.

John pulled the truck forward spraying rocks; the tires caught the truck sped away leaving Andy behind. The Humvees approached quickly. The soldiers fired a couple of bursts after the APC. Andy grabbed the tree at the roots, took a step, swiveled his hips and swung the tree like a baseball bat, throwing it at the truck. The tree made a single rotation in the air and crushed into the first Humvee. The driver was launched through the windshield. The soldier in the turret was thrown into the ditch on the side of the road. The second hummer swerved and skidded away from the wreckage. The driver took it into the ditch, drove around the tree, and headed back to the road.

"Get out of here, Holly. I have a feeling this is going to get ugly."

"What are you going to do?"

"Whatever it takes. Get going." Andy tucked his fists into balls, lowered his head, and began to run at the Humvee. Andy lowered his shoulder and braced for the impact. The Humvee rammed him, the driver unable to swerve.

Holly squeezed her eyes shut but it didn't help. The noise was horrible, even worse than when the tree hit the first Humvee. Holly's sensitive ears picked up each and every noise involved: The slap and splash of human flesh against metal, the grunts of the driver and the soldier in the turret, the rending and twisting of the chassis and the body of the Humvee, and Andy's low, rumbling growl. Every noise seemed to echo and re-echo in Holly's head. It was more noise than she ever wanted to hear, even worse than gunfire. When it was over, she heard one heartbeat. Not three.

She hesitated, and then dared a look. One of the soldiers was laying ten feet in front of her. He was definitely dead. His head was an odd shape, probably fractured his skull on impact with the ground. He had been wearing a black beret, not that a helmet would have helped a lot. Andy was in the middle of the road, only a foot or two from where he had rammed the truck. He lay still, his surgical gown clothing ripped and torn, but Holly could hear the slow, steady thudding of his heart.

"Andy? Andy, please tell me you're okay."

Andy blinked his eyes. He let out a low, wavering groan. "Oh, that was not smart."

"Are you okay? Is anything broken?"

"I don't think so."

"Don't move. Stay still. I'll get help."

"Forget it," said Andy. He rolled to his side, pushing himself to his feet. He arched his back and joints popped. "John will start heading back toward us. Go meet him and get out of here."

"What about you?"

"I'm not going anywhere without Sarah. I will get her out of here even if I have to take on the whole U.S. Army."

"It's a suicide mission," Holly said. "Come back with the rest of us. We come back as a unified team. Once Posey and Kenny are healthy, we'll come right back. We'll use our powers and shove their plans right down their throats! Without you, we're not full strength. Literally."

"Without Sarah we're not full strength. You all are welcome to join me, but I'm not going anywhere without her."

"You're not well! You need to heal."

"Healed enough. Sarah is in danger."

"Andy," Holly tried to reason with him. "You're going to get caught. You may be strong, but they've got a lot of soldiers and weapons!"

"My choice. If I get caught, at least she won't be alone."

Holly tried one last tack, "You're not even wearing clothes!" Andy looked down at the torn and bloody surgical gown around his waist. He scratched his wide, hairy belly and shrugged.

"I won't care if they don't." He gave Holly a mischievous smile and started lumbering back toward the Home, the ratty, dressing gown loincloth flapping around his thighs. He swayed like a loping elephant, each of his thick legs landing heavily in the ground. Maybe it was real, maybe it was just Holly's imagination, but it felt like the ground trembled each time his feet landed. Andy quickly disappeared over a small rise. Beyond the hill lay the way back to the Home. In the sky, smoke was rising thickly from the fire and the flames were coloring the gray, early morning sky a hazy, burnt orange.

Holly felt anchored to her spot. She felt helpless and sick. The brown bat projected a mental image into her brain. The APC was returning. Then, something happened she didn't expect: Her mental link with the bat suddenly filled with emotions of concern and wonder. She looked up and saw the bat darting above her head. It was fluttering and looking down at her. Through its eyes, she could see herself. She could see the look on her face, melancholy changing to confused. The bat flooded her with feelings of concern again. Holly quickly realized that the bat was no longer under her direct control. Her mental command link with the bat had been severed when she was thinking about Andy and Sarah, but somehow the bat had reestablished the link with her. It was projecting its own emotions into her. The bat could read her emotional output. It was worried about her!

The APC rolled to a halt and Holly got back into the cab. "Andy's gone after Sarah."

John seethed for a second, and then punched the dashboard and dented the metal covering.

Dr. Sebbins stuck her head through the window between the cab and the bed. "We've got to get to the safe house. I've only got enough sedative to keep Posey under for about three, maybe four hours. After that, she's going to emerge into a world of pain that I do not think her body will be able to survive. If she doesn't get into the hyper-womb, she *will* die."

"We don't have a choice, do we?" John asked Holly.

She shook her head. "Andy and Sarah can fend for themselves."

"They're going to have to," said John. "How far to the safe house, Doc?"

"About a hundred miles, maybe a few more. We're going to have to get a map at some point, otherwise we'll be lost."

John looked at the road toward the Home. Holly could see him trying to piece together some sort of plan. She could also see the frustration in his eyes that told her he wasn't coming up with anything.

"They'll be okay," Holly said again. John nodded slowly and put the truck back into gear. He did a U-turn and rolled away from the Home, away from Sarah and Andy.

Indigo stuck her head into the cab. "We've got Posey. We escaped the Home. None of us are ever going back into that building. None of us are dead. It's a victory, right?"

"Yeah," John said. "A victory. For now."

Holly didn't say anything. She tried to think of what sort of image to project to the bat that was still following the truck; she wanted to reassure it, to tell it that everything was going to be okay. Her time spent in the minds of animals had already taught her one thing about the "lesser creatures," however: Animals relied on raw emotion and instinct, lies were constructs of humans. The bat kept projecting ideas of assistance and help, but Holly could only send it unsure images of an unsure future.

The sun broke on the horizon and the sky was becoming filled with rosy pink and bright orange. In the side mirror, Holly could see a thin column of smoke rising into the dawning blue.

"Red sky in morning…" John muttered.

Holly wrapped her fleece jacket tightly around her and tried to get a grip on the worry she felt in her stomach. She finished the statement in a whisper. "Sailors take warning."

— End of Book I —

Book Two

Truths and Consequence

Sarah sat on the floor of a chilly, barren jail cell. There was a cot in one corner with a thin, foul-smelling mattress stained with suspicious spots and a gray military-issue blanket like the one Kenny used on his bed in the Home. There was also a combination sink and commode in the opposite corner, the worst humiliation of all humiliations. There was a water tap on the top of the commode, but Sarah couldn't bring herself to drink from it, no matter how thirsty she felt. She couldn't stop thinking it was toilet water.

Her butt was numb from the cold floor and her legs were painfully cramped from being cuffed and restrained. She was still clad in undies and a frayed sweatshirt. Her captors hadn't bothered to give her pants. They had taken the cuffs off her wrists, but there was still a strong, polymer cable looped around her ankles several times and locked tightly with a combination lock. She had tried liked mad to get the cable off her ankle without success. Without her legs, she had no speed, not that she had anyplace to run to inside the cell. She sat motionless for the most part. The only time she bothered to move was when the soldier finally brought food to her cell. She had foolishly been expecting some meager C-rations or something vile and tasteless like bread-and-water. The solider, however, had brought a serving bowl full of steaming, gourmet-quality spaghetti bolognaise, a whole quarter-sheet cake with heavy frosting from a bakery, and a gallon of whole milk. Thinking about it, it made sense; if her captors were hired by the same people who funded the experiments in the Home, they would know what her nutritional needs were especially after using her powers for an extended amount of time: Carbs, fats, proteins, and sugar.

She dove into the food like a wild animal, shoveling the first mouthful into her face with her bare hand. The sauce burned her skin and her tongue, but she was too hungry to care. Still with a mouthful of spaghetti, she uncapped the milk and drank back several slugs. Without pausing to get a full breath, she scooped a handful of cake with her free hand and slammed that into her mouth as well, savoring the sugary, buttery richness.

The soldier opened the door again and waved a roll of paper towels at her. "We did think to provide you with a fork, you know." He tossed in the roll and the door clanked closed behind him, a heavy lock spinning into place with an ominous, final-sounding clack.

Sarah devoured the food. She didn't stop eating until it was all gone and she felt almost sickeningly full. She drank the entire gallon of milk. She remembered reading somewhere that drinking a gallon of milk in an hour was supposed to be physically impossible. She had drunk a gallon in under thirty minutes. Of course, she had also been running faster than the speed of sound not that long ago, so impossible was now a negotiable term.

There were voices outside of her cell, faint voices that drifted down the corridor. The door was made from the same heavy iron as the walls and floors, but there was a small, barred window near head height. Every half hour, like clockwork, a pair of eyes would glance into her room to make sure she was still there and she hadn't hung herself or choked on her own tongue. There were no other windows in the cell and the only light was provided by a fluorescent bulb in the ceiling covered by a metal cage and thick Plexiglas. It bathed the room in a somber, yellow light and filled the room with a constant buzzing drone.

The ride to the town had been mercifully short. She had been forced into the back of a truck by a guard who attempted to take liberties with her body. She had never felt more helpless than she had at that moment. Luckily, the helicopter sprayed gasoline everywhere and the fire started. The guard had left her in the back to help the other soldiers, but she couldn't make an escape. She tried. The second she leapt out of the back of the truck, the officer, the sadist in the red beret, had been right behind her. He had dropped into a low stance and swept her legs out from underneath her with an whirling kick. She crashed hard on the ground and the toe of his combat boot quickly found familiar territory on her collarbone.

Two guards were assigned to escort her after that. Thankfully, two guards kept each other honest and she didn't have to feel the sinister sensation of a gross man's hands on her body. The vehicles in yard of the Home had somehow been drained of gasoline. Extra trucks had been dispatched to carry the soldiers back to the town from whence they had come.

Sarah had never been to the town. She knew it was there, of course. Indigo had snuck over to it a few times and she said that she hung out with a couple of the local kids. Indigo never really talked about the kids. Since John's revelations about what the town's purpose might be, Sarah wondered if there even were kids. Maybe Indigo had never found any. Maybe Indigo's excursions were exercises in futility and she had lied to them all in order to mask her failures. When the truck rolled into town, Sarah looked for the small-town normalcy that she and the others had watched on satellite television shows and read about in books. The town looked as normal as a town was supposed to look, Sarah thought. There were a few old, ramshackle houses, a gas station, a small greasy-spoon diner, and a few bars. The main street was populated with a variety of small cars and pick-up trucks.

Sarah found herself examining everything, looking for American flags or any sort of insignias or notations that would tip her off to what country was commanding the military or where the base was located. She saw nothing, not even a bumper sticker flag or a patch on a soldier's uniform. The cars were varied, everything from American to Swedish to Japanese to German makes. The pick-ups were Chevrolets and Fords. There were a few sports cars, both American heavy steel and foreign coupes. Everyone was speaking English that she could hear, but she also heard hints of foreign accents and she saw a few small clues told her maybe not everything was one hundred percent American.

The license plates, for example: That was the first thing she looked at when she saw the town. The plates were all plain white with black lettering, nothing fancy. They looked like government plates. There were no state affiliations and they were all four digits. Typical American plates are six or seven digits. The ones in town had four black block letters or numbers and had no state or country affiliation that she saw. Also, the cigarettes gave her a clue. In the Home one night, they all had been lying around the TV room watching the first *Die Hard* movie and Andy pointed out that John McClane knew that Hans Gruber was European and not American like he was pretending to be because of how he held his cigarette. Since then, Sarah had been very keyed in on how people held cigarettes in movies or on television shows. The soldiers who were smoking around her and on the streets were holding cigarettes in both an American and European manner. Nothing pinned anything down. American and imported beer cans were visible on the streets.

When the truck stopped, two guards dragged her out of the back. Sarah was in the middle of a set of seven buildings, all plain-colored with dark metal roofs. The buildings were surrounded by a high, tan-colored cement wall topped with razor-wire. The walls faded back to the side of a small, rocky bluff and butted against the stone wall. A chain-link fence atop the bluff extended back into a pine forest. The guards frog-marched her into a plain, tan-colored, two-story building. They lead her into the basement and tossed her into her present confines.

Now, sitting in the cell with nothing to do but think and digest, she replayed everything she saw and heard, desperately seeking some sort of clue. Some good her new-found powers were. She was trapped in a cell, no way to get out, and no idea what to do even if she did. Sarah felt disgusted with herself.

The hollow scuffle of a pair of stiff-soled shoes began to get louder. Someone was approaching the cell. It wasn't the usual guard soldier in combat boots. Boots were heavier, with better soles. These shoes sounded crisp and thin in comparison, some sort of leather dress shoes with hard soles. In moments, a pair of eyes glanced through the cell window and the lock turned, opening the door. An official-looking man stepped through. He wore a crisp dress uniform, again without discernable ties to any single country. He had a bushy mustache and hard eyes. He surveyed her and gave her a brief nod in greeting.

"Subject Two. Codename: Blink. I am General Tucker. You are not being held prisoner. Let me make that clear."

"Sure seems like I'm being held prisoner."

"You are not. You are being held in confinement for your safety and protection. I was brought to understand than you experienced a power manifestation last night when you and the other subjects attempted an escape."

"Last I saw, General, the others weren't attempting, they were actually escaping." Sarah was surprised by her snippiness. She didn't know where she was channeling this brash attitude. She wasn't like that. She was always the good girl, the diplomat, the peacemaker.

General Tucker coughed into his fist. "Yes. That remains to be seen. Dr. Cormair is still in intensive care. As the computer files from the Home have been erased, we must hold you in protective custody until the doctor awakens from surgery and tells us how to best handle the final data recovery in this experiment."

"The files were blanked?"

"Affirmative. Including the analog back-up and retrieval system that was stored...elsewhere. I know that one of your kind, Subject Four, Codename: Psiber, was constructed to be a binary telepath. It seems that the subject's programming was extremely successful. I imagine the subject forced itself into the system and performed a data wipe to confound us. We are not so stupid as to keep everything online where someone who possessed this one's abilities would be able to find it. There are off-line copies of the files we need at another location. It will only take a day or so to access them and have them brought here."

Tucker turned his back to Sarah and peered out the small window of the cell door. "It was brought to my attention that a member of one of the squads under my command was less than...honorable with you. I regret that most unfortunate and unprofessional action occurred. Please know that I have punished him most severely and you will not have to deal with behavior like that anymore."

"What about the guy who nearly broke my collarbone?"

"Captain Krantz? He was doing what a good soldier should do."

"You have a weird definition of 'good soldier' then."

"Yes, well," General Tucker's mustache wiggled in a funny manner that reminded Sarah of Charlie Chaplin. "We will do our best to make you comfortable here. A better mattress can be brought shortly as will a change of clothes. If you require food or beverages, merely ask. The guards will provide whatever you wish."

"But, I can't leave?"

"No."

"And I'm not in prison?"

"You are in protective custody."

"Do I get to ask questions?"

"Negative."

"Sounds like prison to me."

"We expect your fellow subjects to join us shortly. They will be, no doubt, mounting a futile rescue attempt."

"Better hope they don't. From what I saw, we handed your guys their butts back at the Home."

"Trust me, Subject Two: We are prepared to deal with all of the experiments. Each has its own weakness. We have ways to exploit that weakness. Do you really think we'd create a thinking weapon without a way to disarm that weapon? We will be ready for the other experiments." He left without saying another word.

John was tired of driving. He was tired of running. He was just plain tired, really. And hungry. His stomach felt like it was eating itself.

They had only driven the APC for an hour before stowing it and trading it for an ancient minivan from a seemingly abandoned junkyard on the outskirts of a ramshackle town. The engine of the minivan was barely serviceable and John was able to get it running only after cannibalizing a few parts and gasoline from the military APC. The Dodge Caravan was rusted and it smelled of a gag-inducing combination of gas fumes, mouse feces, and mildew, but with no rear seats it was easy to hide in and it had enough room for Posey to be laid on the floor comfortably. She was still unconscious, kept in a coma by Dr. Sebbins.

During the junkyard search, Indigo had found a book of road maps in an old AMC Pacer. Using the pilfered map, the group figured out where they were. Then, they drove toward Pennsylvania taking a bevy of side streets and gravel roads to keep anyone from following them. They were running behind schedule and Dr. Sebbins was beginning to voice fears that Posey would wake before they were able to get her into the hyper-womb of the lab.

"How much farther, Doc?" John asked. The Caravan was beginning to run rougher. The oil in the engine was old and dirty. The van had been sitting immobile for at least five years. It was only going to get them so far before it shuddered into death on the side of the road.

Sebbins checked the map and looked for a sign on the road. They were going down a small farm road that curled and rolled over the countryside in a graceful, playful arc. It was pretty, but it made driving annoying. There was no place to get a good head of steam and John was constantly braking on the corners and gassing the van to get out of them. It was wearing too much on an engine that was already a gamble.

"Only a few more minutes, I hope," Sebbins said. "We passed Barns-dale, right?"

"A few minutes ago," John said.

"Then I think we'll be there in about ten minutes. There is a road off to the left. Take that when you see it. It goes into a valley."

There was a hill in front of them and a well-weathered Amish wagon with a wizened old man holding the reins of a Clydesdale was taking up most of the right lane. John pulled around the wagon and the Caravan belched a cloud of black smoke and backfired; the horse began to shy, the old man suddenly waking out of his sleepy daze and trying to yank the horse back into submission.

The horse suddenly fell back into step as if nothing happened. John looked over to the passenger seat and saw Holly's eyes were glazed over with a foggy sheen. "Nice one," he said.

Holly came out of her trance and smiled. "You just scared him. That was all. I just helped take away his fear."

The road Sebbins told John to take wasn't even gravel, it was a path worn down to two wagon-wheel ruts by Amish buggies. It rolled down through a cornfield and disappeared into a tree-filled valley. John checked the road ahead and behind for a sign of anyone following them, then guided the Caravan into the valley. The van bounced and banged its way through the field road and into the thick forest at the base of the valley. A hundred yards into the trees in a sunny clearing was a small, log cabin that looked like something out of a Laura Ingalls Wilder book. It was covered with moss and lichens and looked abandoned.

"This is it," Sebbins said. John stopped the van, shifted it into "park," and listened as the engine sputtered angrily, coughed a half-dozen times, and then gave up the ghost. John turned the ignition again, just to see if it would start. It was completely dead.

Holly stepped out of the van and stretched. Her eyes were closed and John could tell that she was reaching out and making contact with various animals. He wondered what it must be like; just looking around he could see birds, a few squirrels, and a few anthills. If Holly could hear all of them, it must sound like a football stadium of voices in her head. Thinking about it made his brain itch.

"This is it?" Indigo didn't bother to hide her displeasure.

"Books and covers, Indigo, books and covers," said Sebbins. "The house is merely a façade. There is a laboratory beneath it, hidden well, even from overhead spy cameras using infrared. Dr. Cormair built this to be a secret, even from the people who were funding the Home."

"Why?" asked Holly. She walked over and helped Dr. Sebbins lift Posey's limp body from the floor of the van.

"Because Dr. Cormair was a man of vision," said Sebbins. "He wanted to be ready for anything, including a possible need to abandon the Home and go into hiding."

Kenny was groggy, but awake. With help from Indigo, he slipped out of the back of the van and stood on wobbly legs. "I think I'm going to be sick." Immediately he turned and vomited, splashing the dirty floor of the Caravan. "I'm sorry," he wheezed, wiping his mouth.

"No worries," said John. He slid the side door closed. "We're abandoning it anyhow." John lifted Posey in his arms. She hardly weighed anything. Her skin was still raw and chapped from the constant change. In the two hours they drove from the Home, she had begun to sprout a fine downy material across her back and her upper arms and all along the fine, bony appendages jutting from her back. Sebbins said the down would eventually become feathers. Posey's skin felt hard and spiny against John's flesh. He started walking to the cabin. "First thing's first: We get Posey into a hyper-womb. Then, let's find beds. And food."

"Food is a must," said Indigo.

John shot her a look. "I thought you didn't eat?"

Indigo shrugged. "Telekinesis makes me hungry."

"Rations are down in the lab," said Sebbins. "I can't guarantee they're the best stuff in the world, but until we can get to a grocery story, they're all we got."

"So there is a grocery store?" Holly asked.

"In Barnsdale, not too far away. It's not huge, really a glorified convenience store, but it's got what we need." Dr. Sebbins walked to the door of the cabin and pulled. The door, wet and rotted, fell away. The interior of the cabin was musty and filthy from what looked like animal and flood damage. John took a wary sniff and choked.

"It's still part of the façade," said Sebbins. She found a log in the corner of the cabin and slipped her fingers into a groove in the wood. She tugged hard and part of the log came away revealing a ten-digit keypad. Sebbins typed in an intricate number and then pressed the star and pound keys at the same time. A small part of the cabin floor slid back revealing a circular metal door. The metal door had another keypad which Sebbins quickly disarmed. The door opened and a dim light at the base of the secret entryway flickered to life.

"It's about twelve feet down. John, can you make that climb while carrying Posey?"

"No problem," said John. He shifted Posey to one arm. "She's really light."

"Then I'll go first," said Sebbins, "and you follow immediately after, okay?"

"No," said Indigo suddenly. "I'm going first. Then you. Then John. Holly, you okay to help Kenny down?"

"Sure," said Holly. "No problem."

Indigo gave Sebbins an indignant look. "I don't know if I trust you yet."

"Fair enough," said the doctor, holding her hands up. "There is nothing down there that will hurt you."

The lab was a miniature version of the lab in the Home, but dusty and filled with the smell of plastic, industrial rubber, and computer components that had just been removed from a box. In one corner was a hyper-womb, a long, low bathtub version, not nearly as technical or as pretty as the vertical cylinders at the Home. The rest of the room was filled with monitors, machines, and boxes of parts and tools. As Holly and Kenny clambered down the stairs, Sebbins quickly went to work readying monitors and finding syringes and bottles of serum and sedatives. She began filling the hyper-womb with a neon-orange syrup.

"Holly, undress her. Put her in the hyper-womb, John," said Sebbins. Holly helped remove the clothes Posey was wearing and John carefully set Posey's body on the bottom of the hyper-womb. The serum began to rise up around her naked form, coating her in the orange slime. Her eyes fluttered a bit as the serum reached her eyelashes. Her eyelids opened halfway and John saw a thin, plastic-looking covering over her eyes.

"Secondary eyelids," said Sebbins. She was standing over his shoulder, hooking monitors into Posey's body. "It's almost like a nictitating membrane. Some animals have them for doing things like diving underwater or sweeping clear debris from the eye. Dr. Cormair had them surgically grafted to her about a year ago. He wanted her to be able to use her vision underwater without distortion, if needed. The secondary eyelids will help her do that. They'll also protect her eyes from wind at high velocity so she will be able to fly at incredible altitude and not worry about having to lose sight of anything while she flies."

"So she is going to fly?" Holly asked.

"If everything works as planned," Sebbins said quietly. She slid a needle into the vein on the bottom of Posey's foot and hooked it to a large bottle of a murky fluid. "I don't know how much longer the transformation will be taking place. Cormair tried to program it to go very fast once it started. That's why he devised the hyper-wombs. After it's over, that's when we find out how much she will and won't be able to do."

The serum engulfed Posey completely and finished filling to the top of the chamber. John helped Dr. Sebbins pull a heavy, glass top over the tank and secure it down, making sure it created a strong seal all the way around. "I'm going to pressurize it now," said Sebbins. "It will help her heal." Sebbins hooked two long, black, snake-like tubes into the head end of the tub. She flipped a switch and a generator began to hum. Sebbins turned on a few computer monitors and images flashed to life. One had several cross sections of a crudely rendered brain. Sebbins pointed at it. "This shows me what parts of Posey's brain are active. Her pituitary gland is practically on fire trying to get her through this change. However, if you look at this image," Sebbins' fingernail tapped the glass over the three-dimensional image of brain that was vibrantly pulsating with orange and red light. "This shows activity in the pain receptor areas of her brain. Red is the worst. Orange is almost as bad. You can tell she's in agony. If she was awake right now, she'd probably go insane, go into immediate shock, or go into cardiac arrest and die."

"How come the rest of us haven't suffered like Posey?" asked Holly. "I never had pain when I was getting my abilities."

"Me neither," said John.

"I did," Kenny croaked. They looked over at him. He sitting along the wall with his knees angled up and his head hanging between them. His eyeglasses were pushed up onto his forehead. "Migraines. Like you wouldn't believe. I had 'em at night. Never woke anyone up about them, though."

"I got headaches, too. I don't think they were related to these powers, though," said Holly. "How do you know your headaches were related? Everyone gets headaches."

"All of you will have different experiences," said Sebbins. "Some, like Andy and Posey, will go through major body modification and growth. It will be more painful. Others, like Holly and Indigo, will not have body changes, only sensory changes and stimulation of dormant sections of the brain."

"Let's get some food going," said John. "We need to walk to Barnsdale, I guess. The van isn't going to move and unless Holly can find us a horse to ride, we'll have to go by foot. Too bad Sarah isn't here. Probably only take her a minute or two."

There was a deep silence after John finished speaking. He shouldn't have mentioned Sarah. "I'll go," said John. "If I run flat-out, I should be back in less than an hour."

"It'll be dark by then, John," said Sebbins. "There are some emergency MRE's stored here somewhere. We'll have those for tonight."

"I'm not worried about the dark. I see really well at night."

"We don't want to attract attention, John. You're not...uh...Oh, how do I say this? You're not the kind of person that people around here are used to seeing."

"What?"

"She means you're black," said Indigo. She had a scowl on her face and she was hunched in the corner by the ladder. "We're deep in *gwai loh* territory."

A light dawned in his head and John slumped into an office chair by the monitors. He'd heard about racism. He'd read about it, and he'd been taught about it. He'd even watched movies and TV shows that showed it, but in his life, he'd never had to deal with it. He had lived a protected life, accepted for who he was by the six people with whom he was housed. They never treated him as different and he'd never looked at any of them as different. Only Indigo, for whatever reason, held racial boundaries as important, often researching her Japanese heritage and doing heavy reading on Heart Mountain and the other Japanese-American internment camps established during World War II.

"So, I can't go out because having a black man in town would make people in Barnsdale nervous?"

Sebbins looked embarrassed. "Yes. I'm sorry, John. We'll have the MRE's—they're not great, I know, I'm sorry—and tomorrow, Holly and I will go into town and get more food. And we'll make a plan on our next step."

"We go get Sarah and Andy back," John said. "I don't leave my friends. That's our first step."

"No," Indigo said.

"What?"

"Dr. Sebbins owes us the explanation," said Indigo. "That's our first step. We need to know everything now, Doc. Or did you forget about our deal?"

Sebbins took in a deep breath. "Fair enough. Give me a few hours to situate Posey and give her a full scan, and then check all of you over for injuries and get some scans. Then, we'll eat. Then I'll tell you what I know."

The MRE had been filling—high in calories and carbs—but tasted like old socks. Sebbins had choked it down the best she could. She didn't need a lot of food, not like the kids. She watched as the four of them force-fed themselves a few meals apiece. They groused and whined like normal teenagers, but they finished every crumb and licked their plastic forks clean. They didn't have much of a choice.

After they finished, Indigo put a chair in the middle of the room. "You sit there," she said.

Sebbins took the chair and the four kids gathered around her. Kenny still sat against the wall, looking haggard. John stood off to her right, his arms folded across his chest. Indigo sat in the corner by the ladder, her dark eyes constantly studying Sebbins' face. Holly sat on the floor in front of Sebbins.

Sebbins took a deep breath. "Where do I begin?"

"Why us?" said Holly. "Why pick the seven of us? What makes us so special?"

Sebbins sighed. She licked her lips and chose her words carefully. "Dr. Cormair was light-years ahead of his peers in the study of the human genome. You all know that DNA is like two sets of stairs circling each other, a double-helix, right? Well, the double-helix is comprised of many sets of genes. Normally, they're tightly connected, however Dr. Cormair began to notice something unique about some of those strands. In his studies he learned that some sets of DNA were 'looser' than others, some chains of DNA had greater strength, while the looser ones were poised for change. Cormair believed that it was evolution in action. The DNA chains were waiting for the stimulus to force change. You seven were chosen because your DNA strands were ready for splicing. The bonds between each separate set of genes in your DNA were incredibly elastic. You were selected for the rarity of your genetic profile. You would all be easy to change. You were selected from a pile of literally more than a million genetic profiles because you had the correct genetic flaws to make you susceptible to the splicing process."

"Flaws? So we were less than human?" asked Indigo.

"No, Indigo. You were all on the border of being *more* than human."

"Why take us as kids, then?" said John. "Why take us away from our parents?"

"Children heal faster than adults. We had to wait until you were old enough so your bodies could survive the strain of change, but couldn't wait until you were so old that your body wouldn't change. You were taken at the age of seven because you hadn't begun puberty or your adolescent muscular-skeletal growth."

"And our abilities?" Indigo piped up. "What are we supposed to be?"

"This will take more time to explain," said Sebbins.

"I'm not sleepy and I'm not going anywhere," said Indigo. "I want to know what sort of military project we are."

Sebbins rubbed the bridge of her nose. "Your individual DNA profiles, along with your musculature and your skeletal composition chose what sort of abilities Dr. Cormair could develop within you. Indigo, you would never have survived Andy's strength transformation. John, your brain wouldn't have been able to handle the implants Kenny received. Dr. Cormair studied your chemistry practically from birth. He knew what you could become. For instance, Andy had an extremely rare genotype. He was the first one identified, Subject One."

"Subject?" Holly frowned. "It's Andy!"

Sebbins nodded at Holly. "That's what I would have called him if I were running the show, but the people funding the project, and Dr. Cormair, wanted to keep it at what it was initially intended to be: A project, cold and faceless, with no humanity. You were to be experiments, not people. Andy was the first to be identified and he became Subject One. His project code-name was 'Brawn.' He was an experiment of hyper-strength and healing. He can heal from trauma at an incredible rate and his bones were enhanced to withstand exponentially more force than the average human bone. Right now, his bones are nearly unbreakable."

"How unbreakable?" asked John.

"The average human femur—the strongest bone in your body—can withstand something around six hundred pounds of pressure. It was projected that Andy's body might withstand nearly six hundred-thousand pounds of pressure, give or take."

"You mean we could drop a truck on him and he'd be okay?" John gaped.

"You could drop several trucks on him. And he could probably lift the trucks off of himself, too. His muscles have been genetically and artificially boosted to give him strength beyond anything humans conceive. His bones had to be enhanced otherwise his muscles would have crushed them to pulp when he flexed. He's not invulnerable, though. The problem comes with his skin. That's one of his weak spots," said Sebbins. "His skin is normal skin. It tears like everyone else's. His eyes are vulnerable. He's vulnerable to bullets like everyone else. The only difference is that he'll be able to heal from multiple shots without medical care. The muscles on his body can stop bullets. It's like he's wearing a bullet-proof vest. He is nearly invulnerable to physical damage, but Dr. Cormair hypothesized that he may have a damage limit. Drain Andy of enough blood, or drop him out of a plane and let him fall far enough and he might die, plus his swimming days are over. He no longer has buoyancy in the water. He'll drop like a stone."

"Why did they do all that to him, then? What's the point?" said Holly.

"Imagine him as a human crane or a human bulldozer. He can move machines, rip trees out of the ground, and carry massive amounts of weight. In a forward military area, having one person capable of doing the work of a piece of heavy equipment would be a great boon. He's also a shield. He can protect targets or lead assaults."

"We're all military projects, aren't we?" said Indigo. "We're weapons. Tools for warmongers."

Sebbins sucked in a sharp breath. "Yes." Sebbins paused, waiting for their reactions.

Indigo glanced at John and gave him an almost imperceptible nod. "Go on, Doc," said Indigo. "What about the rest of us?"

"Sarah was Subject Two, codenamed 'Blink.' Her body has been enhanced with tachyons, sub-atomic particles that can exceed the speed of

light. Obviously Sarah cannot exceed the speed of light, but she can sprint
faster than any vehicle on the planet can move. At speed, she should be able
to run across the surface of water. She is an experiment in lightning assault.
Why would you need a gun if you could move faster than bullets and hit a target and be gone before anyone could react?"

"A human sniper rifle," said John. "One shot, one body…no witnesses."

Sebbins' face seemed to grow sadder. "John, you were the third subject.
Codename: 'Elite.' Your body has been enhanced beyond human limitations.
You're stronger than almost every man, except Andy of course, and your stamina is nearly limitless. Your reactions are faster, too. Your brain has also been
enhanced by artificially stimulating areas relating to hand-eye coordination,
balance and grace, and leaping. You can turn anything into a weapon and fire
it with accuracy—from pea shooters to heavy artillery. You are the ultimate
soldier. You can take orders as well as give them. In your education, you've
been hypnotically trained with all the military information Dr. Cormair could
gather so that you react to military situations unconsciously. Your mind will
tell you what to do and how to do it. Your brain is a tactical military supercomputer."

"The ultimate soldier," Indigo repeated. "A modern day Alexander."

John scowled, but stayed silent. Sebbins continued, "Holly, you were
fourth—they called your project 'Animalia.' You've already figured out your
powers, haven't you? Commanding animals, enhanced senses?"

"Yes, Doctor," said Holly. Her voice was thin and her eyes showed the
awe that everyone was feeling. "How do I do it?"

"Your body can secrete pheromone command signals to animals. You
can send out messages and hypnotize animals into following you. You can also
receive their signals and interpret them."

"That's amazing," said John.

"Yes," said Sebbins. "It is. Holly, what I want to know is how well your
interpretation of signals works. Do animals actually 'talk' to you, like in a language?"

Holly shook her head. "They send me messages based on emotions or
actions. I can command them based on the same cues. Different animals have
different perspectives, needs, and reactions. It's not like there are words and
sentences."

"Fascinating," said Sebbins.

"And my telekinesis?" Indigo prodded.

"Ah, Subject Seven, or 'Anomaly' as they called you."

"Anomaly? Screw them."

"Telekinetic ability would make you an anomaly," Sebbins said, her tone
reassuring. "You have had your hypothalamus enhanced both genetically and

mechanically. As you all know now, many emotions are controlled by the hypothalamus and the endocrine system." Sebbins paused and nodded to the pen on the desk. "Indigo—move that pen, please."

Indigo's eyes narrowed and she focused on the pen. For several moments, no one breathed. The pen refused to move.

"Aw, c'mon!" Indigo shouted. "What the hell is wrong with me? I could do it before! You all saw! You all saw me do it! This is complete bullsh—"

The pen suddenly rocketed off the desk and narrowly missed hitting Sebbins. Indigo froze mid-rant.

"Your hypothalamus wasn't engaged when you first started to move the pen. When you failed, you threw a…tantrum, shall we say? When the endocrine system began responding to the hypothalamus, your telekinetic field extended. The angrier you get, Indigo, the more your power works."

"What about the helicopter? I wasn't angry then. I could move that stick."

"Were you scared?"

Indigo didn't answer. She opened her mouth and quickly shut it, slumping back in the corner and crossing her arms petulantly.

"Fear, anger, lust, anxiety, sexual urges—powerful negative emotions of all sorts can all trigger the expansion of your telekinetic field. With time and training, you may be able to do far more."

"What about Posey?" Holly asked.

"Subject Six, called 'Nightingale.' Posey was the avian project," Sebbins said. She sounded as if she were reading from a dossier. "As you can tell from the wings, Posey was grafted with bird-like characteristics. Wings, hollow bones, thin but strong muscles, and even a sonic weapon modeled after an eagle's cry. Posey was intended to be a spy weapon. High or low altitude reconnaissance, undetectable by radar, silent—she could even be an assassin."

"That's sick," said Holly. "She's not an assassin."

"I know she's not. But, if they trained her in the art, she could have advantages that no one else could have."

"Fly in, hit a target, and fly out. Even the most remote targets wouldn't stand a chance. If she could intercept a plane, how easy would it be for her to drop a C-4 charge on the wing? Wing blows up, plane goes down," said John. "I don't know if any counter-terrorism team could stop that."

"What about me?" Kenny said so little that his voice seemed foreign.

"Ah, Subject Five. I could tell you about your abilities…but, I think you're in a much better position to do than I am, right?" Sebbins fixed Kenny with a knowing smile. To her surprise, Kenny returned it. Sebbins couldn't remember Kenny ever smiling.

"What does she mean by that, Kenny?" said John. "Are you okay?"

"I'm fine," said Kenny. A slow smile spread over his face. As it did, the shy, quiet Kenny seemed to fade into the background, replaced by a more confident, more self-assured Kenny whose eyes crackled with fire. "I'm considered a binary telepath, codenamed 'Psiber.' I can mentally manipulate computers and electronics. I have a memory capacity greater than most supercomputers and I can calculate as fast as any microprocessor, hundreds of thousands per second. I can browse the Internet and send e-mail with my mind if I'm in the broadcast area of a Wi-Fi source. However, they haven't been able to find a way to compensate for the physical drain on my body. My body basically serves as a battery for my mind. When my mind works double-time to talk to the computers, my body pays for it. That's why I pass out after big hacks."

"You know all that?" said John. "You been holding out on us, Ken?"

"Before we left the lab, I absorbed all the computers there. It's here," Kenny said, tapping his temple with a slim finger. "I blanked all the hard drives and stored their collective info up here. I know it *all*, John. At least, everything that was connected to that computer system. Even the deep files, the ones they tried to hide under layers of encryption."

"All?" Sebbins said. She hadn't been told everything when she joined. Even after all her service, a lot of the project was still classified to her.

"Well, I know as much as was on the hard drives. Files, e-mails, spreadsheets on our performance during those tests—it's all here. I know a lot, everyone. I know that the United States Government has no idea we exist. I know the true identity of our investors. I know that our parents aren't alive anymore." There was a gasp from Holly, and John bit his lip. Even Indigo raised a hand to her mouth in disbelief. "You weren't going to tell us that bit, were you, Doc?"

Four pairs of eyes fell on Sebbins and she could feel them burning into her flesh. "No," she said. Air caught in her throat and she was barely audible.

Kenny gave a half-smile. "Not like it was a big deal, though, right? We've all moved past them, haven't we? I mean, we all pretty much thought our parents gave up on us. In a way, it's kind of nice to know that they didn't."

"That's why their letters stopped?" Holly wailed. Tears were streaming down her face and she snuffled into the back of her arm. John bit his knuckles thoughtfully.

Indigo just glared at Dr. Sebbins. "You knew?"

Tears began pricking at the corners of her eyes. "Guilty," said Sebbins. "Your families were systematically eliminated as the project advanced. Brothers, sisters, mothers, fathers, and then—aunts, uncles, cousins, and grandparents. Everyone who knew you existed." Holly let out a loud, heart-wrenching sob and buried her face in her hands. "I guess that's why I got so close to all of you," Sebbins continued. "I knew you didn't have families anymore. Please, please forgive me for not telling you."

"All this time, I actually hated them because I thought they just didn't care," Holly collapsed in a heap and sobbed.

"That's cold," said John. "That's really cold."

"They erased our birth records, too," said Kenny. "Anything that could identify us in the world has been eliminated. Technically, none of us exist."

"Did you know that too, Doc?" Indigo hissed.

Sebbins could only nod. So many nights she thought about this information, laid in bed just thinking about it. She had wanted to tell the kids, but Cormair had insisted they not know. *They've already given up on their families,* he'd said. *The anger they feel toward their families will help their abilities develop!*

"I also know about the *other* experiments. I bet ol' Doc Sebbins here doesn't even know about those." Kenny sneered. "December thirty-first of this year, Doc: We were all going to turn eighteen. And what was going to happen then?"

Happen? If anything was scheduled to happen, she hadn't been told. "I have no idea," Sebbins said.

"Liar!" Indigo shouted.

"No," Kenny waved Indigo back. "I believe her. I know she didn't know. It was in an encrypted, classified file deep in the computers, an email exchange between two of the higher-ups. I don't even think Cormair knew."

"What 'other' experiments, Ken?" John urged.

"The other kids—the second project."

"Stop playing with us, Ken. Just let us have it!"

"Seven years ago, in a separate lab, they started another group of kids with strange genetic profiles on the path to becoming enhanced like we all were. They have a super soldier, a strongman, and a bird girl. And they have a few of kids that aren't like any of us."

"There are more kids like us?" Indigo sounded incredulous.

"*Better* than us," said Kenny. "They are benefiting from all our testing in order to enhance their abilities faster. They're us, but tuned-up, better, faster, stronger, and smarter. They are our replacements."

"Replacements?" John said.

"On our birthday this year, as a present, the program at the Home was scheduled to end. Didn't know that either, did you, Doc?"

"No, I didn't!" Sebbins felt anger bubbling up in her. She felt like some newbie junior researcher rather than someone who had given up her life for this project.

"The program was going to end?" Indigo shouted. "That means we could have just walked away free in a few months?"

Kenny laughed. His laugh was something other than human: shallow, breathy, and low. "Free? No. Think about it, Indigo! We're billions of dollars and a decade's worth of astronomically ground-breaking research! We're too valuable to simply be turned loose."

"Jail?" John asked. "Servitude?"

Kenny's voice was flat and hollow, "Termination."

Andy spent several hours lying in a copse of trees not far from where soldiers were picking up the wreckage of the disaster at the Home. The pain of his transformation had kept him from sleeping. He had lain in tall grass, oblivious to the chill of the morning, with tears streaming down the sides of his face as he was wracked with aches and agony, trembling and gritting his teeth to keep from crying out as his muscles bubbled under his skin and his bones increased in mass and thickness. The last thing he needed was to alert some soldier to his position.

From what he gathered, the activity around the Home had quieted down considerably. The soldiers must have assumed that all of the experiments had escaped, save for the one they caught. That would work to Andy's advantage. He might still be able to sneak around, though running might trigger seismic sensors.

He was still wrapped in the flimsy hospital gown. It barely covered him and left him feeling rather exposed. New clothes would be a necessity if he was going to mount a rescue mission, but those clothes would have to be loose-fitting. He wondered if there was something beyond a Big and Tall Men's store, like maybe a Freakishly Big Men's Store.

He forced the pain to the back of his mind and hoisted himself up on an elbow, just above the grass level. Only a few soldiers still milled about in front of the Home and none of them were in a position to spot him in the trees. He could make his way toward town without too much trouble as long as he stayed in the trees.

His feet had grown and expanded during his transformation, shredding his shoes as they did. Each foot was wider and longer. His toes had become thick, bulky rods that jutted out from the meat of his foot and the skin on the soles of his feet thickened and toughened. To balance his enormous bulk, his feet were like steel. With each step, that's what it felt like. Every motion felt as if he was moving in pudding and each step seemed to shake the ground.

The town was on alert. By the time Andy reached the village, the streets were patrolled by armed soldiers. They stood on street corners chatting quietly and smoking cigarettes, their guns hanging idly from shoulder straps. They looked like they were at ease, but from his vantage point, hidden behind a fallen maple, camouflaged by thick shrubs, Andy could see their eyes darting and he could almost sense their edginess. The soldiers were looking for trouble. No one out of uniform walked the streets, and Andy couldn't see if any stores were even open. He could see the gas station on the corner of the town and no one was at the pumping stations.

Andy didn't have a clue to Sarah's whereabouts. John would know what to do in this situation; John was good at figuring out things like that. In class, John was always able to lay out winning strategies in games or projects. Take chess, for instance. John was slick—laying out extensive pawn strategies, utilizing his knights for quick strikes, moving his rooks and bishops in conjunction to pin Andy back deep. Andy just tore straight ahead, going for the quick kills and usually lost his queen before the tenth move. John usually didn't even need his queen.

A loud rumble snapped Andy out of his reverie and he squinted down the road. A dark green Humvee was rolling toward town from the direction of the Home. It was the first military vehicle Andy had seen since he made it to the outskirts. The hummer took a right by the gas station and thundered up the road, past the main street, and to the outskirts north of town. The hummer took another right and disappeared from view as if it had gone down an inclined road that was hidden by a grassy knoll.

If Sarah was being held prisoner, it would make more sense to put her in a military installation than a civilian house. And, if he was going to screw up and sacrifice his queen too early in the match, he figured it would be better to take down the military base than to try to tear down the town. It would be heroic…in a stupid, get-blown-up-and-die sort of way.

There were guards in woodland gray camouflage and black berets about a hundred yards from Andy's present location. Between the edge of the woods where he currently hid and the town, there was nothing but scrub grass and pavement. There was no way he could make a run at them. He'd find himself riddled with bullet holes before he made twenty yards. If he angled away from the guards and headed toward the backyards of some of the houses at the edge of town, he'd leave himself exposed to anyone looking out their window. If anyone saw him, a lumbering behemoth in their backyard would inevitably lead to a phone call to authority figures, and then, most likely, guns.

Rocks and hard places, Andy thought. He thought about the class they had taken on strategies. A wizened professor with a face like a dried apple had been brought in to discuss the battle tactics of Alexander, Napoleon, Hannibal, and other great military minds. There, Andy had been instructed on the art of battle: Everything from tactical movements such as the Hammer-and-Anvil, the Chariot Vice, and Throwing Sand to Disguise the Blade, to the great battles such as Thermopylae, Waterloo, Omaha Beach, Midway, and

Gettysburg. "Do something unexpected," the professor had told them. "A ruse, perhaps. Scare your opponents. Feint! That is the secret to finding a weak spot. Destroy your opponents' confidence. Make them think they've won and then go for the kill."

Andy dug into the dirt with his hands. His fingers, each easily three times a regular man's finger, plowed into the earth with the ease of a backhoe. He pulled up handfuls of black loam, wet and dark. He haphazardly smeared his face and body; he rubbed some in his hair. He waited for a few moments to allow the dirt to dry a bit, fanning it with a wide skunk cabbage leaf, and then it was show time.

He set his feet and put his hands on the trunk of a diseased elm at the edge of the woods. He pushed hard, feeling the surge of power through his core. The elm wavered; roots began to snap beneath his feet as they broke under the stress of being stretched. Suddenly, the elm gave way beneath his hands and fell straight, smashing into the ground. The guards immediately scrambled for their guns. Andy stumbled out of the trees like a drunk, staggering and reeling. He let out a loud, low, moaning wail and fell to his knees. The guards were advancing on him quickly, guns raised; one was already on his radio calling for help. Andy fell face first into the dirt and let his body go limp. In seconds, guards were swarming the area and several medics had arrived on the scene. A thick needle bored into the skin of his upper arm, piercing a vein, and then everything became light and filmy in his mind. He felt his breathing slow and everything went dark.

Andy woke up in a windowless hospital room lit by a droning fluorescent light. The room was a pale, sickly, industrial green color. The walls, the tiles, even the bed linens, all colored in institution green. There was no TV or radio in the room. There was nothing to tell him where he was. A small basket of plastic flowers sat on an end table next to a wooden bureau that was painted a dull off-white, but that was the only decoration in the room. Through a glass panel in the only door, he could see an armed guard standing at the ready. Andy had been strapped down to a metal table in the center of the room with polymer cables, each about as thick as a man's forearm. A few large-bore needles ran fluids into his arm from a hanging bag. There were EKG pads taped to his chest. Everything was quiet. There was no hustle in the hallway and there was utter silence. That meant it was time to make some noise.

Andy closed his eyes and took a few deep breaths. Polymer cables held his wrists to the table, but his arms weren't strapped down otherwise. If he could get his arms free, he was confident that he could tear a new door in the hospital room. Andy inflated his chest, pushing against the cable across his chest and stomach. He tensed his thighs, feeling the cable there, too. He began to curl his hands toward his shoulders, feeling the hard, taut resistance of the bonds. His biceps began to burn and the cable across his chest began to bite into his skin. He relaxed for a second, grabbed another deep breath to inflate his lungs again and pulled. He repeated this several times, each time gaining a little more ground against the wrist cables. Finally, he pulled up hard, one last time, and neither he nor the cables broke, but he had succeeded in stretching the polymer until he could slip his massive fists out of the bonds. Once his hands were free, it was short work to stretch the other cables so that he could wriggle his way to the end of the table and out of the restraints entirely.

He was still naked, save for the king-sized hospital linens. Andy ripped the pads from his chest and slipped the needles out of his forearm. He quickly ransacked the bureau, finding a pair of navy blue sweatpants that looked like they'd initially been made for an elephant. He was able to slip into them with ease. The hooded sweatshirt that accompanied them was a little too small. Andy ripped the arms off, and then ripped slits down the sides from the underarm sections. He also had to rip the neck open. When he put it on, it stretched tightly over his torso, but it was better than being naked. He caught sight of himself in a mirror. Someone had bathed him, shaved the scrub from his cheeks and chin, and brushed his unruly red mop of hair.

The door to the room opened. Andy froze. A man in a military-style gray dress uniform walked into the room. Andy scanned the ribbon bars and hanging medals on the left side of the man's chest. He'd studied the American military; none of the colorful little rectangles were American medals. One looked like a Canadian medal, one of the many service crosses; another medal looked French, but Andy couldn't place it. The epaulets on the man's shoulders each had two stars. Whatever military he was in, he was a high ranking officer.

"Good afternoon, Subject One. It's nice to finally meet you. I am General Tucker, the executive officer of this installation. I'm glad the pants we found for you fit, at least. I'll try to have someone find a better shirt for you. If nothing else, I'll have someone sew you something. Please, have a seat back on the table and get comfortable."

Andy didn't move. He watched the man's eyes. There was no fear, no concern, despite the fact that he was standing before a genetic behemoth capable of tearing him in two with his bare hands. That fact didn't sit well with Andy. It meant the man knew something that Andy didn't.

"How did you know I was awake?"

Tucker smiled and pointed to the floral arrangement. "There is a camera in that basket. Also, the moment you began to strain against your restraints, your heart rate and adrenaline shot up to a point where a warning went off at the nurses' station down the hall. You have been under observation the entire time."

Andy felt like a deflated balloon. Of course they'd be watching him! Why wouldn't they? Andy was at a disadvantage. He was on the defensive, he needed to get on the attack. He took a different tack. "You know what I'm capable of, don't you?"

Tucker nodded. "Affirmative."

"So, why aren't you scared? How do you know I'm not going to tear apart this room? This hospital?"

"Because we have something you want: Your friend, Subject Two."

"Sarah."

"As you say. I am not here to argue semantics with experiments, regardless of what that experiment might think it can do to me. You took a risk coming back to this town. You might have been killed, you know that? You were one of the more risky experiments."

Andy drew himself up to his full height, which wasn't overly impressive, but when he folded his arms across his chest, there was a slight tearing sound as part of the sweatshirt gave way to his sheer, broad mass. "I'm not an experiment."

"As I said, I'm not here to argue. Why don't we take a walk?" Without waiting for an answer, General Tucker turned on his heel and walked out the door. The guard at the door snapped to attention and the general nodded and then turned the corner. He didn't look back to make sure Andy was following.

Andy hesitated. Part of him wanted to follow the general to see what he could learn, and because the general expected him to follow. The rebellious side of him wanted to stay in the hospital room, wait for a while, and then trash the place as only he knew how. Andy sighed and followed the general. As he walked, trailing the general by a few paces, his bare feet slapped against the cold tiles in the hallway, each one making a thunderous noise that seemed to tremble the corridor.

"Quite a step you have there," the general called out, not bothering to look over his shoulder. "The medics estimated your weight somewhere around eight hundred pounds. However, your body fat is at only 2.2 percent. That is amazing in and of itself. You are practically made of muscle." Tucker paused, as if waiting for a response. Andy kept his mouth closed. After a moment, Tucker baited him again. "I saw what you were able to do at the Home. Your strength is impressive."

"You should know. You did it to me," Andy said.

"Dr. Cormair's genetic enhancements surpassed our expectations, you know. We had anticipated you being about half as strong as you appear to be."

"Sorry to throw off your plans."

"Come with me; I want to show you something," Tucker said. He beckoned Andy with a finger but he still didn't look behind him. "I have a feeling you'll want to see this."

Andy followed the general into a gymnasium of sorts. A hard concrete floor was polished smooth and a couple of basketball hoops hung from the walls on either side of the building. There were no bleachers or lines on the floor and a set of double-doors on the far side was open to the outdoors. A gentle afternoon breeze blew in the room carrying the smell of mown hay from a nearby field and a square of sunlight slanted in through the door. General Tucker walked over to the door and took a deep breath. He still wouldn't look over his shoulder at Andy. Andy walked across the gym and stopped a few paces behind the general.

"You presented me with an interesting challenge, Brawn."

"Andy."

Tucker continued as though Andy hadn't spoken. "With the success of your genetic engineering, we now have the ability to create a human tank. Now, stopping your average man, that's not a problem. We have many tools that would allow us to stop an average man. A human tank, though—that's a new challenge entirely. Obviously, we wouldn't want to shoot you. That would be a great waste of resources. Bullets won't harm you enough to stop you. Sure, they'll hurt, but they won't stop you. They'll probably just make you angry. So, we need something that will allow us to take down a genetic experiment such as you without harming the experiment."

A wave of unease washed over Andy. He looked around the room for weapons. Other than the basketball hoops and backboards, there was nothing.

The general continued. "I was told that the medics that found you when you came out of the woods used a hypodermic needle filled with enough tranquilizers to drop a charging bull elephant. It kept you sedated for about five minutes. You started to come out of it and had to be immediately shot up with more tranquilizers. You have the ability to heal extremely quickly. That makes drugs a very inefficient way to prevent you from destroying whatever you choose to destroy, should you choose to destroy something."

"What's your point?" Anxiety was building in Andy's chest. He could sense what was coming.

Tucker turned and faced Andy. "Obviously, your strength poses an interesting problem. Those cables you stretched out in the infirmary have more than five times the strength of steel. Tying you up would be ludicrous, wouldn't it? You could snap the chains like they were licorice."

"Cut to the chase General, or else I'm going to walk."

"Precisely!" said Tucker, a smile appearing beneath his mustache. "That's exactly what I want you to do."

"Say what now?"

"Go out those doors."

"Why?"

"I have a platoon of my most elite soldiers stationed outside. They have a singular objective: Stop you without killing you. Have a good time." Tucker reached into his pocket and took out a flare. He popped the cap on the flare and red sparks began shooting from the top. With a nod to Andy, Tucker tossed the flare out the door and strode back across the gym to the doors where they entered. The doors shut behind Andy with an ominous thud.

Andy backed away from the open doors. He walked to the door that Tucker had just passed through and tried the knob. With his new, massive hands, the doorknob was hard to grip. The door was, of course, locked. Andy pulled on the knob and it ripped straight off the door leaving a hole surrounded by jagged edges. He slipped his index finger through the hole and pulled. The door tore open like a tuna can. Beyond the door, a thick wall of solid steel was blocking the corridor.

A speaker in the wall next to the door began to squawk with Tucker's voice. "What you see before you, Brawn, is nearly two feet of tested blast steel. The entire wall is made from it. It's meant to survive a direct hit from a mid-grade missile. If you try to force your way through it, I'm quite certain the skin and muscles on your hands will tear away before you succeed. Your bones would probably survive, but I doubt you're strong enough to keep punching as you bleed to death. The only way out is through the gauntlet beyond the doors. Good luck." The speaker clicked to static and then went silent.

A strong mixture of anxiety and rage bubbled in Andy's chest. "What if I don't leave the gym, General? I'm just going to take a seat in here and your platoon can go to hell for all I care!" Andy yelled into the speaker. "You hear me? I'm not your guinea pig!"

As if his rant was a signal, Andy heard two loud pops from outside the door. A pair of black cylinders skittered across the cement floor, clouds of white smoke billowing from them. One whiff of the smoke made Andy heave what little sustenance was in his stomach. His eyes watered and his nose and mouth began burning. Blindly, he stumbled toward the doors, toward clean air.

Breeching the doors into the lot around the gym, Andy rubbed his eyes furiously and snorted out a long, nasty stream of mucous from his nose, desperate to stop the burn. He was standing outside a pair of buildings, a large, metal warehouse to his right, and the metal-sided square gymnasium. A large, grassy exercise yard lay to his left. There was a wide paved area between the buildings. Two dark gray Humvees and a pair of white pick-up trucks were grouped loosely around the pavement area. Several uniformed soldiers with strange-looking weapons were standing around the vehicles, waiting for Andy to make a move. Andy spit on the ground, his mouth tasted like bile and his sinuses were on fire. Fine. If this is how it has to be, Andy would go along with it. If they wanted a fight, he could certainly give them a fight.

With a roar that seemed to come from a part of Andy that was more animal than human, Andy lowered his head and charged the nearest pick-up truck. He could hear one of the soldiers shouting commands while other soldiers bustled around, setting up for shots from their weapons. *They won't kill me*, Andy thought. *That will be their biggest mistake.*

Something hit Andy in the back and he felt a massive surge of electricity run through him. He stumbled and fell to his knees. The electrical charge stopped and he was able to regain his senses. He ripped the taser darts from his back. He quickly pushed himself up and lowered his shoulder into the side of the pick-up, nearly bending the truck in half.

"Double the voltage!" a soldier called.

Before they could reset their weapons, Andy slipped one hand underneath the truck and the other grabbed the rim of the high side on the truck's bed. Muscles surging with power, Andy lifted the truck over his head and lobbed it at a pair of Humvees, sending soldiers scattering for cover. The truck landed on the hoods of the assault vehicles with a glorious crush of metal.

A soldier in a red beret with a green-shield patch on the front was screaming into a hand radio. "Bring up the foam!"

"Foam?" Andy shouted. "You're not even trying now." In the distance, Andy began to hear the bass *whut-whut-whut* sound of a helicopter.

A soldier pulled a canvas tarp off the back of one of the Humvees, revealing a silver cannon that glowed with crackling blue light. The cannon began humming loudly. The soldier jumped to the controls of the weapon and charged it, swiveling it to be pointed straight at Andy. "Eat sonic, freak!"

A blast of sound nearly crippled Andy. The high-pitched whine seemed to bore into his ear drums and press spear points into the sides of his brain. His body became jelly and Andy fell to his knees, clapping his hands over his ears in a vain attempt to stop the noise. The sonic weapon was hitting him with a wavelength of sound that penetrated his skin and made his organs vibrate with a sickening tremolo.

The helicopter came into view over the gymnasium. Beneath it, a square, metal container dangled from several cables. As the helicopter passed low over Andy's head, the container opened and a pile of cream-colored foam, a fifteen-foot square block, fell from the sky. Andy, incapacitated by the sonic, could only watch as the lump of sticky foam landed on him, engulfing him.

The foam began to harden immediately. As it solidified, Andy felt his skin becoming colder. Extremely cold. Vapor rose off the foam in wisps of smoke. He needed to fight through the pain of the sonic and break free of the foam or he would be frozen solid! He gritted his teeth and took a sharp inhale of breath. The air around him seemed to be like an arctic storm, it filled his lungs and he felt his body begin to lose strength, to shut down. It was becoming harder to move in the rapidly drying foam. A taser blast, stronger than the first one, made his body seize. The sonic blast battered him. Soldiers swarmed in with hoses and backpacks of the foam, spraying him down with more.

In moments, Andy was frozen. His heartbeat dropped quickly, going hypothermic; he became sleepy. He tried to continue to fight, but his eyelids closed on their own volition and Andy ceased his battle.

From a room in the hospital wing on the second-story of the gymnasium building, General Tucker watched his men immobilize the subject with brutal efficiency. There had been collateral damage. Those Humvees and pick-ups weren't cheap, but it was worth it to personally witness the experiment's display of strength. Tucker turned from the windows and faced a hospital bed.

Dr. Cormair was sitting in the bed, arms folded in a combination of frustration and anger. "You did not tell me that you had developed the foam already."

"Of course not, Doctor," said the general. "It wasn't in your need-to-know capacity. I will not turn overpowered teenagers loose on this world without some way to eliminate each one of them. Brawn was probably the trickiest. The others are vulnerable enough to tasers or sonic cannons. A bullet, if need be, will stop them as well. But, how do you stop something like project Brawn? Incredible muscle density, bullets wouldn't get much penetration, even a large caliber. I doubt a bullet would even be able to get to his heart, provided it didn't hit one of his ribs first. Bullets can't hurt his bones. A head shot would be out of the question. It would just stun him momentarily, at best."

"You are toying with them," Cormair said. He leaned back in bed, casting his eyes to the ceiling. He didn't want to watch the exercise anymore.

"It's all research, Doctor. I thought you, of all people, could appreciate that."

"My research was to further the development of man, General. Not to make sure I could control it."

"Doctor, a horse that cannot be controlled is wild. It's useless to man. It just feeds on resources and causes problems. But a horse that can be controlled was man's greatest boon. Without the horse, how would the Plains Indians have fared? Or how far west could Americans have expanded without horses? Even now, we control horsepower in engines to serve man. Control was necessary to prove usefulness. Doctor, without control, how would a regular, normal man fare against your forced evolution? An average guy trying to stop something like Brawn would be obliterated. Control is what is needed for all things. We need control in order to channel the weapon otherwise the weapon could kill innocents. Without control, releasing Brawn would be no different than dropping a bomb." General Tucker turned back toward the window and watched as his soldiers used a mobile crane to lift the frozen block of foam off the ground and load it onto the back of a flatbed truck. The truck's leaf springs sagged as the weight settled.

General Tucker turned to Dr. Cormair. "We can't wait for you to recover. Time is too short. We will run the final tests on this subject for you, Doctor. I will apprise you of the results."

"And then what?"

"The subject is too dangerous to attempt to confine long-term. Once the data collection is complete, we will terminate the experiment. The same with the other experiments. They have shown that their usefulness is coming to a conclusion." Tucker left the room, the door closing behind him.

Dr. Cormair closed his eyes slowly. Slowly his lips thinned and his jaw clenched. A tear slipped from his eyelid and cascaded to his cheek.

"They call themselves 'The Trust'," said Kenny. "Wholly underground, wholly paramilitary. They're a ghost; they can't exist, they *shouldn't* exist, but yet they do. It's pretty amazing, actually. Even that town they use—Amboy, Ohio it's called—is a front, in case you care. It was a small mining village back in the late nineteenth century, but it turned into a ghost town when the railroads stopped running to it during the Depression. The Trust bought up all the land around that town in the late '70's and early '80's and began using the town as a base of operations. They're preparing for something major, that much is evident from what we all saw last night, and the fact that they created something like us proves it, but exactly what they are preparing for wasn't on the hard-drives."

"A coup," said John. "It's got to be."

"They're not in any way associated with the U.S. Government, then?" asked Indigo.

"Not at all. According to the personnel files I was able to download, they're made up of a contingent of military types from different countries throughout the world, soldiers from different countries who have lost faith in the way their countries do things, the way the world does things. They were recruited through the black market and cryptic ads in soldier of fortune magazines and websites. Some are Americans; there are a lot of Europeans from various countries, a few Middle Easterners, and even a few Asians. They are highly trained and extremely skilled; some are mercenaries, but most are seeking something in which to believe. They're not terrorists…yet. They're financed by private corporations throughout the world. A few eccentric billionaires, and several oil-baron sheiks all have a stake in what goes on as well. They have massive resources, but since they're trying to stay underground, they've had to scrounge for everything from different places. They can't purchase anything in enough volume to alert anyone. It's a lot of black market, no receipt, no paper-trail dealing, followed up by sneaking guns and supplies into the country through unchecked border routes from Canada and Mexico."

"Amazing," breathed John. "Do any of you know how incredible this is? Do you see the scope of this? It's incredible! They able to move completely unrecognized by the government, by any government!"

"They're the military equivalent of a ninja," answered Kenny. "Spoken of as if they're myth, but yet they do exist."

"How do they do it?" asked John. "How is it possible? Why hasn't anyone caught on? Why haven't they discovered this group?"

Sebbins piped up. "The fallibility of human logic and lack of imagination, John. Remember, prior to nine-eleven, the U.S. government was aware of people inside the United States with connections to terrorist cells, but they never imagined that anything with the scope of the destruction of the World Trade Centers could happen. The same goes with this entity: If you have a few people collecting weapons, you might notice it—The Branch Davidians at Waco, for example. But, who could stretch the imagination to think that you could have a whole town's worth of people collecting weapons and training as a whole, functioning, active military base inside the borders United States? It's almost unthinkable. Plus, the Trust has the money to buy and sell high-ranking officials. I wouldn't doubt it if they had a few politicians in their payroll. Probably more than a few," said Sebbins. "I don't know for sure, though. It's not like they let me know how the operation works."

"It's like we're something straight out of the G.I. Joe comics—remember? The COBRA organization was hidden in a town called 'Springfield.' They operated unnoticed until they needed to attack. This is the same thing," said Kenny. "Or maybe they're like the Ku Klux Klan—they can go about their day and you might not suspect anything, but they've got a hood and sheet hanging in their closet at home."

Holly was looking at Sebbins with horror. "And you knew? You knew about this 'Trust' group?"

Sebbins' cheeks flushed red. "I did. I knew the basics of their organization. Not the specifics. I knew they were paramilitary."

"So why did you join?" Holly asked. "I used to trust you, Dr. Sebbins.
I used to think you were different from the rest of the doctors and teachers."

Sebbins put her face in her hands. Her voice wavered and cracked as she
spoke. "I joined because of the money they offered, and the chance to work
the premier geneticist in the world."

"That's not all, Doc," Kenny said. His eyes were lit up like Christmas.
"You want to tell us the real reason?"

Sebbins sighed. She rolled her eyes up to the ceiling and swallowed hard.
After a few breaths, she seemed composed and she looked at them all. "I was
blackballed. I couldn't get a job anywhere else."

"How? Why?" Holly asked.

"Because I destroyed a lab," Sebbins said quietly. "I was hired into a laboratory that was conducting unethical experiments, horrible experiments that
will haunt me the rest of my life: Psychological warfare testing on homeless
people and runaways. You all know that all over the world people go missing
every year and are never heard from again—well, some of those missing people ended up in this lab. They were tortured into insanity for the sake of ques-
tionable science and live out the rest of their sad, pathetic lives in a mental
asylum deep in the backwoods of Georgia, oblivious to who they were and
what happened, their brains turned to goo. It was inhuman. When I found
out, I wanted to turn them in, get them shut down, but I couldn't prove it
without bringing authorities into the lab. However, I couldn't bring them in
without proof. It was Catch-22. I got so fed up with the system that I just
torched the lab. I tried to make it look like an accident, but the higher-ups
knew it was me."

"How would that get you blackballed?" Holly asked.

"When the lab is one of the largest in the world, and they start talking—
you don't get any respect. I forgot how powerful the dollar can be. It wasn't
until I got blackballed did I realize that the cops I went to were already aware
of the lab and its activities. Money gets heads turned and records falsified. I
was left with nothing. I couldn't even get a job at McDonald's. They put a
hammer down on me. This job at the Home was the only one I could get, and
I only got that because my grad school mentor and Dr. Cormair were old
friends. I wasn't in a position to question anything." Sebbins stopped talking.
John could see teardrops heading in the corners of her eyes. She had a glazed
look in her eyes, remembering her mistakes.

"A reject. Figures that's what they'd bring in for us. I mean, if we don't
rate enough to be allowed to live after we turn eighteen, might as well not
waste money on our doctors," Indigo said.

"Ease up, Indigo," said John. There was a tone to his voice that hadn't been there before, a sharp edge to his baritone.

Indigo glared at him and huffed a stray strand of hair away from her nose. "Well, that's what she is. That's what we are! Rejects! Castaways. We were the beta test models, never meant to be released to the public."

"Indigo! I mean it! Be quiet."

Indigo started to speak again, but stopped. She flounced back to her corner and flopped down again, scowling.

John looked around the room. He spoke with a clipped, military efficiency, not his usual voice. "For now, we really can't do anything and we're wasting our energy worrying about what's already been done. We have to move forward. The first order of business is sleep. Then, we get food—real food. Then, we get Posey healthy and go after Andy and Sarah."

"Then what, *Herr Kapitän?*" Kenny said.

John shot Kenny a harsh look and Kenny looked down at his feet. "You might be smarter than I am, Ken, but unless you've got some ideas about what to do, for right now, stow it."

Kenny gave a half-hearted salute and kept staring at his feet.

"What time is it?" asked John.

Holly glanced at the digital clock on the bottom of the computer screen. "It's a little after seven."

"What sort of supplies do we have for sleeping, Doc?"

Sebbins shook herself out of her daze. "Uh, two cots. A few blankets. This wasn't meant to be a long-term facility."

"Doctor, you and Holly take the cots. Ken, Indigo, and I will make our beds on the floor."

"Hey!" shouted Indigo. "Why does Holly get a cot?"

"Because you're supposed to be tough."

"You can have my cot, Indigo. I'll be up watching over Posey," said Sebbins.

"It's kind of early to sleep, isn't it?" asked Holly.

John said, "We barely slept last night, and we were up before dawn, and we did all that running around! Aren't you tired?"

"I suppose I am," said Holly.

John clapped his hands like a football player breaking huddle. "That settles it; let's hit the racks. Dawn will be here too soon."

The morning was already warm, an unusual heat for early in the day. The sun wasn't quite separated from the horizon, and the sky was promising a beautiful day, blue with only wispy clouds in the upper atmosphere.

Kenny slumped back against the wooden wall of the shack. He watched John as the athletic young man did a series of complicated yoga stretches and then broke down to a punishing regiment of calisthenics. Kenny had never been much of an athlete. He was slight and thin, with spindly arms that seemed more bones than skin. He had been through the hand-to-hand combat training just like the other six, but he never really took to it. It was a struggle for him. He didn't want to hit Andy or John, even though they had often reassured him that he couldn't hurt them. He didn't like the feeling of grappling with another person. Maybe that was why he liked his computer so much. It was clean, sterile. There was no sweat coming out of it. It was complex, yet he found it simple and beautiful. Holly could keep her butterflies, to Kenny the true beauty of the world was found in the innards of a PC tower.

Kenny watched John fire off push-ups with machine precision and endurance. John didn't fatigue, he barely broke a sweat. After a solid fifteen minutes of push-ups, John jumped to his feet and pulled a knee to his chest. "I need to run," he said. He looked at Kenny. "You want in?"

Normally, Kenny wouldn't have even responded. He hated running. It was mindless. Kenny could spend seven hours straight at a keyboard and it would feel like five minutes. Five minutes of jogging felt like seven hours. However, the only computers at the remote lab were simple machines, meant to keep the lab equipment functioning and recording data. There was no internet. There wasn't even a stray Wi-Fi signal in the area. The computer components of his brain had effectively been silenced and for the first time in years, Kenny was actually bored and confined. A run was pretty much his only option for entertainment. Holly and Dr. Sebbins had gotten a ride into town from an Amish man, and Indigo was watching over Posey in the lab. He had no other choice for entertainment, so he nodded sheepishly and fell into step behind John.

John led the way to the west, continuing along the old farm road through the trees. John's stride was strong and rhythmic; Kenny bumbled behind him stumbling occasionally and catching himself before he fell, and shuffling his feet more often than not. There was no grace in Kenny's movements. A thin sheen of sweat broke out on John's forehead; Kenny's shirt was soaked with sweat and he kept swiping beads of sweat away from his eyes with the back of his hand.

The farm path led out into some open fields and down into a low valley. A creek ran across the bottom of the valley and it was the sight of the water that allowed Kenny to realize that he'd had enough. He plunged into the creek headfirst and let the water soak his clothes and run over him. He popped his head out spluttering and cupped his hands to bring some water to his mouth.

"I wouldn't," said John shaking his head.

"Why?"

"We're in farm country, unless you hadn't noticed. I'd be willing to bet that we'd find cattle upstream. Where there's cattle, there's probably manure in the water. You could get some sort of nasty disease."

"But I'm thirsty!"

"We've hardly run anywhere," said John. "It's only been about six miles."

"Six miles!" Kenny fell back to a sitting position in the creek. The water swirled around him, covering him to his neck. "That's more than I've run since I convinced Cormair that the physical training was a waste of my time."

John chuckled and reached a hand to Kenny. He pulled Kenny onto the grassy bank of the creek and sat next to him as Kenny stretched out, still gasping for air.

"It's nice to be able to talk to you like a normal guy," said John. "We always tried in the Home, but you were always so closed off, so anti-social."

Kenny shrugged. "Before, I guess I didn't feel like I was important. Sarah was the pretty one, Indigo was the mean one, Andy was the funny one, you were the jock, Holly was the compassionate one, and Posey was the one everyone liked. I guess I felt like there was a need for a shy one. I guess I didn't feel like I was important. The rest of you were always getting tested in all these neat and interesting ways. My testing sessions were done in front of computers. Or I'd play chess with Cormair. It was very low-key. I guess I thought that whatever they were trying to me wasn't important. Now I know why they did what they did and for the first time in my life, I actually feel useful. I guess I have something to say now."

"Well, I should hope so. You really absorbed all that data?"

"Yeah. It was hard, but I was able to do it."

"What's it like?" John asked him.

"What's what like?"

"Talking to computers. How does it work?"

Kenny looked at the sky and tried to formulate an answer. "I don't know if I can explain it. It's like trying to ask you what it is like when your power works."

"I don't really know. It usually works before I'm aware it's working. Yours is different, though. You actually have to think about it, don't you?"

Kenny shrugged. "A little. When I first started realizing that I could do it, it was a little a scary."

"How'd you figure it out?"

"About three years ago, I was fixing my computer while thinking about Holly," said Kenny. "She had told me earlier that day that she'd been keeping a diary on her computer for a few months. I got curious and wanted to know if she'd written anything about me. Suddenly, it was like my brain was in her computer and my eyes were looking at all her files. If I looked at one and wanted it to open, it opened. It was pretty scary. I didn't come out of my room for about two days."

"I think I remember that," said John.

"I realized pretty quickly how to use my powers to hack computers. Pretty soon, it was like tying a shoe. But…"

"But?"

"But the physical strain is hard. Each time I do it, it feels like it breaks down my body a little bit."

"Each time you talk to computers?"

Kenny shrugged. "Just talking to them isn't the hard part. That might kill a few cells, maybe a brain cell or three, I don't even notice. It gives me a little headache afterward. According to Cormair's files, it's less harmful than a shot of liquor. But, getting through a security system, or re-routing a computer's data flow or something like that—something that requires a lot of mental manipulation, that's like taking punches straight to my brain. It uses energy from my body in order to accomplish its tasks. It's like any sort of project, really. You take a board, right? You want to nail it to another board? You drive a nail into it. You've created something new, but you've damaged both boards in order to accomplish your goal. And you can never repair them."

John gave Kenny an incredulous look. "Have you thought about what this means long-term?"

"No. The research I downloaded didn't have any long-term projections. They were going to kill us, remember. They weren't worried about the long-term."

"Well, I'm not planning on dying. I'm not going down without a fight. And if I'm fighting, you're fighting too. Now just think long-term: If you continue to use your power, won't it break down your body to a point where you can no longer move? Maybe even think? It will break you down like Alzheimer's disease or something, won't it?"

Kenny shrugged. "I guess. I never really thought about it."

"Won't it, though?"

John made sense. He usually did. Maybe it was all that military logic that got programmed into him. Kenny shrugged. "I guess it will."

"You have to limit yourself, then. You need to make sure you don't use your power that much. Only use it in dire emergencies. I can't even imagine how much you injured yourself yesterday. If I had known yesterday, I wouldn't have let you do all that stuff."

"I just feel a little sore today, that's all. I'll probably feel worse tomorrow, what with all this stupid running."

"A little sore today? What about next time you have to talk to computers and security systems and such like you did yesterday? You'll hurt worse the day after that. In time, you'll be useless. A shell, an empty husk. No mind, no body, just a shell."

Kenny swallowed hard. He hadn't thought of that. He hadn't been conscious the day before, when they had fought their way out of the Home, but he had been useful. He'd gotten them through the security. What happens if he can't talk to computers? How useful would he be then?

"John," Kenny said. "They're going to come for us, won't they? The people from the Home?"

"Yes, they are. They're probably coming already. Who knows when they'll show up? I would rather go to them, though. We have to free Sarah and Andy. Sometimes it's best to be on the attack rather than sitting and waiting."

"I'll be useless then. I can't help you guys in any way. I'm not you; I can't fight. I can't call animals or fly or move things with my mind. If you don't let me use my powers, I'm nothing! I go back to being unimportant!"

"You can stay here, then," said John.

"Teach me to shoot," said Kenny.

"What?"

"You heard me. In a fight, I'm useless. I've got no strength and there probably won't be computers that need rerouting in a battle. Teach me to shoot."

"Shoot a gun? As in: To take a life if need be?"

"Exactly."

"Kenny, you don't know what you're asking. To actually shoot someone, there's a lot more than just pointing a gun and pulling a trigger. You have to steel yourself for the long-term effects of killing someone. You have to understand the weight of your action."

"And you do?"

"I do. I think it might be part of my programming. It's like there's a small part of my brain that clicks on when I think about having to shoot someone. It cordons off the rest of my brain or something." "I have more control over my brain than anyone in the history of man, I think I can handle plugging a guy who will shoot me if I don't shoot him first. John, teach me to shoot."

"I can't do that."

"You have to," Kenny said. "Look at the facts: We're underdogs. We need every advantage. They never taught me to use guns more than the basics, and those were barely useful on the shooting range. I need more training. Teach me to shoot so I'll be worth something if we get into it with these army guys."

John took a deep breath. "I would rather we didn't shoot anybody."

"Isn't sacrifice a part of battle?"

"Yes…but—"

"No buts. I need some way to attack, to be useful. Teach me to shoot and I'll carry a gun."

John sighed. "I don't like this plan."

"Use your tactical brain and look at the facts. It's the only option I've got."

John sighed again and nodded slightly. "I'll start when we get back. We better head back. Holly and Seb will be back with food shortly."

John led the way back and Kenny stumbled along behind him, perhaps not quite as graceless as he was before. He let his mind wander to the topic of guns. He pictured himself with a sidearm strapped to his thigh like a gun-fighter in the Old West. He saw himself with that gunfighter's limp, a hand hovering above the pearl handle of a Colt revolver. If he could shoot, it wouldn't matter that he couldn't use his power.

When they jogged back to the shack, Sebbins, Holly, and Indigo were already eating a simple meal of soup cooked over a fire and cold-cut sand-wiches. John and Kenny tore into the food with gusto. Between bites, John asked Sebbins, "What's the plan for the afternoon?"

"We wake up Posey."

She couldn't move. Even if she could, she didn't want to move. Every-thing hurt. Needle-pricks of pain shot through her constantly, as if she was lying on a table with a low-voltage electric current. She tried to open her eyes, but they wouldn't respond. She tried to breathe, but found her lungs could barely move, yet she wasn't lacking oxygen. Screaming was impossible as well, her throat felt thick and choked. She could hear things though: scraping sounds, the incomprehensible music of muffled voices, a droning engine—probably a generator. She could also hear a strange sucking noise, a squelch followed by a *chug-thunk*.

Posey began to feel heavier than she had. Whatever she was immersed in was draining from whatever was holding the solution. As the goop rescinded, her face slowly emerged. As soon as her mouth and nose were clear, her body began involuntarily choking up the goo in her lungs. She vomited orange mucous that splattered on the glass shield above her and dripped back onto her. When she vomited, more stuff came out of her nostrils. She could feel it draining out of her ears and away from her eyes. She tried to open her eyes, but a bright light above her made her close them again. She continued to cough up sputum until the last chunks of the gelatin-like substance cleared her throat. Her next instinct was to suck in air hard, filling her lungs as deeply as possible. The exhale wracked her with thick, wet coughs again, but they were worth it. The air was cold and clean and made her head clear a bit with each breath.

There was a loud, sucking *pop* and the air pressure changed. She could tell the lid of the tank was off. She could hear voices again. John's voice. Holly, her best friend forever. Doctor Sebbins was there, too.

What had happened? Posey's memory was cluttered and cobwebbed, like coming out of a dream. Bits and pieces of memories filtered through the fog and embedded themselves in her consciousness. The pain was the first memory to return. She was still in pain, but it was much, much less than it had been. A different memory came back through the mist. She had a sense memory of having four arms: Two regular arms and two spindly, long-boned arms with long, claw-like fingers. The mere thought struck her with nausea-inducing anxiety.

"Posey? Can you hear me?" Dr. Sebbins leaned over the edge of the tank. Posey tried to focus on her face. It was blurry. Sebbins' fingers, cool and smooth, swept Posey's eyes clear of the goo. She was smiling. "Posey, you've had a very long night. You're not out of your change yet, okay? You're past the excruciating pain, but you've still got a lot of the transformation left."

Dr. Sebbins slipped an arm beneath Posey's shoulders and helped her sit up in the tank. Each inch of the motion made her muscles twitch with pain. She was vaguely aware that she was naked. Instinctively, she tried to cross her legs and shift her arms to cover her breasts. It hurt too much and she started to breathe heavier, filling with even more anxiety.

"Its okay, Posey," said John. "We've all seen it all already." Posey almost died from embarrassment.

"Get a blanket, John," said Sebbins. John quickly tossed a blanket over Posey and Sebbins tucked it around her. "Posey, I'm going to lift you out of the tank now. John? You and Kenny go upstairs and get some air, please."

"Got it, Doc," said John. He grabbed Kenny by the shoulder and jerked him to his feet. They padded up the metal rungs and popped the seal on the bunker. John closed the lid behind him, dropping it so that it rang out heavily.

"Indigo, Holly—bring those towels. Start getting Posey dried off. We need to see how far along she's come."

Posey saw Holly's face. Holly gave her a reassuring smile, but the smile was twisted at the corners of her mouth. Holly was the worst poker player of the group. She could never hide her feelings entirely. Posey knew something was wrong.

Sebbins began injecting large hypodermics full of strange colored liquids into Posey's arms and stomach. Holly and Indigo began to gingerly towel off Posey's body, but even the light touches hurt. Posey lied on the cot and let the tears slip down the sides of her face, trying not to cry out in pain.

"You're going to be sore for a while, Posey. The hyper-womb helped you through the worst of the transformation, but your body basically rewrote its programming in the span of thirty-two hours. You have changed a great deal. The hyper-womb helped you through several days' worth of transformations in a short time. The physical toll is great, though. You will have extreme muscle pain for quite a while."

Posey tried to speak, but the words seemed to catch in her throat and she coughed. Indigo handed a bottle of water to Dr. Sebbins and the doctor held it to Posey's lips. Posey drank greedily, suddenly realizing she was thirsty. As she drank the water, her stomach churned and rumbled reminding her how hungry she was.

The girls finished drying her body. Holly slipped cut-off jeans and a tube top onto Posey's body, bringing the tube top up her body from her feet. It wasn't an outfit that Posey would have chosen for herself, and Holly would have known that, so Posey reasoned they must have had nothing else with which to dress her.

"We're going to help you to your feet now, Posey. You're going to feel a little disoriented. You've been out of it for a long time," said Sebbins. Posey had to shut her eyes as they lifted her out of the tank and set her on her feet. She felt motion-sick. Her legs felt swollen and weak. Her feet felt different, too. It was harder to balance.

Sebbins spoke quietly in her ear, "Take a step, Posey."

Moving her legs felt different. It took more focus. It was as if her brain was trying to retrain her limbs to move. Posey exhaled and tried to speak. She succeeded in issuing a low moan. "Keep trying to speak," said Sebbins. "I know you feel weird right now. The more you try to utilize your body as you used to, the faster you'll regain control."

Posey coughed and exhaled again. "How…"

"We escaped, Posey!" Holly blurted. "We're not at the Home anymore. We stole you and came here."

"Andy and Sarah stayed back, though," said Indigo. "We're going to back for them as soon as you're well enough to travel."

Posey shook her head. "How," she coughed again. She couldn't speak above a whisper. "How do I…look?"

Holly's smiled widened to a forced, pained expression of positivity. "You look…good."

Holly, you liar. Posey was desperate for a mirror. Since she was a little girl, Posey had always been self-conscious about her appearance; being tall and lanky with almost no breasts and a big, stupid, hideous nose had always eaten at her.

"Girls, I want to get Posey outside. The sun will help restore her circulation and we'll be able to get her…uh…spread out."

Indigo looked up at the hatch above the lab. "How are we going to get her up the ladder?"

Sebbins sighed. "I don't suppose you can just…lift her out, can you, Indigo?"

"No way. I'm not angry or upset or scared. I don't think I could move a speck of dust."

"Holly, get up the ladder and get John. We'll use some rope to fasten a crude harness and we'll have John just pull her up and through." Dr. Sebbins turned to Indigo. "Get some rope from one of the survival kits over on the far wall, beneath the bottom row of shelves."

"Check," said Indigo. Holly scampered up the ladder and John's face quickly appeared in the hatch. Indigo threw him a coil of rope. John quickly tied off an intricate harness and lowered it through the hatch.

"John," Sebbins called up, "we're going to have to be extremely careful. I'm going to leave it to you to maneuver her through the hatch. Be very careful of her…uh, well…you know."

"No problem, Doc."

Sebbins turned to Posey. She put her hands on her shoulders reassuringly. "Posey, we're going to take you outside now. We need to get you stretched out and there just isn't room down here."

"I can…stretch here," whispered Posey.

"No, not really. I want to get you in the sun."

Posey's memory was still fuzzy; she was desperately trying to piece together a jumble of memories. She could see the hallway at the Home; she had been talking to Holly. And then pain. Pain like she'd never known, pain that seemed to start deep in her chest and radiate out through her very bones. Stabbing sensations were still in her mind. But, it was hazy.

John easily pulled her through the hatch, his strong hands handling her delicately. He untied the harness and cradled her. If she hadn't been so out of it, Posey might have died of happiness.

Sebbins crawled through the hatch right after, with Holly and Indigo on her heels. "Carry her outside, John. We need to get her out of the shade and into the light; the sun will help her get feeling in her limbs faster. There's that patch of grass down the road. Lay her there. Holly, I'll need your help with her, uh…"

"Got it," said Holly.

"What's…wrong with me?" said Posey. "How much…did I change?" Posey saw Holly shoot Sebbins a look. The doctor tried to stifle a sigh.

"Posey, I'm not going to lie to you. You are *very* different to what you remember yourself as, okay? I think seeing yourself right now, before you're ready to deal with it physically, would be extremely detrimental to your healing."

"Oh no," Posey moaned. "How ugly am I?"

"You're beautiful," Holly said immediately; it wasn't sincere, just fueled by reaction.

"Get me a mirror!"

"Not now!" Sebbins said firmly.

John walked quickly into the sun. Posey shut her eyes and tried to lift a hand up to shield herself, but she was still barely more than a rag doll. John knelt and laid her on the ground, moving her slowly and gently. When he stood up, he shielded her from the sun with his body to keep her from being blinded. The rest of her body was being warmed by the heat of from the sun. It was a cooler day, but the direct rays made her sore limbs feel better.

"Posey, this is probably going to hurt," said Sebbins, "but, we need to get you spread out so you don't atrophy." Posey felt the doctor's hands as they slowly began working the muscles in her shoulders. One of the doctor's hands slid down to her shoulder blade—and everything felt very, very wrong.

It was as if her brain had bifurcated into two distinct halves. One half told her she had one set of shoulders, the way it was supposed to be. However, the second half was suddenly telling her that she had a second set of shoulders and that it was perfectly natural. That second half started projecting memories of four arms instead of two and then the fog in her mind cleared and missing chunks of memory slammed back into her conscious mind. Both halves of her brain were fighting for dominance. In an instant, her heart rate shot up and she began to panic. There were memories of things sticking out of her back. What had they done to her?

A look of concern crossed Sebbins' face. "John, I'm going to need a med-kit out here. Go back and get me one now. Fast!" She put her hands on the sides of Posey's face. "Listen to me! You're going to be okay! Breathe deeply!"

"What…what happened to me?"

"You went through the transformation process, Posey. It looks like it was a success."

"What…what does…that mean?" Tears were streaking down the sides of her face now.

Holly stuck her face into Posey's line of sight, tears welling in her eyes, too. When she spoke, her voice wavered as if torn between a lie and the truth. "You're an angel, Posey. You grew wings. Big, beautiful wings."

"Wings?" Posey felt like tossing her lunch, if only she had something in her stomach. Adrenaline, released with the panic attack, was washing pain away from her. She suddenly felt a surge of strength. Her arms shot up and shoved Sebbins backward. There were four limbs on her torso, she could feel each and every one. She stretched the second set—the new set—and the muscles on her back, knotted and tight, fought her, but she was able to sit up, feather-covered wings unfurling behind her like battle standards. She looked down at her feet; they had lengthened, become bonier, more gnarled. Each toe had lengthened and her toenails had become curved and dark like daggers. She was horrified. She wanted to scream and before she could, something else happened—an incredible burst of sound from her throat. Her shriek dropped everyone around her, forcing them to grab their ears in pain. Posey choked off the noise. She saw a broken-down minivan in the trees. Using the panic surge, she forced herself to run to the minivan. Her gait was gawky and uneven and awkward like a vulture hopping over ground. She knelt and looked at herself in the side-view mirror.

She was ugly. Pure and simple. She had become even uglier and she hadn't thought that was possible. Smooth, downy white feathers speckled with delicate brown spots had sprouted along her temples, curving back over her ears. More were over her eyes like freaky eyebrows. Long, straight feathers grew out from behind her ears, curving down her neck and toward her back, going from white to a dark brown in color. Her irises had grown in her eyes; they were at least twice the size they had been. Eagle eyes. She had a poster of an eagle on her wall at the Home. She used to stare at the large, golden-hazel eyes and think about how proud and mysterious they looked. Now, those same eyes stared back at her in a mirror and she only saw hideousness. She looked down at her arms and saw feathers shooting out of the skin on the backs of her arms, growing back toward her back. More feathers had grown from her ankles and the sides of her lower legs. She shook her wings. No wonder Holly put her in a tube top, a regular shirt wouldn't fit over those mutant wings. Posey began to cry—not a teenaged girl's drama-queen weeping or the petulant bawl of an upset child, but a deep, soul-tearing keening that tore through the air with a razor's edge, cutting all who hear it to the very bone.

Holly ran to her side and threw her arm around her waist. "It will be okay, Posey. You will be fine. We'll all be fine. You've got us and we'll get you through this."

Fury suddenly silenced the wail and Posey spun on her best friend, grabbing her by the front of her sweatshirt and almost lifting her off the ground. "You don't know that! You're not some freak from hell!" Posey tossed Holly backward. Off-balance, Holly fell backward hard and her head hit the ground with a heavy bounce. Holly looked terrified for a second, and then her eyes rolled back and her head lolled to the side.

Instinct flooded Posey, an instinct that hadn't existed before. Her brain suddenly commanded her second set of arms to flee and the wings began to churn. With three strong pushes, her feet left the ground. Another push and she was truly flying, slipping through the air with ease. As she gained height, the extraneous feathers on her body picked up the thermal waves coming off the ground. She instinctively tilted her body and an updraft launched her several feet higher. She curled around in a lazy circle and caught the thermal again. In moments, she was several hundred feet in the air. She looked back at the people on the ground. Her eagle-eyes spotted them easily, focusing with perfect clarity. She could see individual strands of hair on their heads.

Tears still combing her cheeks, she forced herself to look away. Freaks don't belong with humans. She was going away. She was going to find herself some rocky peak somewhere, far away from people, and she was going to sit there until she died. She tilted her body into the sun and found a stream of air. With her wings spread to the sides, she allowed herself to glide along the air current and slowly rose into the clouds. In no time, she disappeared into the emptiness of the sky, the only family she knew stood on the ground blow, helpless.

Sarah woke, her teeth chattering and her skin prickling with goosebumps. She was shivering. At some point, the blanket had slid off of her and rolled to the floor. She had been dreaming tormented dreams of horrific tests, vivisections, and being put on display in a zoo. She sat up on the cot and wrapped the blanket around herself, closing it in front and trying to get warm. Her hands were bandaged, but they didn't hurt nearly as much as they had the night before and the swelling was down considerably. She unwrapped the gauze from her hands and surveyed the damage. There was only a bit of discoloration. She was healing very quickly. She closed her eyes and shivered, concentrating on tightening her muscles. She tightened her thighs until they shook with strain, her toes curled and her legs began to tremble. Her legs were still bound tightly by the cables. If she wasn't a prisoner, why did it feel so much like she was?

She hopped over to the door of the cell and peered out the little rectangular window that was in the middle of the door. The clock on the wall across from her cell told her it was in the late afternoon. Past the locked metal gate just outside the corridor where her cell was, she could see a couple of guards sitting at a table. One was doing a crossword puzzle and the other was eating some sort of pasta dish. The sight of food made Sarah's stomach rumble. She called out loudly, "Hey—can I get some food in here?"

She stood up and saw the guard doing the puzzle lay down his paper and get on his feet. He walked to a refrigerator a few feet from the desk and pulled out a tray. On it were several sandwiches pilled high with meats and lettuce and tomatoes, a small bottle of mustard, a dish of mayo, and a gallon of milk. Sarah backed away as the guard opened the door with a key. He gave her a half-smile and handed her the tray, quickly closing the door after she took it.

Sarah collapsed to the floor in the middle of the room and did nothing but inhale food for several moments. The sandwiches and milk were very chilled, and she was already cold, but they tasted amazingly good. She poured mustard over them thickly and bit down hard. Mustard slopped out of the sandwich and onto her thigh. She wiped it off with her fingers. She rubbed the mustard between her thumb and forefinger for a moment. It was slippery. She looked down at her bound ankles. The cables were tight, but they weren't like handcuffs. It was just cable looped around her legs, binding them together. Sarah pushed herself to her feet and looked out the window at the guards. They were still just sitting there. Quickly, Sarah bent over and squeezed the contents of the mustard bottle between her ankles and the cords, trying to move her legs to allow the thick yellow smear to coat everything between her skin and the polymer cable.

Pulling with her legs and pushing with her hands, she tried to pry her ankles out of the cords. They were slippery, but they were still tight and they were unyielding. She took a deep breath and began again. This time, she could feel her Achilles tendon bulging beneath her skin like a steel rod. Her feet flexed as she pointed her toes. They were like hardened metal. The skin on her feet began to pull and scrape, despite the mustard lubricant, but Sarah tried to block out the pain. She kept pulling and pushing. She gritted her teeth and hissed a breath out between her lips. In an instant, Sarah went from the intense pain of her skin ripping and pulling to the joy of accomplishment: Her right foot suddenly slipped free of the bonds. Sarah collapsed to the floor and used her right foot to push the cables off her left foot. Her legs were free. She glanced at her feet and saw red streams mixing with the smears of mustard. The thin skin on the top of her foot, and a few patches near her ankles had split open. She grabbed the blanket from the cot and held it on the wounds. It hurt, but not badly.

She stretched her long legs, flexing her toes as she did. She could run now. She needed some blood flow back in her legs, but she knew she could run. She stood and steadied herself with a hand against the wall. She bent deeply at the knee and righted herself. As she did so, she thought of the rest of the group. She needed to find them.

Sarah knelt and opened the flap in the door again. "I'm done!"

She moved back a few feet and took a deep breath. The guard's face appeared in the window of her cell and Sarah heard the key in the lock. The second the door began to swing open, Sarah clicked to speed and hit the door for all she was worth. The impact blasted the door open and sent the guard into the wall of the corridor so hard that he put a hole in the drywall and slumped to the ground unconscious. The other guard began to leap from the desk, but Sarah hit him like a missile. She drove him into the cinderblock wall behind him, trying to slow up enough to keep from putting her hands through his chest. He gave a sick grunt and his eyes closed; he slid to the floor in a heap. Sarah hoped she hadn't killed him. She walked back and pulled the keys from the first guard. Keys might help her escape, but she had no idea where to go.

The hallway outside of the jail area was empty. Sarah listened for noise and could hear a few low murmurs of people talking, but it all sounded like it was coming from behind doors. All the tricks from all the spy movies she'd seen in her life started to pop into her mind. She checked the corners of the hallways for cameras. She let her eyes drift down the length of the hall, and there in the middle of the hallway was the tell-tale dark plastic half-globe that protected a camera.

She ducked back below the window in the door and pulled her thoughts together. The memory of one of those "mysterious world" shows came into her mind. She and Andy had stayed up late one night and watched this episode about UFOs. It had talked about a phenomena called "rods," weird rod-like images that couldn't be seen with the naked eye, but showed up on film as blurry wands of light. One of the skeptics interviewed showed how a bird, moving at top speed, could show up as a rod. It also showed how, if a bird moved fast enough, it could barely be seen by a video camera. The believers tried to give their side, and show how they clocked the rods at more than 300 miles per hour, much, much faster than even a Peregrine falcon could dive. Sarah could go faster than the speed of sound. She didn't know where the corridor led, but she reasoned that as long as she kept moving and moved fast enough, the cameras wouldn't even be able to pick her up, let alone some security guard half-asleep starting at a black-and-white CRT monitor. She just had to make sure she kept it under the sound barrier. To create a sonic boom in the hallway would probably not be the safest way to keep a low profile.

"To hell with it," Sarah whispered. She shoved the door open and blasted out of the jail, in less than a heartbeat she was at the end of the hallway slowing up greatly to negotiate the ninety-degree corner, and then flying up the stairs. At the top of the stairs, she wrapped around and flew down another hallway, her feet barely feeling the cold floors as they moved. Every time she passed a bulletin board or a poster in the hallway, the vacuum behind her ripped it from the wall and left it flipping down in her wake. It felt like she was playing a video game, one that was moving too fast to comprehend. She reacted from gut instinct, not thought. Her legs propelled her down the halls, changing direction before her conscious mind had a chance to register the turns. She turned down a set of stairs and went to the bottom. Ducking under the final set she stopped and tried to get her bearings. She was breathing hard, still unable to get a breath when she moved that fast.

There was a small map on the wall next to the doorway into the next corridor. Sarah glanced around for a camera and couldn't see any. She snuck over to the map and tried to read it. There were no words on the map, only odd codes with numbers and letters. The numbers meant nothing to her, but she supposed if she were in the military like everyone else in the complex, things like "GS-102" would mean something. The map showed the entire installation, six buildings in a loose U-shape surrounded by a wall. From the outlines of the rooms in the building, she guessed that she was in some sort of office building, lots of small, square boxes in a row. Maybe a hospital? The corridor beyond the doors she was next to led to a new building, a larger one with a large, wide room like a gymnasium or an airplane hanger or something. There was a definite exit in the next building, though. It had to be. It was labeled in red with a fire icon and an arrow on it.

She tried the door: It was locked. The keys she carried would probably get her through it, but the door at the other end of the corridor was most likely locked as well and there was a camera globe in the ceiling. I could chance it, she thought. Maybe the guard wouldn't watch that monitor at that moment. It would take her a few seconds to try different keys if the key that opened the near door had a different lock. She would need a lot of luck, but she didn't have a better plan.

At that moment, an ear-splitting siren above her head began to wail. Above her, in the stairs, she heard feet thundering around, and men calling out directions. Her escape had been discovered.

Several rather choice words raced from Sarah's lips. She was pretty much out of options. She began trying keys, flipping through the ring as fast as possible. Once she found the right key, she flung open the door and raced to the next door. Different locks. She tried more keys. Nothing was working.

A male voice suddenly came over an intercom, "Visual with the prisoner. MM—128. Move to intercept. MM—128."

A pair of guards suddenly appeared at the bottom of the stairs. Sarah ducked below the narrow windows in the door and moved against the wall. The doors opened as the guards came in and Sarah crushed the first one against the wall, grabbed the door, and raced past the second one, lashing out with her fist as she engaged her powers and sending him spinning. Her hand was throbbing, but she didn't slow down. Sarah flew up the stairs. At the next floor, guards were racing down the hallway. The male voice on the intercom was trying to keep tabs on her position, constantly relaying coordinates. Sarah kept moving up. She banged around the landings and kept moving. At the top of the stairs, she was left with only one set of doors. She grabbed the handle and ripped it open, engaging speed as she did and launching down the hall.

A guard came around the corner at the end of the hall moving in slow motion. She lowered her shoulder and rammed him, smashing him into the wall, and kept going. The hall was long, very long, but she made it to the other end in an instant. There was a room to her right and another corridor.

"Suspect confirmed: GS-400 Hallway. Consider dangerous. Use non-lethal force. There is a no-kill order. Repeat, use non-lethal force." They were closing in on her position quickly. Sarah could hear them thundering up the stairs at both ends of the halls. She could try running through them, but with each body in her way, she would be slowed. She would have to go out a window. Moving quickly, she began trying doors in the hallway. Locked. Locked. Locked. The lights in most of the rooms were dark. Sarah kept trying.

Finally, one door gave way. Sarah slipped in and slammed the door behind her. There was no lock on the inside of the door. Sarah grabbed a chair near the door and wedged it under the handle like she'd seen them do in movies.

"Who is there?"

Sarah spun around. It was a makeshift hospital room. A TV on a mobile cart was playing some mindless daytime TV program. A long window on the far wall allowed a few speckles of sunlight to filter through gauzy curtains. There was a bed in the center of the room surrounded with a few machines and a wooden armoire along the other wall. Sarah couldn't talk. She looked for some sort of escape, but leaping from the window was the only way out.

"I say again, who is there?" the voice was crisp and even. Sarah recognized it in an instant.

Sarah hesitated, she didn't want to speak if the doctor was going to rat her out.

"Who are you?" repeated Cormair.

"Sarah, Dr. Cormair. It's Sarah."

"Sarah!" Cormair's sounded surprised.

Sarah moved to Cormair's bedside. He looked much older than she remembered, as if he had aged a decade in a few hours.

"Sarah, what are you doing?"

"They had me, Doctor. I was a prisoner. I got free, though. I used my powers. I'm going to escape. I've got to go find the others. Please don't tell the soldiers that I'm here!"

Cormair leveled his gaze at Sarah. His stern countenance softened. "They are coming. You know that?"

"I do."

"Open the window."

"What?"

"Just open the window! Hurry!"

Sarah went to the wall. "There are no locks or anything. This window doesn't open!"

Cormair pointed at a chair in the corner. "Use that! Smash the damn thing!"

Sarah grabbed the chair by its back and swung it into the glass, shattering it and throwing the chair through. A rush of wind swept into the room billowing the drapes.

"Get into the armoire!" Cormair commanded. "Do not move! Do not even breathe until I tell you to!"

Sarah climbed into the closet and slipped the door shut, holding her breath. She could hear the door to the room burst open.

"She jumped, you idiots! She shattered the window and leapt!" Cormair shouted.

Sarah heard a soldier's voice. "She jumped! I repeat the subject is in the yard! The subject is in the yard!"

Fuzzy and metallic, a voice answered over what must have been a handheld radio. "I don't have visual confirmation! I repeat: No visual I.D."

Cormair's voice berated the men in the same acidic tone that Sarah had heard so many times before. "You morons! Of course you cannot see her! She travels at the speed of sound! She could run past you and kill you before you even felt the breeze!"

There was flurry of cursing and shouting. The alarm klaxon kept blaring its obnoxious scream and the male voice shouted instructions. Sarah held her breath and waited. Cormair called to her lowly. She crept out of the armoire and looked around.

Cormair looked sad, his eyes looked dark and morose. "In a moment," he said, "a nurse will come in to check on me. You need to knock her out. I do not have any medication so you will have to hit her. Aim for the spot where the neck joins the skull and swing hard. If you can, engage your speed powers just before you start to swing. You should connect with more than enough force to render her unconscious. Once she is out, take her uniform and put her in the armoire. That should get you out the door without too many problems."

"Why would you do this for me? I thought you were one of these jerks."

Cormair shook his head. "I suppose I was, though that was never my intention. I regret that I might have been one of them once. I am not any more. It's all over for me. I am old, Sarah. I have made some mistakes."

"Like what? I don't understand."

A tear crept to the corner of Cormair's eye. "I was so focused on the research, on the experiments, on succeeding, that I forgot the most important thing: My kids. You all are my children. *My* children. My creations." Cormair put a hand over his eyes and sobbed once. He inhaled sharply and wiped his eyes. "I tried to keep it hidden, to not let it show, and for that I am wholly sorry. Over the last ten years, I watched you all grow and learn. I monitored your existences. From afar, I shared in your joys, celebrated your triumphs, and mourned your failures. It has been my greatest joy to watch you all grow and become adults."

Sarah was both touched and revolted. The Dr. Cormair she knew was cold and cruel, a driven taskmaster. The Cormair before her was a frail, sad old man, hurt and bandaged, gaunt and pale, a shadow of the man she knew.

"Sarah, do you think…Can…Can you forgive a stupid, prideful old man?"

"Dr. Cormair, I…I don't know what to say. I…I don't know if I can say anything."

"You don't have to say anything. Just escape. Get out of here."

"Where, though? Where do I go?"

"There is a town called Barnsdale. It's in Pennsylvania, near the Dutch Amish country, about two hours from here. I set up a lab there in a valley. The valley is very low and I built the lab underground with a lead shield over the top of it to keep them from being able to scan for you. Go there. The lab is beneath an abandoned cabin far back in the woods. If the others escaped with Dr. Sebbins, that's where they went. It had the equipment Posey would have needed to survive her transformation. I don't know if I can help you any more. Just get out of here and run. Don't look back. Just run."

"I will, Doctor. I'll get there as fast as I can go, but what about you?"

"Don't worry about me. I'm an old man and they need me to complete the data on their experiments. I will be fine."

The door to the room suddenly opened and the nurse walked in. She was a bit shorter than Sarah and a redhead instead of a blonde. Her scrubs would have to do, though. Just as Cormair said, Sarah engaged her powers and cracked her fist across the back of the nurse's head. The woman collapsed in a heap. Sarah shook her own hand wildly. "Oooh! That hurts so much!"

Sarah stripped the nurse to her skivvies and donned the blue surgical scrubs. She dragged the woman over to the bathroom adjacent to the room and laid the woman in the bathtub. Cormair instructed her to put an icepack on the woman's neck to help the headache she would undoubtedly have when she awoke.

Sarah stood at Cormair's bedside. "Do you want me to tell them anything when I get there?"

The tears were flowing openly down the old man's cheeks. "Tell them...that I'm sorry."

"I will." Sarah walked to the door and paused.

"And Sarah," Cormair said.

"Yes, Doctor?"

"Please tell them that I am sorry about Andrew. I was powerless."

Sarah's heart stopped. Cold sweat broke out on her body. She tried to speak but no sound came out. She licked her lips and tried again. "What did you say?"

"Andrew's death. I was powerless to stop it."

"Andy...is dead?"

"He came here. I imagine he was looking for you. They caught him with a prototype freezing gel-foam that I had designed long ago. I didn't know they actually manufactured it. It's my fault he's dead. My heart is broken."

"They killed him?" Sarah couldn't breathe.

"The experiment was over," said Cormair. "He proved his powers; he became a liability. Andrew became a very big liability."

"Killed?" Sarah felt her world crumbling.

"He was taken to a lab for final tests, and then he was to be terminated for dissection and final data recovery."

Sarah was scared, more scared than she had ever been. It was as if Cormair was telling her that goodness and kindness had been purged from the world. Andy was her best friend, her compatriot, she...loved him.

"Doctor, is there a chance he's alive still?"

Cormair shrugged. "Possibly. He was taken not too long ago. But don't throw effort at foolishness! If he's still alive, he's under heavy guard! Trying to free him will only result in your capture as well! Don't be stupid, girl! Run! Run now!"

Sarah set her jaw defiantly. "No. Not without Andy."

Holly stood and stared at the sky for a long time after Posey flew away. She stared into the horizon until the sun became too bright in that direction. She kept hoping that Posey would reconsider and come back. Holly had tried to follow Posey as she flew with a robin that she had been able to mind-capture, but as soon as Posey flew outside of Holly's power range, Holly lost her control on the robin and subsequently lost sight of her best friend.

Dr. Sebbins went for a walk by herself. Indigo had locked herself in the minivan for a while, insisting she didn't want to be disturbed. John went into the bunker to eat and Kenny just sat on a fallen tree and aimlessly scratched the lichens on the trunk with his finger.

Holly was still standing in the spot where Posey had knocked her out. Posey had never been violent, never even really been angry. Holly could still feel the strength in Posey's arms. Posey had really hurt her, not so much with the physical shove, but with the intent behind it. Posey would never be violent, never lash out like she did. Somehow, the transformation had made her do it.

Holly had a twisted feeling in her gut, a raw anger at the whole project. Her parents were dead. Her brothers and sisters were dead. Her best friend was gone. All because of this stupid, stupid project. It wasn't fair. Holly didn't want to pout, but she couldn't help feeling like the world had gone out of its way to wrong her. Why did she have to have the DNA strands that Cormair had been looking for? Why did she have to be taken away from her family? Why did she have to suffer the surgeries and implants and training?

The side door to the minivan slid open and Indigo slouched out, her eyes slightly red. She walked over to Holly and stood next to her. "She's gone, isn't she?" Indigo asked.

Holly nodded. She couldn't bring herself to talk.

"How's that bump on your noggin?"

"I'll live," said Holly. "Just a little headache, that's all."

"Do you think we'll ever see Posey again?"

"I don't know. I've never seen her upset like that. It's been over two hours, hasn't it? That should be plenty of time to cool off, shouldn't it? She would have come back by now if she was planning to come back."

Indigo made an odd sucking noise with her mouth. "I don't know. If it was me, I'd be gone at least a day or two—enough to make you all worry about me a lot. Then I'd come back and refuse to talk to any of you."

"Posey doesn't run, though. She was the one who always wanted to talk out her problems."

"Maybe she'll come back."

"Yeah," said Holly. "Maybe. I hope she does. I hope its soon."

At that moment, John stuck his head through the trap door in the shack and called out to them. "Indigo! Holly! Kenny! It's time to start planning our rescue! Come into the bunker!"

"You're the only one in the bunker," Indigo called back. "We're all out here. You come out here."

John conceded and climbed out of the bunker. He sat on the log next to Kenny and looked up at the sun over the trees. "It'll be dark soon."

"What's the plan, Fearless Leader?" said Indigo.

"I don't have one," said John.

"You're the super soldier," Indigo said. "You're supposed to be our tactician."

"We're miles from anything. We don't have a car. The five of us walking through small towns will draw way too much attention to us. So, we're kind of stuck unless someone has a plan."

"I can help," said Kenny.

"Kenny, you're not allowed to use your powers," said John.

"But, I can help! Let me walk to Barnsdale. There has got to be some Wi-Fi signal there. I can use that to hack a bank and get us some working cash. That cash can buy us a car. Bingo! Problem solved! We load up and roll back to the Home and find Sarah and Andy, grab them, and run."

"No, Ken," said John.

"Why not?" Holly asked. It made sense to her. "I think he's right."

"Kenny's powers are slowly killing him. He's not doing it."

"What?" Holly looked at Kenny. He looked sheepish.

"I'll explain it later. Right now, it's not important. We can sit here and do nothing or I can get us a set of wheels and we can go get Andy and Sarah."

"No, Ken! We'll find another way. Holly?"

"What? I can't get us a car."

"Can you get us horses?"

"Horses? We're going to ride back to the Home?" Holly said. "It's over a hundred miles! That's ridiculous."

"We're going to have to ride until we can get a car. Can you find us horses?"

"I don't know. Let me check." Holly closed her eyes and extended her mind. She let her energies ebb out, spreading over the area like a rolling tide. She released pheromones and started making contacts with animals. Bugs and spiders were abundant. Smaller, lesser mammals were hunkered down in nests or warrens. The careful, nervous signals of deer came back to Holly, highly anxious creatures always ready to bolt. A flock of wild turkey sensed Holly's pheromones and the tom, a big sturdy bird with a fierce sense of territory, began to puff and strut. A mountain lion made contact, private and solitary, its thoughts stark and sad compared to the herd animals. Holly felt the presence of a lot of creatures, but there were no horses. She retracted her energy field and came back into her own head. She looked over at John and shook her head.

"Well, just because there are none around here right now doesn't mean that aren't any around here. We all saw them when we were coming down the road. This looks like Amish country. There's going to be horses."

"So you want me to steal some poor Amish guy's horses?"

"I still think you should just let me reroute a few bank accounts," said Kenny.

"Life or death situation only, Ken."

"We can do this without your powers right now, Kenny. Save 'em for when we need 'em," said Indigo.

Kenny slumped back dejected; the light in his eyes seemed to fade out. He held his arms out to the side and looked at John. "See? Useless."

A few nearby animals suddenly raised alarms in Holly's head. She could hear them interpreting a predator. Holly zeroed in on a crow in a tree and asked him for an image of the predator. The crow answered, drawing a human female image in his mind and projecting to Holly. Sebbins was coming back.

Holly stood up and looked in the direction the crow was pointing her. Dr. Sebbins was walking slowly toward the shack, her head down, hands shoved deeply into the pockets of her white lab coat. Holly could taste the sadness radiating from the doctor.

Sebbins walked over to them and looked around, making eye contact with each of them. "We'll stay here for tonight. It's too late in the day to go anywhere. We've got food in the shelter. We've got beds. We'll rest tonight and start early tomorrow."

"What about a car, Doc?" said John.

"I'm going into town right now. There's a stash of money in the lab here. I'll buy a used car and be back as soon as I can."

"You want me to go with you?" asked Kenny. "In case you need a computer hack?"

"No. I'll be fine."

"What do we do while we wait?" asked Indigo.

Sebbins shrugged. "Lay low. Don't cause any problems. If you practice your powers, do it in the bunker."

"Why?" asked Holly. "I've been using mine out here."

"I know," said Sebbins. "Just...trying to keep any chance of being discovered to a minimum. I know Dr. Cormair hid the building of this lab from the Trust, but we're not typical of this area of the country. Someone saw us. They may have ignored us, or they may have remembered us. If the Trust has feelers out, those people who saw us may remember where they saw us and give the Trust a lead to follow."

"Will do," said John. "I'm going to teach Kenny to shoot on the run. It's okay if we bust out the weapons down there, right?"

"Use the handguns," said Sebbins. "There should be silencers down there, too. We don't need noise."

"Silencers? Cormair thought of everything, didn't he?" John whistled lowly.

"Not everything," said Sebbins. "He didn't think his project would be terminated."

"You believe that?" said Kenny.

"I do," said Sebbins. "I think he knew they might have done that and wanted to protect his research. Why else would he build a bunker like this?"

"Good point."

Sebbins took of her white coat and folded it neatly, laying it over a fallen log. "I'm going now. If you make a fire, keep it small. It's almost four now. If I jog a few of those miles, I should be able to make it to town before five. I'll be back as soon as possible."

Holly watched Dr. Sebbins walk up the worn tracks in the grass toward the paved road. John retreated into the bunker and returned with nine-millimeter handguns and silencers. He gestured to Kenny and the pair of them walked deeper into the woods, presumably to set up a shooting range. Indigo stood up and dusted off her pants with her hands.

"You going to go practice your powers?" said Holly.

"Might as well," Indigo shrugged. "Nothin' better to do, right?"

"I guess."

"Maybe I'll figure out how to use them without being an emotional wreck or a blinded-by-anger bitch."

"Try acting," said Holly. "Remember when we watched that show about Stanislavski? Bring back an emotion from your past and use that to project a new emotion in your current situation."

"That's not a bad idea. Thanks, Hol. I'll try that. Maybe I can use the time I caught John and Andy looking through my underwear drawer. Should be able to lift a car with that sort of anger." She turned and walked into the shack, disappearing through the trap door.

Holly felt very alone. Usually when all the others went on their own little jaunts, Holly could always count on Posey. She and Posey would go for walks together, or sit in Posey's room and flip through fashion magazines and watch *Pretty Woman* for the billionth time. When they were first brought to the Home, Posey and Holly had sought each other out for solace, never quite vocalizing their sadness over being separated from their families, but it went unspoken between them, a bond that made them closer than friends. When they were younger, they spent their free time with Barbie and stuffed animals, graduating to DVDs and iPods as they got older. They comforted each other with popcorn and grape sodas after surgeries or brutal testing sessions, and dreamed pie-in-the-sky dreams about what they were going to do when they left the Home. Now, without Posey, Holly felt utterly lost. Willfully ignoring Sebbins, she sat and searched the skies with her powers, recruiting any bird in the area to her cause and patching into their vision to comb the area, desperately hoping to find Posey flying back or hiding in the scrub somewhere nearby. She stared into the middle distance, her eyes glazed with the aura of her abilities.

The mountain lion was growing angry with Holly. It was trying to get away from her infringing power. Holly began to busy herself with trying to calm the agitated animal. She submitted thoughts of kindness and comfort. The lion kept pushing back with images of territory and threat. It started to become a game. Holly issued images of tummy scratching and food, trying to get it to crawl out of its den and come down to play with her. The mountain lion tried to clear its mind. Holly eventually left the cat alone, turning off her power.

Suddenly, there was a small tickling in Holly's brain. She concentrated again and the little brown bat made contact with her again. He followed the van on the drive, and then followed Holly to the lab site. He had been somewhere nearby, asleep, for most of the day.

"Hey, little buddy," Holly said smiling. She projected images of food and got an orange from the bag of fruit in the shack. She used a knife to cut it in half and spiked the orange on a broken twig in a low tree branch. The bat fluttered out of the woods, landed on the orange, and began lapping at its flesh.

Holly sat back against the stump and watched the bat eat. Its feelings were contentment and trust. It seemed genuinely happy that Holly was there and was extremely grateful that she was feeding him. Holly sent him warm images: kindness, sympathy, love, care—anything she could think of to make the bat more comfortable. The animal seemed truly at peace around her. Getting a crow to bring her flowers or getting deer to walk up and take grass from her hand was the extent of how she used her powers until now. She was beginning to realize the full range of possibility for her powers. She could see through an animal's eyes or get them to perform tasks for her. She could register the moods of animals and understood how they thought, but the connection with the bat was different. When she broke her control of an animal, it had always bolted as it would have with any other human being or just moved away from her, oblivious to the link she had just created with the beast.

But the bat—the bat was unique. It was as if the bat was actually interested in her, as if it wanted to be friends. It was more than a pet-master connection: When she had severed her powers from the bat, the bat was still seeking her out. The bat was curious.

Holly held out a finger and gave a mental prod for the bat to fly to her, a suggestion, not a command, just to see how it would react. The little creature flapped away from the orange and landed hard on her hand. It was light and its body fur was incredibly soft. She thought about rabies, but decided that the bat was thinking a little too clearly to be in the throes of a brain disease. Holly remembered reading that bats almost always had body parasites like lice. She sought the little buggers out and used her powers to make them all crawl off the bat. She tried not to throw up as they did that. She also tried not to make a more distinct mental link with the parasites. She kept it to blunt commands and then tried to pull her powers back quickly. She made a clear link with a tick she found on her leg one night not too long ago and was repulsed by the arachnid's single-minded thought process: Feed, feed, feed, feed, feed.

Holly wished she could communicate with the bat as she would to another human. She wanted to know what being a bat was like. She wanted to be able to discuss concepts of higher order thinking. Not that she ever did that with Posey or anyone else, of course. With Posey, the closest she ever came to higher order thinking was wondering what her first kiss would be like or what her wedding colors would be. It would still be nice to have the bat be able to relate to her in sentences or anything other than emotional reactions and rebus-like imagery.

Holly tried to teach the bat about names. She tried to get the bat to understand the concept of titles, but it was pointless. Animals don't name things; scent works better.

The sun had dipped below the horizon and night was coming on quickly. Holly shivered. Her thoughts drifted back to Posey, alone in the dark somewhere, scared and confused. They hadn't been raised with religion in the Home, but Holly remembered church from her childhood. She bit her lip and whispered a prayer to God—any god that would listen, really—to keep Posey safe.

A pair of headlights came around the curve on the roadway. Holly could hear the sound of the tires slowing, and then the headlights turned down the field road. With her enhanced senses, she could make out Dr. Sebbins behind the wheel of a battered, solid-side Ford Econoline van. The engine was raw and loud. The body of the van was leopard-spotted with rust. Dr. Sebbins brought it in beneath the cover of the trees next to the shack and killed the engine. The van sputtered for a moment and wheezed to silence.

Sebbins climbed out of the driver's seat. "It's not much, but it will do."

"Looks rough, Doc," said Holly.

"Doesn't smell that good, either," said Sebbins. "I got it from an independent dealer on the edge of town. He only had a handful of cars, but he was willing to deal in cash with minimal paperwork. Where is everyone else?"

"Indigo's in the bunker. The boys are shooting somewhere off in the woods."

"Well, can you go get them for me, please? We'll have a bit of a cookout and then get some sleep. Tomorrow, we'll head back for the Home and see about getting Andy and Sarah." Sebbins paused and squinted at Holly. "Holly, what *is* that thing on your lap?"

"A bat."

Sebbins shuddered. "Why?"

"It's the one that saved us."

"Here? It followed us?"

"Yup," said Holly.

"Amazing," said Sebbins. "Why?"

"I'm not sure. I think he likes communicating with me. I think he was lonely."

"It told you that?"

"I don't know that animals have a thought process for 'lonely'," said Holly. "I could imagine cats and dogs do, after all they live with people and get used to company. But wild animals certainly don't. If they did though, I'd bet he was lonely."

"Does he have a name?"

"I call him 'Bat.'"

"Good name. Go get the boys."

"Will do," said Holly. "C'mon, Bat." Holly tossed the little animal gently into the air and it quickly began flying around her in frenzied circles. "Go show me the boys."

The bat broke off from its arc and shot into the sky. With her sensitive ears, Holly could barely make out the constant tick of the animal's echolocation as it zigzagged its way through the trees, toward the faint *ping-ping* sound of silenced handguns being fired.

Holly could see through the bat's eyes, a dark, fuzzy blur of motion. In her mind, she could see how the bat "saw" with its echolocation—a strange, low-res computer screen of lines and shades. She couldn't tell where the solids were and where there was open space in which to fly, but she somehow just sort of knew by using the same instinct the bat used. As the bat tracked the sound of guns and the boys' voices, Holly began to get the line-and-shadow images of humanoid shapes. She followed the bat's telepathic signals and found Kenny and John in moments.

"Sebbins is back. She wants us to come in for dinner," Holly said.

Kenny didn't look up. He calmly raised a handgun and squeezed off several rounds. In the dim light, Holly saw a couple of puffs of dirt and grass and then heard the metallic clunk of a bullet hitting and empty metal can.

"You're getting better," said John. John raised a gun himself and squeezed off six rounds as fast as he could. The can leapt into the air with the first bullet and kept climbing as each bullet kept it juggling.

"Amazing," said Kenny. "I wish I had hand-eye coordination."

"Did you guys hear me?" said Holly. "Food. Us. Now."

"Keep your pants on," said John. "We're coming."

The bat suddenly swept low in front of them. Kenny jumped backward. "What was that?"

"Don't shoot it!" Holly said. "That's the bat that saved our lives."

"I wasn't going to shoot it," said Kenny. "You got to teach that thing that dive-bombing people isn't polite."

"He was eating. He goes where the bugs are."

"He's not coming into the bunker tonight," said Kenny. "I don't think I could sleep with him buzzing around."

"He'll stay outside. He has to eat," said Holly. "That's what bats do at night, you know. They have to eat a huge amount."

"So do I," said John. "Let's go."

They walked back to the cabin, Holly leading the way with Bat's assistance. John and Kenny descended down the ladder into the lab. Holly looked at an open space in the sky where Bat was darting around, grabbing at mosquitoes. "I'm going in now," she said. "I'll be back later." As she broke the mental link to her furry friend, she felt its last mental signal: Sadness.

They ate silently in the bunker. After Sebbins had told them about buying the truck, there was nothing to say. What happened to Posey was an elephant in the room. The hyper-womb was still out in the open, still with traces of the orange syrupy goo.

Holly couldn't help but reflect on the dwindling number. At one point, there were seven kids, Cormair, Sebbins, Mrs. Miller the housekeeper, and a bevy of doctors, teachers, and others who filtered in and out of the home. Now, it was down to only four kids and Dr. Sebbins. Holly did not like the way the math was working. She kept wondering who would be next to go?

There was no television or radio in the bunker. There was nothing to do after eating, so they simply retired to bunks. Holly and Indigo took the canvas cots again, while the other three curled up on the floor. Once the lights were turned out, only a few green glowing balls on the power buttons of some of the computers and the icy blue light of a single computer monitor lit the room. After ten minutes, the monitor went into sleep mode and the room became oppressively dark. Holly lay on her cot and stared at the ceiling. Thoughts raced through her head, but she couldn't grasp them and make them stay for any length of time.

Impulsively, she let her field of telepathy crawl out beyond her head, scanning the bunker for bugs or mice. Occasionally, she let it crawl out beyond the metal walls of the bunker, scanning the surface for Bat or other nocturnal animals. She was able to locate the mountain lion quickly. When her mind linked with the beast's, Holly found it scattered and confused, a palpable sense of fear flooded into Holly from the animal's mind. What could scare a mountain lion? Holly forced herself to link into the animal's eyes and see what it was seeing. With the cougar's exceptional night-sight, she could make out the outline of a man, helmeted and carrying a weapon—a soldier. Quickly, Holly used the animal to scan the area. Soldiers were creeping toward the bunker. Bat's telepathic signal suddenly blurted into her mind, a panicked screaming, nothing but sensations of terror and worry. It almost overloaded her brain. The little creature's whole being knew nothing but fear, but not for itself, only for Holly.

Holly leapt out of bed. "They've found us!"

Indigo heard Holly's scream and leapt from her own bunk. "Where? Who?"

Holly pointed at the door to the bunker. "There are soldiers out there. They're coming this way! Bat showed them to me!"

"Calm down," said Sebbins. "They don't know where the bunker is. We're safe in here."

"They'll find the hatch," said John. "It's sitting in the center of the cabin, big as life. We didn't hide it."

"They'll still have to get past the door lock," said Sebbins. "They don't have the key-code."

"It's not a big lock, Doc. A little C-4 will blow it wide open."

"John, what do we do?" Holly said.

"Can we make a break for it?" asked John. "It's no good to hide in here. We need to get out, get to the van, and run for it. Do you know where the soldiers are?"

Holly's eyes clouded and rolled back into her head. After a moment, her eyes cleared and she shrugged. "Bat can't tell me where they are exactly. I know there are some over by the bluff to the northwest, but that's all I can give you right now."

John rolled out of his sleeping bag and pulled several handguns out of a weapons locker. He tossed one to Kenny and one to Holly. He gave Kenny a light flare as well. Indigo stuck out her own hand. "Lock and load, worm-head," she said. John handed her a gun and nodded. Indigo checked the clip and slammed it back into place in the handle.

"Only use the guns in a life or death situation! We don't want to become killers!"

"Why not?" Indigo said. "They were going to kill us in December." Indigo knew from her psychology classes that there was supposed to be a greater good, that if she lowered herself to the level of an enemy, then technically she lost the battle, but she had never been able to buy that sort of rationale. The law of nature was kill or be killed.

"No guns!" John shouted. "I'll go first. Then I want Indigo to follow behind me—be ready with your telekinesis, Indy. I may need the back-up."

"I can't do much!"

"Dirt in the eyes is all I'll need. I trust you can manage that."

"What if they're wearing goggles?"

"Then remove their goggles and throw dirt in their eyes."

"I think I can do that," said Indigo. She could feel the tickle in the middle of her head where her new powers were aching to be used. Pens weren't much of a trick, Indigo wondered if she could get enough anger or fear or hatred to generate a large telekinetic field, do some real damage. She was already feeling very scared.

"Holly," John continued. "You follow Indigo. Stay in contact with your pets. Sebbins, you next, and Kenny, you bring up the rear."

"If I can shoot, I'm going to," said Kenny.

"Only if necessary!" shouted John. "I'm not too keen about us having to kill our way out of here."

"Kill?" said Holly. Indigo shot her a look that was, at best, a cross between "don't worry" and "stop being such a girl." That was always one of Indigo's biggest problems with Holly and Posey—they never knew when to man up and put down their dolls. Indigo prided herself on being tough. She was always the smallest and the lightest, but she had no problem stepping up to Andy or John when they needed it. She even would stare down Cormair when the situation called for it.

Indigo followed John up the ladder. He moved like a panther, silent and strong, and disappeared into the darkness above the hatchway opening.

Indigo pulled herself through the hatch and saw John's shadow hunkered down by the door, listening. Before she could even whisper, John's hand shot out and his finger pressed against her lips. She could make out the faint shadow of his head shaking. Holly was out of the tunnel next. She pressed herself to Indigo's back. Indigo could feel her shaking with nervousness.

"There are at least five of them, but less than ten," Holly hissed. "Bat says the nearest one is about twenty yards in front of the shack, near the van."

John slipped a small, square item from his pocket. "Flashbang. Close your eyes. Be ready to attack. Kenny, after this goes off, I want you to shoot the flare into the sky. It will give us enough light to spot and attack. Holly, if you can animal-up any target, do so as soon as the flashbang goes off, okay?"

Holly nodded. Indigo squeezed her eyes shut and jammed her fingers in her ears. A moment later, there was a loud pop and white light pushed hard on her eyelids. There were screams of pain right outside the shack as the flashbang overloaded the night-vision goggles of the soldiers.

John was out the door in an instant, Indigo on his heels. John was a tornado, whirling and moving almost too fast to comprehend. He was on top of the nearest soldier in a heartbeat. Indigo watched him unleash a flurry of punches into the man's chest, neck, and face and saw the man's legs go to jelly and he collapsed in an unconscious heap.

Indigo tried to remember where she heard screams and scanned the darkness. "Kenny! Flare!" There was another pop as Kenny fired the flare gun and the sky was suddenly filled with a sparking orange light that illuminated a wide circle on the ground.

Indigo spotted a soldier crouched in tall grass near the shack, rubbing his eyes. "There's one!" She felt a surge of anger when she saw him and felt that tingle in her brain expand. She took control of her telekinetic field and threw an invisible wall of energy at the soldier. It hit him like a fist and knocked him backward.

"Another over here!" shouted Kenny. Indigo whipped around and saw a larger soldier lumbering toward them, a gun in his hand. He was shouting commands, but Indigo only heard a blur of words that made no sense. John attacked the man, a kick to the side of his knee that buckled him, a fast elbow to the man's temple that knocked him to the ground. John finished with a flurry of fists to the man's face.

"Get to the van!" John shouted. "Sebbins, get the van started! We have to roll out of here!"

Sebbins took steps toward the van and a voice rang out from the grass. "They're trying to run!"

Indigo tried to locate the source so she could take him out, but even with the light from the flare, she couldn't find the soldier.

Suddenly, another soldier's voice shouted out, "The adult is expendable!"

The crisp thunderclap of a gun shattered the night. Dr. Sebbins cried out and dropped to her knees.

"Seb!" Holly screamed.

Everything seemed to slow down. Holly dove to Seb's side. John drew his sidearm and began firing blindly into the grass. Kenny struggled to pull his gun from the holster. Soldiers began to pour out of the grass. Indigo began to feel a new kind of fear: Fear of death, fear of more experiments, fear of ending life as a pile of data, a general terror began to sweep through her. Close on the heels of this terror was a different emotion: Rage. She was sick of being afraid, sick of feeling helpless. The hub of her telekinetic power within her brain began swelling. Indigo looked down at Sebbins, a rosebud of blood spreading rapidly across the doctor's chest. The force in Indigo's brain was screaming to be freed. Indigo caught sight of a soldier from the corner of her eye and whirled in that direction, flinging her arms wide as she did and releasing the pent-up fear and anger in a telekinetic bolt. The soldier was slammed backward as if he had been hit by a locomotive. His body rag-dolled into the trees, cracking into a large oak sending bark and splinters flying. A rush of power and adrenaline flooded through Indigo's body. She felt the energy of her powers crackle through her and awaken every inch of her body. Joy flooded through her, as if her brain had been crying out for her to find this hidden strength. The joy fueled her powers further.

Another soldier stood up and leveled a strange-looking gun at Indigo. It fired with a small flare of light and a hollow "poik" sound. Indigo stuck out a hand and froze the projectile, a feather-ended tranquilizer dart, inches from her palm. She flipped the needle in the air so it pointed back at the soldier and sent it flying into the soldier's neck faster than the gun had fired it. The soldier clapped a hand to his neck and fell into the grass.

Indigo turned on her heel and saw two more soldiers. She unleashed a bolt at the nearest soldier and sent him cartwheeling into the sky. He flew above the treetops and fell back toward earth, slamming hard into the ground and laying still.

John dispatched the last soldier with a rapid combination of punches and kicks and the action ceased. Everything became quiet and still.

A searing pain shot through the center of Indigo's head. It made her drop to her knees and clap her hands to the side of her head. Her vision dimmed to black and her chest tightened until it was hard to breathe. As quickly as the pain came on, it dissipated until it was an aggravating throbbing in her temples. Indigo took in a deep breath through her nose. What made her hurt so much? Was it a repercussion from using her powers?

"Damage check," John's voice snapped Indigo out of her daze. "Is anyone hurt?"

"John, please help me!" cried Holly. She was kneeling by Dr. Sebbins' body and pressing her hands over the wound. Even in the soft light of the still-burning flare, Indigo could see Holly's hands were slick with blood. "It's bad, John," said Holly. "Real bad."

John gently pulled Holly's hands off the wound. The bullet had hit the doctor in the right side of her chest, just to the right of her sternum. The blood was dark, darker than Indigo thought it should be. All of them had been trained in anatomy and physiology. They had all learned basic First-Aid techniques, but this type of wound was beyond any of them.

John frowned. "I don't think it hit her heart," he said, "but..." his voice trailed. Indigo knew he didn't want to finish the sentence. It was a bad wound. Sebbins wasn't going to live. Her labored breaths and rasping, gurgling coughs could tell them that. She had blood in her lungs.

Holly was biting her lip so hard that a thin trickle of blood was seeping out the corner of her mouth. Her eyes were welling with tears. Kenny swiped his wrist across his eyes and sat back, hugging his knees to his chest.

Indigo felt that telekinetic hub of her brain begin to swell again. Sorrow and sadness swamped her mind. She choked back a sob and knelt next to Holly. She reached down and picked up Seb's hand.

Dr. Sebbins turned her head toward Indigo and Holly and coughed, blood flecking her lips as she gasped for air. "Not...gonna..."

"Don't talk," said Holly. "You're...you're going to be okay."

Sebbins smiled weakly. "Bad...liar."

"We're gonna get you to a hospital, Doc," said John. "Just save your strength."

Sebbins shook her head. "Don't...not gonna...make it." Coughs wracked her body and she spit up a horrid amount of blood.

Indigo cleared her throat. "Seb, I'm sorry I was such a bitch to you." Sebbins squeezed her hand. "I...You didn't deserve it. I just...I don't know why I did it. I never meant it. I was just being an idiot."

"I'm sorry if I was ever short with you," said John.

Sebbins slowly reached a hand out toward him and he took it. "Never." She licked her lips and coughed lightly. Blood flecked her lips. "Don't bury me...just go. Get...Sarah and Andy."

"We won't just leave you!" said Indigo.

"Don't...be stupid," said Sebbins. "Get away...from these people. Take care of each...other..." Sebbins coughed again, she went rigid and struggled for a moment, and then she gave a shuddering, breathy heave. Her head lolled to one side.

Indigo felt the doctor's hand go slack. Indigo reached a shaking hand to Sebbins' neck and felt for the pulse she knew wasn't going to be there. "She's gone," said Indigo. She felt tears pricking at the corners of her eyes.

Holly slumped over against Indigo and sobbed. Kenny's face was buried in his arms and his back was shaking.

John cleared his throat and spoke quietly. "I'm not going to just leave her here."

"Bury her?" Indigo asked.

"I aim to," he said. "But first, we have to get those soldiers stowed. Kenny, get some rope from the shelter."

Holly stood up. "I'm going to get a shovel," she said. "There are entrenching tools in the shelter. I'm going to start Seb's grave." She sobbed again. "I hate this."

Kenny returned with a coil of rope. John cut lengths with a pocketknife. "Let's get the soldiers tied up. Take away any communication devices and pile them by Sebbins' body. We'll save one and destroy the rest."

Indigo walked over to the soldier that she had thrown into the sky. She started to loop the rope around his wrists and stopped. He wasn't breathing. She frantically felt for a pulse. None. "John! Help! What did I do?" Panic clutched at her heart. She hadn't meant to kill this man. Indigo blew breaths into the man's mouth and began chest compressions. John was at her side in a second and began assisting her.

While she applied steady compressions to the man's chest, she began babbling. "I wasn't in control. I didn't control my power. I had a big surge of emotion and I unleashed it without thinking! I didn't mean to hurt him."

John puffed breath into the man's mouth. "I know, Indigo. I know."

"Did you see me? Did you see this man? I accidentally threw him really, really high. He fell really far." She was babbling and she couldn't stop herself.

"I didn't see it."

"He fell really far!"

"I know, Indigo," said John. He felt the man's neck for a pulse and shook his head. Indigo continued with the chest compressions. John pushed her away. "You're not pushing hard enough!" John straddled the man's body and pushed once, then pulled his arms back. "His chest is crushed. He's done."

"Oh, please no," Indigo breathed. "I killed him."

"They killed Sebbins. They were going to kill us eventually. It just happened. Let it go," said John. "Things like this happen in war."

"I killed a man," said Indigo. She felt her world spiral. "I...killed him." Her mind started flicking to thoughts of whether or not the man had a family, if his parents would be sad. She thought of the man possibly having a dog that might be at home, waiting for its master to come back and feed it. It was all too horrible. Indigo fell to her side and began bawling.

John grabbed her and sat her up. His large, strong hands held her by the shoulders and he looked at her. "Indigo, don't do this. I need you here. Now. We don't have time for this. This is war. The first rule of war: People Die."

"But nowhere in that rule does it say that I have to be the one who kills them!"

Kenny came out of the woods. "There's another one dead," he said. "Looks like he dented a tree with his body."

"I killed two of them!"

John shook Indigo. "This is not the time to fall apart, Indy! We need you here and now!"

"I killed two men!"

"What did you think you were doing when you sent him flying into a tree?"

"I wasn't thinking! I just did it! I didn't think about where he would go, or if he would hit a tree!" Indigo was blubbering now. She was angry at herself for crying, and even angrier at herself for killing those men. Killing didn't feel like she thought it would. It was hollow and empty and dark.

John pulled Indigo to his chest and held her. "Indigo, calm down. It will be okay."

"Says you!" said Indigo. "I don't have ten years' worth of military programming rolling around in my brain. I'm not some advanced weapon ready to kill everything I meet."

"Then think about our philosophy classes: Soldiers understand that death is a part of their job. These men were professional soldiers, paid to give up their lives if need be. This wasn't a couple of innocent bystanders. They weren't a pair of eighteen-year-old kids sent to a foreign land because their government was ironing out grievances; they were hired guns, willing to kill for their cause."

"It doesn't make what I did right."

"It's going to be part of this whole mess we're in, Indigo. These men are dangerous. They want to capture us, torture us with tests, and eventually kill us. Once they decide that they have enough information for their research, we're going to be killed unless we fight back. We can run for a while, we might even be lucky enough to get Andy and Sarah without combat, but eventually the day will come when we have to fight. When that happens, people are going to die…whether it's us or them."

"I won't kill again," said Indigo. She meant it. "I can do other things with my telekinesis. I don't need to kill."

"If that's how you want to play this, that's fine. I don't blame you," said John. "Maybe you'll be able to do that."

"It's not like G.I. Joe, is it?" said Kenny. Indigo looked at him with a raised eyebrow. Kenny shrugged. "Remember when we were kids, John? We would watch G.I. Joe cartoons on TV?"

"Yeah," John smiled slowly. "I loved those shows."

"Every time one of the Joes would fire a rocket or a laser at a Cobra vehicle, the vehicle would blow up, but every pilot would bail out and parachute to safety. Laser blasts flew everywhere and no one even got nicked."

"And I show up and kill two men with a whim, a thought. G.I. Joe never did that," said Indigo.

"That's why I said it's not like G.I. Joe," said Kenny.

"You going to be okay, Indigo?" asked John. Indigo looked up into his brown eyes and nodded.

"Do I have a choice?"

"No. We've got work to do. Can you help Holly with Sebbins' grave while Kenny and I tie up the other soldiers in the shack?"

"I'm burying the soldiers, I killed," said Indigo.

"We don't have time for that."

"John, I'm taking care of them," Indigo glared at John. "I killed them. I am going to bury them."

"And I said we don't have time for that! We get Seb buried, and we roll."

"John!"

"Indigo! I am leading this team! We have to go. We can't waste time digging holes for those men. It's taking enough time to bury Sebbins! I am sorry that you feel guilty, and I will help you get through that some day in the future, but right now we must leave."

Indigo felt a snap in her brain and she spun on her heel toward the area where Holly was digging. She grabbed chunks of ground with her powers and ripped plots of earth from the ground, creating three neat, square holes in the ground, each nearly five feet deep. She let the mounds of earth fall at the heads of the graves with a thud.

John did a double-take, looking from Indigo, to the graves, to Indigo again. He opened and closed his mouths a few times like a guppy. "Okay, I guess we have time to bury them."

"It's the least I could do," said Indigo. A shotgun blast of pain coursed through her skull and she turned her back to John so he wouldn't see her crying because of it.

John lowered the first of the two guards into the grave Indigo made. Indigo lowered the second one telekinetically. John crawled out and watched Indigo fill in the two graves with dirt. Then, he looked at Dr. Sebbins' body.

Dr. Sebbins had been different than the other researchers and scientists that had made their way through the Home. She had reached out to John on a personal level. She had made the time to get to know each of the seven individually, to find out what they liked to do and what they liked to watch on TV. She threw a football around with John and Andy. She taught Holly and Posey to put on make-up. She even showed Indigo how to sew so that she would be able to make her own clothes. John knew she had even reached out to Kenny, though he didn't know exactly how.

As he watched Indigo gently lift Sebbins' body with her telekinesis and lower it into the ground, he felt a gnawing in his chest, a hollow, painful emptiness. He didn't feel like crying, though. Maybe that was part of his programming, part of his training, but he knew there wasn't going to be tears. Kenny's eyes were wet. Indigo had stains down her cheeks. Holly was a wreck. But John just stood there like a statue, a soldier standing honor guard.

Sebbins lay in the grave. Her face looked different, changed. There was no worry in her face anymore, only a simple serenity. Indigo lifted the final mound of dirt and began to move it into place above the grave.

"Hold it, Indigo. Someone should say something," said Kenny. The dirt gently drifted back to the head of the grave.

"Does anyone know what religion she was?" asked Holly. They looked at each other and shrugged. Holly looked at John, "You are the best speaker."

"I don't know what to say," said John.

"Make it up. Just say something, anything," said Indigo.

John took a deep breath. He had never attended a funeral. He had only seen a few in movies. From what he'd seen, there didn't seem to be a right or wrong way to do a funeral. John looked at the sky for a moment. Nothing was coming to him. He focused on the star Deneb. Sebbins had been the teacher who taught them about astronomy, taught them the names of the stars and the constellations. "Sebbins wouldn't have wanted us to be sad," he said. "She would have wanted us to go on and do what we needed to do. She came with us at the risk of her own life. She knew that she could have stayed at the Home and been safe. Maybe she could have even gotten a new job. Who knows? But she chose to come with us because she really cared about us, and because it's what was right. She didn't deserve to die. She deserved a better life than what she got. She was one of the good guys."

"Do…do we say 'Amen'?" asked Kenny.

"I don't think so," said John. "It wasn't a prayer."

"Remember that movie we watched last month?" asked Indigo. "The one where the cop died? Remember how everyone who was at the funeral walked up and threw a handful of dirt onto the coffin? Should we do that?"

"I don't see why not," said John. He stepped forward and took a fistful of black dirt. He stepped to the edge of the hole and let it sieve through his fingers. "Good-bye, Seb." The dirt spotted her white coat.

One by one, the other three stepped up and followed suite. Then, Indigo slowly lowered the dirt back onto Seb's body, letting it settle gently over her corpse. Indigo stepped back and touched her hands to the side of her head for a moment. She seemed to sway.

"You okay?" John asked.

Indigo shrugged. "I'm better than Seb," she said. She wiped her hand under her nose and a long smear of blood appeared on her wrist.

John grabbed her wrist. "What's that?"

Indigo yanked her hand back. "It's nothing. Leave me alone."

"Are you bleeding?"

"No."

"Is that because you used your powers?"

"No!" Indigo snapped. "Leave me alone, John."

"John!" Kenny called out. "One of the soldiers is awake!"

John gestured toward the soldier and beckoned Indigo to follow him.

"If you're going to interrogate a brawny soldier, a five-foot, ninety pound Asian girl is not really the muscle you bring along to intimidate someone," said Indigo.

"Just follow my lead," said John. He walked into the cabin, grabbed the soldier by the edges of his flak jacket, and lifted him to his feet in a single move. "How did you find us?" John hissed through gritted teeth.

The soldier glared at John but said nothing. John glanced at Indigo; she thought she saw him wink. Suddenly, John dropped his right arm, and brought it back across the side of the man's face. The crack of bone-to-bone was like a thunderclap. The soldier huffed for breath.

"How did you find us?" John asked again.

"You realize they're not going to just let you go, right kid?" the soldier wheezed. His spoke with a thick Russian accent. "No matter where you go, no matter what you do, they're coming for you."

"You see this girl over here?" John said jerking his head toward Indigo. "You know who she is?"

"The brief said she was called 'Anomaly.'"

"Then you know what she can do?"

"Telekinetic."

"She can sculpt your brain into a new shape inside your skull," John said. Indigo started to say that she couldn't, but John silenced her with a look. Even in the dim light of the still-crackling flare, she could tell that John didn't need her input.

John continued, "She can squeeze your heart into a tiny ball inside of your chest. She could crush your balls with her mind. If you don't start talking, I'll let her do it."

The soldier relaxed. "You think you scare me, kid? You think you're some sort of big, bad scary man? You don't know what you're up against." There was a crunching noise and the soldier's face broke into a wide smile. The man's body went rigid and his face went slack, his eyes became vacant and dull.

"Damn!" John shouted. He threw the man to the ground and jammed a finger into the man's mouth. In a second, he brought out a small piece of crushed plastic. "Suicide pill. These guys don't mess around."

"They carry them in their mouth?"

"Only place to do it. Stuff it between your cheek and your gums by your molars. If you're caught and captured, bite down and it makes certain that you never give away any secrets."

"That was impressive, John," said Indigo. "I never knew really saw you as a hero type, but you really handled that situation like you knew what you were doing."

"I don't," said John. "I'm channeling Clint Eastwood."

"How do you think they found us?"

"I don't know. No idea, really. If I had to guess, I'd say they had GPS in our brains or something. Or maybe something got flagged when Seb bought the new car. They probably had to run checks on her license or something. That would show up to anyone doing a vigilant computer monitoring. They probably tracked her to this spot with a satellite or something, flew the soldiers in with a helicopter. I don't know for sure, though. I don't know how many resources these guys have at their disposal."

"If they know that Seb bought a car, then they know what we're driving and they'll be looking for it."

"And if the Trust is as big as Ken said it is, then they'll be coming after us and they'll be everywhere."

"So, what do we do?" asked Indigo.

"Occam's Razor," said John. "The simplest solution is best."

"And what's the simplest solution?"

"We drive. We get in the car and drive. We go back to the Home, find Andy and Sarah, and wreck that place. If we can make enough smoke, someone important who isn't involved with the Trust will see it and investigate."

"So the four of us are just going to storm a small, fortified army base?"

"Got a better idea?"

"I think there's probably some quote about being backed into a corner that's appropriate here, but I can't bring it to mind," said Indigo. "We could run, but they'd kill Andy and Sarah and still come after us, wouldn't they?"

"I don't doubt it for a second."

"It's our only choice, isn't it?"

"If we run to the U.S. Government, I'd be willing to bet they'd experiment on us themselves to figure out what the Trust did."

"So, it's us against everyone else?"

John nodded. He looked over at Holly and then to Kenny. "Seven of us against all of them…and three of us are missing right now."

"But, we have Holly. She can get animals to come help."

"'Let my armies be the rocks and the trees and the birds in the sky.'"

"You watch Indiana Jones movies way too much."

"All we need is the 'Raiders March' in the background."

Indigo sighed. "That's the problem with real life: The soundtrack sucks."

— End of Book II—

Book Three
Razing Hell

Ten Years Ago

The bus pulled up in front of the Victorian building and the soldiers on board herded the seven, scared children toward the front door. Posey was crying loudly; Holly was crying softly. Indigo just looked mad. Kenny looked frightened, but said nothing. John had set his jaw and stared fiercely at the guards. Sarah wavered between being angry and crying, but the big kid, a rotund, obese little boy who had sat in the back seat drawing funny cartoons in an old notebook for the whole ride spoke up in a loud, brazen voice. "Hey, great! A house! I hope they have lunch!"

Sarah was shocked. The boy smiled broadly at her and she suddenly felt less scared. The boy seemed to be unafraid and unconcerned. "What if they don't?" she asked him. "What if they don't have lunch?"

"Then I'm going to eat the tires off this bus." He grinned broadly, his round, freckled cheeks shining.

Sarah laughed. She hadn't meant to laugh, as she hadn't laughed since her parents had told her that she was going off to a special school, but she couldn't help it. Something in the way he said it, something in the way he delivered the line that tickled her.

They started to walk up the front steps to the building they would come to know as the Home. "My name is Sarah," she told the boy.

"My name is Sarah, too!" he said. "Actually, it's Andy, but wouldn't that have been weird if my name had been Sarah? What would my parents have been thinking?"

Sarah laughed again and she suddenly stopped being scared. She was apprehensive about this house, the soldiers, and the men in the coats, but she wasn't scared anymore. There was something about the big, lumpy kid that put her instantly at ease.

Throughout the first weeks at the Home, Sarah sought out Andy's company at every opportunity, and he sought her, as well. When she went through her first surgery, Andy somehow snuck into the recovery room with her favorite candy bar. When he went through his first surgery, she brought him leftover pizza.

The thing Sarah admired most about Andy was that he was everyone's friend. No one could make him angry and he never angered anyone else. Indigo used to get angry at him over the fact that he never made her angry.

From day one, Sarah and Andy were nearly inseparable. Posey would tease Sarah that she was in love with Andy, but Sarah never really considered it love. He was just Andy, her buddy. Her partner-in-crime. Her confidant. Just…Andy.

The Present

Sarah snuck back through the halls of the hospital building and into the basement. Dr. Cormair's diversion had emptied the building and focused the search for her outdoors. She kept her head down, fluffed a few strands of hair into her eyes to conceal her face, and walked quickly and purposefully down the empty halls with her hands jammed deeply into the pockets of her scrubs top. She got to a staircase at the end of the hallway and walked down, winding her way to the bottom. She needed someplace to hide, someplace where no one would ever think to look for her.

She opened the first door she came to and peeked in. It was a small laboratory. A computer screen in one of the corners had a program still running. Someone would come back to this room, Sarah thought. She moved to the next room, an empty classroom. There was no place to hide among the skeletal desks. The next room was a bit chilly; a single shielded fluorescent light illuminated the room with a sickly, pale cast. There was a tiled floor and a table in the middle of the room with a drain at one end. One end of the room was a tall, metal wall with four thick, heavy doors arranged in a two-by-two pattern. Sarah had seen a room like this before in a movie.

It was a morgue.

She shuddered and tried to keep her jaw from chattering. She fought her revulsion and stared at the four square doors in the industrial cooler. It would be disgusting. It would be frightening. But, if she needed a place to hide where no one would look, she could do worse than to hide in a body vault. At worst, she told herself, it would only be for a few hours, just enough time to let the base calm down and stop looking for her.

Her stomach doing flips, she crossed the room and yanked open one of the bottom doors. She slid into the vault feet-first and lay on the slab, teeth chattering out of the general creepy sensation rather than the cold of the refrigeration. Her enhanced stamina kept her from being affected by the cold, but she still didn't like it. She didn't like the prickly stinging or the constant chill. She didn't like how the end of her nose felt when the temperature dipped. She closed the door at her head, easing it to point of the lock, but not letting it lock completely.

A thin beam of dull gray light slipped into the body chamber from the crack in the door. Sarah realized that she wasn't in her own, private box. The morgue cooler was a large, open square with two body shelves above, and two below. She let her eyes adjust to the dark and cast a worried glance to her right. There, on the other lower bed, lay a body.

Instantly, Sarah felt a scream well up in her chest. She fought it back down, struggling to get her fear under control. She pushed the door to her vault open slightly and let more light into the cooler. Sarah's heart jumped again.

It was the guard who had assaulted her in the truck. She recognized his fire-scarred face instantly. His body was naked and prepped for burial. He had been punished, "...most severely," as the general had told her. Sarah saw the bullet wounds in the man's chest and stomach. Three small holes dotted him.

She tried to make herself small, sliding over as far to the left as she could. She tried not to think of the corpse sixteen inches to her right. It was only for a little while, she told herself. She just had to hide for a little while. Andy needed her. She could deal with laying next to a dead man for a couple of hours if it meant freeing Andy.

The hours ticked by slowly. It seemed like forever before Sarah finally felt confident that the base had been lulled back to thinking she was gone. She threw open the door to the body vault and pulled herself out, sprawling on the floor next to the cooler. She spent a few seconds shuddering and brushing the creepy sensations of death from her arms.

Sarah slipped out of the morgue, into the basement hallway, and headed for the stairs, walking up three flights until she came to the ground floor. She walked out into the dark night and surveyed the compound.

A tin-sided warehouse with a brown tin roof near the northern edge of the compound was fully illuminated, and a steady stream of activity surrounded it. Soldiers stood on guard outside a large, brown garage door and a single jeep stood at the ready, a fifty-caliber machine gun mounted in the back. Sarah even spotted the sonic gun that took her down at the Home. She was willing to bet that the warehouse was where Andy was being held.

Sarah started walking directly toward the building, head down, keeping an easy, casual pace. A few soldiers noticed her, but none of them seemed to care. A couple of nurses had been milling around all day. The closer she got to the warehouse, the more apprehension built inside her. She could feel her knees quivering and the butterflies in her stomach were doing crazy loops. A horrible thought occurred to her: What if her powers kicked in involuntarily? Suddenly becoming a blur of color and motion was bound to attract attention.

She walked past a patrolling guard, keeping her face down and letting her hair hang into her eyes. Sarah tried to keep her pace from quickening. She felt like she was going to get stopped any second. Her panic instinct was screaming for her to click into speed and find someplace to hide.

She walked toward the guard post outside the warehouse. A tall, mustachioed soldier stood watch, an assault rifle slung over his shoulder. He extended a hand and stopped her. "State your business."

Cold sweat exploded all over her body. Sarah cleared her throat and tried not to sound like a teenager. She reached deep into her book of movie clichés and said, "I just got sent over here to relieve the duty nurse on the experiment."

The soldier raised and eyebrow and shrugged. "She just started two hours ago."

"She was covering for another nurse. I'm the night-shift replacement." Sarah held her breath. Her heart was racing. She couldn't bring herself to look him in the eye. She felt like everything she said was a paper-thin lie that the guard was going to pick up instantly.

The guard used a small hand-scanner to check her ID card. The red light on the end of the hand-held tool went from red to green. The guard shrugged. "Whatever. Have a good night. It's been pretty quiet since this afternoon."

Relief poured through Sarah's body, it replaced her fear with a sudden, rash bravado. She chanced banter. "How is the experiment?"

"I dunno," said the guard. He spoke with the hint of an accent. French? Maybe Quebecois? "I haven't seen him. Some of the guys from inside told me he was a big, ugly bastard, though. I guess he's supposed to be like some sort of Incredible Hulk or something."

"Neat," said Sarah checking her anger. She shouldered past the guard and entered the warehouse. The door had two hallways, one to the left and one that lead straight from the door. The main body of the warehouse building was to the left, so Sarah strolled down the hall. She glimpsed a surveillance camera in the corner of the hall and made sure to keep her pace steady and her head down.

A door at the end of the hall opened into the main body of the storage area. Corrugated steel siding rose two stories to a slanted ceiling supported by thick I-beams. Around the edges of the building were cargo-netted boxes of supplies stacked on wooden pallets and a few odd vehicles, jeeps and Humvees, some in various states of disrepair. Andy was in the center of the room. Sarah hesitated at the door. She had to resist the urge to spring into speed and annihilate the first guard she saw.

Andy looked like something out of a twisted carnival. He stood atop a platform encased on four sides by Plexiglas. A plastic tube jammed into his nostrils was running to a humming oxygen machine next to his cage. He was motionless, coated in some sort of thick gel. Steam rose off the goo and every few minutes, a blast of frothy white foam would shoot out of a black, rubber nozzle hanging from the ceiling. The foam slowly turned to clear jelly and began to steam. Each blast from the foam gun sent a wave of arctic air through the room. They were freezing him to death.

Through the gunk, Sarah could see Andy's face. His eyes were closed and mouth was slightly open. Wisps of gelatinous slop dangled from his lips. His skin had a slight bluish quality about it. Across the warehouse, someone dropped something large and metallic. Andy's eyes blinked open and Sarah saw him glance across the room at the noise.

He was still awake! He was conscious! Sarah had to choke down her rage. It wouldn't do him any good if she suddenly snapped and went super-speed around the room. A patrolling guard was walking toward her with slow, measured strides. Sarah ducked her head again and forced herself to walk into the room. She spotted another nurse in a small booth with dark, tinted windows along one side of the room. She made a beeline for the booth and walked in, her heart beating wildly in her chest.

The nurse barely acknowledged her. She was middle-aged, overweight, and plain with a frog-like face. She was watching some sort of machine that was delivering lines of information onto a computer terminal. "Hey," the woman said. She didn't even look up.

"Hey," Sarah said again. "I'm...uh...new here."

"Whatever," the woman said. "You know what you're doing?"

Sarah couldn't believe the woman just bought what she said. "Sorta. I mean, they went over most of it in...uh...a briefing?"

The nurse looked up. "Briefing?" She made an odd grunt noise. "Staff meetings? Those are pretty useless."

"Uh, yeah...tell me about it," Sarah said.

"How'd you get assigned to the freak show?"

"Freak show?"

"These genetic things they're doing? The freaks? If General Tucker wasn't so committed to these stupid kids, I'd just as soon gas the lot of them. Playing with God's domain is going to get these numbskulls in trouble."

"Gas them?" Sarah's hands were trembling.

"Sure. Load 'em into a trailer and just fill it with hydrogen cyanide or something. I know I took an oath that said I wasn't supposed to do any harm and whatnot, but I figure joining this outfit caused me to renege on my military oath and commit an act of treason, so I might as well start breaking as many oaths as I can."

"Sounds...like solid logic...to me," said Sarah. She was confused. What was this woman talking about?

"I heard that those mutants broke out of Cormair's operation. Tucker's ordered the project to be terminated as soon as we recover them."

"Terminated?"

"Yep. With the five that ran last night and the fact that the one girl broke out of the brig earlier today, Tucker decided that the experiment is over. The big guy here is pretty safe, but the rest need to be recovered for final data collection."

Sarah almost vomited. "Terminate. That…sounds like a pretty good idea. Can't have those…uh…freaks…running free, right?"

"Right."

"What are you monitoring?"

"His muscle activity. Since he got drenched with the cryo-gel, his muscles have been behaving strangely. Take a look." The nurse held up a stack of paper and Sarah took it. There were a bunch of graphs and charts that made no sense to Sarah. There were even some notations near the charts, but it looked like it was written in a different language. It made no sense to her.

Sarah flipped through the pages, looking at nothing in particular, but frowning as she did so the other nurse wouldn't think she was confused. "Wow…that's…unusual. What am I looking at?"

"The cryo-gel basically made his muscles freeze out to the point where he shouldn't be able to feel them, but he seems to still be generating some muscle activity. It's pretty amazing. I guess that's the chance you take when you turn a kid into a genetically enhanced killing machine."

"You sure it's not some sort of adverse reaction to the cold?"

"Eh…pretty sure."

"Is there a way to check it? Make sure he's not in pain or something?"

"Nope. The only way to check would be to shut down the foam distributor above him. If that happens, the foam will steam away in time and he'll slowly gain feeling in his extremities. Once that happens, I'm pretty sure he'll destroy everything in this room. One of the grunts told me he can pick up a truck and throw it the length of a football field."

Sarah bit her lip. Shut off the foam gun and Andy is free. She checked the contraption on the ceiling and traced its power conduits across an I-beam to a small converter box on the floor along the wall behind Andy. She could make a sprint. She'd probably be able to hit the converter box hard enough to crush it, severing the cables and disrupting the power flow. It would take some time to get the unit back online and in that time, Andy could get free…but the guards would come after her. And they must have some sort of foam agent that can travel, otherwise how could they have stopped Andy in the first place, Sarah reasoned. She cursed under her breath.

"What was that?" the nurse asked.

"Oh, nothing."

"Talking to yourself is the first sign of insanity."

"So is working here," Sarah blurted. She froze. She shouldn't have said that.

The nurse looked up at her and then broke out into a guffaw. "You got that right!" She went back to looking at her charts, still chuckling. Sarah blew out a low, slow breath of relief. She slid into a chair and pretended to be going over a chart, but in reality she just stared at Andy. She watched his eyes, closed again, and screamed at him in her mind, trying to let him know that he would be all right, that she would help him.

The world around Sarah erupted in a haze of red emergency lights and blasts of a metallic alarm klaxon. She leapt off her chair. "What is that?" Soldiers began yelling orders and scrambling for weapons and vehicles.

"Lockdown," the nurse said. She opened a drawer and pulled out a handgun. "You stay here. Keep the door locked until I come back."

"What's happening?"

"Hard to say. I need to talk to the guard on post duty. Could be that those freaks are back to rescue Lumpy over there." The nurse bolted from the office slamming the door behind her.

Andy's eyes were open. Sarah stared at his eyes. He flicked a glance in the direction of the nurses booth and looked away, then suddenly looked back. Sarah couldn't help but smile. Andy winked one eye at her.

The nurse ran back and banged on the door. Sarah let her in. "What's the story?"

"They just found one of the nurses from the hospital ward. She'd been knocked out and left in a closet in Dr. Cormair's room. That means the girl that we thought ran away could still be on base somewhere using that nurse's security badge to get past clearance points."

Sarah's heart began racing again. "What happens now?"

"They're going to start scanning badges until they find the badge that the nurse lost. Then, they're probably going to shoot the girl with the badge. At least that's what I'd do. If she showed her face in this warehouse, I'd probably volunteer to stomp the mud hole in her back."

Sarah couldn't stop herself. She engaged her powers—just a little bit. She used a short, powerful burst to launch herself forward, swinging her fist up into the woman's double-chin. The woman's lower jaw snapped up into her upper jaw with such force that her incisors cracked in half. The woman's eyes rolled up into her head and her body went slack and rolled forward into Sarah's arms. "Mud hole that, you fat bitch."

She dragged the woman's body to the bathroom in the corner of the small office and sat her on the toilet. She tugged the badge from the woman's chest and tossed her own pilfered badge into the tank on the back of the commode.

A soldier in a black beret and holding an assault rifle was banging on the door when Sarah walked out. She opened the door for him.

"Catch you in the can?"

"Yeah. Bad timing, I guess." Sarah flushed red.

"We've had a security breach. I need to see your badge."

Sarah held out the white plastic card and the guard scanned it with an optical reader on his belt. The reader beeped for a moment and flashed a green light.

"You're clean," the guard said. "Keep an eye out for any nurses who aren't where they're supposed to be." He paused. "Aren't you a little young to be a nurse?"

"I'm twenty-one," Sarah lied. "I graduated early because I took summer courses."

"Really?" The guard gave her a sly smile. "You...maybe want to have a drink in town with me sometime?"

Sarah flicked a glance at Andy without thinking. "I've got a boyfriend."

"He must be a lucky fella. Where's he work on base?"

"What?"

"Where does he work on base? I was just wondering if I knew him."

"Oh, he...he's in...in...computers."

"One of the IT nerds, eh? Figures. They make all the money. Well, if that ever goes south, you let me know, eh? I'll take you out for a celebratory dinner."

"Oh, you'll be the first guy I call. You can bet on it."

"I'll hold you to that. What's your name?"

Sarah balked. She couldn't use her real name and the guard had just scanned a code bar on her stolen badge that probably pushed information to the screen on the reader. "Uh...you know what it is already, don't you?"

The guard smiled. "Of course. It's on your ID. But it's still polite to ask." The red lights overhead kept flashing.

"Don't you have to get to work?" Sarah asked.

"I suppose. I'll see you later, Sarah."

"What did you say?" Sarah began to shake with fear. How did he know?

"I said I'd see you later, Sarah." He gestured at her name badge. She grabbed it and looked down. She chuckled to herself.

"That's right," she said, trying to cover her momentary panic. "Because you read it on my badge..." What were the odds the nurse was named Sarah, too? That had almost been a colossal mistake on her part.

The guard winked again, spun on his heel, and went to scan the badge of the next soldier in the facility.

Sarah collapsed into a chair. She couldn't believe she'd actually lied her way out of that mess. Of course, she realized, now Andy has no nurse who knows how to watch over his health while he's in that horrible goo and every soldier on base is looking for a super-speedy teenager. She picked up a chart and walked out of the booth. She went to the front of the block of gelatinous slop that was Andy and looked at the chart. She chanced a glance and could see him squinting down at her. His eyes were laughing, even if the rest of him couldn't.

"What do you think you're doing here?" Sarah murmured lowly. "Did you come to rescue me or something stupid like that?"

Andy blinked. A single, very direct blink.

"You're an idiot," Sarah sighed. "I would have been free and clear now if it wasn't for you."

Andy rolled his eyes upward as if to say, *I am an idiot.*

"Are you okay?"

A single blink.

"Does it hurt?"

Andy rolled his eyes. Sarah couldn't tell what he meant, but she was certain there would have been some sort of silly comment that would have made her laugh.

"I'm going to get you out of here somehow. Don't even squint at me, Andrew! You came back for me and I'm not leaving without you! You think I'd be able to sleep knowing I left you here to your doom?"

The foam cannon overhead shuddered and another glob of freezing goo dropped onto Andrew's body forcing him to close his eyes. Steam rose from the foam and it quickly turned to jelly. Sarah could feel the chill from the material. "I'm going to get you out of this, I promise."

Sarah glanced around the room. Aside from the nurses' station and the crates and vehicles, there was nothing else on the first level. However, in the far corner of the room, raised up on a platform that jutted out awkwardly, a technician was hovering over a control board, idly watching gauged and occasionally fiddling with dials and switches. If there was going to be a control booth for the foam gun that would have to be it. The only problem was going to be how to get up there.

Sarah walked back to the nurses' station and grabbed the stack of printouts. She walked back to the corner and climbed a steel rung ladder up to the deck. The control tech gave her a strange look. "Hey, can you maybe turn down the…thing?" Sarah said. "It's messing with these readouts."

"I have orders to maintain current levels," the tech said. He was a younger man, barely much older than Sarah.

"Please? I'm supposed to finish these tests before…termination." It was hard to choke out the word.

He scowled, but reached out and twisted a dial slightly. Sarah made a mental note of which one it was. She glanced out at the warehouse and made sure no one was watching. She jumped to speed in an instant and cracked the tech across the temple with a high-speed rap of her knuckles. The tech rolled back off his chair and hit the floor. Sarah twisted the dial all the way until it wouldn't twist anymore. Then she pried it off the terminal.

Sarah walked back to the nurses' station, sat in a chair, and watched the foam cannon. There were no more blasts from its nozzle. She watched the goo recede from around Andy's eyes, and then it drew back from the rest of his face. No longer impeded by the jelly, she watched him inhale deeply, his nostrils twitching and his chest expanding. More gelatinous gunk sloughed from his shoulders as he did. It would only be a matter of time before Andy could move again.

Then they would leave. Together.

Kenny huddled in the back seat of the minivan. John was driving—extremely fast—and Indigo was riding shotgun. In the middle seat, Holly was sitting primly, having a silent conversation with her new friend, Bat. The little vermin had been allowed to ride inside the van with them and Holly had let it sink its claws into the upholstered ceiling. It creeped Kenny out, the way Holly's eyes glazed over when she would tap into that place in her brain that allowed her to talk to animals; her eyes glowed a rather disturbing white, like someone with advanced glaucoma. Kenny just sat in the back, his hand in the pocket of his windbreaker grasping the handle of the Beretta.

As John guided the van back toward the Home and the town the Trust owned, Kenny felt the familiar itch in his brain when they crossed pockets of Wi-Fi and longed to reach out and scan the 'Net. Keeping John's words in his mind, he didn't. He resisted the urge to jostle through some firewalls and probe people's secrets. He tried to focus on the fact that when they reached Amboy, when they ran into the soldiers of the Trust, that he might have to take someone's life.

In his history classes, he was always taught that loss of life was just a part of war. It was one of those things that happened. In philosophy classes, they had lengthy discussions about war. What if it was part of a grand, karmic scheme for someone to die in a war? Would taking their life still be bad if they were *meant* to die? Kenny tried to convince himself that if he had to shoot someone, it was part of that grand karmic scheme. Like John said, though: It was all well and good to think about it; it would be something entirely different to have to squeeze a trigger and watch someone fall.

None of them really spoke on the way to Amboy. Indigo had a map on her lap and uttered directions to John every so often, but other than that, only the radio filled the silence. They listened to the news broadcasts and listened for stories about a strange birdwoman, or about gunshots in the Pennsylvania

Dutch country, or even about everything that went down at the Home two nights previous. Nothing was reported.

Morning had broken shortly after they began driving and eventually, gnawing hunger pangs hit the group. As soon as they passed an open McDonald's, John pulled over. The Golden Arches lay outside of a sleepy little town just east of the Pennsylvania border. The four of them walked into the restaurant and up to the counter, disheveled and tired. John leaned over to Kenny and whispered, "I'm glad I've seen them do this in the movies." He walked up to the counter and smiled at the woman standing at the register.

John cleared his throat, surveyed the breakfast menu for a moment and said, "I will take four number two value meals with large orange juices."

"Will that be all?" the woman asked.

"I don't know. What do you guys want?"

"Same," said Indigo.

"Sure," said Kenny.

"I'll only have three of them," said Holly.

"Is this some kind of joke?" asked the register-lady.

"Only if you don't get them quickly enough," said John. "We're starving."

It took some convincing, but eventually they were given their meals, and each carrying trays laden with food, the four of them moved to the booth farthest from the counters and tucked into their meals.

"I've been thinking," John started through a mouthful of hash browns and orange juice. "I think I've got a plan."

"Give it to us," said Indigo.

Kenny looked over at John and raised his eyebrows. "How can you have a plan? Do you even know what we're going up against?"

"I can guess. I figure there's got to be a single main gate, heavily guarded. There might be a sniper. There'll be a main barracks that soldiers will pour out of the second someone trips the alarms. I bet there'll be some weapons that are meant to neutralize Kenny's telepathy, Indigo's telekinesis, and Holly's animal powers."

"No weapons to neutralize you?" asked Holly.

"I'm not bulletproof. A well-placed shot I don't see coming will neutralize me without a problem."

"So, how are we supposed to get in the gates without setting off the alarm, find Sarah and Andy, and then get the hell out?" Indigo blew her hair out of her face with a petulant huff.

"I can get into the compound; I'm sure of it," said John. "The only problem is going to be getting the three of you into the compound. If there's only a main gate, we're going to have to find a way to disarm the alarm before we charge the gates."

"I can do it," said Kenny. "It's a snap. Just get me to a computer that controls the alarms and I'll have them off inside of a minute."

"No, Ken," John started, but Kenny cut him off.

"Hey—if this isn't a call for me to use my powers, I don't know what is. They put them in me for a reason. This is what I do. Get me over the wall, I'll shut the base down."

John scowled.

Kenny stared him down. "This is what I do. If I am eventually going to lose my mind, I might as well do some good first." Kenny could see John fighting it over in his mind.

Eventually John conceded. "Okay. I'll get you over the wall. Your job will be to disable the alarms, blow their computers, and nuke everything else, okay?"

"Computers, alarms, communication relays, I should be able to nuke all of them."

"I'll lead the assault on the main gate, then," said John. "Holly, I'll need you for diversions. How many animals can you gather?"

"I can issue a general distress call and see, but until we get there, I won't really know. I can only work with what's around me."

"Can we stop and get some?" asked Indigo.

"What?"

"Animals. If you can control them, what's to prevent us from stealing a panther from a zoo? We could load it into the van."

John looked at Holly. She shrugged. John said, "That's so crazy it might actually work."

"Where is a zoo near Amboy? Or a farm?"

"There's open country all over Ohio, we could probably find something wild," said Holly.

"But, something offensive, something weapon-grade like a big cat?"

"Maybe," said Holly. "There was a cougar near the shelter. There are reports of big cats in places big cats aren't supposed to be every year. Ohio does have a cougar population. They're not that easy to command, though. They're really independent. I think maybe a gorilla or something more social might take orders better."

"Well, there was that gorilla farm right next to the Home. We could stop there," said Indigo.

Holly's mouth dropped open, "There was a gorilla farm?"

"Of course not, ditz! Where are we supposed to find a gorilla? A cat could hide behind a seat! You can't hide a gorilla!"

"Hey—keep it down," said John. "People might think we're insane."

"As if ordering enough food for a football team makes us normal."

"Indigo, hush." The look in John's eyes silenced her. He was exuding the aura of a leader; it seemed to ebb off of him in palpable waves. Kenny felt like he would be willing to do whatever John asked of him. Kenny wondered if maybe that was part of John's genetic alterations or if it was just something inherent and inexplicable within him. "Whatever you can do to help, Holly, whatever you can bring to the party will be good. You're going to serve like an archer. If nothing else, you'll be able to find insects and birds, right?"

"Always. Except in winter. No bugs then."

"Then, we'll take what we can get. Swarms of insects. Plagues of locusts, if possible. Rain bees down on them. Whatever you can get, throw at them. Hit them from a distance with your pets."

"What about me?"

"You are going to be the heavy artillery, Indigo. You're going to have to use your telekinesis to take out any soldiers in front of us."

"I won't kill again," said Indigo.

"You don't have to. Just push them away. Keep your emotions in check and you won't have any accidents."

"Just keep them in check...sure. You make it sound easy."

"When we get there, Holly will start gathering her armies and running recon with Bat. Indigo, you'll stay hidden. Kenny will go over the wall with my help. After that, you're on your own, Kenny, for good or bad. No heroics, Ken. Don't overuse your powers. Take out the bare minimum of security and then get out of there."

"Got it."

"I'll double back and pick up Indigo. Once the alarms are dead, we'll launch the animals. They'll serve as a distraction while Indy and I bust in and grab Andy and Sarah. Then, we shut down as much of the base as we can. I'm sure I can figure out a way to blow some building boilers if we can find them. Let's make it impossible for them to track us and do a little damage to their whole operation."

"Then what?" asked Holly.

"Then we get out and run to the hills."

"I meant about Posey."

John sighed and looked down. "I don't have any notion of how to find Posey, Hol'. I think she may be gone. I mean gone for good."

"So we just leave Posey? Just forget about her?"

"If she wants to come back, she will. Until that happens, we're kind of in a tough spot, aren't we?" said Indigo. "It's not like we can force her to be here. It's not like we can just summon her back to us."

"In case you all have forgotten, we're the only family we have anymore. Our parents, our siblings, they're all dead! I'm not just going to let Posey go, too!"

"Holly, this is a subject for another time and another place. Posey is untraceable right now. We know exactly where Andy and Sarah are."

"Fine." Holly sat back and folded her arms across her chest.

"Has everyone eaten enough?"

Kenny glanced at the table, a disaster of wrappers and empty cups. "I have."

"Then let's get back on the road. They won't be expecting us to hit them during daylight and we can probably get back to the Home within the hour and scout out where our hits will be."

Andy could feel the goop loosening. The cold was lessening. His arms and legs were beginning to tingle with the sickly pain of frostbite. He watched Sarah in the nurses' station and patiently waited for a moment to break free of his prison. He could feel anger in his gut, and he wanted to release that anger all over the monkeys who taunted him while he was frozen. He couldn't move, but he heard their insults. He was absolutely aching to smash some faces. Given the size of his mutated fists, one punch would do it. Thinking of that cheered him a little.

Now that the pain had stopped burning through him, Andy was able to reflect on his new abilities and savor the memories of actually uprooting a tree and tossing a car like he was something out of a comic book; he actually began to enjoy his lumpy, misshapen form, to see the bright side to it. He'd always been a somewhat heavyset; it was nice to finally have an excuse for being a fat guy other than just being lazy and having a weakness for Ring-Dings and Mal-lomars.

He tentatively flexed his fingers. It hurt to curl them, but he was starting to gain movement. The jelly, cold and oily between his fingers, was losing its solidity slowly but surely.

Andy started to take stock of the room: Two guards stood by the large garage doors, one on each side, each armed with an AK. A guard sat on a stool by the door. He was armed, but the gun was on the ground next to him. A pair of grease-monkeys were rooting in the engine of a Jeep, occasionally taking out parts and pausing to light new cigarettes.

Andy knew he'd need to act quickly once his movement came back. He looked for something to throw. If he could throw something big enough, he could take out the two guards by the door and then rush the other guard, hopefully hitting him before he had time to take out his gun. He could probably throw the crate that held an air conditioning unit. It was right next to him. It would take out the guards if he could bowl it through the both of them. Then he could charge the lackey whose gun was on the ground. He wondered if he'd be able to make his legs move fast enough.

He looked over at Sarah. She could move fast enough. There was no doubt to that. When she first engaged her newfound abilities, Andy had watched as she blinked out of existence, moving too fast to register with his eyes, he had marveled at the swath of destruction she had left. She could do the damage necessary at speed, but how could he tell her?

His knees were stinging and his thighs began to burn. He gritted his teeth and shifted his weight. His left leg moved forward ever so slightly. The thaw was starting to go faster. He inhaled hard through his nostrils. Warm, wet air filled his lungs. It felt better than the cold, sterile air the nose-tubes had been feeding him. He felt stronger instantly. He pulled his leg again and found it easier to move in the goo.

Andy looked up and locked eyes with Sarah. She had seen him move. In an instant, Sarah opened the door of the nurses' station. She walked forward and pressed her hands to the Plexiglas. "Can you move?"

Andy took in another deep breath. He nodded slowly.

"Then we do this and we do it fast. We hit this place like a ton of bricks and we get the hell out. Sound good?"

Andy nodded again. Sarah smiled. "I've got the three guys with guns. You hit the mechanics." Andy took several sharp breaths and he lifted his hand and pulled the oxygen tube out of his nose.

Sarah snapped into action. In a blink, she went from one guard to the next and knocked all three unconscious. Andy dragged his feet from the goop that surrounded him and grabbed the oxygen machine. He bored his thick fingers into the top of the metal and bowled the machine toward the mechanics. It smashed into their legs before they could dodge and tumbled to the ground. As they struggled to get up, Sarah suddenly appeared between them. She grabbed the backs of their heads and racked their skulls together.

"Wow! That was a little Rambo of you, wasn't it?" Andy coughed out. His voice crackled and he spat out clear ooze.

Sarah winked at him. "I guess it was." She retreated back to the nurses' station and brought out a towel. "Here. Let me get that gunk off of you." Andy dropped his head and Sarah laid the towel over him. She began to slough off the remainder of the foam residue. "Thanks for coming back for me...you big idiot."

"I am nothing if not a hulking moron."

Sarah traced her finger over the veins in Andy's shoulder. Her touch was warm through the residue. Andy looked over at her hand. "I guess I look like a big freak, don't I?"

"I can't believe what they did to you."

"It wasn't so bad; I could barely feel the cold. I just couldn't move."

"No," said Sarah. "I mean, what they turned you into. Have you seen yourself?"

"Not really, but I can tell that I look like something hideous."

"You're like the Incredible Hulk."

"No. More like the Thing. The Hulk would eventually turn back into Dr. Banner. The Thing had to stay hideous. I'm the Thing."

Sarah reached up and took Andy's face in her hands. "You're still Andy. You'll never stop being Andy. And Andy was beautiful to me."

"Thanks, Sarah. Really." Andy dropped his face and his eyes met hers. There was a long, awkward pause. Neither knew what to say. Andy felt himself blushing. He wondered if blushing still looked the same now that he was a genetic freak. "Is this the part where we're supposed to kiss? Because I'm willing to bet someone, somewhere saw what just happened on some kind of camera and all hell is about to break loose."

"Then we'll make it quick," said Sarah. She leaned up on her tip-toes and touched her lips to Andy's. "We need to talk once this is over."

"Why?"

"Because I love you," said Sarah.

"Sounds good to me," said Andy. "Are you sure?"

Overhead, the alarm klaxons began to sound. "As sure as I'm sure we're going to be in a world of trouble in a few seconds."

"Bring it on," said Andy. "Nothing like a little life-threatening danger to make you feel alive."

"Do you love me?" asked Sarah.

"Since the first second I saw you."

"If we weren't about to be assaulted by a small army, I would kiss you again."

"You ready to run, Fleet-feet?"

"You ready to bash through a door?"

"Let's do this." Andy lowered his head and charged the corrugated steel garage door.

Finding a space to put Kenny over the wall was the easy part, as the main part of the base was anchored at the side of small cliff. Pine trees were thick on the hillside and moving between them offered plenty of cover. There was an occasional patrol of two guards, but they were easy enough to avoid. John was able to lead Kenny over the hill to a spot where a pine tree offered a few low-hanging boughs to climb up, move out along a limb, and allow Kenny to leap and make it over the razor wire curls above the ten foot chain-link. Kenny landed hard and awkwardly, but if he was hurt, he didn't show it. John tossed him a Beretta and then passed two clips of ammo through the fence.

"Remember what I said: Don't panic, breathe deep, and only shoot if you intend to kill."

Kenny jammed one clip into the gun and cocked it. The other clip went into his pocket.

"Make sure the safety is on," said John. "I don't want to see you jam that thing into your pants gangster-style and blow off your twig-and-berries."

"Good thinking." Kenny double-checked the safety.

"You know where you're going?"

"I will. I'll have to use my powers a bit to trace the signal feeds to a source box, but I'll find it and I'll hit it."

"Don't go overboard. Only do as much as you have to do; I don't want to see you fry your brain over this. Just take care of the alarms and get out."

Down the fence line, a cherry red light sitting atop a fence pole began swirling as if cued from John's line. "Is that an alarm?"

"I think it is," said Kenny.

"Did we set it off?"

"I don't think so."

"Are you sure?"

"No, but I really don't think we did. We didn't touch anything that could have triggered an alarm and I don't see any cameras out here."

"Damn!" John punched the tree in frustration. "Go! Run! Stay low and don't get your head blown off!"

"I'm going!" Kenny turned and started running, his awkward gait carrying him stiffly over the terrain.

"Stay low!"

"I can't run and stay low! You just do what you have to do! Don't worry about me! I'm a big boy. I can take care of myself." Kenny disappeared in the pine trees.

John turned on his heel and started a flat-out sprint. His muscles began to process oxygen more efficiently, his breathing slowed, and his body became a machine. He moved with a fluid grace. He'd left Holly and Indigo on a hillside just outside of the main gates of the compound, hidden in the thick scrub.

From there, Holly was supposed to gather her "army" and Indigo was supposed to lay low until John returned.

If the alarms were going off and he and Kenny hadn't tripped them, then it meant that Indigo and Holly were spotted, or Sarah or Andy was doing something stupid. Either way, it greatly affected John's plans and complicated his life to a degree he had hoped to avoid.

In moments, John had broken from the forest edge and saw Indigo crouched behind a bush watching for him. She shrugged and pointed at the base. John stopped running and looked over at the walls. The alarm was still blaring and he could see soldiers mobilizing.

John gestured for her to stay where she was. He made the break across the open field toward the hill and sprinted to the top.

"We didn't do a thing!" Indigo said.

"It's got to be Andy or Sarah then. We've got to move fast. Where's Holly?"

"She's off gathering creatures like you told her to. She said there wasn't anything near the base. She had to go off into the woods and the fields around town here. She's been gone about five minutes."

"We can't wait for her. You and I will have to do this ourselves."

"What do we do then?"

John held up the gun. "I'll go hit it as hard as I can through the front door. You stay down until I tell you to come. If you see me go down, don't be a hero: I want you to get out of Dodge like the devil is after you. Go blend in somewhere and hide. Have a normal life."

"Seriously?"

"As normal as you can make it. If you have to go, try to use your powers as little as possible. Just do what you have to do to get by."

John sprinted down the hill as fast as he could. It was roughly two hundred yards to the guard post by the front gates. There were two soldiers guarding the entrance with rifles. They were facing away from the entrance, though, looking in toward the center of the complex instead. They didn't see John coming. It only took him fifteen seconds to close the gap from the hill to the entrance. His footsteps were so light and so quick that by the time one of the guards heard him coming, John was already airborne with a flying kick. He buried his foot into the neck of the first guard while he reached out with his hands and ripped the rifle from the hands of the second guard before he could pull the trigger. John landed lightly and swept the butt of the gun up and into the guard's chin. Both men were unconscious.

John slung the rifle across his back. He gestured to Indigo and she made her way down the hill quickly. The two of them slipped into the compound and sprinted for the nearest cover: a jeep just inside the entrance. They slid underneath the vehicle and Indigo rolled under the rear axle. John slipped the rifle off and handed it to her.

"I won't kill, John."

"I know. Wait here. If anyone spots you, blow out their kneecaps."

"I hate guns."

"You didn't mind the handgun I gave you last night."

"That was before I had to look into the eyes of the two men I killed. Now I hate guns."

"You hate dying more, right?"

"I suppose."

"Shoot 'em in the kneecaps. If they're still idiot enough to pull a sidearm, shoot them in the hands, too."

"What are you going to do?"

"I'm going to find Andy and Sarah."

A jeep suddenly burst into view from behind the edge of a building. It was flying end-over-end through the air and smashed into the ground sending bits of metal and asphalt flying.

Indigo looked at John with wide eyes. "That'd be Andy, I'm guessing."

"Stay alert," said John. He pulled himself out from beneath the jeep and headed toward the sounds of battle.

Kenny made his way down the rocky terrain as best he could, though it felt like he was crawling instead of running. He accessed his power slightly, searching for signals. The familiar tickle of data processing through his brain was euphoric. He wanted to sit and indulge it. He let a few websites crawl through his brain before he could stop himself, and then had to refocus to find the source of the alarm signal. It was coming from a small, square building in the most remote corner of the compound. The data stream from the building was like a flashing arrow pointing out its location. His brain reveled in the flow of information. Kenny didn't want to stop the data streams and it took him several seconds to push it out of his mind. The instant he did, a dull ache began at his temples, reminding him of the price he had to pay for using his ability.

Kenny came to the edge of a small cliff. He sat on the edge and pushed himself down the steep incline. He had intended to drop to a foothold and slow his descent, but the speed of his fall was too great. He missed the jutting rock he'd intended to grab and slid the length of the steep, sandstone cliff, slamming into the ground at the bottom. He felt something pop in his ankle.

It was slight, only a sprain, but it still hurt like crazy and hampered him even more.

He stood on one leg for a moment, shaking his injured foot to take away the sting. Then, half-hopping, half-limping, he angled for the communications center as quickly as he could. Each time his right leg touched the ground, pain shot up his leg. The expanse of ground between the cliff and the communications building was wide open but exposed to the guard post at the north end of the complex. Kenny checked the tower. There was a guard in there, but he appeared to be sighting down his rifle at some sort of activity in the compound. Too lucky, Kenny thought. He limped to the nearest door and put his hand on the card reader on the wall. He discharged a data stream and the light on the door blinked from red to green. Kenny slipped inside unnoticed.

Once inside, the central control almost screamed his name. The flow of electricity and signal practically illuminated the path to the computer core of the base like neon road signs. Kenny tip-toed down a hallway toward a metal blast door. The door was locked with a computer-controlled lock. Kenny put his hand over the control pad and separated the lock with his powers. Sweat burst on his forehead and the pain in his head became intense. He felt weak in the knees. The doors opened and Kenny almost fell into the room beyond. A single guard manning a computer turned and saw him. The soldier leapt to his feet, sending his flimsy chair flying.

"Stand down!" the guard yelled, fumbling for a weapon on his belt.

Kenny slipped his hand into the waist of his jeans and pulled the Beretta. "You stand down."

The guard froze, and then slowly raised his hands. "Don't do anything stupid, kid. Face facts—you ain't getting out of her alive, you know. Might as well just lay down the gun and give up."

The gun in Kenny's hand felt like it weighed fifty pounds. His arm was straining just to hold it level. "Get on the ground. Put your face to the floor," Kenny said. He was trying to remember all the dialogue he'd ever heard in cop movies and TV shows. The guard slowly got to his knees and laid face-down on the ground. "Which of these controls the security around this place?"

"As if I'd tell you."

"Good point. Then I guess I don't need you," said Kenny. He cocked the pistol and aimed it at the guard.

"You wouldn't. Look at how you're shaking," the guard said. He pushed himself up on one elbow. "You don't got the stones, kid."

Kenny lowered the pistol. "You're probably right. I'm not a killer."

The guard started to slide a hand slowly toward the holster at his side. "Just lay down, kid. It's over."

"I'm not a killer," Kenny repeated. "But, I think I might be a kicker." He swept his leg forward and put the toe of his shoe into the guard's teeth. The guard rolled with the kick, spinning away but spitting blood and teeth. He started to pull his weapon but Kenny was faster, following up with a second kick to his wrist, sending the pistol sliding across the room and under a cart laden with servers.

"You little bastard!" The guard spat a thick glob of blood and saliva. He had a gap in his mouth where several teeth used to be. "I'm gonna tear you apart with my bare hands!"

Kenny swung his leg again, intending to connect a toe to the man's temple. The soldier was ready this time. He caught Kenny's ankle and yanked, toppling Kenny's balance and dragging him to the ground. Kenny kicked away from the soldier's grip and tried to get back to his feet, but his sprained ankle buckled under him and he fell back to the ground. The soldier was on him in an instant. The man was much, much stronger than Kenny and he was better trained than Kenny. Kenny felt a fist slam into his lower back; he felt a sharp, stabbing pain. The soldier dropped another heavy fist into Kenny's lower back on the opposite side. This time, the stabbing pain was across his whole lower back, as if both of his kidneys had ruptured. It knocked the wind from his chest.

Kenny turned over onto his back just in time to catch another fist full in the stomach. The soldier hit him again, this time on the underside of his ribs. Kenny felt like his lung was collapsing. Another fist connected with his side and there was a roar of thunder. The soldier groaned and then slumped across Kenny's chest. Blood splatters dotted Kenny's face and a hole in the soldier's chest poured blood over Kenny's torso, warm and slick.

Kenny gasped for breath. His right ear was ringing. His hand and wrist ached from the kickback of the gun. He let the weapon fall from his hand and it clattered loudly off the metal floor. He felt frozen in place. A dead man was laying on him. He'd been the one holding the gun that killed him. He hadn't meant to pull the trigger. He didn't even remember pulling the trigger, but the blood was evidence enough.

Kenny pushed the soldier off of him. He dragged himself back to a standing position. He'd seen the men that Indigo had killed the night before, but this was different. He knew why Indigo had broken down and cried. He fought the urge to run screaming from the room. The computer array beckoned. He took his eyes off the dead man and summoned up all his will power to concentrate on the task at hand.

Kenny dropped to his knees in front of the server stacks and tried to regulate his breathing. This was a super-system, a huge interlinked array of computers. This wasn't like busting through Cormair's firewalls on the tiny computer he had in the Home. This was going to cost him. He knew he was going to hurt after this hack. He knew he'd probably loose consciousness. He extended his hands and began a tentative data hack. The sudden, surging, pulsating rush of signal almost swallowed his mind, as if he was being swept away by rapids. The base ran a *massive* network. Kenny waded into the data streams and started to pick his way through the jumbles of controls. He found the security systems and shut them down piece by piece, disabling each piece as he did. He found the gate controls and threw them open. He disabled the fire alarms and emergency safety systems. He hacked into their closed-circuit cameras and filled every monitor he could with static. He deleted every file and folder he came across. He wanted to stay in the stream and keep hacking, raze the entire network to the ground and make certain the Trust would have a nearly impossible time picking up the pieces and starting again, but the stress of the hack was taking its toll. His brain was screaming. Reluctantly, he withdrew from the hack and fell back into his physical body, drained. He collapsed on the floor and gritted his teeth as the headaches roiled through his brain and his body convulsed in pain.

"Good job, Subject Five," the brusque voice of General Tucker made Kenny's eyes snap open. The general stood above him, holding the Beretta. Tucker continued, "The second the alarms went down, I knew you were here, and I knew right where you'd be. I'm glad to see all the research and equipment we spent on you didn't go to waste. You're everything we hoped you would be. I think this display of your abilities is all the end data research that I need. You were an amazing achievement. However, I'm certain that Psiber 2.0 will be a much better operating system."

Waves of stark, bleak pain ripped through Kenny's body. Agony mixed with adrenaline and he struggled to fight his way to his feet.

"Subject Five, like all technology eventually becomes, you are now obsolete." General Tucker squeezed off two quick rounds. The first one hit Kenny in the upper chest above his heart, the second tore into Kenny's guts.

Kenny never heard the gun. The bullets seemed to hit him in slow motion. He stumbled backward into the server rack and slowly slid to the floor. His vision began to tunnel, a dark void on the edges of his sight illuminated by a brilliant gold light. Kenny felt his breath rattle in his chest. His vision went dark and then he felt nothing at all.

Powerless would be the only way to describe what Indigo was feeling. She lay motionless under a jeep, trying to blend into the grass as best she could. She was sweating, partially because of the heat, partially from fear. Fear churned in her gut like surf crashing on a rocky shoal. The fear generated power, though. She could feel the skittery, crawling sensation of emotion in her brain that fueled her telekinesis. And that scared her just as much as the prospect of death.

She would not kill again. She didn't even want to injure. She had always thought that she could handle death, she had thought that it wouldn't bother her, but it had more than she ever imagined it would. It was worse than anything she'd seen in any movie. She wanted to swear off violence. No death, no pain. She didn't have the stomach for it. So when it came down to fighting, what good was she? She was a liability.

Indigo could hear the sounds of battle. Wrenching metal, the screams of men, and the staccato bursts of gunfire filled the air. She couldn't see John or Andy. Occasionally she saw a blur of color whip past the open space between the buildings and she knew it was Sarah. More soldiers were running into the battle from the main gate. The off-duty soldiers from the town must have been mobilized. There seemed to be dozens of men with guns running by her hiding spot. She felt exposed, as if one of them would look over and spot her at any second.

The sky seemed to grow darker. Indigo chanced a glance, rolling over once to be under the middle of the jeep so she could crane her neck to see. A thick cloud of blackbirds, thousands of them, blotted out the sun over the compound as Holly's army arrived. As the swarm neared, dozens of birds began dropping out of the sky, swooping down in smaller groups to peck and scratch at the soldiers.

Indigo looked back over her shoulder and saw Holly standing on the hill where she and John had just been. Holly was standing tall, her brown hair whipping wildly in the wind. Indigo began to hear incessant buzzing. Thick swarms of bees, wasps, flies, and beetles began to push into the compound, zigzagging through the soldiers and causing panic.

"It's the animal controller! She's here!" one of the guards shouted. "Find her and kill her! The animals will go away!"

Indigo heard another voice above her. "I got her." A guard in one of the small sentry posts on top of the wall was sighting down a sniper rifle at Holly. Fear, anger, and rage suddenly flared up in Indigo's heart and she lashed out with a telekinetic punch that hit the guard in the back as he pulled the trigger. Indigo panicked, realizing that she had launched out full-force. She tried to rein it back in, to divert its course. There was an extreme shockwave of pain in her brain as she did. The force bolt hit the soldier in the elbow, bumping his shot at the last second. He spun in the tower, but he wasn't knocked out of it. Indigo breathed a sigh of relief.

In the field on the hill, Holly suddenly spun to her right and fell out of sight in the long grass. The birds and insects stopped their focused attacks and began to dissipate.

Indigo's heart was in her throat. She couldn't run to Holly. She was trapped where she was, but what if Holly was hurt? Or dead? Indigo didn't even want to think about that possibility. She willed Holly to stand up, to regroup her animals. Indigo squeezed her eyes shut. She needed to get to Holly's side.

"Sarah!" Indigo screamed as loudly as she could. Her voice cracked as she shrieked into the upper octaves. "Sarah! I need you!"

She had given away her position. The soldiers heard her and she knew it. Several began walking carefully toward the jeep, weapons at the ready.

"You come out of there, little girl, and we won't hurt you. We're just going to take you in," said one guard with a southern drawl.

Indigo threw a telekinetic whip along the ground, a low, heavy burst of force that hit the guards in the shins and upended them hard. Their guns fell as they hit the ground and Indigo picked the rifles up with her mind and lifted them to the roof of the warehouse building.

A soldier called out, "It's the Jap! This one can do things with her mind! We need to get to one of the disruptors."

Indigo caught movement out of the corner of her eye, a flash of color. Sarah. Indigo screamed for her again. She pulled herself out from under the jeep and shrieked. The flash of color suddenly diverted course and Sarah was in front of her in an instant, barelegged and out of breath.

"I need to get to that hill *now*! They shot Holly!"

"No sweat," Sarah said. She grabbed Indigo's arm and hefted her into a fireman's carry. Suddenly, Indigo's world became a blur of colors and a rush of wind, and then jolted back to clarity. She was next to Holly, who was still prone. There was another blast of wind as Sarah accelerated back to the fray.

Indigo gently rolled Holly onto her back. Holly's eyes were wide and she was trembling. "Am...Am I dying?"

Indigo looked down at Holly's stomach. A small dark spot was slowly growing near the waistband of her jeans. "Don't be stupid," Indigo said. "You'll be fine." The bloodstain was spreading at a frightening rate. Indigo tore the sleeve from her coat with a telekinetic push. She bunched it up and jammed it to Holly's side. Holly moaned loudly as the fabric touched the raw wound. Indigo heard voices; the soldiers were coming after her. They had abandoned their rifles for a futuristic-looking weapon that reminded Indigo of a Star Trek phaser. Anger welled up in Indigo and she threw up a telekinetic wall and began to bulldoze the soldiers back to the compound. She saw the sniper in the tower taking aim. She threw up a wall in front of herself; the bullet was slowed by the force shield and dropped to the ground harmlessly. She threw another telekinetic punch, hitting the soldier in the face. He fell backward beneath the wall of the guard tower, out of sight. A wave of wicked, biting pain shot through Indigo's head and radiated down her spine. It was so intense that it made her eyes water. She pressed her hands to the sides of her head and squeezed as hard as she could until the throbbing receded to a manageable level.

"These guys are starting to piss me off," she muttered. Holly's face was ashen and she was trembling. Shock. Indigo grabbed her by the shoulders. "Holly! Holly, you gotta stay with me! We need you! Andy and John and Sarah can only fight for so long, Holly. We need your powers!"

A hint of color seemed to come into Holly's cheeks and her eyes lost the faraway look. She blinked hard and tried to speak but no sound came out.

"Holly, listen to me: If you cannot get us a diversion of some sort, we are going to be in a heap of trouble. Big time trouble, Hol. You have to dig deep here and summon up something."

Holly's eyes suddenly welled with tears. One slowly filled the corner of her eye and slid down her cheeks to her ear. She slowly shook her head. "Can't do it." Another tear slid down the other cheek.

"What do you mean you can't do it? I'll help you. I'll hold you up. You just worry about the pheromones or whatever it is you do."

"Too tired," said Holly. "Can't...focus. Never summoned that many animals before..." Holly's eyes closed and she started to go slack in Indigo's arms. Indigo shook her and Holly's eyes blinked open. A few more tears slipped from her eyes. "I'm sorry, Indigo. I failed." Holly closed her eyes and Indigo heard her breathing change into a lower, shallower rhythm. She had passed out.

"Holly?" Indigo shook her again. Holly's head rolled to the side, her eyes still closed. "Holly? Wake up!" Holly remained unconscious. Indigo stripped off her own jacket and covered Holly with it. She took a good look at Holly's left hip. The sniper's bullet had hit her just off the iliac crest of her pelvis, more of a deep graze than a piercing wound. It was bleeding plenty, though.

A sudden explosion from the compound shook the ground and a fireball shot into the air over the warehouse. The gunfire and sounds of conflict ceased. Indigo held her breath. Plumes of black smoke rose into the air, clouding the sky. As quickly as it stopped, the gunfire and sounds of violence started again. Indigo released her breath, shuddering.

Something reached her ears above the battle sounds, a rapid, chattering, clicking noise, thousands of high, short whines in succession, a massive wall of sound. Indigo turned and looked behind her, toward the thick forest to the east. A dark cloud of flittering, jerky movement was beginning to emerge from the leafy shadows. It moved as a whole in an amoeba-like fashion, stretching and shrinking, oozing forward and retreating. Objects seemed to be darting in and out of the cloud. Indigo squinted, and suddenly she realized what was coming.

Bats.

Sarah raced back to the fray after dropping Indigo at the top of the hill. She wanted to stay and help Holly, but John and Andy needed her more at the moment. Without Sarah there to deflect bullets, Andy was a sitting duck. Bullets couldn't kill him, but he had already taken better than two dozen hits and he was slick and stained with his own blood. He was slowing down. Sarah could see that the blood loss was taking its toll on Andy.

When they first broke through the steel doors of the warehouse, the soldiers took up defensive positions around a perimeter and fired on them. Sarah had stopped the initial volley of bullets with a bare hand. These were no longer the rubber, non-lethal, riot-control bullets they had used at the Home, they were now metal slugs meant to kill, not immobilize. The bullets had torn up the skin on her hand. When she ran past Andy, she paused long enough for him to bend a shank of steel around her hand like a steel boxing glove to protect it. He had taken a clip of bullets in the back during that time. If it hurt him, he hadn't let Sarah know.

Sarah sprinted around the compound, a blur of motion too fast to comprehend, knocking bullets from the air and keeping the soldiers off-balance by slapping gun barrels when she could. None could get a bead on her as long as she was in full speed and when she needed to breathe, she would race to a far corner of the compound, stop, suck in as much air as she could, as quickly as she could, and then race back to help Andy. The legs of her nurses' scrubs had been shredded quickly from her speed. The top was becoming frayed rather quickly as well.

Andy was an unleashed machine of destruction in the compound. If he could grab it, he bent it. If he could throw it, he threw it into something else. If he could jump in the air and wreck it by landing on it, he did so. He wasn't restraining himself. There was something frightening and terrible about his actions; Sarah could tell he didn't care if people died or not. If they were in his way, they were going to get crushed. Andy's skin was cut and torn and bleeding freely so that he was stained a dark crimson. He looked like the villain from a slasher movie, more frightening than anything John Carpenter or Clive Barker ever dreamed because he was real.

John had come into the fight after Sarah and Andy had been battling their way toward the front gates for almost five minutes. Sarah didn't know where he'd come from, but she was thrilled to see him. John had mingled into the fight like a ninja: One moment there were men firing at them, a split-second later those men were laying on the ground and John was standing in the middle of the bodies. John had made it to the center of the compound where he had taken refuge behind a jeep that Andy had already smashed. It lay a few feet from the front wall of one of the buildings, giving him the reassurance that no one was sneaking up on him from behind. He had collected the rifles of several soldiers and was using them to keep the soldiers from moving any closer. Firing with uncanny accuracy, John's shots were disabling, but not lethal.

When he first got there, John gave Andy and Sarah a briefing on Posey and Sebbins, and where Ken, Indigo, and Holly were and what their plans were. Sarah had to swallow her initial shock at Sebbins' death. It was neither the time nor the place to mourn.

When Sarah returned from saving Indigo, John was crouched behind the jeep with a rifle at the ready and Andy was lying on his back on the ground next to John. Sarah joined them. She cowered behind the jeep, sidling next to Andy. "What do we do now?"

John stood quickly and squeezed off three rounds. He hit a power coupling and a shower of sparks exploded from it. The power line fell from the coupling and hit the ground near where the soldiers were taking cover. A few of them had to bolt from their position to avoid it. John shot again and one of them went down hard, clutching his knee.

"Why haven't they hit us with explosives?" John wondered aloud.

"They tried," said Andy.

"What do you mean, 'tried'?"

Andy chuckled. "They tossed a grenade at us. Sarah practically caught it and sprinted it back to them. She was back here by the time the thing went off. I think it killed one of them. If it didn't kill a guy, it made a few of them really unhappy."

A loud volley of gunfire strafed the wall of the building, startling them.

Sarah craned her neck and glanced at the soldiers hunkered down around the compound. There seemed to be dozens of them. There was nowhere they could go.

"We're not getting out of this, are we?" asked Andy.

Sarah put her hand on his shoulder. He was sticky with blood and sweat. "Don't say that," she said.

"I'm being a realist. There's too many of them. We either have to kill every man on this base or we go down."

John turned and shot again. When he dropped down he spat on the ground in disgust. "More bad news: They finally brought out that disruptor that they used to shoot Sarah the other night."

"They're looking to end this, aren't they?" asked Andy.

"I think so," said John. The sound of a helicopter became audible. Sarah instinctively looked up at the sky.

Andy sighed. "They're going to freeze me again, aren't they?"

"Probably," said Sarah.

"We gave it our best shot," said Andy. "We tried. We failed. I hope Holly, Ken, and Indigo get out of here. Sarah, maybe you should go, too. Take John. If you go fast right now, you should be able to make it. Get out."

"No," Sarah said. "You came back for me. I'm not leaving you."

"Don't be stupid," said Andy. "Suicide is not an answer, here. You got to get out. Get out, get away, and get our story told to someone, anyone who'll listen. If you stay here, you're going to die."

"Andy's right," said John. "We have to go."

"No!" Sarah shouted. "You go, John. I'll get you out of here. But, I will not leave without Andy."

"You're being stupid," Andy said. "I'm too heavy, too slow, and too big a target to get out of here alive. If they're going to freeze me again, I'd rather not get you caught up in it as well. I'm prepared to go down right now. I'll give them a great fight, but I'm prepared to go. This is my time. It's over for me."

Sarah blinked back tears. "This isn't your time! You never even got to have a life, yet! Andy, listen to me: They already took our lives. None of us have ever been allowed to be free. We have to leave and find out what it really means to live."

Andy reached out a meaty hand and touched Sarah's arm with his fingertips, a surprisingly gentle touch. "Then go. You live for both of us. Go out and have the greatest life ever. You owe that to me. You have to go."

Sarah's throat felt tight and her lower lip was wavering. "You don't understand, Andy: I don't want a life where you're not a part of it."

"And you don't understand," Andy said. "If you don't sprint outta here, I'm going to pick you up and throw you as far as I can."

"I'll be back here in five seconds."

Andy rolled his eyes. "You just have to be difficult about this, don't you?"

"I told you, I'm not going. Besides, if I try to get out of here with John on my shoulder, I'm not going to be able to get enough speed to outrun that sonic cannon. They'll just take me down and I'll be no better off than I am now."

Andy staggered to his feet and ripped the hood of the jeep from its hinges. With a backhanded toss, he winged the hood like a Frisbee and it neatly bisected the disruptor. Sparks exploded from the wreckage like a Chinese firework. A fresh hail of gunfire answered his attack and Sarah watched in horror as several new wounds suddenly exploded on his chest. Andy dropped back down to the ground.

"Are you all right?"

"As good as I'm gonna be," Andy wheezed. "Just don't put your fingers in the hole and I'll be fine. The disruptor's gone. Get out. Get out now."

Sarah felt her heart breaking. She slowly nodded. Tears began flowing freely. She leaned down and kissed Andy gently on the lips. "I'll always love you," she whispered.

Andy smiled up at her. "I'll love you for the rest of my life," he said. "The fact that it's only going to last another five or ten minutes shouldn't deter you from finding that statement incredibly romantic." He reached up and traced a massive finger down the side of her face, teasing a curl of hair. "Now go."

John knelt down next to Andy and clasped his hands around Andy's hand. "You have always been my brother."

"From another mother."

"If I can ever avenge your death, I will," said John.

Andy shook his head. "Not worth it, man. Just go. Get Kenny, Holly, and Indigo. Get out of here. Enough with the good-byes, just go!"

Sarah looked at John. "You ready? I'm only going to be able to run maybe two hundred yards, tops, with you on my shoulder before I have to stop to breathe. And that's if nothing gets in my way and I don't have to contend with really uneven ground."

"It'll have to do."

"I'll distract them so you can get out of here," said Andy.

"We have to find Kenny before we get out of here," said John. "Which building will be the communications center?"

Sarah pointed. "I saw it earlier when I was sneaking around looking for Andy."

"Then we go there first, get Kenny, and we go."

"Then go," said Andy. He rolled to his feet. "*Theirs not to reason why...*"

Sarah didn't want to wait for him to finish the quote. She grabbed John and nodded at Andy. Andy dug his hands into the jeep and began to lift. Sarah put John on her shoulder and engaged her speed. In a heartbeat, she and John were at the doors to the communications array.

She looked back at Andy and watched as he lifted the jeep above his head and hurled it across the compound and into a fuel tank. The tank split open and high octane fuel gushed out in oily, rainbow streams. A stray spark from the electric cable John shot down earlier ignited the gas fumes. A stream of blue-white flame shot across the compound to the tank and caused a massive explosion. Shrapnel blasted outward over the compound, a massive fireball shot into the sky, and thick, black smoke rose slowly into the sky. Several pieces of flaming wreckage landed on or near some of the other buildings and vehicles. The hungry flames lapped at fuel sources, a stray bit of wood or a jeep tire, and spread quickly. Buildings began to smolder and then turned into fully-fledged flames and began to burn voraciously.

Andy was standing completely exposed amidst a ring of burning buildings and vehicles, roaring at the soldiers in defiance, a savage in tattered, blood-soaked, bullet-riddled sweatpants. Many of the soldiers ran to get fire gear to extinguish the flames, some recovered from the explosion and launched a barrage of gunshots at Andy. Sarah closed her eyes.

John shot the lock off the door. He opened the door and shoved Sarah inside. "Don't watch," he said. He put his arm around her shoulder and led her down the hall.

Sarah felt her body begin to break down. Her legs felt like string, it was getting hard to breathe. She started to slide to the floor but John slipped his hand under her arm and lifted her back to standing. "Be strong," he said. "Andy made his choice. He might be the only reason we escape."

"That helicopter is going to drop that gel on him, you know. They're going to freeze him and then kill him."

"I know," said John. He stopped. "Oh, Kenny," he whispered.

Sarah looked up and saw Kenny's body slumped back against the computers, his shirt soaked in blood.

John dropped to the ground by Kenny's side and felt frantically for a pulse. Sarah slid helpless to the floor and wept. "This can't get any worse."

John clutched Kenny's head to his chest. "There's a pulse. It's very weak, but it's there."

"What do we do?"

"We need to get him back to the Home."

"What? Why?"

"We need a hyper-womb. A hyper-womb can keep him sedated while his body heals. We'll steal a hyper-womb and a couple of tanks of that oxygen fluid stuff out of the basement labs, load it into the back of that old pick-up truck in the shed, and we'll take him someplace where we can fix him."

"N...no," Kenny whispered. John looked down at him.

"Kenny?"

"Not done here," Kenny said. He half-opened one eye. "Need to finish the hack...kill their network..."

"No, Ken," said John. "You've done enough."

Sarah crawled over to them. "You've done more than enough," said Sarah. "It's over. We're going to get you out of here and get you well."

"Too late for...me," Kenny coughed; it sounded like liquid was in his lungs. "Not going to make it."

"Stop saying that," John said.

Kenny lifted a hand and dropped it heavily on top of a rack of servers. His eye closed and his head dropped. A trickle of blood oozed from the corner of his mouth.

"Is he..." Sarah couldn't bring herself to say the word.

"I can't feel a pulse," said John. "We got to get him to the Home right now. You take him. You can get there a lot faster than I can, even if you have to stop every couple hundred yards."

"Kenny's a lot lighter than you. I can go farther."

"Then take him and go, Sarah. Get him to a hyper-womb. Get him healed."

"I don't know what I'm doing with that stuff!"

"It's like Sebbins told us, it is full of medicated, oxygenated syrup that allows the body to speed healing and recovery. Just fill a tank and stick him in it. I don't know that you have to do much more than that."

"What if it's not that simple? What if I have to do more?"

"If he stays here, he's dead. At least the womb gives him a chance, even if it's a slim one."

John was right. He always was. Sarah got to her feet and tried not to collapse; she felt so weak and sick. With John's help, lifted Kenny to her shoulder. She tried not to think about how lifeless he felt or how frail he was.

"How are you going to get out of here?"

"I'm going to try to sneak out. Do me a favor, though."

"What?"

"On your way to the Home, stop and tell Indigo and Holly to run. In case I...you know..."

Sarah nodded, the lump in her throat felt like a boulder. She could hardly breathe with the heaviness in her chest. "You're not going to leave, are you? You're going to go down with Andy."

John gave her a half-smile. "I'll hold their attention as long as I can. Just take care of Kenny."

Sarah wanted to say something, complain, argue, shriek in anger, anything—but she didn't have the energy anymore. It felt like her world was collapsing around her and she couldn't do anything about it.

There was a crackle of electricity in the room. The tangy scent of ozone filled the air. Sarah looked at the computer and servers. The lights across the servers were blinking wildly. One by one, the servers began to arc blue electric bolts and in a puff of smoke and a flash of light, each one burned itself out, melting components and destroying any information or programs. The monitors exploded sending shards of glass flying across the room. The computers began to smolder and smoke poured from the vents as motherboards melted and chips fried.

John laughed, a short, choked-off laugh that was balanced somewhere between mirth and sadness. "He did it. The nerdy little hacker did it."

"Kenny fried the computers?"

"When he touched the computer, he must have gone back in to overload the system. It might have cost him his life."

"Not if I get him to a hyper-womb fast."

"Go. Do your best."

Sarah nodded and walked to the door. She pushed it open and stepped into the light cautiously. She could hear Andy, still screaming profanities and smashing everything he could. The sharp tattoo of gunfire answered every crash of metal and Andy's roars of pain and anger answered the gunfire. She looked toward the gates. Something wasn't right. "John? John, come here! You've got to see this." John jogged up behind her and looked over her shoulder. A cloud of darkness was coming toward the base.

"What is that?" John whispered.

"No idea," said Sarah.

The cloud was coming quickly. It seemed alive, a moving, pulsating mass. "It's animals," said Sarah. "It's a massive cloud of animals."

"What kind?"

"I don't know. It's too far away."

"Remind me to give Holly a big ol' kiss the next time I see her," John said. "If...I see her again," he added.

"I guess this is the big diversion she promised. The bugs and birds were helpful until they left. But, Holly was shot. She probably wasn't able to keep her powers going. She must have regrouped, though. She must be okay."

The cloud grew closer and Sarah could make out an audible clicking noise. She suddenly realized what the cloud was. She made a face. "Oh, gross..."

"Bats," said John. "Tons of 'em."

The swarm of bats hit the compound like a biblical plague. One second, there were none, the next second, they were everywhere at once. The air became thick with a living, leathery-winged, brown-furred snowstorm. Their squeaks and chatter was a constant drone. The air was stirred by their wings creating buffeting winds. The stench of their fur, ripe with the oppressive scent of guano, permeated everything in the compound. The fluttering, darting mass of animals carpeted everything, providing a swirling, moving curtain in which to hide.

Andy stood in the middle of them, battered, beaten, bloody, and more tired than he had ever been. He hadn't eaten in what felt like forever and his arms and legs ached as badly as when he first began his transformation. The painful stings of the gunfire had stopped. The soldiers were screaming and shooting at the bats, but the more they screamed, the more the bats attacked. A soldier broke through the living wall in front of Andy, several large bats were clinging to his face, biting and flapping as he beat at them in blind panic. The bats swirled around Andy's bulky form, not even grazing him with wingtips as they flew. Andy smiled. If nothing else came of it, at least every soldier on this base would have to endure a long and painful series of rabies shots. Holly's powers were amazing. Andy began lumbering toward the entrance. As he moved, the bats parted and he walked freely in their midst, the animals enveloping him like a living shield.

He walked over to an air conditioning unit outside of a building and lifted it off its base. The helicopter was nearing. He could see the container dangling beneath it that dropped that freezing goo. Andy twisted the unit from its moorings and began a slow hammer-spin. He released the metal cube and watched as it arched lazily through the air and into the spinning rotor of the helicopter. A ghastly metal-on-metal crunch ripped the air and the helicopter plummeted, slamming into the ground. The gel container cracked open like an egg, spilling its contents in a wave of icy froth. Bats and soldiers were covered. The soldiers, lacking Andy's metabolic processes and enhanced tissues, were overcome quickly, the gelatin mixture practically lethal to them. The bats that were splashed stood no chance. Their wings froze, their bodies went rigid, and they fell out of the sky dead. More bats immediately took their place, dropping out of the swirling column in the sky and filling in the holes in the attack.

Andy kept walking through the cloud of bats. He couldn't see the gates of the compound, but he figured he was headed in the right direction. He caught glimpses of soldiers running amok, slapping at bats, and seeking shelter. Andy laughed out loud. It felt good to laugh. A minute ago, he was wondering if there was any sort of experience after death, and now he was going to walk out of the compound without further injury.

An engine roared behind him and Andy spun around, ready to smash the hood down with his fists. He stopped short. John was behind the wheel of a big Dodge pick-up. John leaned out the window and jabbed a thumb at the truck bed. "Get in, big boy. I got us some wheels."

"Where'd you steal that from?"

"Motor pool. I ran over and grabbed the keys off a desk. The bats were everywhere; no one even saw me do it."

"Holly is the best," said Andy. "She's getting a big hug later." He walked behind the pick-up and eased himself up onto the tailgate. The tailgate immediately snapped off and Andy rolled to the ground. Andy stood up and eased himself back onto the back of the truck. The shocks protested, but held. "I feel like cattle," said Andy.

"You smell like cattle," said John. "Hold on, I'm going to fly. We have to get to the Home."

"What? Why?"

"Kenny's hurt. Sarah already went there to get him into a hyper-womb." John punched the gas and the pick-up tires screeched on the asphalt. Hidden by the cloud of bats, John guided the truck to the entrance and smashed through the flimsy drop-arm barrier at the sentry post.

As they broke free from the compound, the lights in the buildings began to flicker and then go dark. Andy watched gleefully as the power boxes around the compound and the adjacent town sizzled and exploded in golden waterfalls of sparks. Inside the buildings, wiring caught fire and plumbing backed up. Every computer in the installation melted down, every hard-drive erased, every motherboard destroyed itself, every back-up memory drive began to smoke and spin data to nothing. Every building went dark, everything with a power cable fried, and every computer became an expensive paperweight. The electrical surge spread into the town outside the compound, with the electrical system melting in every store, every building, and the gas station on the main thoroughfare. Computers throughout the town destroyed themselves. In minutes, the town was devoid of working technology. The army of bats abated their attack and lifted into the air, dispersing in a myriad of directions, and becoming pinpoints of darkness in the blue of the sky. Soldiers lay scattered on the ground and hiding under jeeps, bleeding and traumatized. Buildings burned and black smoke drifted over the compound. Flames, stirred by winds, spread and burned the grass, already dried brown by the late summer drought. The ghost town turned military outpost became a ghost town once again.

When the Home came into view, Andy tensed involuntarily. He hadn't expected to see its dormers and purple-shingled roof ever again. John pulled into the half-circle drive in front of the Home and slammed the truck into park. Indigo leapt out of the passenger side and Andy eased himself off the back of the truck, Holly cradled in his arms. Holly was the second-smallest of the group, behind Indigo, and in Andy's cartoonish arms, Holly looked like a child.

"I sent Sarah ahead with Kenny," John said. She was supposed to get him into a hyper-womb. I want to get him loaded into the truck and get him the hell out of here. We'll go far away and get Kenny healthy."

"What about Holly?" asked Andy.

"Holly will be fine," said Indigo. "It was a flesh wound. The bleeding has stopped. She just needs to get bandaged."

Andy looked down at the gash in Holly's upper hip. "Looks like she needs stitches. Maybe Sebbins…" He stopped. Indigo and John were frowning at him. "Aw, I'm sorry. I forgot."

"Let it go," said John. "It's all right."

Indigo opened the front door of the Home. She and John walked in easily. Andy had to negotiate his new body through the doorframe, walking sideways like a crab.

The Home was still and silent. It had always given Andy the sense of being like a library, save for when Indigo and Posey were screaming at each other over nothing or he and John were wrestling in the TV room, but now there was a new level of quiet, an almost funerary quality about the room. The four of them strode through the entry, into the kitchen, and walked down the long, back hallway to the basement steps that led to the labs. Indigo paused at the refrigerator and pulled out a package of bologna and a jar of mustard. She grabbed a loaf of bread from the counter.

"What?" she hissed when Andy shot her a questioning glance. "Like you're not hungry."

The basement was dark, save for the dim exit signs. They walked down the long hallway and into the lab. The large room was cast in shadow, only a small, shielded light over the tank in the corner was lit. In its narrow cone of light, Sarah was kneeling by the hyper-womb. Kenny's body bobbed in the neon-orange syrup. He was in silhouette, a scarecrow dangling in space. Sarah looked over her shoulder when they entered. She didn't get up.

Andy paused. Sarah was the type who would run over and throw her arms around them. She celebrated the smallest achievements with hugs. He used to tease her about it. Andy cocked an eyebrow at Sarah. She flicked her eyes toward the dark corner of the room. Andy spun toward that direction and stopped short. A man sat in the corner in a plush office chair. Andy immediately wanted to charge him and smash his face.

"Don't do anything rash," General Tucker said in a cold, monotone voice. His thumb shifted slightly on the remote and suddenly Andy felt paralyzed as electricity coursed through his body. He dropped to his knees. Holly tumbled out of his arms to the ground in front of him. The shock was severe on his thick, insulated body. Indigo, John, and Sarah were on the ground, writhing in agony. Even Holly awoke from unconsciousness and moaned.

"For those of you who have not met me yet, I am General Tucker," he said. His thumb shifted again. The electrical surge stopped and the agony ceased. "I am the overseer of the project that created you. I must admit, I had hoped that you wouldn't be quite so predictable, that perhaps you would have realized Psiber was beyond healing and given up a lost cause, but I suppose if you had done that, I wouldn't be able to see this project through to its end."

John rolled to his feet and faced the general. The shock of the electricity hit them all again and they were forced fetal by the pain.

"Don't do anything stupid, Elite," said Tucker. "Didn't you ever wonder why this room was made mostly of metal? We had it built to be a shock-cage. There are electrical conduits under every inch of the main floor. Over here, on the rubber mats by the computers, I'm protected. However, you all are standing on a lightning bolt, if I so choose to make it feel like that. If we were going to deal with over-powered adolescents, we needed a way to take them down if they got out of hand during experiments. Electricity works. It's faster than Blink, stronger than Brawn, and can neutralize everyone in between. Granted, it hurts Brawn a little less than it hurts, say Anomaly there, what with all the metal in its brain and down its spine; I could only imagine how much that hurts when I hit this button." For good measure, the general jolted them all once more. "The only one of you who gave me concern was Psiber. That subject might have been able to tap into the electrical workings of the shock-cage and reroute the streams or shut it down, so I was lucky enough to be able to neutralize it earlier." Tucker lifted a large caliber handgun from his lap and gave it a small shake for emphasis. "We'll lose some data because of that, but one out of seven isn't too bad."

"Six," said Indigo. "Posey's gone."

"Ah, yes. Nightingale. The experiment will turn up eventually. A bird-girl cannot hide forever. When it makes a mistake and shows up somewhere, we shall bring it in." Tucker's smugness made Andy want tear off the man's left arm and beat him to death with it.

Tucker continued, "I give you all credit; you all are more impressive than we thought you would be. However, it's time to end this little jaunt and finalize the experiment so that we can move on to the second phase."

"Second phase?" grunted John. "What do you mean, 'second phase?'"

"The next generation, Elite. Our second group. Since Psiber accessed our computer system, I'm sure you know about the second group. They are the real subjects. You were all only the rough draft. We never intended this experiment to make it to full completion. All those implants and tests we gave you over the years were vital to your growth as a project. However, we need to examine the damage and changes all our meddling caused your bodies over the past ten years. To do that, we need to see our implants again."

"Kill us, you mean," said Andy. "Cut us open and dissect us."

"Unfortunately, yes," said Tucker. "That was always in the cards, even if Cormair didn't know it. We had hoped to be able to run a full battery of tests after your abilities fully manifested, but you have all proven too dangerous for that to happen. We were able to pull some basic data on Brawn while it was in stasis, but for the most part, we will be unable to get the full data we need from your living bodies without your full cooperation. Thus, your corpses will have to yield the final data."

John chuckled lowly. "You don't have any data anymore, Tucker." There was a blast of electricity that made Andy's brain feel as if it was starting on fire.

"That's *General* Tucker to you, experiment."

"Your data is gone, *General*," John spit out the word with venom in his voice. "Kenny hacked your system. It's done. He blitzed all your data. Your whole town is shut down. Kenny nuked your compound from the inside."

Tucker smiled. It was a wide, knowing smile that made Andy's stomach yaw. "Are you so naïve as to think this was our only compound? Did you honestly think we only had the one base? True, Psiber did put a bit of a bug in our plans, perhaps set us back a whole year, maybe two depending on the extent of the damage, but rest assured, we have been storing all data in several locations. We would not be so short-sighted to put all our eggs in one basket; no, no…as a matter of fact, the reach of the Trust is far longer than you could even begin to expect."

Andy's stomach finished its acrobatics, settling somewhere between his feet. He didn't feel defeated when they caught Sarah. He didn't feel defeated when they froze him in Jell-O. He didn't even feel defeated when he was certain he was making his final stand in the center of the compound, but Tucker's admission was the final nail. It was over.

"How are you going to do it?" asked John. "Bullet in the chest like you did Kenny?"

"Far too messy," said Tucker. "Electricity will eventually stop your hearts."

"So do it already," said Andy. "I'm sick of waiting for it."

"I need a team in here, first," said Tucker. "Doctors, scientists—I don't want your bodies to begin to decompose and chance losing that data."

"So when do they arrive?"

"Soon, Brawn. Very soon."

"Then the plan is to just keep us shocked and immobile until they get here?"

"Correct."

General Tucker flicked the switch once more and Andy felt the crackling inferno of power fire through his body once more.

The curtains along the windows stirred slightly with the breeze from the broken window. The room smelled of smoke. When the fuel tank exploded, the winds pushed tendrils of smoke into the room. No nurse came to check on him. He hadn't even seen a nurse since the alarms had sounded. He had sat there, breathing the acrid smoke, crying silently as his children battled the soldiers in the compound.

He had been such a bloody fool! All those years he spent silently relishing their achievements, watching from afar as they grew into adults, eavesdropping on their conversations to find out more about them as people and not just guinea pigs as he was supposed to regard them. Now it was too late; he'd kept them at arm's length for a decade because of his stupid, stupid fanaticism about his work and now Dr. H. Bromwell Cormair was going to die alone, a bitter old man, without family, without friends, and without anything to show for his lifetime of research. He closed his eyes and tilted his head to the ceiling. It was all over. Everything was over.

Cormair reached over and pulled the IV from his left arm. He slipped the pulse oximeter from his index finger and let it fall to the ground. The plastic clattered loudly on the tile floor. One by one, he peeled the sensors from his chest and let them flutter to the floor. The power was out. None of the machines were working anyhow. It was pointless to keep them on. Finally, he pulled the oxygen tube from his nose and exhaled slowly. His body hurt. He had internal injuries from the shot Indigo gave him. He felt broken inside. A pair of doctors had patched him up as best they could, but they were little more than field medics. Their skills and medical resources were grossly limited. Cormair knew it would only be a matter of time before he died.

He exhaled again slowly until his lungs felt empty. He resisted inhaling as long as he could. He began to feel light-headed. He felt as if he was receding into himself. The pain in his chest and stomach lessened and ebbed into the ether. He could no longer feel the uncomfortably firm mattress beneath him or the scratchy hospital linens. He concentrated on the darkness so long that he began to feel as if he was spinning in crawling, lazy arcs. He separated from time and space and began to drift into oblivion.

Was this death? Was this how life came to its conclusion? What was that line from Hamlet?

But that the dread of something after death...
The undiscover'd country from whose bourn
No traveller returns...

Thoughts and images raced through his mind. Time ceased and for a moment he thought days had passed. Perhaps years. The logical voice in the back of his brain told him it was only minutes, but then the irrational, illogical voice would counter, asking if he knew *how many* minutes. One? A thousand? A billion? He saw his research, the kids—*his* kids—the fog of old age seemed to clear and he began to remember his childhood with stunning clarity: His mother standing in front of the old stove, baking something for the Sunday meal. His father, austere and proud—a true English gentleman—wearing a waistcoat for each meal with that old, tarnished watch fob dangling across his thin belly. There was no watch at the end of it. He had sold it in England to get the money to come to America, but he kept the fob as a reminder of his York origins. Cormair felt his skin begin to crepitate with sensations of unease. Somewhere, in the tiny part of his brain that was keeping an eye on reality and the present began to sound a mental alarm. Cormair began to escape from the darkness flooding his mind. He left the images and the sensations behind, spiraling back up into the light from the depths. In seconds, he was in his hospital bed, scratchy linens and all. He opened his eyes. The room was still dim; the power in the building was still off. The curtain by the broken window stirred again. The room was empty. Cormair closed his eyes. He exhaled again and waited for the darkness to return. The hair on the back of his neck stood up and he opened his eyes again. Behind the curtains, he could make out a shadow, a human form crouched like a gargoyle on the windowsill. The shadow didn't move. Cormair could feel eyes watching him from behind the gauzy drape. He pushed himself up in bed further and reached a shaky hand to the bedside table for his glasses. "I know you're there," he said.

The figure didn't move.

"I know you're there...and I'm sorry, Posey."

The figure behind the curtain cocked her head. Cormair watched the silhouette. She didn't move.

"I imagine you came to exact some form of revenge? You're bitter about what you've become and I believe you probably wanted to make me pay somehow? Perhaps you were going to steal me from my bed here and fly me into the stratosphere and then drop me so that I had time to think about what I'd done as I plummeted to my death? Or maybe even higher than that? Maybe the mesosphere? Can you fly that high, Posey? Could you breathe up there? Will your wings still provide lift in air that thin? Please, dear girl, come out from behind that curtain and let me see you. Let an old, dying man apologize to your face."

Slowly, with a careful, graceful movement, the silhouette reached forward and gently pulled back the curtain. She stepped off the windowsill and crept forward in short, awkward steps. Posey stood before her creator, a feathered, winged girl, Cormair's greatest achievement in gene therapies and biological enhancement. She was the very pinnacle of a half century of work. Cormair's breath caught in his throat. He leaned forward in the bed, squinting. He scanned the curve of her folded wings, the smooth feathers that framed her face and curved out of her collarbones and gently sloped over her shoulders. He looked down at her feet, the toes curled and sharp like an eagle's talons.

Posey stepped closer. In her eyes, Cormair saw no remnant of the gawky, awkward teenager he had known, only a hard, bitter woman filled with anger. Her voice was low and cold, "You were right. I came here to kill you. I was going to fly you out over the mountains, then drop you, but I wasn't going to do it from the stratosphere. I was going to drop you just high enough to break your legs, but not kill you. Then, I was planning on sitting in a tree and see what sort of carnivore found you first. I was going to watch while a bear or a wolf tore you apart."

Cormair could feel the hatred in Posey's voice. She truly despised him. His heart broke further.

"Do you see what you did to me? You had no right! Do you hear me, *Doctor*? No right to turn me into a freak of nature, an abomination! There's no way to reverse this! Even if I cut off these stupid wings, my feet will always be gross, horrible claws and I will continually grow these stupid feathers! I was always homely, and I accepted that. I knew no one was ever going to fall in love with me because of my face, but now I am beyond homely! I am truly ugly!"

Cormair shook his head fervently. "No! No! Posey, you are beautiful. You are the most beautiful woman I've ever seen."

Posey's golden eyes flashed with flame and ire and her face became a twisted snarl of disgust. "Look at me, Doctor! I am ugly! Ugly, ugly, ugly!" Posey crossed to his bedside and moved her face in front of his. "Look at me! Do you see what you've done to me?"

"I had no way to predict the results of what I was doing in an aesthetic sense, Posey. If I could, I would have made certain that you would have enjoyed the results. I was creating something new, something beyond human limits! Can you not see that? Can you not look in a mirror and realize that you are something—someone who is greater than everyone around them? You are better than beautiful! You are glorious! You are a miracle! You are truly one-of-a-kind creature. True, perhaps by human standards, you might consider yourself ugly, but you limit your thinking! You have to see yourself by new standards, standards of beauty that have never existed. Posey, you are a prototype, the first of your species. You are a new creation with unique DNA, *Homo Aves*. And far as that species goes, you are, by far, the most beautiful."

Posey grabbed the front of Cormair's hospital gown and yanked him forward. Her strength surprised him. She shook him so hard that his jaw bounced and his teeth clanked together.

"Do you honestly expect me to buy that crap? I am the *only* member of my so-called *species*, Doctor! I don't want to be glorious or unusual! I want to be a regular eighteen-year-old girl who dates and gets her heart broken and has a first kiss and marries and enjoys life! Now I will *never* get that chance! No one will ever love me! I will never have a normal life!"

Cormair slumped over. It was useless to argue. He had nothing he could say to her. For the first time in fifty years, he saw himself as a true monster. What rights did he have to play god? "I know."

"You condemned me to this living hell!"

"I know," he repeated.

"Why? What sort of sick man does this to a child?"

"A man who was so blinded by his work that he forgot to see you as children."

Posey released his gown and Cormair fell back against the bed. "I was going to kill you, Doctor. But I'm not going to do that now."

"Why?"

Posey turned her back to him and looked out the window. When she spoke, her voice had a faraway, hollow quality about it. "Because I want you to kill me."

"What? Posey, don't be ridiculous! You may not be able to live this idealized, magical, movie-version 'normal' life that you think you have to have, but you can still have a life, a long, fulfilled, and interesting life. Think about the possibilities! If you escape this compound, if you get out of here right now, you have the ability to go anywhere you want to go! You are almost immune to cold—you could go live in the Yukon. You can use your wings to ride thermals to almost any destination! You have the ability to get to get to any mountain peak in the world! You could be the greatest explorer the world has ever known!"

Posey turned back to Cormair. Her cheeks were wet with tears. "But I will have to do it alone."

"You have the others, your brothers and sisters."

"They look normal. They can blend into a crowd. They can hide in plain sight. I might be the greatest explorer in the world, but what good would that do if I can't even go to the mall and buy a shirt off the rack? I don't want to live life being stared at, being singled out and humiliated. I want to die."

"You do not need me for that, then. If you want to die, go die."

"I want you to kill me because watching your research die off will hurt you more than bears tearing your limbs from your body."

"To hell with the research!" Cormair shouted. "The research is already terminated! Kenny erased the computers in the Home and there is a standing order to kill all of you! My research is over. I do not want to see you die because it would be like…No, it *will* be watching my own daughter die before my eyes and I will not stand for that." Cormair felt a pain shoot through his chest. The fingers on his left hand began to tingle. His breath became short.

"Now listen to me," he said, attempting not to show the pain. "Go back to the Home. In my room near the labs, my bedroom not my office, there is a hidden panel behind the dresser. Behind that panel is a metal box. That box has a key in it and a letter from my lawyer. Take the key and the letter to First National Bank of Erie in Erie, Pennsylvania." His entire left arm went numb and a wave of agony rippled through his body stopping his breath. Cormair drew in another short, hard breath. "The key is for my safety deposit box. In it you will find seven hundred thousand dollars and an envelope. The envelope is very important to me; it was my most treasured possession. Get the money and divide it amongst yourselves. It is money that I funneled away from the project for years. It is why you all had to endure gruel and small portions for dinner some weeks. It is why sometimes there was only oatmeal for breakfast. I often lied to the Trust to get more money for your meals and clothing and stocked it away for you should this day ever come. Consider it the best I could do for an apology." The pain was apoplectic.

"I can't just waltz into a bank, Doctor!"

He could barely get a breath. "Get one of the others to do it! Posey—you will not kill yourself. Please, do not end your life. Promise me! Promise a stupid old man that you will fight for every breath!"

Posey hesitated. She swallowed hard. New tears were flowing. "I…can't promise…"

"You must!" Fire was burning in Cormair's chest and his veins felt like they were crawling with flames. "Promise me!"

Posey opened her mouth and no sound came out. She swiped her eyes with the back of her wrist. She nodded slowly before uttering, "I…Promise."

"You can never go back on the promise you make to a dying man," said Cormair. His breath was coming in short, sharp bursts. "Now go! Get the key. Find your brothers and sisters and live! Go forth into the world and live your lives!"

"I will, Doctor."

Cormair took in a final breath. His lungs no longer wanted to work. He hissed through a clenched jaw, "And Posey…please tell them…I love them. I love you all."

Cormair seized in pain, and then he went limp. His eyes closed and he spiraled into the darkness, tumbling end over end into nothingness.

"...*from whose bourn*
No traveller returns..."

It was all John could do to keep breathing. Every time he moved in the slightest, the general would light them up with a jolt of lightning. Each wave of electricity felt like it was burning his muscles. Each wave of electricity made keeping thoughts in his head more difficult. He wanted to lash out, to do something heroic that would save his friends, but nothing came to his mind, his tactical supercomputer brain had gone offline.

Tucker checked his watch. John could see a hint of frustration in Tucker's eyes. John couldn't keep his tongue in check. "What's the matter, General? Your team late?"

"They will be here. I'm afraid Brawn's little tantrum damaged some of the gear in the warehouse needed for the vivisections. They are making repairs and looking for back-up equipment. It's just taking them a little longer than I had anticipated." For good measure, the general blasted them once again.

"I'm getting a little tired of that," growled Andy.

"You and me both," Indigo moaned.

John's jaw kept clenching involuntarily, a side effect of the electricity. With all their combined powers, with all their abilities, they were held powerless against one man with a remote control. It was unbelievable. He'd actually had the time to get over to the Home and sit down and wait for them. That meant that he had to have departed the compound well before Sarah had left. He had shot Kenny, and then made it to the home before the girl who can run faster than any car could drive.

Something in John's brain clicked, the tactical supercomputer rebooted and began making connections. Tucker had left before Sarah! He hadn't been in the compound when Kenny's final hack had taken effect. He hadn't seen the power go down or the electrical fires. He hadn't seen the computers melt down. Tucker was oblivious to the fact that his compound was cleansed of all technology that had been plugged into a wall socket or hooked into Wi-Fi. Something in John's gut told him that Tucker's team wasn't coming. Their computers were shot. Any medical machines that were on the electrical line were now useless. Kenny had put a big whammy on the Trust and Tucker was oblivious to it.

"Hey, Tucker," said John. A jolt of electricity went through him. "Sorry, *General Tucker*. I got five bucks in my pocket here that says your team isn't coming and you're not going to kill us."

"Elite, when you are dead, I will take that money. I'll use it to buy a nice bouquet of flowers to place on the steps of this place in your memory."

"Seriously, General," John tried to sound aloof. "I don't think they're coming. Why don't you try to email them or something?"

Tucker gave John a patronizing smile. "Psiber hacked the computers down here. The experiment neutralized the intranet we had between here and the installation. The computers in the building are all useless as well. It made sure to blank their hard drives."

"I know," said John. "He downloaded everything in the hard drives into his brain."

Tucker leaned forward. John could see he was suddenly interested. "Downloaded the hard drives?"

"Every last bit. All the data this place had, from Cormair's private log to Holly's trigonometry homework, is rattling around Kenny's brain."

"Can it download the information again into a computer?"

"Probably," said John. "If his body gets healed, that is. He's not much of a cyborg with a pair of bullets in his chest." John watched Tucker's eyes flick to the tank where Kenny's body floated in stasis. "Of course, if death is the only end for us, I doubt he'll even bother to help you out. Shame, too. There are a lot of things Cormair did that he never told you about, I'm sure. Having Cormair's files? That would probably make your version 2.0 whatever go a lot smoother, a lot faster. You might even get it done sooner than you think."

Tucker's eyes jumped from the tank, to John, and then back to the tank. Tucker broke into a haughty, toothy grin. "Nice try, Elite. Very good. You actually got me thinking for a minute. But, in the end, there will be no deals. I can't let you all just go free to be traipsing about the county with paranormal abilities. We need the information contained within your bodies to complete 2.0, not Cormair's files."

"Well, I think you're going to have to take whatever information you need by yourself, General. Your team is dealing with Kenny's little virus. He smoked your whole compound. We watched every building's power blow out as we left."

Tucker stared hard at John for a long moment. He reached into his shirt pocket and withdrew a flat communicator. He pressed a button on the side and murmured into it, "Tucker to Krantz." After fifteen seconds, he repeated it loudly, "Tucker to Krantz. Answer me, damn it." Only silence answered him. Tucker tossed the communicator aside muttering curses under his breath.

"I guess we'd call this an impasse, General. Perhaps a stalemate? You uploaded all this tactical military knowledge into my brain and it is constantly figuring out the best angles for me to do things. Right now, it's coming up blank. If there were any way that I could take you down right now, I would know. Right now, you've got us down. We can't even make a move without you bringing us back down to the ground with that little power button of yours, and you can't kill us because you need your precious information."

Tucker inhaled sharply through his nose. John could see him puffing out his chest in frustration and trying to decide what to do next. When he finally spoke again, he was no longer smug and aloof. "The problem with your *uploaded* information, Elite, is that your information only deals with battle tactics and combat under fire. In a situation like this, you don't possess a military man's thinking ability. Improvise, Adapt, Overcome. Unless bullets are flying at you, you don't have the ability to think like a soldier."

"And you do?"

Tucker snorted. "Of course I do."

"A soldier in a paramilitary organization, an anti-American organization at that. You're a traitor to the country who taught you to think like a soldier!" John knew he'd pay for that outburst. When the shock subsided, John could feel a trickle of drool rolling down his cheek. Tucker had really let them have it. John looked over at Indigo. Her eyes were closed and John couldn't tell if she was breathing. Holly was awake, she looked at John with scared, pleading eyes.

"What is the ultimate objective of my mission, Elite?" asked Tucker.

John rolled his head back to look at Tucker. He knew instantly where Tucker was going with this line of questioning. "Terminate the experiment."

"Now, if you have all that military tactical information rolling around in that big, soldier's brain of yours, perhaps you can tell me what a soldier is supposed to do if he has a series of objectives to complete toward a goal and some of those objectives are rendered impossible?"

John dropped his head back. "The ultimate objective is the only objective that matters. If other objectives are rendered impossible or might interfere with the completion of the ultimate objective, those objectives should be shelved until a later time. Complete the ultimate objective at all costs."

"Excellent," said Tucker.

"What's all that mean, John?" grunted Andy.

"It means that he's going to kill us."

"What about the—"

"They'll just have to get what they can, when they can. Complete secondary objectives in a time frame that won't interfere with completion of the ultimate objective."

"It's a shame, really," said Tucker. "Millions of dollars of research and development, the finest geneticists we could hire—we had to kill them after they left here, you know—and all that time and effort in training and teaching you…It's all wasted now. A successful beta-test that leads the way to a better version."

"What do you mean by that?" asked John. "We're not defective."

"You are defective," said Tucker. "In order to get your bodies and minds to do what we wanted, we were unable to condition your minds the way that we wanted. Dr. Cormair tried to raise you as normally as was possible in that environment to make certain your minds developed as normally as possible. Television, music, internet access—all the things that normal adolescents have access to in their daily lives. Even that old *Playboy* magazine you found in the culvert by the road two years ago, Elite. That was placed there for you to find so that you could experience the full range of normal, adolescent teenage male behavior. Did you honestly think your luck was that unbelievable?"

"I had hoped."

"You were raised to be independent and free-thinking. That is a major defect for the purposes the Trust has in mind for this project."

"Can't be assassins if we were taught to value life, right?" said John.

"As I said: A major defect."

John glanced over at Indigo. She had opened one eye. He looked at her, staring hard, trying to mentally project the idea of taking the remote from Tucker's hand into her brain. As if she could read his mind, Indigo gave her head a slight shake and whispered, "Can't do it…No fear, no emotion. The shocks are too much."

John looked over at Holly. He could see her eyes were clouded over, a white haze. She was trying to summon animals. John hissed, "Holly?"

The fog left her eyes and she shook her head. "Can't make contact," she whispered.

He craned his neck to look at Sarah. Her eyes were closed and she was twitching slightly.

John looked at Andy. The big lug was still bleeding from a few bullet wounds. His skin was pock-marked with battle damage and even his forehead showed a few gashes and tears where bullets had bounced off his nearly unbreakable skull. Andy whispered, "I'm slower than you are, man."

John began to run battle tactics. How can he get up fast enough to avoid the electro-shock? Once up, where can he go where Tucker won't be able to shock him and take him down? And the gun—Tucker was in possession of a handgun. At a distance, John could anticipate the trajectory of the gun from the positioning of the barrel and dodge the shot. In close range, that would be trickier. If he could do a push up hard enough to roll to his toes and then jump sideways as hard as he could, he would probably be able to get to the edge of the metal flooring. Then, from there, he would be able to reach Tucker with a leaping kick. He'd have to take the gun out first, then the remote. He knew that Tucker didn't stand a chance against him in hand-to-hand; Tucker was older, gone to seed. John took a few quick, priming breaths. He'd only have one shot at this.

"Distract him?" John whispered to Andy.

"How?"

John couldn't answer that. He shrugged. Andy shrugged back. Andy suddenly curled fetal and rolled away from John while groaning loudly and clutching his stomach.

John sprang to action, kicking off the ground with a cobra's speed and flinging himself sideways. The second Tucker caught motion out of the corner of his eye, he thumbed the remote. Indigo, Andy, and Holly screamed. John landed on the protected area and rolled to his feet. He jumped again, whipping around in a circle and extending his leg in a textbook roundhouse kick. Halfway through the motion, something bit into his side and he felt every muscle in his body go tense at the same time. It felt like half the muscles in his body were being torn from his bones. John crashed to the floor and the pain continued. When it stopped, John couldn't breathe, he couldn't move.

"A taser," said Tucker. "Did you think I wouldn't plan for the chance that you'd try something stupid, Elite?"

John looked up at Tucker. The wires for the taser had come out of the end of the remote control. John's head fell to the floor, defeated. He was angry at himself, angry that he hadn't anticipated a taser, only the gun. It was a major tactical blunder. He had become so focused on the victory, he forgot that defeat was possible.

Tucker shocked him again. "Valiant, though. It was a great attempt. It is a marvel to see you in action, Elite. But, I think you have outlived your usefulness. I can't wait any longer." Tucker pulled out the gun clicked the safety. He pointed it at John. "As punishment for your heroism, I think you shall watch the other experiments die."

Tucker clicked the remote again and John heard the hissing crackle of electricity coursing over the floor. He heard Holly shriek in pain and Indigo groaning. Andy began to convulse. John began to smell the burning hair and the sickly sweet stench of burning flesh. He closed his eyes. The words of one of his old history teachers echoed in his head. You can't beat the system. The system will always win…

The world suddenly exploded around John's head. He clapped his hands over his ears and clenched his jaw to keep his teeth from rattling out of his mouth. The noise—so much noise. John opened his eyes and saw Posey standing in the doorway, an angelic shadow. Her screams immobilized Tucker. He was clutching the sides of his head in a futile effort to lessen the intensity of the noise. The remote had fallen into his lap.

When the scream stopped, it seemed to linger in the air, a heavy reverberation that echoed in the ears. John didn't know what was worse, the taser or Posey's incredible scream.

"Who are you to dare hurt my friends?" Posey's voice was hoarse and guttural, raw from her scream.

"He's General Tucker," said John. "He is the man who was in charge of this whole place! He's the reason we became experiments in the first place!"

Posey's eyes narrowed to slits. She spoke in a tone that John had never heard emanate from another living being, a voice low and thick with loathing and anger. "You are the one who made me ugly?"

Tucker struggled to recover. He fumbled for the remote and the gun. "I will deal with you in a minute, Nightingale!" He hit the remote again and pushed himself out of the chair. "A shock cage! You cannot help them!"

Posey's face devoid of compassion, cruel and demonic. Her golden eyes glittered with rage.

"To shock me, I would have to touch the metal!" Posey sprang into the room and her wings shot out to her sides. With a heavy downswing, her wings propelled her at Tucker. Tucker raised the pistol and fired a single, panicked shot. The bullet clipped Posey in the shoulder, but she didn't slow down. She spun her body in the air and landed on Tucker's chest with her feet. As John watched in horror, she sunk her toes into Tucker's chest and pulled back, tearing bloody gashes in his flesh. The remote and the gun clattered to the ground from his hands. Posey's wings beat the air madly as she tried to stay aloft.

"How dare you?" Posey shouted. "These are my friends, my brothers and sisters. Who are you to think you can harm them?"

"Nightingale, stand down," Tucker grunted. Posey's talons flexed deeper into his flesh and he growled with rage and pain. "You will pay for this, freak!"

Posey dropped onto the General's chest, grabbing him by the collar of his shirt and crouching on him like an eagle on a perch. "You will pay for making me the freak. You turned me into this…this thing!"

Tucker surged forward and tried to knock Posey away. She lost her grip on his collar and her right foot came free of his chest with a sickening slashing of flesh. She beat her wings wildly, trying to remain aloft. She kicked awkwardly, trying to maintain her balance and flight. Posey's foot shot out, talons flashing through the air, and her toes sliced across General Tucker's neck. Tucker's eyes became wide, terrified discs and he gurgled in shock. He clutched at his neck, blood seeping through his fingers. The general coughed and convulsed, and then slid to the floor, his eyes slowly glazing over with the glossy, endless stare of death.

Posey fell to the ground, her eyes locked on the general's body. She watched his life ebb. Silent tears began to run down her cheeks and slowly curled into a fetal ball.

John crawled over to her and wrapped his arms around her, sitting her upright, and holding her tightly to his chest. Posey pushed her face into John's body and wept. Holly and Sarah were by Posey's side in an instant, each clutching her from either side. Indigo knelt behind John and draped her arms over his shoulders, wrapping her arms around his neck. John could feel Indigo's frail body shaking with sobs. Andy knelt by them all and reached out his hand to gently stroke Posey's head with an oversized finger.

The rest of the world ceased to exist for a time.

Andy carried Kenny's hyper-womb out of the basement by himself. He and John slid it into the back of the pick-up truck, secured it with ties, and then covered it with a tarp, tying it down tightly. Posey and Holly gathered the key and the letter from Dr. Cormair's room. Each of them gathered clothes and personal trinkets from their rooms. None of them had much they wanted to save. Indigo and Sarah took whatever food they could find in the kitchen and packed it into plastic bags. Some they loaded into the pick-up truck with John and the rest they put into the old farm truck that was in the back shed of the Home. Sarah drove the pick-up out of the shed and left it to idle next to the white truck.

They gathered on the lawn in front of the Home. Andy draped his arm around Sarah's shoulders. Holly and Posey stood close to each other. Indigo stood with her hands on her hips, John towered behind her with his hand on her shoulder.

"This is it, then," said John.

"Yes," said Sarah. "We finally leave here."

"Before we go, I want to do something," said Posey.

"What's that?" asked John.

"I want to burn this place to the ground."

"The smoke will alert the soldiers in Amboy that we're still in the area."

"Then let's start the fire and go," Posey's eyes were locked on the front door, her jaw set in grim sorrow.

John looked at Andy and nodded. Andy went to the shed by the side of the house and brought out the gas cans they used to refuel the lawn mowers.

Sarah brought out some old two-by-fours and some rags. They each wrapped a rag around the end of the stick and Andy doused the rags in gasoline. John used the cigarette lighter from the truck to light them.

One by one, each of the six stepped forward and tossed their torches onto the home. Posey took a seventh torch and flew it to the roof. She dropped it on the old, lichen-covered shingles and drifted back to the ground. "That one was for Kenny."

The greedy flames quickly devoured the old, dry wood siding of the Home. In minutes, the flames had circled the building, engulfing the base and climbing the sides, spreading until every inch was swallowed by the flames. The wood crackled and black smoke drifted to the sky in a thick cloud. The Home became a funeral pyre for their childhood as lab rats.

They watched silently for a moment before slowly retreating to the vehicles. John and Indigo took Kenny. Andy got into the back of the other pickup and Sarah and Holly covered him with a tarp. Sarah and Holly got into the cab and followed after John and Indigo.

Posey lingered at the Home for a moment. She put a hand to her cheek and wiped a tear away. Then, she pushed herself into the air and in moments she became a dot in the empty blue.

Epilogue

Begin Again

At precisely ten in the morning on a Tuesday, a mousy young woman in plain clothes with plain brown hair walked into the First National Bank of Erie in Erie, Pennsylvania with a key, a letter, and a backpack. She limped slightly, favoring her right leg. She was led to the safety deposit vaults and, with the help of a letter from a lawyer, was granted access to a vault to which she possessed the only key. A clerk took the box pulled from the rows of safety deposit boxes and put it in a small room with a locking door. The young woman entered the room and the clerk heard the door lock. In several seconds, she emerged from the room, the vault box empty and her backpack full. She thanked the clerk and walked out of the bank.

No one took notice of her. She wore sunglasses and kept her face turned away from the security cameras. The security guards never saw her because they were too concerned with capturing a small bat that had somehow gotten into the bank and was causing a minor panic amongst the female tellers and some of the patrons.

The bat was never captured.

An hour later, two pick-up trucks were parked at a remote scenic overlook atop the bluffs around Lake Erie. Near the picnic area at the overlook, down a well-worn dirt path, in a thick copse of trees, six young men and women lay in the grass devouring an enormous fast-food lunch, talking…and laughing for what felt like the first time in their lives.

The white, letter-sized envelope lay in the middle of the picnic blanket amongst the stacks of cash. They hadn't opened it. Each of them was dying to of course, but they hadn't opened it. Instead they talked about the future and enjoyed resting in the shade.

"When I asked for thirty burgers, I thought the girl's eyes were going to fall out of her head!" Sarah broke into giggles. "And the fries! She was like, 'Uh…did a bus pull up?' I wanted to say, 'No, it's just my boyfriend!'"

"I'm hungry!" said Andy sitting in the middle of a small mountain of cardboard burger wrappers.

"I'm going to have to get a decent job if I'm going to keep you fed," said Sarah.

"I'm going to have to eat more if you get a decent job," said Andy. He smiled and pushed Sarah lightly on the shoulder. She grabbed his arm and held onto it. He picked her off the ground easily and held her aloft. She slid off his arm and fell to the ground next to him. He rested his mammoth hand on her shoulder.

"So, you two are really...like..." Holly didn't know how to phrase it.

"In love?" Sarah suggested.

"Sure, that works," said Holly.

"Ew," Indigo deadpanned.

Sarah looked up at Andy and he looked back at her. "I guess we are," said Sarah.

"As if no one could see it coming," said John. "Jeez, you two were practically married from day one."

"I suppose I'm happy for you," said Indigo. She didn't look happy.

"What's up with that face?" asked Andy.

Indigo's face darkened further. She chewed on her lip thoughtfully for a moment and then turned to John. "What are we going to do now? This is all fine and good, but you know they're not going to just let us go. The Trust will come after us, won't they?"

"No doubt," said Sarah. "They're probably already searching for us. We're the only ones who know their secrets."

"I didn't want to bring this up while we were having fun, but I've thought it through: We have to split up," said John. "Together, we're going to be too conspicuous. I think they'll be expecting us to stick together. We can't do that; we need to blend in more. We have to go places where we can blend in and become part of the background. Use fake names, get cash-only jobs where we can. Don't buy anything big like a car. Stay off the radar. We have enough money to get a decent start, so let's use that to our advantage. We have to figure out where that whole 'phase 2.0' project is going on and shut it down. People like Tucker and the Trust can't be allowed to ruin more kids' lives for their twisted purposes and they can't be allowed to run a coup on the government."

"So, we're going to go all superhero on another base?" asked Sarah. "We barely made it out of the first one. We would have all died if it hadn't been for Holly."

"What?" asked Holly. "What do you mean? I got shot, remember? I was unconscious for most of it."

"You know," said Sarah. "Bringing all those bats like you did was amazing."

Holly stared at Sarah, confused. "What bats? I brought birds and bugs, but when I got shot, I stopped."

"There was a mountain of bats! They were freakin' everywhere. They saved us."

"I didn't bring any bats, though. Other than Bat, of course…" A slow, serene smile spread across Holly's face. "It was Bat. He did it; he brought them. It wasn't me."

"No freakin' way," said Indigo.

"Are you kidding me?" said Andy.

Sarah raised her eyebrows and whistled lowly. "That's truly amazing."

"I'll say," said John. "We owe that little flying rat our lives."

"Hey!" said Holly. "He's not a flying rat!"

"I didn't mean it in a bad way," said John. "I figure if he pulls something like that, he's one of us and deserves to get ribbed the same way I tease Andy about his hourglass figure."

"You're just jealous, Stringbean," said Andy.

"Well, he's not a rat," said Holly indignantly. "He's sensitive."

"Bring him down here," said John. He pulled a plastic dipping cup of honey out of a bag and peeled off the top. "He deserves to eat with us." John set down the honey and in a moment, the little bat darted into their view and landed on the blanket, pulling itself forward and lapping greedily at the honey.

Holly laughed. "He's sending me images of what bats consider thank-you like placing dead bugs at your feet."

Andy touched some of the still-healing bullet holes on his chest and stomach, and then reached his hand to stroke the bat's head gently with his index finger. "Little guy really saved my bacon. You can tell him that he'll always have a place to eat at my table." The bat raised its head and chattered happily at them.

"Back to serious matters," said John. "We have to split up. I'm going to take Kenny. I need to get him healthy. I don't think we can take down a base without his powers."

"What if…Kenny doesn't…" Indigo started.

John cut her off sharply. "Shut up! Don't even think it. Kenny will be all right. Sarah got him to the tank in time. I refuse to believe anything else!"

"Kenny will be okay in the tank for a while," said Holly. "If what Sebbins told me at the remote lab in Barnsdale was correct, the tanks can hold enough oxygen in the suspension for about two days before you need to get them oxygenated again."

"I'll get him someplace soon," said John. "After we're done here, he and I will get a place near here."

"You want me to stay with you?" asked Indigo.

John shook his head. "We need to split up. It's for the best. Easier to stay hidden."

Indigo huffed and blew a stray strand of hair from her eyes. "Fine."

"I think it would be best if we went to different areas," said John. "Really split up. Does anyone know where they'd like to go?"

"I want to go south," said Sarah immediately. "The desert. I hate the cold. Besides, I need someplace devoid of people where I can hide Andy."

"Yeah, I seem to have lost my action-hero physique and Statue of David looks."

"Indigo, how about you?" asked John.

Her eyes shot daggers at him for a moment but said, "A big city. I'd like to be someplace exciting, someplace where you can go out at night. I'm tired of being cooped up in the country. Besides, where better to hide than a big city? A thousand people pass by every day. Who can remember a single individual?"

"Anyplace in particular you thinking about," asked Sarah.

"Someplace with other Asians. Maybe Seattle. Maybe San Francisco."

"What about you, Holly?" asked Andy. "You and Bat going to hit up the big city?"

Holly shook her head. "No. I'm a country girl at heart. I need to be someplace where I can see cornfields and rolling hills. I'm going to try to head out to the west, get a job working with horses on a ranch, maybe. I'd like to work with horses."

"Posey?" asked John. She had barely spoken that afternoon. She sat removed from the rest of them, a few feet back from the picnic blanket, occasionally using her wings to fan herself.

"Dr. Cormair told me to live, to explore. I think I might do that. Maybe head west with Holly for a while, then maybe find someplace else to be. See the world. Maybe I'll find a deserted island in the Pacific to live on, or maybe I'll go scale mountains like Cormair told me to do."

"He loved us? Cormair really said that?" asked Indigo for the fifth time since Posey had told them of her final moments with the doctor.

"That's what he said," said Posey. "He also said that the envelope had something important in it."

"It's just hard to believe, you know? All those years of him being gruff and demanding…and he was a big softy. Just doesn't seem right," said Indigo.

"You know," said Holly, "when you think about it, I think that even though he was cold and distant, I think we all loved him back to a degree. At the very least, we respected him."

"Yeah," said Andy. "When I played Cormair in chess, I tried harder than I did when I played John. Didn't matter, I still got my butt handed to me, but I wanted him to think I was smarter than he thought I was."

"Ditto," said Sarah. "During tests that he oversaw, I tried harder than I normally would."

John leaned forward and picked up the envelope. "This was his most prized possession? Doesn't seem to be a lot in here," he said. He slipped a finger behind the pasted flap and tore an access swath in the paper. He turned the envelope upside down and tapped it gently. A small photograph slipped out and fell to the blanket.

"That's it? What is it?" asked Andy.

John picked it up and examined it. He smiled and passed it to Holly. "It's us."

The picture was a black-and-white snap of their first day at the Home. They were gathered on the porch, giving the camera forced smiles while they tried to hide their fears. Andy was in the center, a porky little boy with a broad grin. Sarah was next to him, pretty and thin. Holly and Posey were the book-ends on the first row, Holly a shy violet behind messy hair, and Posey, tall and gangling with thick glasses. John, Indigo, and Kenny stood in the second row. Kenny's face was plastered with a dark, serious look, the same look they would all come to know so well over the coming decade. Indigo was a tiny china doll, looking more like a three or four-year-old. John had his arms folded across his chest. When he first arrived at the home, he was skin stretched over sticks. There wasn't even the faintest hint of muscle on his seven-year-old body. And in the back, standing behind them, Dr. Cormair was looking down on them and smiling. A genuine smile.

"Did you ever see him smile?" asked Sarah. "I never did. Not once."

"Look at him," said Holly. "It's like he's happy to have us there."

Indigo said, "There's something strange in that look."

"He looks paternal," said John. "He saw us as children that day. He might have blocked that over the next few years in order to do his research, but that day, at that moment, it looks like he thought we were *his* kids."

"Will wonders never cease?" said Andy.

Posey cleared her throat. "Does anyone…mind…if I keep this picture with me? There are almost no pictures of us growing up that aren't for scientific documentation. I think the only ones we have are the few we'd taken of each other. It's nice…to remember."

"Go ahead, Posey. It's yours," said John. "It's the least we could do after you saved us."

With that, John stood and began cleaning the clearing. "It's time to go," he said. "I have to get Kenny someplace where I can set up the oxygen system for the tank."

"So, this is it, then?" asked Holly. "We go away from each other?"

"For a while," John said. "Until we know where the Trust is hiding their other project. Or until the Trust finds us."

Holly swallowed hard. Her eyes were welling with tears. "I'm going to miss you guys."

Sarah wrapped her arms around Holly. "We'll miss you too, Holly."

Andy held out his arms, "Come on, Spaghetti-head, how 'bout a hug?"

John and Andy embraced briefly and separated. "You've been a better brother than any real brother could have been," said John. "Thanks."

"You too," said Andy. "I'm going to miss seeing your stupid hair every day."

Indigo stood. "This is getting too mushy for me," she said. She picked up her stack of cash and slipped it into her pockets. "I am going to hitch out of here. I can't handle more good-byes."

"Don't hitch," said John. "Get a bus ticket or something."

"I'm a telekinetic," said Indigo. "Anyone tries anything funny and I'll crush their balls with my mind."

Sarah and Holly hugged Indigo, and surprisingly the often stand-offish Indigo hugged them back.

"Be good, Wings," Indigo said to Posey. "Don't pull an Icarus on us."

Indigo turned to Andy. "I'll miss you most of all, Scarecrow."

"Be good, Midget," said Andy. He gently tapped the end of her nose with his oversized finger.

Lastly, Indigo looked at John. She wrapped her arms around his chest and John bent his head to hers, touching his cheek to her forehead. Indigo broke from the embrace, turned on her heel, and walked away without glancing back.

"I suppose Andy and I had better go too," said Sarah. "It's going to be a long drive for us."

"Can you give me a lift to the bus station?" asked Holly.

"Certainly."

"I'm going to get a ticket west."

"Anyplace special?" asked John.

"I'm not sure. Maybe Sheridan, Wyoming. Saw a special about it on TV once. I think I'll like it there. There are horses out there. Posey, you going to come with?"

"I'll follow your bus," said Posey.

The trio walked away from the picnic site to the old pick-up. Andy lay in the back of the truck, nearly filling the bed, and Holly and Sarah tied the tarp down over him. Then, Sarah and Holly climbed in the cab. The truck started with a minimum of fuss and they pulled away, heading down the road, back toward Erie.

John and Posey stood together amidst the trees. "You'll be all right?" asked John.

Posey shrugged. "When I first came out of that hyper-womb and I saw what I had become, I panicked. I spent that day flying as far away as I could. I found a lake and landed on the shore. I spent hours staring at my reflection in the water and crying and I guess I sort of snapped. I wanted revenge. I wanted someone to feel as badly as I did. I made up my mind to kill Dr. Cormair."

"You didn't, though."

"No. He gave me options for my life that I hadn't thought about. He told me that I could do things, see the world. Then, he made me promise not to kill myself. But, you know what really got to me? What made me change my mind?"

"What?"

"My biggest fear was being alone, that no one would ever love me and that I would be forced to withdraw from everyone everywhere."

"And?" prompted John. "You know you will most likely have to withdraw. You can't just go to the grocery store or what-have-you."

"And I realized," said Posey ignoring John, "that being alone was what Cormair did his whole life. He lived a solitary life despite having people around him at all times. He was utterly alone. If he did that for so many years, I realized I already had it better than he did: I have Holly, and you, and the others. I might be ugly, but at least we're all freaks in this together."

"I don't see ugly," said John. "Only Posey, the same girl I grew up with. That will never change."

"I guess I'm going to have to come to my own terms with how I look," she said. "It's not going to be easy. I'm not happy with this."

"I know," said John. "I think it will get easier over time. Are you going to be okay with the...you know, the..." John made a half-hearted gesture toward his neck. He didn't want to just blurt out, *Are you okay with slicing open a man's jugular veins and watching him die?*

Posey took a deep breath and let it out slowly. "I never killed anything before and I never thought I would. Well, spiders and mosquitoes, but they don't really count, do they?"

"It's not easy," said John. "I'm programmed to do it if necessary, and I would have if Tucker hadn't tasered me, I was prepared to do it, but you..."

"They made me this way for a reason. They gave me talons, John. Big, wicked daggers on all of my toes. They must have expected me to have to kill someone eventually, right?"

"Doesn't mean you have to like it."

Posey smoothed out the feathers on her forearm. "You know, what scared me the most is that after it was over and I was able to process it, a part of me enjoyed it, and it was more than just revenge or saving my friends. There was something else behind it that I don't know how to describe. It felt right. When I felt his flesh tear open...I felt...good."

Before John could speak, Posey turned and ran to the edge of the bluffs. She leapt into the air, throwing her arms out and snapping her wings to their full span. She flapped once, twice, and then caught a thermal. She rose quickly, spiraling into the sky, and disappearing into the clouds.

John watched until her ivory wings winked out of sight. The wind began to pick up slightly and John noticed the ash leaves were beginning to show silvery undersides. A storm was coming.

He hoped it wasn't an omen.

In the Washington D.C. office of Senator Abraham Uriah, the honorable Senator from the great state of Ohio was concluding a meeting. The meeting was about a construction company looking to circumvent a D.N.R. order to cease plans to build on a protected wetland site, and a small suitcase full of cash. Uriah glad-palmed the developer's hand and smiled a wide, cheesy grin. "George, I think we can easily come to an agreement on this matter. Now what say we have a drink and a cigar?"

With a practiced move, Uriah gestured to the expensive leather couches in his office where a cut-glass decanter of an extremely pricey Armagnac and a pair of snifters waited on a silver tray alongside two hand-rolled cigars. They were extremely fine cigars, but they weren't the prized Cubans, although Uriah did have a few of those stashed away for extra-special occasions.

Uriah poured his guest two fingers of brandy and poured another for himself. He sat back against the couch and used a beautiful, brushed-silver Zippo to light his cigar before tossing the lighter to George.

"This is a pretty nice bit of hooch you got here," said George. "I've never tasted anything better."

"It's from a vineyard in France that I know. The proprietors and I are on good terms. Every time I get over to France, I make certain to buy a few bottles of their best and mail it back home."

"Now, about those D.N.R. orders..."

"George, you don't have to worry about a thing," said Uriah waving a manicured hand dismissively. "When you get back to Ohio, there will be a federal order overturning that mandate from the D.N.R. Your project will go ahead. After all, what are a few ducks and geese compared to a country club convention center that will bring in millions in revenue and provide jobs for the good men and women of Ohio?"

"I'm glad you see it my way, Senator," said George. "The D.N.R. doesn't seem to think the same way you and I do."

"Unfortunate. Progress is vital to this nation's success!"

There was a knock at the door to the Senator's office. A ruddy-faced young man stuck his head in the room and waved a small sheet of paper at the

Senator. The man had a fresh sheen of perspiration across his forehead. "Sorry to bother you, Senator Uriah. I have some news about your Aunt Sarah."

Uriah's brows furrowed. "What did you say, Peterson?"

"Your *Aunt Sarah*," Peterson said with particular inflection. "There's been a development in her condition, sir. A drastic change."

Uriah stubbed out his cigar in the ashtray on the coffee table. "George, I'm sorry to cut our meeting short, but this is important, a family thing—you understand, don't you?"

"Oh, absolutely," said George. He stood and stuck out a hand. "I appreciate your time, Senator. I hope the next time you're back home, you'll swing by the site and see how it's coming along."

"I'll do that, George. I will be sure to do that. Look forward to it."

Uriah's assistant showed the developer to the door then bolted it closed behind him. He dropped his voice, "Senator, I have some bad news."

"What is it?"

"The Amboy base is in ruins. Project Evolve is a wash—the experiments have escaped."

Uriah's face flushed with anger, his usual tanned and toned skin flaming to a vibrant crimson. "Damn, damn, damn. Get Tucker on the phone immediately. I want his head on a platter!"

"Tucker's dead, sir. From what Captain Krantz told me, it looks like one of them tore out his throat."

"What about Cormair?"

"Dead as well. Heart attack."

"Why didn't they call sooner?"

"The binary telepath destroyed all the communications equipment in the compound. The overload of power at the base shorted out all of Amboy, as well. Krantz had to drive to a spot a few miles from the base just to get the cellular signal to be able to call."

"Did any of them get stopped? Do we have any bodies?"

"No sir. From what Krantz tells me, he thinks they all got out alive."

The brandy snifter in Uriah's hand shattered under the force of his grip. Glass cut deeply into his palm but he didn't notice. He threw the remnants of the glass at the wall and kicked the coffee table as he stood up. The decanter tipped over and cracked. Armagnac slowly pooled on the expensive oak.

"Tell me something, Peterson—What the hell good is a hired army that can't stop seven snot-nosed kids? They had everything they needed. We spent billions! Billions, Peterson! No expense was spared, nothing was held back. Do you have any idea what the Trust is going to do when they hear about this?"

"I know, sir. It's bad."

"Bad? Bad, Peterson? Bad is an understatement. Bad is only the tip of the iceberg!" A vein bulged on Uriah's forehead.

"What would you like me to tell Captain Krantz?"

Uriah strode to the window and stared into the distance. His lip curled in anger, but he inhaled deeply and his face became impassive. Some of the color in his cheeks faded. "Tell Krantz to disassemble the Amboy base. He is to break the town down, leave no traces—at least nothing that can be discovered too easily. Use explosives to collapse the underground structures. Tell him to salvage what he can, but destroy what he can't. And give Krantz a field promotion. He is now Colonel Krantz."

"You're bypassing Major and Lieutenant Colonel?"

"I am, damn it. He was Tucker's second-in-command at the Amboy base. I want him to be in charge now! He'll have the most intelligence about the experiments."

"Understood. I will tell him to disassemble the base, sir. Anything else?"

Uriah rubbed the bridge of his nose with the hand that wasn't bleeding. "Contact the McKinley Base. They are to get phase 2.0 online as fast as possible. I want those projects ready to go inside of a year. Six months if they can."

"A year, sir? I don't know if that's even possible."

"They're still a little young, but we're going to need them sooner than later if we're going to maintain anything even resembling the Trust's original time-table. Their evolutions will have to be artificially accelerated."

Peterson paused, "Uh, Senator, won't that cause problems with their development? Dr. Cormair's files were very clear—"

"Do you see a lot of options here, Peterson?"

"No sir."

"Then I guess you had better just carry out my orders now, shouldn't you! They are to artificially accelerate the evolution!"

"Yes, sir. I'll start making phone calls right away." Peterson rushed back to the door and unlocked it.

"Peterson?" Uriah turned away from the window.

"Yes, Senator?"

"One more thing: Tell Krantz that I want him to form a commando unit. I want him to find the nastiest, most lethal, savage, inhuman animals we hired and I want him to put them on a seek-and-destroy mission for the seven."

"Yes, Senator," said Peterson. He slipped out the door and shut it noiselessly behind him.

Uriah plucked the small shard glass out of his palm and wrapped his silk handkerchief around the wound. The white silk stained to red. He strode to the window behind his desk and looked out over the Washington skyline. He could see the White House in the distance.

He would still get there, he told himself. It will take patience, that's all. He would still get there. It would happen, all in good time.

John sighed heavily and did a belly-flop onto the mattress in the corner, the only furniture in the room, save for the folding chair that served as a television stand for a thirteen-inch Dynex. The cramped, single-room efficiency apartment was dingy, and the neighborhood it was in was horrible, but the landlord took cash and didn't check references or credit. It was all John could find. Kenny lay suspended in the womb in the opposite corner. His body was technically still alive. The womb monitored an extremely slow, but steady heartbeat. The bullet holes had healed nicely in the first four days, even after John's ham-handed removal of the metal slugs from his friend's chest. Kenny had been in the gel for almost a week. He was showing no signs of waking. John had been on a near-constant vigil, hoping that Kenny would suddenly open his eyes and tap on the glass front of the coffin-like hyper-womb.

John picked up the laptop computer he'd purchased at a department store not too far from his apartment. He was piggybacking on someone else's Wi-Fi. As soon as he could find a way to get broadband without having to give a social security number, he would get his own; he didn't like to steal signal from others. He logged into his web-based email account and checked for messages. Other than a few spam emails for Viagra and cheap airfare and hotels, there were no waiting messages. He tried to tell himself that the others were still looking for a place to live, still settling into routines. Maybe they hadn't had time to get a computer yet, or if they had, maybe they were having problems getting to an internet connection.

John put the computer down and rolled onto his back. He draped an arm over his eyes and yawned so hard it felt like his skull was going to split into two. He needed sleep. A good night's sleep and then maybe he'd feel better. He'd been awake for most of a week, save a nap here and there. His body couldn't do that. He needed to rest and recharge. In seconds, John's breath deepened into the slow, rhythmic cadence of sleep.

The screen-saver on the laptop stopped its scrolling and the desktop appeared. A progress bar popped into in the center of the screen as an instant messaging program downloaded onto the computer. The IM program opened and ran through set-up protocols. A message window opened in the middle of the screen with a loud, somewhat melodic *ka-chunk* sound.

John's head jerked up and he glanced over at the screen confused and disoriented. A line of text was in the box.

Ps1ber: *John? Are you there? Can you read this?*

John looked at the handle of the user trying to contact him. Then, he looked over at the hyper-womb. Kenny's body still floated in the fluid. Another line of text suddenly appeared beneath the first one.

Ps1ber: *John, you have to type. I can't hear you if you're speaking. Just type. I already set up everything for you.*

John keyed in a response.

Elite: *Kenny? Is that you?*
Ps1ber: *Who else would it be?*
Elite: *Are you all right?*
Ps1ber: *Never better.*
Elite: *Are you accessing the internet from the hyper-womb?*

The last line of text gave John a chill.

Ps1ber: *John, I **AM** the internet...*

About the Author

Sean Patrick Little grew up in Mount Horeb, Wisconsin and now lives in Sun Prairie, Wisconsin. He has wanted to be a novelist and a comic book artist since second grade. His love for the graphic novel genre began at an early age with an addiction to *X-Men* comics.

When not writing, Sean enjoys playing guitar and bass (poorly), playing video games (also poorly), and rooting for Wisconsin sports teams (even when they are doing poorly). He is an alumnus of the University of Wisconsin—Whitewater.

He still reads comic books.

Other Works by Sean Patrick Little

The Centurion: The Balance of the Soul War
iUniverse, 2007

"The Wendigo"
A short story to be published in *The Gents of Horror* anthology
Edited by Jennifer L. Miller (release: October 2009)

Lightning Source UK Ltd.
Milton Keynes UK
UKOW04f1827310817

308364UK00001B/98/P

9 781608 440665